Knight in Shining Suit

Jerilee Kaye

DEDICATION

To my parents, Angel and Norma, who always believed in me.

To my aunts and uncles, who always believed I would be a writer since I was three years old.

To my sisters and brother: Kathie, Roland, KC and Kaz, who made me as crazy as I am now.

To Joe, Debbie, Ralph, and Mai, friends who have always supported my writing and took time to walk inside my head.

To my own Knight in Shining Armani, Sam, who made my own "ever after" come true.

To my little angels, MarQ and KeOn, who will always make me feel young at heart.

Finally, to all Wattpad fans of Knight in Shining Armani, who made this book an even more amazing journey.

CONTENTS

	Acknowledgments	i
1	Motif	3
2	Entourage	13
3	Diamond	23
4	RSVP	35
5	Bridal Car	47
6	Place Card Holder	57
7	Wedding Garter	67
8	The Wedding Night	75
9	Honeymoon	85
10	Arrhae	97
11	Guestbook	107
12	Wedding Favors	117
13	The Maid of Honor and The Best Man	127
14	Bridesmaids and Groomsmen	145
15	Heirloom	153
16	Bells	163
17	Contraception	175
18	Flowers	183
19	Usherette	191
20	Arranged Marriage	197
21	Wedding Anniversary	201
22	I Do	217
23	Bond	227
24	Veil	239
25	Vellum	247
26	Bridal Registry	257
27	Prenup	267
28	Guardianship	273
29	Kiss	279
30	Tulle	285
31	Something New	293
32	Something Old	303
33	Something Blue	313
34	Something Borrowed	319
35	Wedding Album	329
36	Present	339
37	Ring	351
38	The Venue	367
	Epilogue	377

ACKNOWLEDGMENTS

Big thanks to:

My parents, for pushing me to pursue my love for writing;

My sisters and friends who listened to my crazy ideas;

Joe, for the artistic inspiration and for professional photos for my future book covers;

Debbie, for sparking the idea for this book;

MarQuise, for always making me laugh.

Sam, for inspiring my Ever After.

Lauren Boyles and Trisha L. for your initial edit and comments.

Kathleen Consuelo Antic, for the literary advice.

Kim Burger, my editor, for the wonderful job you did for this book.

To all Wattpad fans of Knight in Shining Armani, for your love and support. I would not be able to do this without you.

1.
MOTIF: a dominant color.
In choosing a color motif for a wedding, keep in mind the colors that mean something in your relationship, and what you want to attract in your future.

"We'd like the colors moss green and brown," Estelle, the happy bride-to-be was saying to me and my best friend Nicole. I watched her dreamy eyes and her happy smile and I couldn't help wondering if I looked as ridiculous as that when I was planning my own wedding.

Nicole smiled back at her enthusiastically. "That's a good combination. So…"

"Jungle-like," I suggested, cutting Nicole off mid-sentence.

Estelle stared at me for a moment and her dreamy smile threatened to fade from her beautiful face. "Excuse me?"

Nicole glared at me with a hidden message that said: *Please, just shut the hell up if you can't say something nice!*

"What she meant was… earthy," Nicole said smiling back at Estelle and from the somewhat constipated look on her face, I could tell that she was trying her best to pass on some of her enthusiasm back into the bride-to-be.

"No. I meant jungle-like. If I meant earthy, that's what I would have said," I said bluntly, which gained me another glare from Nicole. This time her hidden message was: *You're so dead!* I raised a brow at her and flashed her a crooked smile that was meant to say: *I already know that!*

"Excuse me? Do you… have a problem with me?" Estelle asked reluctantly.

I sighed. "No. I'm sorry, sweetie. I don't have a problem with you. I have a problem with green. Moss green to be exact. And since you're in Malibu and are planning for a beach wedding, maybe you should take a look at gold, yellow or orange and red, with maybe a bit of indigo?"

I thought Estelle would tell me to get lost right then and there. It didn't really matter. I didn't care anymore. Weddings used to be my thing. However, because of the recent events in my crappy life, it now gave me pain to see a happy, blushing bride-to-be. It's easier for me to imagine that maybe on the night of their fiancé's bachelor party, he might actually be humping the stripper inside the big cake!

"I'm… sorry, Estelle. I know you like green…" Nicole started apologizing on my behalf. She didn't even bother to glare at me anymore. She knew that I couldn't care less and we'd only look unprofessional if we spent half the time glaring at each other.

"My fiancé likes green. I… in fact, like… orange."

"Unfortunately, I don't see green and orange going together with your theme. I hope you are paying for the wedding," I said under my breath.

"Actually, I am," Estelle said raising her chin proudly.

3

I smiled at her. "Good for you! Then you should plan it the way you want it. That way you get to keep your wedding ideas in case your fiancé decides to marry someone else at the last minute!"

"Might I have a word in private, Astrid?" Nicole asked me with a grave look on her face that she was not even disguising in front of Estelle anymore.

"Sure," I said, smiling sarcastically. Then I turned to Estelle. "Please do consider choosing between orange and green. If I were you, I'd make it worth my money. Think of things that are green..." I said trailing thoughtfully. "Hmmm... like vomit."

"Now, Astrid!" Nicole stood up, pulling me by the arm.

When we were outside the office, Nicole gave me a good slap on the face. It actually stung.

"Are you awake now?" she asked me angrily.

"What's your problem, Nic?" I asked, rubbing my cheek with my palm.

"Pull yourself together, Astrid! Or you're not only going to lose your dream wedding, you just might lose your job as well!" she said to me. "Now, stay here and I will talk to Estelle... *alone*!"

Nicole started to go back to the conference room.

"Nic!" I called and she turned back to me with a raised brow. "If she picks orange, will I at least get a credit for talking her into it?"

She glared at me one last time, then she turned on her heel towards the conference room, hoping to repair whatever damage I might have caused.

I went to the pantry to get myself a cup of coffee. Nicole's slap wasn't powerful enough to wake me up. But I knew she had a point. If I continued talking to Estelle the way I did, I would have another complaint lodged against my name.

Last week, a client withdrew their account with us because the tulip-loving bride couldn't forget the story I told her about a psycho killer, murdering brides on their wedding nights and laying them on a bed of tulips afterwards. I made up the story of course, but I didn't know she had such a wild imagination! So the groom refused to have us do their wedding, claiming we had traumatized his blushing bride-to-be. And now I'm pretty sure that if Estelle still chooses green, everything about her wedding will remind her of vomit.

And speaking of vomit, it makes me want to do so when I look around the office and see reels of lace and bows of different colors. A single bow, a single lace, makes me want to puke!

I picked up a bow that strayed on my table. There was a phrase inscribed on it: *Yours Forever*.

I snorted and threw the string in my garbage bin. *Forever* is such a big promise. I don't believe that any man can keep a promise as big as that. That's why divorce happens left and right. Any girl would be a fool to believe in *Forever*. I, for one, will be damned if I ever believe in that word again!

I was so lost in my own thoughts that I didn't notice that Nicole was already standing in front of me with a giant scowl on her face. I stared up at her for a while and then I sighed.

"Okay, okay. I'm sorry, I messed up," I said, throwing my hands in the air.

"No, you did not mess up, Ash! You deliberately sabotaged that meeting!"

"I did not!"

"You did too!" she said angrily. Then she sighed and sat in the chair in front of me. "What is happening to you, Ash?"

"Nothing," I replied. That was a lie. I know exactly what was wrong with me.

"You used to believe in this. This company is twice as big as it was when it started because of you. You've worked on this for five solid years and you were the best employee this company has ever seen. And now… you're throwing it all away. And in the process, you're also jeopardizing my future along with yours."

"No, I'm not!" I said defensively.

"Yes, you are! And not only are you jeopardizing our futures, you're also jeopardizing the futures of the engaged couples who will step into this office!" Nicole let out a frustrated sigh. She stared at me, shaking her head.

I could go on and on in this imminent circle of denial forever. I could argue with her all I want, but I knew that she was right. I was being a bitch. And I was being difficult. And I couldn't stand to see another wedding in my life again. At least not yet.

"What do you want me to do?" I asked her. "Do you want me to file my resignation?"

Nicole rolled her eyes. "No, silly! But I think you should take some time off! I think that you should refrain from talking to engaged couples… until you get back on your feet." She tried to smile encouragingly.

I sighed. "I guess you're right. The sight of this very place I used to love makes me want to puke already! And I don't think I can stand to see another wedding again. Please! The thought of it not ending in happily ever after is enough to make me want to hang myself!"

"Good! Because that is exactly what our clients want to do after they meet up with you!" a familiar voice said behind me.

I didn't have to look to know who it was. Fiona Lewinsky stood in front of me with a glare on her heart-shaped face. She claimed she was meant to do weddings because the shape of her face alone spells love. I had to roll my eyes the first time I heard her say that. And it still makes me want to roll my eyes now.

"Fiona..." I sighed. "I think I need a little holiday," I said to her.

"Take one permanently. You're fired!" she said to me without blinking.

Nicole stood up in shock. "Fiona! You can't do that! You owe half of your success to her! She made you rich, for crying out loud! She's going through a rough patch. Anyone in her situation would be upset! I think you're being too harsh."

Fiona raised a brow at her. "She deserves it! I lost two clients in one week because of her."

"She gave you almost a thousand of them since she came to work for you!" Nicole argued. "We wouldn't be where we are had it not been for her."

"The reason why she was that good is because I taught her well. I've given her one week to mope and cry over her broken engagement. It's been three weeks already! She's getting worse. I can't jeopardize my business because her fiancé left her at the altar!"

"That's not true!" I spoke for the first time since she fired me.

"Yes! That's not true!" Nicole agreed. "You didn't teach her anything. She was fresh, dynamic and creative. And she was the one who came up with the most ambitious concepts we ever used on the weddings we did for years. Right, Ash?" She looked at me as if she was begging me to defend myself.

I took a deep breath. "What I meant was... it's not true that my fiancé left me at the altar," I said in a serious voice and Nicole stared back at me, unable to wipe the shocked expression off her face.

"That's great dear. At least it didn't get too embarrassing," Fiona said without even a hint of emotion. "Now, before every other bride-to-be ends up having your unfortunate fate, I suggest you go. You're jeopardizing my business. I thank you for your services, but I already lost two clients because of you, I cannot afford to lose any more."

I didn't know if I felt heartbroken because of what she said. Sure, it was sad to see your boss not seem to care about you, especially since she owes half of her company's growth to you, but at the same time it was also a relief to know that I need not make another bride's dream come true. It's been difficult for me since I, myself, was a bride-to-be, but the engagement did not last long enough for me to make it to the altar.

"Fine," I murmured. Then I took my cell phone and my bag. "I do expect to receive my full benefits, Fiona."

She raised a brow. "Compared to the amount of business I would lose because of you? I'll be happy to give you your severance pay on a silver platter!"

I rolled my eyes at her one last time and then I marched out of the room. Nicole was on my tracks the minute I got to the elevator.

"Get back in there Nic, if you don't want to share my fate," I warned her.

"You are out of your mind, Astrid! You should fight this! She owes you that much!" she insisted.

I shook my head. "Did you really think I didn't want this?" I asked her. She opened her mouth to say something but no sound came out. "Goodbye, Nic. I'll see you later."

"I'll talk to you later," she said as the elevator door closed behind me.

I exited the building and hailed a cab. There, in the backseat, with only the cab driver as company, I lost it. I cried my heart out.

***

The new Mr. and Mrs. Bryan Bryans! I heard the host announce excitedly. I held on to my new husband's arm happily.

Bryan smiled at me gently, his eyes were teary. He leaned forward to give me a kiss on the lips.

The place was magical. The garden just outside the church was covered in moss green and brown fabrics. I was warm in my pristine white gown. I wanted a long train, but Bryan had been afraid that he would somehow trip on it. I figured that was just his one request so I settled for a waist-length one. The long lacy sleeves of my bolero jacket covered my arms. It barely showed flesh. My gown reflected the prudent, virginal bride that I was.

The cake was a perfect two-tier with little green flowers on its base. The cake topper was the traditional bride and groom locked in a sweet embrace.

My bridesmaids, who were dressed in elegant moss green and brown swirled gowns, danced around us. With the two-inch heels that I wore, my violet eyes were at almost the same level as Bryan's brown ones. He wasn't tall, but it really didn't matter to me. He was my groom, my husband. He made this dream wedding come true. He agreed to make it my way, exactly the way I dreamed it would be.

I danced happily in Bryan's arms. Then the host announced a change of partners and I was whirled out of Bryan's arms. I looked around to find where he had gone. And then I saw him… in the middle of the dance floor, dancing happily with a bridesmaid wearing a revealing moss green gown, a flower tucked on her right ear. She looked at me and a mischievous grin flashed across her beautiful Barbie-like features and then she laughed the most malicious laugh I have heard in my entire life.

"This is my wedding!" I shouted at her. And then I fell to my knees, crying.

7

I felt someone reach out for me and force me to stand up. It was my least favorite person in the world, Adam. He shook me and said, "Pull yourself together!"

"I can't..." I said.

"Will you wake up, Astrid?" he shouted at me.

I felt him shake me more intensely.

"Wake up!" he shouted.

The world whirled around me. I forced myself to open my eyes. I found myself staring into a pair of intense blue eyes, outlined by a handsome tanned face. I stood up from my bed and stared back at Adam.

He raised a brow at me.

"Are you okay?" he asked me.

I took a deep breath and tried to steady myself. Then I slowly nodded.

"Your phone has been ringing non-stop," he told me. "I can't concentrate and I've got a pleading to submit tomorrow."

Adam is sort of my cousin, but we're not really related by blood, although we grew up together. He was my cousin's half-brother. Ever since we were kids, we never got along too well. He's too frank, too tactless. He says what's on his mind, regardless of who will get hurt or who will look like a fool.

I don't really know why I ended up in his apartment after my whole world fell apart. I shared an apartment with Geena, the beautiful Barbie doll in my dreams. She is my first cousin, and has been my closest friend ever since I was a kid. I've slept over at her house more than I've slept in my own bed. That was why it was just natural that we live together after college. Only, it wasn't really my apartment, but hers. Uncle Jack, Adam and Geena's rich father, made sure they were well provided for.

Between the two of us, Geena was the wild one. She wasn't always smart, but with her charm and looks, she survived all the challenges that came her way. Well, if she got away with humping my fiancé behind my back, she can get away with almost anything. Or maybe I was just too trusting... too naïve!

My ex-fiancé is an orthodontist. He is goal-oriented and ambitious, much like me. When Geena needed a job that didn't really have a lot of pressure, Bryan took her in. I was not worried. They both loved me. They would never betray me... or so I thought.

Back when I was still clueless, Adam had been dropping hints to me; sometimes in the form of a very sarcastic remark, but since I was so used to him being rude, I just tuned him out.

So one evening, I planned to surprise Bryan at work. I was about to open the door when I heard him and Geena arguing.

"You have to get rid of it!" Bryan said angrily.

"I'm not going to get rid of it! I may have done shameful things in my life, but I will not kill my own baby!"

"Astrid will find out!" Bryan argued.

"And you still plan to marry her after getting me pregnant!?" Geena asked angrily.

"I already spent a fortune on that wedding she planned! It was too extravagant! What do you want me to do? Call it all off?"

"Oh, really? So you want *me* to call off *my* pregnancy instead?" Geena asked. "I can't believe you're even considering that! Perhaps you should have considered checking your ten-year old condom before you jumped on the sofa with me!"

"Are you sure it is even mine?"

"How dare you, Bryan?" Geena fired at him. "We've been sleeping together for six months! I've never let any other man touch me except for you!"

"So what do you want me to do? Choose between my wedding and your pregnancy? It's a difficult choice to make, you know!"

At that point, I couldn't take any more. I barged into the room, which shocked them both. I stared at both of them, pasting a bored expression on my face.

"Oh, sweetheart... we were just having a discussion about... a patient." Bryan struggled to lie.

I narrowed my eyes at him. "Really? Which patient? Your unborn child?"

They were both shocked to hear me say that.

"I've been standing here long enough and I assure you, I need no explanations from either of you." I struggled to keep my voice calm. "Bryan, I know it is a very difficult choice to make. A man like you will not have balls big enough to make a decision like that. So, why don't I make it for you?" I took a deep breath. "You both stay away from me for the rest of my life! In case, you were too dumb to understand, Bryan... the wedding is off!" Then I turned on my heel.

"But... I already spent a fortune on that damn wedding!" Bryan said angrily.

I turned around so I could face him. "Well, then I'll send you all your receipts and you can see if you can get any refunds!" I stormed out of the room.

I went home immediately and gathered my clothes and as much stuff as I could fit in one suitcase. I didn't have anywhere to go at that time. I couldn't face my friends yet. I was too embarrassed. They already didn't like Bryan that much because they thought he was self-centered and egotistic. I had defended Bryan, saying that at least he was faithful to me. And now, this!

Before I could even have second thoughts about leaving Geena's apartment, I went to the person who knew what was happening even before I knew it myself. And I sincerely hoped that person considered me as family all throughout these years.

Adam never liked Bryan. He always told me that my boyfriend was up to no good, or that he only thought of himself and he would only make me cry.

When he was suspecting that things were happening between Bryan and Geena, he would say things to me like:

"You're so naïve, Ash!"

"Open your eyes sometimes and stop trusting too much!"

"Sometimes, the people you trust the most, Ash, are the ones who betray you the deepest. Look around. You just might understand what I am saying."

So when I came to him that night, I didn't have to explain anything. He saw that my eyes were swollen and that I was carrying a suitcase with me. Without a word, he opened the door wider to let me in.

"How long have you known?" I asked him.

"Does it matter how long I have known?" he asked back. Although he sat beside me on the couch, he offered no arm or shoulder for me to cry on. Adam isn't a very touchy feely person. But it meant a lot to me that he made me feel that he was there for me.

"How could they do this to me?"

He sighed. "The more important question is, what are you going to do about it?"

"She's pregnant!" I said.

For a while, Adam was silent. I could tell he was brewing his anger all inside him. Then finally he said, "I suppose I should beat the hell out of Bryan for getting Geena pregnant. But right now, I want to give him a shiner more for what he did to you."

I stared up at him. He smiled, which is something he rarely does. "You grew up with me, Ash. You, too, are like a sister to me, believe it or not." He chuckled humorlessly. "Now, what happened to Geena, she's an adult now. She should know that her actions have consequences. I can't beat up Bryan if Geena participated in the act so willingly. But you, on the other hand... it was not fair what they did to you."

Adam took me in, but it had always been on a temporary basis. He's a little bit of a woman-hater... I think. A woman's presence in his luxurious bachelor flat would probably kill him little by little.

But I was glad that he allowed me to live with him... until I get my act together. I intended to find my own apartment. If only the rest of my friends were rich enough to rent a two-bedroom flat, I could crash in with one of them. But until then, I'd be the parasite living in Adam's guest bedroom.

"Are you okay?" Adam asked, giving me another gentle shake.

I nodded.

"You were in all afternoon. Aren't you supposed to be working?" he asked.

I shook my head. "Not anymore."

He raised a brow. "Your boss sacked you?"

I sighed and then I nodded. "Apparently, I am no longer recommended to stand within ten feet of people who are getting married."

"I can't say I blame your boss," he said. "You made this breakup the center of your universe, Ash. You have to stop this. You have to pull yourself together. Dwelling on what would have been will only make you twice the loser."

"I'm not a loser!"

"Whatever." He rolled his eyes. "But it looks like that from where I'm standing. No house, no boyfriend, no job."

"Right. Remind me to look for an apartment as soon as I can stand up."

"As soon as you get a job, you mean," he said.

"Yes, that too."

He sighed. "It's no secret that I want to keep this apartment all to myself. But right now, Ash, I'm the only one you have. I don't have a choice. I can't disown you. But I hate to see you deteriorating every day. A week of moping is fine. It's been almost a month now. You're in worse condition than you were the first time you showed up on my doorstep."

"I... I don't know what to do, Adam," I admitted.

"Yes, you do. Go out with your friends. Party all night. You can sleep around if you want. Even I won't judge you," he said. "Just get out of bed and stop moping."

"I'm not moping!"

He snorted. "You don't convince me."

I rolled my eyes and lay back on the bed.

"By the way, your mother called me. She asked if I've seen you. When was the last time you talked to her? She was very concerned."

"Last week. Took her a long time to call you."

"Honestly, I am the last person in our family that they would expect you to run to," he said, standing up from the bed, and then he headed towards the door.

"Adam..." I called.

He turned back to me.

"How's... Geena? Bryan was asking her to get rid of the baby. Did... did they go for it?"

He raised a brow at me. "Why do you want to know? They can go to hell for all you care. Don't ask again! Because even if Bryan's on his knees begging for forgiveness, I will be the last person to tell him where you are!"

"Is he asking for my forgiveness?"

He sighed in frustration. "The only reason he'll do that is because he wants back the sixty grand he already spent on your wedding preparations!" With his last barb cutting through me, he strode out of the room.

Adam can be ruthless and careless with my feelings, but somehow, I appreciate it that he doesn't lead me on or tell me lies just to make me feel better. I can always count on him for the brutal truth. Maybe that's why I ran to him when I found out about Bryan's affair. Because I felt that I had been surrounded by lies for too long. And for once, I wanted the truth. No matter how painful it was.

2.

ENTOURAGE:

A group of people surrounding an important person or persons… like the bride and groom in a wedding.

I met up with my friends. I could tell that they were all getting bored with me. I whined about the usual things. Like how I had known Bryan since I was in college and we had been friends first before we dated and how I've known Geena since we were little and never in my wildest dreams had I imagined that she would betray me like she did.

Dannie Jones, my gay best friend, became the most impatient of my group. He had listened to me enough, I guess.

John Green, my guy best friend, was the angriest at Bryan for what he did to me.

Nicole was the most sympathetic for my feelings.

"I wonder how he is now," I asked.

"Oh, for crying out loud!" Dannie muttered. "Ash, please! Don't do this! You're beautiful, you're smart! You have your whole life ahead of you!"

"No, I don't! I'll be thirty in a few months!"

"You'll be thirty in twenty-three months." John muttered. "That's plenty of time to score a guy who is a lot better than Bryan!"

"But we've been together for two years! Do you know how much work that took?"

"A lot! Particularly since you have been withholding sex!" Dannie said brutally.

"But what is wrong with… no sex before marriage?"

"Nothing! Only that you open him up to readily available sluts within a mile proximity," John said.

"Look, Ash, if he couldn't wait, then he isn't the guy." Nicole said. "And if he really did love you, he wouldn't have the nerve to sleep with Geena. If he had an inch of decency in his body, he would have remembered that Geena is your cousin!"

"Relationships are not important to a horny guy," John butted in.

"Apparently!" I rolled my eyes.

"So, now what are you going to do with your life?"

I shrugged. "Drink it away?" I asked sarcastically and took another gulp of my beer.

"Look at you, Ash! How can a gorgeous girl who's sweet and smart waste her life over a loser like Bryan? I mean, no offense, but he's not nearly that hot!" Dannie said in a frustrated voice.

"And he's short. What is he? Like five feet tall?" John chuckled.

"Hey! He's five feet six!" I said defensively. "And his chocolate eyes are dreamy."

"His eyes are brown! As plain as brown could be!" Dannie argued.

"I just… couldn't think of a reason for him to do that to me," I heaved another frustrated sigh.

John rolled his eyes. "I can. But you're not going to like it…"

"Sex?" I asked him. "He only needed to wait three more months… after we're married."

"Well, apparently, he can't wait nine months. Haven't they been sleeping with each other for a good six months already before you even found out about them?" Dannie asked.

"For all you know, Ash, he could have proposed to you because he wanted to get you to bed," John suggested.

"Not with the size of the ring that he gave me!" I said. Bryan gave me a two-carat diamond ring. It cost a fortune. He wouldn't splurge on that if he was only after the sex, would he?

"Speaking of the ring, where is it?" Dannie asked.

"In my jewelry box," I replied.

"Hmmm… you should have returned that weeks ago," John said.

"Hell no!" Dannie argued. "Don't return it! Pawn it!"

"No! I'm not going to pawn that ring!"

"And why not? You want to hold on to it and reminisce about the good times you spent together whenever you look at it?" Nicole asked in an irritated tone.

"We did have some good times."

"This is not the time to be thinking about the good times. That's a no brainer. Right now, for you to get over him, you have to think about every single annoying thing about him and every single irritating thing that he has ever done to you," Nicole said.

"True. Right now, you have to think of him as a monster. He has no heart. He has no conscience," Nicole said. "This thing that you are in, he brought this upon you. Everything that he was before you broke up with him, was nothing. That's not the person that he is now!"

"You need a makeover. Find a hobby. Get a gym membership. Learn to play the guitar."

"Or you can always find a job," John suggested.

"I hope you have been saving money."

I sighed. "Of course. But… unfortunately, I used some of it to pay the florist."

"I hope you had the guts to ask for a refund from them," Nicole said.

I shook my head. "I gave all the receipts to Bryan when we broke up. I wanted him to refund all those payments so that he'll know how difficult it was for me to make those arrangements while he was humping my maid of honor!"

"So, let me get this thing straight," John said. "If he was able to refund the money *you* paid the florist, it means… he cheated on you… and you paid him to do it?"

"Shut up, John," I told him, although I understood the irony he was aiming at.

"That settles it then! You have to pawn the ring," Dannie said. "With the size of that thing, you can pay for your own wedding."

I snorted. "That is, if I still want to get married. I think I completely lost faith in love. If I see or come to another wedding in my life, I think I'll hang myself! I don't believe in weddings anymore."

"Really? Then why do you still believe in engagement rings?" John asked.

"Why don't you want to pawn it for its worth? If you don't want to use the money for your future wedding, then use it as a down payment for your own apartment," Dannie suggested. "That could be at least ten grand. You'll have a long way to go with that! And trust me, hon, you deserve it."

"I wish you would display the same angst about Bryan as you do about weddings and happily-ever-afters," Nicole said. "If only you would be as optimistic about getting over Bryan as you were about the doom of the weddings of the couples we were handling."

I knew it was downright pathetic. During the first week, I was so mad at Bryan. He was a liar. He was my best friend before he became my boyfriend. How could he treat me like that?

Then I was so mad at Geena because in my opinion, she should have stopped things from happening. Bryan is merely a man. A man who had been harboring his sex drive since we started dating. His testosterone levels were probably shooting sky high like a rocket when Geena showed a little bit of flesh.

On the second week, I was mad at myself. I thought it was my fault that I was a self-righteous virgin who believed that a relationship these days can go a long way without intimacy.

On the third week, I was just mad at love itself… for leading me on, for making me think that there is a happily ever after in store for me.For making me believe that the dream wedding I had in my head since I was ten-years old could turn into a reality.

And now… I just didn't know what or whom I was mad at anymore. A part of me hurts so much that sometimes, I think it would have been so damn easier if I just ran back to Bryan's arms and forgave him. But a bigger part of me cannot trust him again. Not anymore. A part of me says that I have made it three weeks without him, with this pain. I can make it a few more. And then healing will come for sure.

When I got home that night, Adam was on his way to his deck with a beer on his hand.

"Half-pint," he greeted me.

15

"I'm not a kid anymore, Adam."

"Ha! See? I learn something new every day," he said sarcastically.

I rolled my eyes and started to head to my room.

"Hey, wait up," he called.

I turned back to him.

"Join me." He motioned towards his deck.

I raised a brow. "No. Thanks. I better go to bed."

"And do what?" he asked with a raised brow. "Sleep? Mope? Dream that the bastard is going to magically develop a conscience for you?" He shook his head. "Come on, Ash. I've known you all your life. You're smarter than that. Maybe you just need a little push. Come, drink with me at the deck. It's time you and I have our heart to heart talk."

I sighed and followed him towards his deck. The moonlight was beautiful. The sea breeze instantly blew on my face. I sat on the chair beside Adam's. He handed me a beer.

I took a gulp and waited for him to say something.

"It's been three weeks, Ash," he started. "And you're looking worse." He sighed. I didn't reply. "Don't tell me that I don't know anything about pain, about love and heartache. Trust me, I've had my fair share. Maybe that's why I am what I am now. I've been hurt too much before."

For the first time, I saw Adam in a different light. The cold, ruthless façade... the brutal truth he always speaks regardless of who will get hurt... Now, I understood. He experienced pain. He had been lied to in the past. He had been betrayed before... that created the man that he is now. A man who believed that brutal truth, no matter how much it hurts is still a lot better than the sweetest of all lies. And thus, he always says what is on his mind. He speaks the truth, as he sees it. He doesn't lead people on.

"What?" he asked, when he realized I was staring at him intensely.

I snorted and took a gulp of my beer. "Well, I guess this is probably the first time I've seen evidence that you have a heart."

He chuckled. "Hard as it may be to believe... yes. I do have a heart. Oh! I meant... I *did* have a heart."

"So what happened to you?" I asked him.

He snorted. "I've blocked out some memories. So I can't really tell you."

"But you just said you've had your fair share of love and heartache. Surely you must remember some things."

"If you lose, don't lose the lesson," he murmured. "I may have chosen to forget the incidences in my life that tore me apart, but I didn't forget the lessons they taught me. So, though I may not tell you what happened to me exactly, I can still give you advice."

"Okay, knock yourself out, *big brother*," I said sarcastically.

16

"Hey, I have known you since you were kid. We grew up together. We may not be related by blood, but guess what? I was probably the only brother you've known."

"Yeah. And Geena was the only sister I've known. And look what she did to me," I said glumly.

"At least we've never been best friends when we were growing up. You used to hate me."

"What makes you think I don't still hate you?" I raised a brow at him.

"Fair enough," he said coolly. "But at least you don't expect me to be nice. If I say something that hurts your feelings, remember that I've always been like that."

"You're the first one to teach me how to be immune. To tune it all out."

"Yes. But you're not a very good student, are you?" he asked.

"Why do you say that?"

"Because that's what you should be doing now. Tuning out. I don't think you know how to."

I sighed. "There are times that I thought I could. But then again… sometimes it gets so hard. It was painful." Tears rolled down my cheeks. "It still is painful."

"I know," he said. "Don't think that it will go away soon. It's physically hurtful. Like your chest aches. You know, that's why they call it heartbreak. Because you really feel like your heart is breaking. It's not just an emotional pain; it's a physical pain too. And you have to face it, Ash. There's no running away from it."

"I know. But it's difficult not to remember how things were. You know I didn't only lose a boyfriend… or a fiancé for that matter. I also lost a best friend. Geena's been there through most of my childhood. She was a sister. And I can't stop hurting over the fact that the two people I loved and trusted the most did this to me."

"Geena has always been liberated. You know that. You were the only person in the world who trusted her too much. She was spoiled. But you worshipped the ground that she walked on. She made out with one of the guys you dated in high school one hour after you broke up with him. But still… you never expected anything less of her."

"That's why I still couldn't believe she'd do worse than make out with my ex-boyfriend! God! Now, I hate her!"

Adam snorted. "Really? And what about Bryan? Don't you hate him?"

"I should. But…" I sighed. "We've been through a lot. And… well, maybe I also drove him to do what he did…"

Adam was silent for a while. Then he asked, "What… what could you have done that would drive him to cheat on you over and over again… for six months… maybe more? And with your cousin?"

I sighed. I stared at Adam for a long while. And then I replied, "What he got from Geena... he never got from me, you know."

Silence.

A long, deafening silence.

I stared at Adam. He was looking at the sea view. His thoughts were not visible on his face.

"Adam..." I called. He finally looked at me. "I can't believe I am going to ask you this... but please... *say something*! For once, I'll be glad to get a reaction from you."

He recovered from the shock and then he chuckled. "Alright. Even if you're not going to like what I am about to say or how I'm about to react?"

"Yes," I replied quietly.

"So you are saying that you guys never... had sex or attempted to have sex?"

I nodded. "I have a no-sex-before-marriage thing. Bryan knew that. We've been best friends even before we got together, you know."

"And he never even attempted to ask?"

I shrugged. "He did. Just once. But I was firm then. Now, I'm not sure anymore."

"How long since he last asked before he proposed to you?"

I sighed. "Maybe... maybe about a month after."

Adam took a gulp of his beer and then he sighed.

"What, Adam?" I asked. "Please..." I pleaded. "You said you'd say what you think no matter what. And I promise I won't get mad."

Adam took a deep breath and then finally, he said, "Alright. I just think that even if you and Bryan had gotten married... it wouldn't have lasted forever. You wouldn't grow old with this guy."

"Yeah. I don't think Geena could keep her mouth shut for too long."

"No, no." Adam shook his head. "That's not what I meant. I think Bryan proposed to you because he wanted to have sex with you. He thought marrying you was the only way he could have you. He probably even thought you two would last for a long time. But that could be just lust talking in his head. Who knows how he would feel about you afterwards?"

I stared at Adam for a long moment. I couldn't believe what I was hearing.

"It's not easy to hear, Ash. I know you loved him. Maybe he loved you too. But then again, he's probably more eager to sleep with you than to think past the commitments of marriage. If that was the case, then it wasn't going to last anyway."

I didn't say anything. I took a gulp of my beer and stared ahead into the dark horizon. I heard the calming sound of the ocean. Inside, I was a mess because I realized, no matter how hard it was for me to accept it,

Adam might be right. Maybe Bryan thought marrying me was the answer to everything. We'd been best friends for years. And we did love each other. If marrying me was the only way he could get to me, then why not? It's not like it was hopeless to work out, right? There was a chance that it could have.

"Now… since I seem to always be the bearer of bad news, I won't make this any easier for you. You have to know, Ash. The sooner the better."

I looked at him like he just grew an extra head. I didn't get what he was trying to say.

He was staring at me wearily. I could tell that he was measuring me, weighing what my reaction was going to be to something that he said… or worse… something that he was just about to say.

I raised a brow at him in challenge. This gave him encouragement to continue. He sighed and took an envelope from the table beside him. He handed it to me.

"Breathe, Astrid," he whispered.

I stared at the elegant magenta envelope in my hand. The edges were trimmed neatly and at the center were engraved characters B & G.

I recognized the envelope pretty well. I had seen it before when I approved the sample of what would have been the invitation for my wedding to Bryan. Exact same color. Exact same style.

My hands were shaking when I opened the envelope and pulled out the card inside. My breath caught in my throat as I recognized the paper material used, the fonts on the front and the elegant style of the card. I admired the card company for getting the last minute modifications I asked them. There were flowers and hearts embossed around the card. At the center, the letters B and G were engraved in the font of my choice, Vivaldi.

Bryan and Geena
Bound by love forever…

Even the words were chosen by me… but my name had been replaced.

The date was… the same date as my own wedding would have been had I not caught Bryan cheating on me. The ceremony would be in the same church where my parents got married. The reception will be at *King's Lagoon Resort*, where my reception would have been.

Tears rolled down my cheeks as I crumpled the invitation in my hand.

"Easy, Ash," Adam said, reaching out for my hand and taking the invitation away from me.

I stared at him helplessly.

"Everything's the same…" I croaked.

Adam shook his head, trying to smile at me ruefully. "Not really. As you can see, I am no longer part of the entourage. And... well, you are no longer... the bride."

"They stole my wedding, Adam! Bryan was supposed to cancel the arrangements!"

"Well, apparently marriage is Bryan's solution to everything," Adam said, rolling his eyes.

"How could he?" I sobbed. "How could they do this to me? Don't they have... decency? Or conscience? How could they?"

I was getting out of control. I was shaking and raging with anger. I knew I might begin hyperventilating any minute if I didn't calm down. I was losing it.

I grabbed Adam on both his forearms and tried to shake him.

"They cannot do this to me!" I cried. "You have to stop them, Adam! They cannot do this!"

Adam took both my arms and tried to pull me to him into a tight hug.

"Sshhh..." he said. "Breathe, Ash. You need to take deep breaths!"

I shook my head and struggled to be free of him.

"I need to talk to him. I need to talk to her! To both of them! They should still feel some sort of affection for me!"

Adam shook me gently. "Astrid!" He raised his voice. "Get a grip on yourself! They're not going to change their minds about it! Do you think they didn't know all these things would hurt you? More than you've already been?" He shook his head. "They do! And still they chose to do it! They still chose to hurt you! They're not going to suddenly grow a conscience for you just because you found out about it! You were meant to find out about it, Ash! That invitation was yours! Not mine!"

I stared back at him for a while, unable to believe what he was trying to tell me.

"Pull yourself together, Astrid! You're a strong, independent woman! It's killing me to see you torn up like this," Adam pleaded.

"How..." My lips were shaking. Tears continued to stream down my face. "How... how..." I kept on sobbing, unable to let a comprehensible sentence out.

Adam shook his head. "How could Bryan do this to you?" He shrugged. "Only goes to show the type of man you were about to marry. How can Geena do this to you?" He raised a brow. "Oh, you might be surprised just how much Geena envied you since we were kids, Ash."

I stared back at him. "What?"

"Geena is a spoiled brat. She was not content with what she had. Always wanted what the girl at the next table ordered. And that girl is you. She didn't like it that you were happy with your career while she didn't have a job. You were great at what you did and you were doing something you loved. Dad would always tell her to be more like you. Focused. Goal-oriented. When she was jumping from one boyfriend to another, Dad would always say how much he admired you for sticking it out with one guy. She was dating dropouts and spoiled rich kids… you were having a relationship with an orthodontist. She hated that. She never showed you… or you were just too naïve to notice."

I closed my eyes. I didn't know. I thought Geena was my best friend. I always went to her whenever I had problems. She's seen me at my weakest. I didn't know that she had harbored so much hatred for me. I always thought she was the lucky one.

I, on the other hand, was just a typical girl next door. My eye color is weird and I wear dark blue contacts all the time to make it appear blue rather than violet.

I was unpopular in high school. I was smart, but I wasn't cute or glamorous. I had a major crush on the most popular guy in school, Kevin Moore. He was the captain of the football team, and he drove a shiny convertible. He was my lab partner. Then he was my first date, my first kiss, my first boyfriend. Since he was popular, and I wasn't, we kept our relationship low-key. He was rich and I was middle class. I get why he wasn't proud to be seen with me. My meeting with his rich parents was a disaster. At dinner, they were trying to be polite, but my lack of experience in using the crab cracker made his mother show her real spots. And according to her, I wasn't posh and well bred enough to be with her son. Kevin dumped me the next day.

"Babe, you didn't think a guy like me would fall for you for real, did you?" he asked. "Besides, I've got the whole world in my hands. I need to explore!" And then he made his moves from one rich girl to another.

That was the most devastating day of my life. Well, until Bryan decided to knock up Geena, of course.

Geena knew what I went through. She knew all my insecurities, all that I didn't like about myself. She knew why I stayed away from rich, popular guys. Kevin Moore and his mother damaged my self-esteem big time.

How could she envy me? She was little Ms. Perfect! Malibu Barbie in the flesh! Every guy in this town wanted a piece of her. She never had to work for money. Her father kept her well provided for. Me? I had to live with her because I couldn't really afford my own place. Sometimes, I jogged to work. She drove a pink convertible.

Bryan was all that made me happy. But Geena had to steal him from me. And this wedding… she knew I've been dreaming about this ever since I was a little girl. I had this planned out in my diary since I was ten. And she…she took it all away from me.

I sat back on the chair. Adam knelt down in front of me so he could look into my eyes.

"What am I going to do, Adam?" I asked.

He sighed. "Get up," he said. "That's the first thing that you should do. *Get. Up.* Get your act together. Then keep moving forward. *Never* look back."

I wiped the tears from my eyes. "I don't think I can."

"Yes, you can. It's difficult, I know. But you can. You can rise above this. Don't let them defeat you, Astrid! I've known you all your life. You're better than this. You are stronger than this," he said encouragingly. "The first thing you need to do is… accept that Bryan is never coming back. Accept the fact that you have lost Geena too. Accept the fact that in this round… you've lost. You're heartbroken. Acknowledge the fact that you are in pain and suffering. And then what? What are you going to do about that?"

I stared up at Adam, and though my stunned brain was slow to react, I knew he was right. Nobody said this was going to be easy. But what am I doing? What have I been doing?

I've been moping! I've been letting this whole breakup be the center of my life, with no plan or intention of moving forward.

Bryan and Geena cheated on me. They are going to have a baby. They are going to get married. They will have the wedding that I planned for Bryan and me.

And now what? What does the future have in store for me? I was heartbroken, I was homeless and I was jobless. What was I going to do about it now?

"The pain is going to be there for a long time, Ash. It's not going to go away anytime soon. But it doesn't mean you won't do something about it. It doesn't mean you shouldn't move on with your life. The pain is going to be part of it. You know what they say? If it doesn't kill you, it should only make you stronger. And hey, what do you know? You're still alive, aren't you?"

I took a deep breath and then I closed my eyes.

Somehow, a light bulb seemed to have flickered inside my head… for the first time in weeks. I smiled slowly at Adam. "Yes, Adam. I'm still alive…"

3.

DIAMOND:

The strongest and hardest mineral. Commonly used in engagement rings to symbolize the unbreakable bond between a man and a woman.

For the next few weeks, I spent my time job hunting. I tried to steer clear of weddings for now. I knew that I was still in pain, but acknowledging the pain didn't really mean adding up to it or provoking it in whatever way.

But by end of the week, I still had nothing. I was still the same clueless girl I was weeks ago.

"Hang in there, sweetheart." Nicole said to me one night we decided to check out the new bar in the city called Oil Rig. "You'll find one. Although, you would have found one already, if you just went back to wedding planning. You were famous before. People loved your work. It would have been easy to get a job with the competition."

I rolled my eyes. "What's the point of planning other people's weddings when I don't believe in love anymore? If my own wedding is being realized by someone else?"

"Speaking of that, are you... going?" John asked.

"Hell no!" I replied quickly. "Why would I go to the wedding of my ex-fiancé and my ex-best friend? Especially if they didn't have the decency to change a thing that I planned when I was supposed to be the bride? Geena is a classic! She stole my fiancé! And she stole my wedding ideas! She's... a..." I sighed. "She's a... I don't know the word!"

"A thief?" Dannie suggested sarcastically.

"More than that! She's a lying, stupid, conniving bitch!"

"And Bryan?"

"He's a cheap, indecent, spineless son of a bitch! They really deserve each other!"

"Great!" Nicole clapped her hands. "We're getting somewhere! At least now you hate him enough to admit that you need to get back at them for what they did to you."

"How can I get back at them?" I asked.

"By showing them that you are happy," John said. "That you're beyond this. That you're over him. That you've moved on. And you're a lot happier now than when you were with him."

I snorted. "Okay. So I'll get my revenge in... five years! Tough! They won't even remember me by then!"

"They may not even be together in five years, who knows?" Nicole muttered.

"You don't have to be really happy. You just have to show them that you are. Even if you are still breaking inside. You don't have to show them that. You just need to let them see that you are happy, even if you aren't," John said.

"You mean… for the show?"

"Yes," Dannie said. "But the minute you start feeling better about it is the minute you will start getting over him! And you can do it, doll."

I smiled. A new sense of excitement filled me. And for the first time in months, I felt a little lighter and little bit happier.

I raised my bottle to them. "Cheers?"

"Cheers!" they agreed and we all took a gulp of our beers.

"So, how about pawning that ring?" Dannie said. "It can get you out of Adam's apartment."

"Come on, sweetie. No need to hold on to it. He isn't worth it. The memories aren't worth the pain that came afterwards," Nicole said.

"At least get it appraised. See how much you would get for it should you decide to cash in on Bryan's memories." John suggested.

"Worthless memories." Dannie piped in.

Well, the bastard deserved it for all that he did to me. After all, he owed me for the flowers on his wedding!

The next day, I was feeling a bit more cheerful than usual. My friends were right. It was Bryan's fault that the wedding's off. I was the injured party. I guess it wouldn't hurt to at least see how much the ring would be worth in case I truly decide to sell it. Besides, I couldn't be in the charity of Adam forever. I know I was putting him in a difficult position with his family since Geena is his sister.

I met with Nicole and Dannie and we went to the mall to get the ring checked out.

"Okay, my frame of mind should be… I am over him and I have a new boyfriend," I said, smiling dreamily.

"Hmmm… the first part is easier to believe than the second. Who is this mystery guy? Or don't tell me you have totally sold out your values and you decided to hook up with Adam."

I wrinkled my nose. "Adam? Eeww! Incest!"

Nicole laughed. "So who's the man?"

I shook my head. "No one yet. But if I accidentally run into Bryan or Geena, that's what I will tell them. It doesn't have to be true. But I'll raise my chin and that's what I'll say. I'm happy as a bird! And I'm no longer a virgin! I've given myself up on a steamy night of passion with my boyfriend, who I am very much in love with!"

"What's the name of your boyfriend?" Dannie asked challengingly.

"None of their damn business," I replied chirpily.

"Bravo!" Nicole said pulling me into the next jewelry store she saw.

I reluctantly gave my ring for appraisal at the jewelry shop. The guy at the counter gave me an apologetic smile. Instantly, he was able to deduce that it was an engagement gone sour.

"I'll see what rate we can give you," he said.

We waited for five minutes, looking at other rings and trinkets displayed around us. I could only heave a sigh looking at the diamond engagement rings in front of me. I must admit that Bryan's ring, apart from the big stone, didn't really have much style.

"Excuse me, Ma'am," the guy finally called us.

We approached him. My heart was pounding. That ring showed how much Bryan valued me, or loved me. Pawning it didn't say much about how much I valued him no matter what he did to me. And God knows I did value him… too much!

The guy looked at me uncomfortably. "I'm..." He took a deep breath. "I'm… sorry. But no jewelry shop will buy this."

"What? Why?" Nicole asked.

The guy lowered his voice so that only me, Dannie and Nicole can hear him.

"Because, I'm afraid that this is a fake," he said. "The diamond is not real."

"What?" I asked in shock. I knew my face was turning crimson. "That can't be!"

I picked up my ring and looked at the engraving inside to make sure that they had not switched it. It's still there—the date that Bryan proposed to me.

"Ma'am… this is cubic zirconia. The value of which is… I don't know… a couple of hundred at the most?"

"What?" Nicole asked, completely shocked.

"You didn't notice?" the guy asked. "I'm afraid that even the band… was just plated."

"I'm not a jeweler, how am I to know?" I asked sarcastically.

"I'm really sorry," the guy said. He smiled at me ruefully.

I took my ring back. I thought I was going to faint any minute. How could I have been so stupid? He proposed to me with a fake stone? What? He really thought I was so stupid that I wouldn't notice? That no one would notice?

How cheap did he take me for?

"Ma'am…" the guy at the counter said. "I'm really sorry." He handed me a card. "Do come and visit us again. We're giving you a privilege discount card which you can use on your future purchases."

I nodded, trying to prevent tears from rolling down my cheeks. "Thanks," I said weakly.

"Let's go," Dannie said to me.

I seemed to be floating mindlessly towards the exit. I wasn't looking in any direction, wasn't actually seeing anything when I collided with another customer who was entering the store.

I caught a whiff of sweet masculine perfume as I felt strong arms wrap around me in an iron grip, preventing me from falling flat on my butt.

Instead of pulling away from the stranger, I leaned my head on his broad shoulder and for a moment there, I felt comfort… just when I needed it the most. I held onto him and quietly let the tears seep out. Because I needed it. I needed a shoulder to cry on. Someone to hold me as I let reality slice through me. I needed someone to be strong for me at that moment when I felt the weakest… when the pain enveloped me ruthlessly.

"Are you alright, Miss?" I heard him ask, his solid chest rumbled beneath my face as he spoke.

Slowly, I turned my head upwards and found myself staring at a pair of dark sunglasses. His black bangs fell over his dark brows, one of which was raised as he stared down at me.

My mind went blank as his face and his presence filled my senses. I took in his handsome face, the sweet masculine scent of him, the hint of concern in his voice, and the feel of his arms around me.

"*Are. You. Okay?*" he repeated, this time louder and with more emphasis to every word.

I nodded as reality slowly returned to me.

Slowly, he released me, making sure I was steady enough to stand on my own. Then he took a step back. It was only then that I saw what he was wearing. White shirt and black leather jacket.

"Take it easy, okay?" he said. And with a final nod, he went inside the store, leaving me standing outside, still in awe.

"Okay, enough embarrassment for the day," Dannie said, pulling me away.

"Gees, Ash. For a moment there, I thought you were going to go hysterical in that poor soul's arms!" Nicole teased.

After walking one block with my friends, I finally snapped back to reality.

"That guy was real?" I finally asked.

"Who? Dark-haired Ken Doll?" Dannie asked back.

I nodded.

"Yeah," Dannie replied. "And he is *sooooo hooottt!*" And for a while, I thought Dannie was going to cry. "I haven't seen him before!"

"Big city. You can't know everybody who lives here!"

Then I remembered how his arms wrapped around me. In that instant, I felt warm, comforted… safe. I felt the comfort that I had been looking for since I found out about Bryan and Geena.

I looked at the ring that I still clasp in my hand and I remembered how Bryan made me believe his ring was real… along with his love.

I stopped in the middle of the sidewalk. I started crying again.

"It wasn't even a real diamond!" I wailed.

"Oh, God! Here we go!" Dannie rolled his eyes and pulled me along with him and Nicole.

"Did you hear what the guy said? It was worth only a couple hundred bucks!" I continued crying. "How could he do this to me? I thought he loved me then! And this ring... this ring was the symbol of how much he valued me, that wretched son of a bitch!" And I threw the ring on the street.

"What are you doing? You could have sent it back to him to tell him that you know!" Nicole said, running after the ring.

But then a beautiful white sports car came rushing past in front of us and ran over my ring.

"Oh no!" Nicole panicked.

"Nicole! You're going to get yourself killed! Get back over here!" Dannie shouted.

Nicole quickly crossed the street to pick up my ring... or what was left of it. True enough, the huge stone had been smashed leaving only the gold plated band.

"Thank you!" Nicole called after the car angrily.

"I don't need it, Nicole!" I said to her. "This confirms what we already know. Just... throw it away!"

"You'll never know. You just might see Bryan one day and make him... I don't know... *eat this*!" Nicole said angrily. "How could he do this to you, Ash!? I thought... I thought you two were best friends. I thought you were soulmates."

"Is this how cheap he thought I was?"

My friends hugged me, making me feel better. Or at least they tried.

I still couldn't believe it even until that evening when Dannie, Nicole and I went to meet up with John at Oil Rig.

John was speechless almost the whole time. He was shaking his head as he took large gulps of his beer.

"Say something, will you?" Nicole said.

John shrugged. "I can't really say anything except that... I thought Bryan couldn't sink any lower!"

"A freaking cubic zirconia! He said he spent a fortune on that ring!" I said. I drank my beer. "How could he trick me like this? How couldn't I have known? I was a wedding planner, for Christ's sake!"

"You plan weddings, honey. Not engagement parties. Your job begins long after the ring has been placed on the bride-to-be's finger," Dannie pointed out.

Now I realized that for the years that we had been together, Bryan and Geena must have thought me naïve. I was this... pushover, who worshipped the ground that they both walked on... like they couldn't do anything wrong in their lives. I did almost everything they asked me to. God! I'm such a fool!

My sorry thoughts were interrupted by a phone call from my mother.

27

"I... have to take this call, guys," I said. I quickly dashed to the nearest exit of the bar and answered my phone.

"Are you okay, sweetie?"

"I've been better, Mom," I replied.

"Well... I'm sure... if you're still in touch with your cousin, Adam, your invitation has reached you by now. I know it may come as a surprise."

"Yes! It was a *shocker*!!!" I muttered sarcastically.

"I know what they did to you was horrible, sweetheart," my mother said apologetically.

"There are no words for it, Mother!" Tears instantly rolled down my cheeks but I refused to let her hear me whimper.

"But sweetheart, you and Geena... you've been the best of friends all your lives. I mean... you can't really miss this one time event in her life."

"Mom? What are you saying?" I asked her. "Are you... saying that Geena and Bryan will last forever?"

"Oh, sweetheart. You aren't... over him yet, are you?"

"Wow, Mother! It's only been two months since I found out that my boyfriend for years had been sleeping with my best friend for life! I'm not really made of stone, Mother!"

I heard her sigh at the other end of the line. Then she said, "This is going to be tougher than I thought."

"What's going to be tougher, Mom?"

She took a deep breath and then she said, "Sweetheart... we were hoping you would come."

"Where?"

"To... the wedding."

Right that instant, I thought I was hearing things. I could not believe what my mother just asked of me. After running what she said over and over in my head, I still thought I was hearing things.

"Mom... wha... what did you just say?"

"Sweetheart... We know that it was wrong what they did to you. But... this is our family. Geena is like a daughter to us, too. You grew up together. You were best friends all your lives. It's tradition to have a reunion during big events in a family member's life and Geena's wedding is a big event. You may be mad and hurt about the whole thing, but you and Geena... you go back a long way, sweetheart. You two will kiss and make up and you will learn to forgive Bryan. You were also best friends. You would... feel sorry someday if you missed this wedding. I heard it's going to be grand!"

"Oh Mother! I am sure it will be!" I said very sarcastically. "After all, I planned the whole thing! This was supposed to be my wedding Mother! Bryan's and mine! The fact that you think I can get over their sleeping together behind my back, and lying to me for months so easily is unbelievable, Mom! Geena may have been my best friend all my life, but now... she's just some bitch who broke my heart, stole my fiancé, and ruined my dream wedding!"

"Sweetheart... please. You can just show up for an hour at the reception. Say hi to your relatives. Say hi to Uncle Jack. It would mean a lot to him for you to be there."

I sighed. *Uncle Jack.* He's like a father to me. And whatever he gave Geena when we were growing up, he also gave me. Like when he went on trips and gave Geena a doll when he got back, I had the same one too. Even when we were in college, I was like a daughter to him. And I love him. But... if he loves me, wouldn't he understand why I wouldn't make it to Geena's wedding?

"Sweetheart... please. If you can't do it for Geena, please do it for Uncle Jack."

"Mother... I'm sure, Uncle Jack would understand and forgive my absence," I said.

There was silence on the other end of the line.

"Mother?"

"Think about it, dear. You have another three weeks."

"Mom, it doesn't matter if I had three years to think it over, I'm not going." I went to hang up the phone, but one small, vindictive part of me made me raise my phone back to my lips.

"By the way Mom, Geena's pregnant. That's how I found out about their affair." I only listened long enough to hear my mother's brief gasp and apology before I hung up the phone.

I still couldn't believe it when I came back to our table.

"What? Geena has more bad news for you?" Dannie asked, quite alarmed.

I sighed. "No. But my mother does."

"Is everything okay?"

I smiled sarcastically. "According to her, everything will be just peachy if I attend the wedding."

They all groaned.

Nicole was almost furious. "Excuse me, I know she is your Mother, but what is she thinking? Does she not care about you at all?"

"I don't think she understands what it feels like to be cheated on or to be forced to call off your wedding. Or to see your dream wedding happening to someone else." Tears rolled down my cheeks.

Dannie and Nicole put their arms around me.

"Look up, sweetheart," John said. "Better things are coming your way. But for now, you need to hold your chin up high."

I smiled at them. "Thanks, you guys," I whispered.

"Just make sure that if you do choose to attend that wedding, you will not be attending it alone."

I raised my brow at John.

"Well, make sure that you go with a guy. A date. Some guy who's ten times hotter than Bryan and can't keep his hands off of you. We guys really hate that!"

"Really?"

He nodded. "You've dated Bryan longer than he's ever dated Geena. He's had the hots for you ever since. But he never had you… right?"

I rolled my eyes. "Of course! I've been holding it off until my wedding night."

"So, somewhere in the back of his mind, he still wonders what it would have been like to have you… to touch you more intimately. And maybe he just might still have some feelings for you."

"If he had feelings for me, he wouldn't be marrying Geena!" I muttered.

"He's a cheapskate, Astrid! He wanted his money back! Or make the most of it, if the refund option was not available!" Nicole said crossly.

"It's only been two months. He was madly in love with you for years. Chances are… he still has some feelings for you. It may not be what it used to be, but… there's still a shred of that emotion there. And the lust thing is definitely still there because it was never satiated," John continued.

"So, what are you saying?"

"I'm saying, show up with some guy who's so handsome and so hot, even Bryan would want to sleep with him if he were gay. And make sure you two get too close for comfort. Send out signals that you've already slept with this guy."

Dannie beamed. "That's like a slap in the face for him, isn't it?"

"And nobody in that wedding will ever feel sorry for you for what happened. They will think, if this is the prize you got for losing Bryan, then you were much better off," Nicole agreed.

"Not only should he be hot, but he should be a lot more than an orthodontist," Dannie said. "He should be a third-generation millionaire, trust-funded, Ivy League graduate."

"Wow," I breathed. "And what does he do for a living?"

"He should be running his family business or have investments here and there," Nicole suggested.

"And show up in at least a Boxster," John added. "Bryan loved cars!"

Now, I must admit that a part of me got a little bit excited about the whole thing. But then again… I'm wide awake and still sober!

"That is really great, guys! But how will I ever nail a guy like that? And in three weeks? *Where* will I find a guy like that?"

They all fell silent after that. Whether because they thought it was impossible for me to end up with a guy born with a silver spoon or because they thought the time limit was too short, I wasn't sure.

I took a gulp of my beer again.

"Well?" I asked finally. "I've lived here for years and I haven't met a guy like that. That's our first problem. And guys like that only seem to go for supermodels, that's our second problem."

"Think positive, Ash. You could stumble upon a guy like that, you know."

"And you have to remember, I *never* go for the rich and famous," I said.

It was my thing since Kevin Moore. In my version of a fairytale romance, it's the brave, honorable knight who took home the princess, not the spineless prince charming. The rich kids I went to school with were all bullies, with nothing to show for themselves, except for the flashy gadgets and cars that their parents gave them. I swore off guys like Kevin. He taught me not to hope that I would be enough to hold his heart or attention forever.

So I always turned down the rich jocks that attempted to ask me out after Kevin. I wasn't impressed with their wealth. I preferred a middle class guy who was smart beyond his years, and was responsible enough to focus on long-term goals. Someone who would be loyal and would make me the center of his world.

"Bryan knows that perfectly well, too," Nicole said.

"Well, then that might work out well for you, too," John said. "He'll know how much you have changed since you broke up with him. That will make sleeping with this new guy even more believable."

I forced a smile at them.

"But… three weeks is a short notice. Even if you do find him and date him, how would you get him to be all over you in time for the wedding without giving him an impression that you're a slut?" Dannie asked.

"I know! Love potion number nine!" I muttered sarcastically.

We sat there for a while, contemplating our scheme. I must admit that it was perfect. If I go, even for the sake of Uncle Jack, I don't want to look like a fool at that wedding. I don't want to be pitied. And I don't want Bryan to think that he was better off, or Geena to think that she had taken everything away from me. I wouldn't be able to stand the sympathetic looks of my aunts and uncles, even of my parents and grandparents. And I would especially not withstand the sneers of Geena's friends.

Actually, thinking about all that, I wondered again, why I was contemplating going to this wedding. It would be much safer to just stay at home.

31

"Guys, I... I don't think I should go at all. Why are we even discussing this?" I said to my friends. "No. I will be firm about this! I will stay at home... and sulk!"

****

That night, I told Adam all about the ring that Bryan gave me. He didn't even offer a reaction.

Then, I proceeded to tell him about my Mom's phone call, persuading me to attend the wedding and my friends' suggestion to find a date for that night.

"Your Dad would understand if I don't go, right?" I asked him.

He shrugged. "Yeah, he would. But it would warm his heart to know that... there is hope that you will forgive Geena for what she has done to you."

I groaned.

"But your friends are right. You should go with someone who is like a slap in the face for Bryan. Someone that Geena herself would drool over. You already know she has envied you all her life. Even though she has Bryan now, it's still a hard habit to break. So, I suggest you show up happy to that wedding... should you choose to go, that is."

"But Adam... how will I get a dream guy like that to fall for me in three weeks? Considering, I don't even know where to find one!"

Adam chuckled and then he said, "Oh, little Astrid. Your soul is too good, you don't know how to conjure evil plans, do you?"

"What?"

"Find that guy, Astrid. Smoking hot! That's all you need to do."

"Where?"

He shrugged. "You go out more than I do. I don't know. In bars maybe!"

"Even if he's smoking hot, he needs to be rich, smart, has a great career and he must be in love with me."

Adam laughed so hard, I actually started to feel insulted.

"What, you jerk? Tell me!"

"He doesn't have to be all that," Adam replied. "He just needs to be from out of town and not know anyone in the city."

"And?"

"And then you ask him to pretend he's rich. A nice suit would do the job. As long as he's not dumb, had a little bit of high school education, he's good to go. Nobody in our family questions guests scientifically. Well, except for me. But I'm on your side here. So, I'll keep my mouth shut."

"Adam...*are* you insane?"

"Are you desperate?" he asked back.

I sighed and didn't answer.

32

"If you can't get him to say yes to the whole charade as a date or as a friend, pay him. I'll lend you the money. Or better yet, I'll pay for it myself. Whatever takes you out of this misery! Even for just a day!"

"You really are insane!" I rolled my eyes.

He shook his head and put an arm around my shoulder.

"No. Sometimes I've wished you really were my little sister, too." He smiled at me encouragingly and gave me a kiss on my forehead.

I sighed and then started to head to my room. Then I looked back at Adam.

"Thank you, Adam. You're a great brother," I said and then I headed to my room.

4.
RSVP:
Répondez s'il vous Plaît, meaning, "Please Respond"

I'm not going. I'm not going.

At least that's what I kept telling myself over the last two weeks. Now, it's one week until the wedding and no phone calls from my mother begging me to go. Not even an encouraging look from Adam.

So finding mystery Alpha Male is out of the question. Until I received the call that I thought I would never receive.

"Sweetheart, it's Uncle Jack."

I took a deep breath. "Hey, Uncle Jack! How's it going?"

"Not bad," He replied. "How are you?"

"I'm…fine, Uncle Jack."

He sighed. Then he said, "Sweetheart, I know that what Geena did to you is just… unforgiveable. I… couldn't believe it when I found out. I know how hurt you must have been."

"It's fine, Uncle Jack. I'm… over it." I lied.

"If you won't make it to the wedding, I would definitely understand," he said.

I didn't answer. Somehow, there's a hidden message there. *Does he or doesn't he want me to attend the wedding?*

"Astrid… I'm sorry. For Geena's behavior."

"It's fine, Uncle Jack. You don't have to apologize," I said weakly.

"You've been like a daughter to me too. I know your pain, sweetheart. Like I said, I am deeply sorry for what Geena has done. And if you can't find it in your heart to forgive them… I wouldn't hold it against you."

I took a deep breath and went silent for a while. And then finally, I said, "You must be excited for the wedding, Uncle Jack. You'll be walking Ge… her down the aisle."

His tone finally lightened. "Yes. It's a proud feeling to be walking your little girl down the aisle. It's… probably going to be the happiest day of my life…" He trailed off, realizing that he probably said too much.

"It's okay, Uncle Jack. I know you feel very proud. And I will attend the wedding. For you. So your joy will be complete." I didn't know why I said that. But I guess, I really love Uncle Jack. Enough to sacrifice my pride… just to make him complete on that day.

For a while there was silence, then I heard his heavy intake of breath. "Oh sweetheart, sweetheart…" he started saying. "Sweetheart, you don't need to do that."

"For you, Uncle Jack," I said, trying my best not to cry. "I will do it for you."

He sighed again and I thought I heard tears in his voice when he said, "Thank you, Astrid. You're a wonderful woman. And someday, you're going to meet somebody who will make you happier than you have ever been."

Now, I really cried. "Thank you, Uncle Jack. That means a lot to me. I'll see you next week."

After I hung up the phone, I must have cried for hours until it dawned on me that I had a bigger problem now.

If I were to bite every bit of my pride, I would do so with dignity and grace! Even if it's just for the show.

I stood up from bed and called all of my friends and asked them to meet me at Oil Rig.

Adam had a smirk on his face when I walked past him in the living room.

"Ten grand," he said to me.

"What?"

"That's what I'm willing to pay for your date," he said without even blinking an eye.

"Wow! Why so generous?"

"Because you're more desperate now than you were two weeks ago."

"You're not kidding, are you?" I asked, narrowing my eyes at him.

He shook his head. "I don't have a sense of humor, Ash. You know that."

When I met my friends at the bar, I told them about my sudden problem.

"We could have found the perfect guy by now if you had only decided two weeks ago!" Dannie complained.

"I know guys! Now, I'm just plain desperate."

"Where are we going to find your perfect guy? And how?" Nicole asked.

"Adam," I replied.

"Adam? Are you crazy! He's your cousin! Even if you are not related by blood, you grew up as cousins!" Nicole said, clearly abhorred by the idea.

"No, silly! Adam gave me an idea. He said, I only need to find a super hot guy and the rest is easy."

"Are you forgetting? We want super hot, super rich, evidently smart and successful?" John reminded us.

I shook my head. "We only need super hot and maybe desperate for money!"

They all looked at me as if I just lost my mind.

"Adam is willing to pay a guy like that to pretend to be smart, rich and head over heels for me."

"How much money?"

"Ten grand," I replied.

Nicole sucked in a deep breath, Dannie's eyes went wide and John almost choked on his drink.

"Wow! That's a lot of money!"

"Well, he will have expenses. He needs to rent a suit and a nice car. Plus he needs to… *act*. And act well!"

"What's in it for Adam?" Dannie asked.

I shrugged. "Like you, he's was my punching bag too, remember? He sleeps next door to me when I cry at nights. It must have been excruciating to live with me for months now. If I know him well, I think he's willing to pay ten grand for a change of scene. Or maybe he's hoping this is the push I needed to get my act together soon so I can move out of his crib and move on with my life. Plus, he's rich. Ten grand is nothing to him."

"Okay, so your guy only needs to be sexy and handsome and must have a little bit of education?" John asked.

I nodded. "He must be in on the deal. He must pretend to be smitten with me."

"And you won't mind if this guy kisses you all over, puts his tongue down your throat, and his hands all over your ass?" Nicole asked.

I took a gulp of my beer. "If he's super hot, maybe not." I know that once I see Bryan and Geena all lovey-dovey, *I* just might put my tongue down this stranger's throat!

We all agreed to scout for that hot guy who will be perfect for our scheme.

"Remember, he must rent or borrow a luxury sports car, if he doesn't already own one. And he must come in an expensive suit," Dannie reminded everybody.

"Oh, oh! Wouldn't it be nice if he rents out the most expensive hotel room in the resort where Geena and Bryan will have their honeymoon?" I asked.

They all stared back at me.

"And what if he proposes to me on the same night? With a big diamond ring! A real diamond ring! That would really steal Geena's thunder! And that's only fair since she stole my wedding anyway!"

"Ten grand? Not going that far," John chuckled.

"I'm sure there are rental diamond rings out there. We'll return it after a day."

"Ash, don't you think that's going a little too far?" Nicole asked with a worried expression on her face.

"*They* went too far, Nic! They cheated on me and they stole my dream wedding! Plus, they made me pay for their florist! Every single discount they got for their wedding was because of me! Because those suppliers thought *I* was going to be the bride! Now, *that's* cheap!"

John shook his head and took a gulp of his beer.

Dannie nodded "I'm sorry, Nic. But I agree with Astrid. The only way she can get back at them for what they did to her, is to shine brighter than the bride on her wedding day, and to make the groom ask himself, *what the hell was I thinking?*" Dannie smiled at me. "I'm with you, Ash. Let's find you the perfect man for the job!"

I was all set and excited for the next day. We were all supposed to reconvene at the Oil Rig Bar with pictures of prospects that I can choose from.

I'm was going 'men shopping' and for the first time in months since Bryan proposed to me. I actually felt a tingle of a thrill go down my spine.

The next day, as I was rushing to the Oil Rig, Adam handed me an envelope.

"What's this?" I asked him.

"A down payment," he replied.

I looked inside the envelope and found a check amounting to five grand.

"You're really serious, aren't you?"

"I keep my promises, Ash. And I know you need this more than ever. You can give this to your guy as an act of good faith. He can rent a suit and a nice car with this. The other half, he'll get after the party," he said.

"Adam, seriously, why are you doing this?"

He put an arm around my shoulder and pulled me towards him. "I hate weddings! I'm willing to pay for a little entertainment."

I laughed and reached up to give him a peck on the cheek.

"Thanks anyway," I said.

"Good luck. Make it worth my money, Ash," he called in a teasing tone.

When I arrived at the Oil Rig, none of my friends were there yet. I sat in the bar and ordered a margarita.

"The best margarita in town for the beautiful lady," I heard the bartender say.

I looked up and found myself staring at the most striking green eyes I have ever seen in my life. Long dark lashes framed his eyes. He was wearing a white cap over his dark hair and had a stud earring on his left ear.

"Can you sign, Ma'am?" he asked. It took me a while to realize that he had already asked me the question twice.

"Oh." Was all I could say. He nodded slightly and his lips curved into a crooked smile, revealing a deep dimple on his left cheek.

I was pretty sure that my hands were shaking as I signed the slip he handed to me.

"Thank you," I said.

"You're welcome, Madam. Enjoy your drink. Just call for me if you need anything else," he said, grinning.

I might have been in a relationship for too long because, for the life of me, I could not tell whether he was flirting with me or not. But since I had almost lost everything I had worked for, there was nothing I could say to him that would make me sink any lower. Bryan and Geena have totaled me out, thank you very much!

"And what name would I ask for?" I asked, mustering all the confidence I could manage, and hoping to God that my voice didn't sound squeaky.

He flashed me a brilliant smile that made my world turn upside down and every nerve in my body tingle. His aristocratic face suddenly turned boyish and mischievous with a perfect smile that showed another deep dimple on his other cheek, and his perfect set of teeth.

"Ryder," he replied.

I nodded. "Alright. Thanks, Ryder."

He stood there for a while, and I knew he was waiting for me to say my name. Then after a couple of seconds, he figured out I was not going to give it to him. I grinned back at him instead.

"Alright. Perhaps when I bring you your next drink." And he gave me a wink.

I knew I was blushing from head to toe. How could I be flirting with a guy like *that*? When I was with Bryan, I didn't care about how I looked or who looked at me. I always thought I'd be with Bryan until the end of my life. And what he thought about me was the only thing that mattered.

But now, flirting with the bartender who looked like he just stepped out of the covers of a magazine gave me a new string of confidence. I actually felt... womanly... beautiful!

I sipped on my drink, trying to get his face out of my head, but I just couldn't. The memory of his perfect smile and his perfect features were playing in slow motion in my head. I almost forgot that it'd been an hour and my friends hadn't showed up yet.

"Fancy another glass?" Ryder came back and asked.

I looked up at him and because he was so breathtakingly beautiful, I nodded instead of saying something.

My phone rang. It was John.

"Sorry, doll. I can't make it tonight," he said. "My sister had a little emergency and I needed to go take her."

"Is she okay?"

"Yeah, she's fine. Just a little cut on the elbows and knees. But other than that, she'll live."

"Okay... what about the prospects?"

"Well, I can't find anybody else who would agree besides Jonathan. And I thought Jonathan was... not extraordinary enough for your taste."

"Besides the fact that we never got along? He's an ogre!" I muttered.

John laughed. "Easy, Ash. Beggars can't be choosers."

I sighed. "Find somebody else okay?"

Nicole sent me a text message that she couldn't make it either. She had to work on some presentation that needs to be finished by tomorrow.

When I saw Dannie's number appear on my phone, I was getting hopeless.

"Sweetie, I'm sorry." It looked like he was going to come up with an excuse then decided to be honest. "Who am I kidding? I'm on a date. I didn't mean to be, but you know Jasper? I've been dying for him to notice me in the office and finally, he asked if I wanted to hang out tonight! You understand right?"

"Do I have a choice?" I asked.

"Don't worry. I might find some prospects for you. I'm going to a house party tonight!"

"Dannie! Chances are, you're going to a gay house party! And there's no hope for me there."

"Well, you said your guy just needed to look the part. And act it out. You didn't say anything about being straight."

"Oh, that would just be nice." I groaned. "Just enjoy your party. And please... find me a straight guy!"

I heard a suppressed chuckle from the counter as soon as I hung up. I saw Ryder smiling crookedly, and although he was not looking at me, I knew the smile was for me.

I raised a brow. "You shouldn't eavesdrop on other people's conversations." I said sipping my margarita, not looking at him.

"I wouldn't have, if your voice wasn't that loud," he said, approaching me.

"Oh, sorry," I said. "People talk loud in bars, you know. Well, you should know."

"Yes. I know," he grinned. "So, what's the quest for a straight guy for?"

Lie! I told myself. But somehow, the liquor in my system and the frustration I felt for being stood up by my best friends were wearing me out.

"Not just a straight guy. But a straight guy who's willing to do anything for a couple of grand."

He raised a brow. "You're not doing porn, are you?"

I stared at him, clearly abhorred by the thought and then I burst out laughing. "Oh my God! No!" I said when I finally found my voice. "Well, it's not porn, but it does involve the part of playing lovers."

"Now, I'm intrigued. What could a girl like you possibly need a straight guy for?" he asked me.

"You wouldn't believe me if I told you," I said to him.

"Try me," he said with a grin.

"It's a long story," I said.

"I'm here all night," he insisted.

"Yeah, but you're working."

"It's a lax night," he said.

I narrowed my eyes at him. "You're pretty persistent, aren't you?"

He shrugged. "I'm a straight guy. Who knows? I just might be able to help you out."

"Oh! As if!" I rolled my eyes. "You don't strike me as desperate."

He raised a brow. "Everybody has needs, honey."

I sighed. "Okay, where do I start?"

"From the top?" He grinned. As he flashed me that gorgeous smile, I couldn't help thinking, *I could go to bed with this guy!* Then I shook myself back to reality. I took the last gulp of my margarita.

"Perhaps you should give me another margarita first."

"Right away, Ma'am," he said.

He disappeared for a while and when he came back, he handed me another margarita and a bowl of cheese sticks.

"Margarita and cheese sticks, on the house," he said.

"Wow! All these for the pathetic story of my life?" I asked, taking a bite of a cheese stick.

"Well, some stories are worth paying for," he smiled.

I sighed. "Okay. I don't really see the point why I should be telling the tale of my somewhat…sad life to a complete stranger, but whatever."

He leaned closer to me and my breath caught in my throat. "What color are your eyes?" he asked.

"Oh… they're… blue," I replied.

"You're wearing contacts," he said.

I nodded. "My eyes are bluish violet."

He took a step back and smiled. "Nice color. Why do you want to hide that?"

"It's… too different."

"Different is good," he said. "So, what's the story of your life?" he asked. He picked up the champagne glasses in front of him and wiped them one by one as he listened to me.

"Okay… so three months ago, I had everything. A wonderful fiancé I was in love with… the job of making dreams come true… a best friend who is also my cousin, who I grew up and lived with most of my life." I was trying my best not to cry again.

"My life was perfect. I was planning the wedding of my life. The wedding I had pictured in my head ever since I was a little girl. But... three months ago, I found out that my fiancé was sleeping with my cousin. And he knocked her up. To cut a long story short, my world fell apart. I lost my job because I could no longer picture the perfect wedding, or imagine happily ever after. The apartment I was living in belonged to my cousin... I couldn't bear to live there anymore. I had to crash at my cousin's brother's place temporarily... until I get a job or my act together, whichever comes first." Again, I was reminded about how sad my life was.

"I was at my lowest point... or so I thought. A couple of weeks ago, I found out that my ex-fiancé and my cousin would be getting married. And to make matters worse, the wedding I was planning months ago is still going to happen. All of it! From the invitations to the reception right down to the florist! All of it was going to happen exactly as I had planned. But not to me." I took a deep breath. "Everything is going exactly as I had imagined it would be since I was a little girl... except that... I'm not going to be the bride."

I didn't know that I was crying until Ryder reached up and wiped my tears with his thumb. He had a serious look on his face. He didn't say anything, but I knew he understood how I felt.

I took another deep breath.

"And worse, I have to keep a straight, brave face in front of my family. I'm going to attend the wedding."

He raised a brow. "Surely they can't ask that of you."

"Oh, they can. Her father was like a father to me too. I'm going to do it for him. But God! I can't be there alone!"

"And what do you need a straight guy for?"

"I need some guy to pretend to be my boyfriend... to pretend that he can't keep his hands off me... to be so in love with me... so I can keep my dignity," I replied.

"You not only need a straight guy," he said, his eyes narrowed. "You need to make everybody think that you are a lot better off."

I was taken aback by his analysis. Apparently, Ryder's IQ was higher than I gave him credit for. I admired how immediately he was able to deduce my desperation.

I nodded. "The wedding's in a week. I'm desperate. I'm... willing to pay if necessary."

He looked like he was taken aback, but then he chuckled. "That's cute," he said.

"If I ask you, will you help me?" I asked boldly. It's now or never... while the margarita is still effective in my head, I had to say it.

Ryder seemed like a man who had been through a lot in his life and it would probably take a lot to surprise him, but I could see that I had done just that with flying colors.

"I'll… pay you. I'll make it worth your while," I said.

He chuckled and then he leaned his face closer towards mine. "You might not be able to afford me, sweetheart," he said.

"Everybody has a price," I said, refusing to back down.

"True," he said leaning away from me. "I'm not sure I'm for sale though."

"Ten grand. One night. All you need to do is rent a nice suit, come in a fancy car, maybe a Boxster, and rent a diamond ring… or something that will pass as a diamond ring, at least two carats in size."

He raised a brow. "You really are desperate, aren't you?"

I took a deep breath and stared back at him. But I didn't say another word.

"Why the ring?" he asked.

I took a sip of my margarita. "You wouldn't believe it if I told you."

"I find a lot of things you've said to me tonight hard to believe, but damn, I still believe you. So try me again," he replied.

"My fiancé gave me a two carat diamond ring when he proposed. He said he worked hard for it and that it represented how much he valued me. When we broke up, my friends convinced me to pawn it to get back at him. I was jobless anyway, and I could use the money. I went to the jewelry store and had the ring checked out… it turned out to be cubic zirconia, gold plated. I couldn't believe it. What a fool I'd been! I rushed out of the shop crying like a baby." I didn't realize it, but tears were rolling down my cheek.

Again, Ryder reached out to wipe my cheeks with his fingers. When I looked up at him I saw that his expression was soft, like his heart just broke for me, too.

"Do you really think I'm capable of making your ex-fiancé feel like a dwarf?" he asked softly.

I giggled in spite of my tears. "Needless to say, you're a hundred times better-looking than he is. Plus, he's just an inch taller than me. He's short to begin with."

He chuckled. Then gently, he squeezed my nose.

"Alright. I'll help you out. You name the time and the place."

I looked up at him and searched his face. And somehow his expression was warm and genuine. It seemed that my story moved him and he was helping me out just to… help me out. Not just for the cash.

"You need to rent out a nice suit. I might be wearing something violet at the wedding. Their motif is green. I want to make sure I will stand out."

He laughed. "Alright. I'll be your knight in shining Armani."

43

"Plus, you need a good cover. Tell them you graduated with honors from an Ivy League school. Doesn't matter where exactly. Just make something up. You invest money here and there. You have a six digit monthly income."

"You really are going to murder your ex, aren't you?"

"I want to make him cry!" I muttered. "As much as I want to save myself from a little humiliation."

He laughed. "Then I won't disappoint you."

I took out the envelope in my bag and wrote my name and contact number on it.

"This is… a sign of good faith. You'll get the rest after the party," I said, handing him the envelope.

He stared at it for a while and then he took it. But he didn't open it to see what was inside.

"How will I find you?" I asked him. "What's your full name?"

"I won't be here for the rest of the week. But I'll be back in time for your wedding," he said. He took my hand in his and wrote something at the back of my palm. I stared as he wrote his number gently. Then slowly, he brought my hand to his lips and gave it a gentle kiss. "It's Ryder … Ryder W-Woodson," he whispered.

I knew I was blushing from the kiss he gave me. He saw my expression and he laughed.

"You better get used to it," he whispered. "Your knight in shining Armani will be doing more than that at the wedding."

I swallowed hard and I knew I couldn't control my blush anymore.

"Okay. So, I'll get my bill now," I said.

"On the house," he replied.

"No, no. This is separate from our deal."

He shook his head. "I'll just take it out of your deposit."

I stared back at his handsome face and I realized that he was serious.

"Th… Thanks."

"You're welcome, Astrid," he said, saying my name for the first time. I realized I hadn't given it to him, but I had written it on the envelope.

"I… better go," I said.

He nodded. "Are you going to be alright? Do you want a ride home?"

I shook my head. "I'll be fine."

He nodded again. "I'll see you next week then."

I'm pretty sure I was still shaking when I got out of the cab in front of Adam's place. In fact, I was still shaking when I entered his house. He was there, having some drinks on his deck.

"So, how did it go?"

"Well, my friends all stood me up."

44

"So not good?"

I shrugged. "I can't really say. Because... since they left me alone, I got to chat with the bartender. And... oh my God, Adam! He is *hhhhooooootttt*!!"

"Boundaries, sweetheart. Boundaries!" he scolded me.

"Alright, I'm sorry. What I'm saying is, this bartender was so pretty. Like he just stepped out of the covers of a magazine. He looked classy and aristocratic and yet, when he smiled, it seemed like a million fireworks just burst into the room."

"Ash... I get it, okay?" Adam looked at me sternly.

"Right. So, to make the long story short, I ended up telling him that I needed a guy to pretend with me for this wedding. And I ended up asking him if he was up for the job."

"And he was?"

"At first, he wasn't. But then I told him the story of my... fake ring. He must have realized how pathetic I am and... how desperately I needed help. So he agreed."

"And you gave him my check?"

I nodded. "Yeah. I'm sorry Adam. I didn't bargain. Ten grand."

He shrugged. "You'll get the rest next week. So, you told him he needs a cover?"

I nodded. "I will call him tomorrow when I'm not too tipsy anymore. Just to give him the specifics."

"Great! I can't wait to see the look on Bryan's face."

I smiled at Adam. Then I reached forward and gave him a peck on the cheek.

"Thank you, Adam. I don't know what I would do without you."

He smiled back at me and ruffled my hair. "You're welcome."

When I went to bed that night, I was smiling. I remembered Ryder's handsome face and how he looked when he kissed my hand.

With a grin still on my face, I thought, *where have I been all these years?*

5.
BRIDAL CAR:
The car that carries the Bride and the Groom after the ceremony; usually adorned with flowers and signage saying "Just Married!"

I picked out a bright lavender outfit that accented my curves, bared my shoulders and exposed my long perfect legs. I was going to tease Bryan… with something he never had. Something that he should have been having by now, had he waited.

I used to be a little bit on the conservative side when I was with him. But they'd stripped me of almost everything so what did I have to lose?

I went to the salon to color my hair. I tried a multi-colored hairstyle. Blonde, red, reddish brown, dark brown and a few black strands. When the hairdresser was finished, I thought I looked cool and my hair looked stylish. As a benefit, no one could tell what my natural hair color really was.

No contacts anymore. When I put on my gown, it emphasized the violet hue of my eyes that, according to my friends, is just beautiful.

I wore light makeup and I curled the edges of my hair. When I slipped into a pair of silver sandals and went downstairs, Dannie and John just applauded. Even Adam was clearly impressed.

John whistled at me.

"You look fab, sweetheart," Dannie said.

Adam smiled at me. "I'm glad to see you this way. No doubt you will be the most beautiful woman in the ballroom tonight. Bryan won't even know what hit him."

"Thank you, guys!" I said to them.

Apparently, Geena approached Fiona to get an on-site, on-the-day wedding coordinator. I told Nicole to volunteer for the job. It would be nice to have one more ally in the party besides Adam.

I had been coordinating with Ryder most of the week. His cover story was that he graduated with honors at Harvard. He's an entrepreneur. His family owns a couple of restaurant chains in New York. He invests here and there. I asked him to rent a Boxster for the night and a nice Armani suit. I also asked him to rent a ring for the night or buy a fake one that could pass as the real thing. We even agreed to rent a room in the resort to leave no doubt that Ryder and I were for real.

Bryan would be eating his heart out! He knew I never, and I mean *never*, go for super wealthy guys. He knew I preferred a guy who had more time to work on relationships than meet with his business associates. He knew I wasn't looking for something grand. I wanted a simple, but happy life. Quiet and comfortable. And moreover, I would never sleep with a guy outside marriage.

Well, he was in for the shock of his life!

The doorbell rang. Adam went to get it.

I double-checked to make sure that Adam's check was in my purse... Ryder's full payment.

"I look fine?" I asked Dannie nervously.

"You're a goddess!" he assured me and John agreed.

We all waited anxiously for my date to come. I was beginning to wonder what was taking Adam so long. Was he interrogating Ryder already?

Finally, Adam came back into the room and behind him was a breathtaking god dressed in a black silk Armani suit. His raven hair combed smoothly in place. He was wearing a pair of dark sunglasses and for a while I thought he looked familiar. He was not wearing a stud on his ear and the guy I was looking at now was ten times classier than the Ryder I met at the bar. It was almost hard to believe that this was the same guy.

"Hello, Astrid. We meet again," he said.

"Oh my God!" I heard Dannie hyperventilate behind me.

"Hey... Ryder." I tried...*hard*... to keep my voice steady.

Only Adam seemed not so pleased with my choice and I wondered why. He had a cold expression on his face and somehow I knew that he was biting his tongue to keep his thoughts from spilling out loud, which was obviously painful for him.

"Shall we?" Ryder asked.

I nodded. He took my hand in his and gently, he intertwined our fingers. I caught a whiff of his cologne... sweet, yet masculine.

Adam raised a brow at me.

"Oh, sorry. Ryder, this is my cousin, Adam. And these are my friends John and Dannie."

It'd been ages since I last dated someone new, I completely forgot about the necessity of introductions.

Ryder politely shook their hands. Dannie was quite ecstatic to shake his hand, but I could tell the squeeze that Adam gave Ryder was a warning of sorts; probably some macho 'big brother' thing. I raised a brow at Adam. He merely nodded at me coolly.

Finally, we said goodbye to them. Ryder took my bag and led me outside towards a sports car and immediately, my breath caught in my throat.

Now, I don't know much about cars, but I know an expensive, flashy car when I see one.

He opened the passenger door for me.

"Mademoiselle?"

I smiled at him nervously and then I got into the car. He put my bag in the trunk and then he went around the car and sat beside me on the driver's seat.

"You're staying at the resort tonight right?"

I looked at him. "You're not coming with me?"

"Only if you'd like me to."

"If you left, that would make this all sound fake, right? Although it is fake. But... they don't know that."

"Yeah. They don't." He smiled and I had to keep my breathing under control.

He started to drive. It was going to be a long ride to the resort where the reception is going to be.

"What type of car is this?" I asked him.

He laughed. "What does the ex-fiancé drive?"

"A Porsche Boxster."

He nodded. "Don't worry. If your ex knows about cars, he knows what this car is worth."

"Yeah, he has a thing for expensive cars. But what is it? Just in case somebody at the party asks what car my..." I trailed off, not exactly sure what to call him.

"Your boyfriend for now, your fiancé by tonight," he supplied with a grin on his face.

I swallowed hard; somehow, even I couldn't believe that I scored a guy like this.

"Okay. Just in case somebody asks me what car you drive."

"It's an SLR McLaren," he said.

"Mental note taken," I breathed.

"What more do I need to know about you? Brothers or sisters?"

I shook my head. "Geena was the closest thing I had to a sister. And she tore my world apart. She's Adam's half-sister. Adam isn't actually related to me by blood, but we grew up together. He's a lawyer, which works great for him since he's probably the most tactless person I know. Says what's on his mind even though it hurts. He was the only one who dropped hints on me that something was happening behind my back. At first, I thought he just wanted to make me miserable. I didn't listen. So when the shit hit the fan, he was the only person I trusted. He took me in."

"He sounds like a good guy," Ryder whispered.

I nodded. "I only realized that now. In fact, he's the one writing you the checks."

Ryder just raised a brow at me and then stared ahead.

"Will ten grand cover all... your expenses? I mean, you offered to rent out a room for us. And this car seems more expensive than what I asked you to rent..."

He reached out for my hand and squeezed it.

"Sshhh…" he said. "Relax, love. Let's not talk about it. I have it all under control."

"And the ring?"

He chuckled. He surprised me by pulling my hand and brushing his lips against my fingers.

"You won't see the ring until tonight," he said. "Pretend you don't even know about it."

I laughed. "Alright."

He intertwined our fingers and it surprised me how relaxed he was. Like he's known me for a long time.

"You're nervous," he said, squeezing my hand. "You need to lighten up a little bit. Remember, you're on a mission. And you need to accomplish it with flying colors."

I leaned back on my seat and tried to relax a little. But inside, my heart was hammering wildly against my chest. Whether it was because I'll be seeing the two people who hurt me the most or because of the tingle that Ryder's hands were sending down my spine, I was not sure.

"Just give me a recap," he said. "I'm supposed to act in love with you. I can't get my hands off you and I only have eyes for you in the whole room."

I nodded. "Pretty much."

"Okay, so how did we meet?"

I froze on my seat. I realized that I had spent so much time making sure that Ryder had the perfect cover that I forgot that I must also have the perfect love story for us.

"God! I forgot that!"

"Hmmm… how about at the bar. Oil Rig. You're there a lot, aren't you?"

"Yeah I am."

"Okay, so we met through your friend John. He introduced us and I fell in love with you at first sight."

"Wow! You believe in that?"

He stared over at me under those pitch-dark shades and even though I couldn't see his eyes, I could feel a blush creep over my face.

"Hey, we're going for the rebound story of the year, why not go the extra mile?"

I giggled. "I admire your imagination. When did we meet?"

"Two months ago. But you'd lost your faith in love then. I was pretty persistent. Let's say I sent a dozen roses to your apartment for a month until I finally got you to go out with me, and I haven't let you go ever since."

"Have I met your parents?"

He shook his head. "But you do speak to my mom on the phone a lot."

"Where are they?"

"They're in Manhattan. I'm just in town for my latest business venture."

"Where do you live in Malibu?"

"Let's say a few blocks from Adam," he replied.

I laughed. "Okay, I'll say it's the three story house with the huge wrap-around deck facing the beach."

He smiled. "Yeah. It could be that house."

"God, I hope no one in the party would know the owner of that house! Otherwise, we're doomed."

He smiled again. "The city's big enough. You have zero percent chance of running into the house owner there to nullify our story."

"Have we slept together?" I asked, laughing.

He squeezed my hand. "Of course! I can't get enough of you."

I laughed. "My ex is going to eat his heart out if he hears that!"

"Why? Was he possessive of you?"

I shrugged. "Let's just say that he also didn't get enough of me."

Ryder stared over at me, as if asking me to elaborate. I smiled and winked at him.

"Maybe that's why he cheated on me," I said rolling my eyes.

"He must be a loser then," he said.

"Why did you say that?"

"Because if I had you, I wouldn't think about touching anyone else."

I forgot to breathe right that instant. When I finally recovered, I forced a laugh. "Right. Keep that frame of mind. You need it to make it all real."

"Not a difficult job, love," he murmured.

"I'm twenty-eight years old, by the way," I said.

He smiled. "I'm two years your senior."

"I'm jobless right now. But I'm looking."

He shook his head. "Why not say you're looking to put up your own business?"

"Me? Put up my own business?"

"Yeah. With me in your life, I have influenced your entrepreneurial skills."

"Wow! It'd be awesome if that were true!"

"Why not? Do you want to be an employee all your life? You've got the skills, the know-how, the contacts, and even the portfolio."

"But I don't have the capital."

"Ah-ah-ah… Are you forgetting? Your rich boyfriend invests here and there. Why can't he invest in you?"

"Trust me! My relatives will be watching out for that! And they would know if it didn't happen within the next few months!"

"In the next few months you will have your act together. You could always say something more interesting and a little bit less risky came up."

I stared at him and realized how brilliant his plan was. "You really have the answer to everything, don't you?"

He laughed. "Just years of talking to a lot of people."

I realized that Ryder was smart. And being a bartender in a classy bar like Oil Rig exposed him to a whole lot of different people. He seemed like a person who likes to listen to people's stories. And he was quite a charmer. I felt confident that we would be able to pull this off. And I had the feeling that even Geena would hyperventilate at the sight of him. Bryan would be practically salivating with envy! That is... if John's right and he still had feelings for me.

We chatted, polished our plan and then I must have fallen asleep for a couple of minutes. It was at least an hour drive to the resort.

We arrived at the hotel with perfect timing. A bridal car was parked in front of us.

"That's them?" he asked.

"Unless there's another wedding happening here tonight," I replied nervously.

Ryder took off his shades and placed them on top of his head.

"So, now, we're officially together," he said to me.

I nodded, my heart pounding in my chest.

He smiled gently. I could drown in the deep green of his eyes.

"Permission to become your boyfriend, Ma'am," he asked politely and I couldn't help smiling.

"Permission granted, Sir," I said, giggling.

He stared at me deeply in the eyes. My breath caught in my throat as I watch him lean forward and brush his lips against mine. It was a soft, gentle kiss. When he pulled away, I thought he took my heart with him.

"Do... do I need to start getting used to that too?" I asked, stuttering slightly. I felt completely dazzled by this man.

He raised a brow and grinned at me. "Oh no, love," he replied and just before we went out of the car, he said, "Not just that!" And he gave me a rakish wink.

My heart pounded as I watched him exit the car and go around to open the door for me. I saw Bryan and Geena just getting out of the bridal car in front of us. Before I got out, I caught a glimpse of Bryan looking at Ryder's car with *lust*.

I felt a thrill creep through my veins. Operation Revenge was starting to work exactly as planned.

"Come, love," Ryder said, holding his hand out.

I took it and slowly stepped out of the car.

Ryder took my hand and pulled me towards him. He leaned closer to my ear and said, "I forgot to tell you. You look breathtakingly beautiful. I'm the luckiest man on earth today!"

And because I couldn't say anything to that, I just laughed. He pulled me towards him and gave me a kiss on the forehead as his arm wrapped tightly around my waist.

He tossed his key to the valet. "We have bags in the back. Take it to our suite," he said and gave him our suite number.

Then, with him wrapped all around me, he led me towards the hotel. As we walked past Bryan and Geena, surrounded by some of their bridesmaids, Ryder kissed me on the lips.

We didn't look over at them, I didn't know whether they were looking at us or not. It was like Ryder and I only had eyes for each other.

When we entered the hotel, Ryder took a glance back, while I buried my face on his chest.

"Is that your ex?" he asked.

I nodded. "Are they looking?"

"Yeah. Bride, groom and entourage," he replied chuckling.

Hearing that, I stopped and faced Ryder. Then I stood up on my toes and gave him a chaste kiss on the lips. As I pulled away, he leaned forward and recaptured my parted lips, deepening the kiss. I could barely support my weight on the tips of my feet, my stance became shaky and I gripped Ryder's shoulders for balance. I was glad when his arms wrapped tightly around my waist.

When I broke the kiss I could not bear to open my eyes. It had been a while since I'd been kissed like that. In fact, I couldn't remember ever being kissed like that… like I was the center of someone's world. The kiss was sensual and enticing, but also reverently gentle.

He leaned his forehead against mine and sucked in a deep breath.

"Even if you didn't pay me… your kisses are worth it all," he said.

Staring up at him with his gorgeous green eyes, I laughed for the simple joy of the moment.

He took my hand in his and led me towards the lobby. I saw a familiar face there. Nicole was dressed in an understated cream, silk gown. She had a headset on and I couldn't help sighing.

"You miss it that much, huh?" Ryder asked.

I nodded. "I was fired by my boss because I lost faith in ever afters."

He reached forward and touched my cheek softly.

"You, of all people, deserve an ever after, love," he said to me. "Even if you don't believe in it, it still believes in you. And someday, it will find you."

I almost cried when he said that, but Nicole interrupted my thoughts.

"Astrid!" She beamed. She came over to me and gave me a hug. "Wow, you look like a goddess!" Then her eyes drifted on to my date and I could tell she fought hard to keep herself from drooling over Ryder, whether it was for my benefit or hers, I don't know.

"Nicole, this is Ryder. Ryder, Nicole. My best friend."

"Oh, it's so very nice to meet you, Ryder," Nicole said, shaking Ryder's hand. "I must say, you do not look last minute at all."

I had to glare at Nicole for that. But Ryder simply laughed. "Sometimes, the choices you don't prepare for are the best choices you'll ever make."

"So true!" Nicole said. "Okay, I see the bride and groom arriving. I'll see you later. Go and kick some butt."

"It was a pleasure to meet you, Nicole," Ryder said.

When Ryder took my hand to lead me towards the terraces, I stole a glance back at Nicole. She was staring at me.

"WOW!" She mouthed and gave me two thumbs up. I couldn't help smiling, I was proud of myself for the perfect choice I made.

"Shall we go to the party now?" I asked him.

"Depends on you," he said. "Are you anxious to go in?"

"No. Not really. If they followed my program too, there'll be a first dance after they are introduced formally as Mr. and Mrs. I don't want to be there for that!" I said, shaking my head and wrinkling my nose.

"Come, let's go watch the sunset while we have some drinks."

He led me to an open-air restaurant facing the beach. He ordered light beer and I ordered a margarita.

"Isn't it too early to be drinking?" I asked.

"You might need a little help pulling this off," he teased.

"I do not!"

"Sure you do. You tremble so much when I kiss you. Like… you're new at this or something."

"God, I hope that's not your ego talking!" I groaned. "Didn't it occur to you that maybe I haven't been kissed for a while? I need a little time to get used to it again."

"Really? You didn't attempt to date after you broke up with him?"

I shook my head. "To… to tell you the truth, I'm still in the stage of accepting how my life suddenly turned a three-sixty," I said sadly. "I was mostly mad at my cousin. She was the lucky one, you know. She was always the beautiful one, Barbie doll in the flesh. She was popular, rich, and had a loving father who gave her everything. I was the one who followed her around like an avid fan. She was always the center of attention and I didn't mind that. I didn't care. I had Bryan. He was my best friend before he became my boyfriend. And I was… comfortable with him. I thought myself lucky to have found him."

"He didn't kiss you much, did he?"

I raised a brow at Ryder. He had a teasing grin on his face.

54

I sighed and shook my head. "I guess I didn't know how much kissing two people needed to do. I didn't mind when I was with him. We were comfortable sitting together, just cuddling and being close to one another. I felt safe with him. Like I belonged. That was all that mattered to me."

"But that's not all that matters," Ryder said. "You have to have passion. Like when you walk into the room, your scent fills his senses. No one else is more divine or more beautiful. No one else can capture his attention. I mean, comfort is good. Comfort is what you get from knowing that the other person can't feel that kind of passion for anyone else but you."

For a guy who looked like a model, I was surprised to hear these words from Ryder. He spoke like he really did believe in happily ever afters.

"You're a romantic, aren't you?"

He snorted. "I'm a bartender remember? I'm the shrink behind the counter filled with liquor."

I had to laugh at that. He was right. His job required him to talk to strangers. So many people go and sit alone in the bar, drinking their problems away into the wee hours of the night, and they only have the bartender behind the counter as company. I knew this from experience, because I was once one of them. And it was easy for me to talk to Ryder about *my* problems. That was the whole reason he was here with me.

"Are you over him?"

I stared at the beautiful sunset ahead of us.

"I'm mad enough at him to stop crying over him," I replied.

"That's good enough. Because to tell you the truth, sweetheart, he's not worth it. You know what they say? The only guy who is worth your tears is the one who won't make you cry at all."

"Wow! Ryder! You must have snapped right out of a romance novel!"

He laughed. "I have a sister," he said. "She's a hopeless romantic. Got her heart broken three times."

"You seem like a protective big brother."

He smiled. "Yeah. Paris is still a baby to me. I try to be there for her as much as I can. Even if it means having to listen to all her guy problems or listen to her quote passages from all the romance novels she loves reading… or writing. She's quite talented."

I could tell that Ryder held so much love and affection for his little sister. I admired that. It made me wish I could have shared something like that with a sister or a brother. But Geena was the closest thing to a sister that I ever had and… look where we are now.

"Did you punch those guys who broke your sister's heart?"

"Just one. The one who slept with another girl. The two others went to another country. Geography is a difficult obstacle to overcome in a relationship. I can't really blame the guys. It's better they were honest with her than cheat on her."

"She's lucky to have you," I murmured.

Ryder reached for my hand and brought it to his lips.

"And any man would be lucky to have you, Astrid," he said gently. "That ex of yours... he's not it. He's not the one for you. Every single good thing that he did to you has been nullified by the things that he did after which were downright cheap and distasteful."

I squeezed his hand and smiled at him.

"Yeah. What kind of guy proposes with a fake engagement ring? The one that you get inside a candy bar for free!" I muttered.

"It doesn't show how he valued you. It shows his value as a man," he said. "Please tell me that he at least paid for something in the wedding."

"Oh, he paid for almost everything!" I said. "I threw all the receipts at him and told him it's his job to refund his money from all the suppliers."

"And instead of refunding, he thought of using all your arrangements... albeit, you are no longer the bride," he said shaking his head. "He is one of a kind, isn't he?"

"And I paid for their florist," I said.

"Don't expect him to pay you back," Ryder teased.

I squeezed his hand. "Thank you for being with me, Ryder. I couldn't have made a better choice for a date tonight."

He stood up from his seat and pulled me up on my feet. "Come on. Let's show your ex what he's missing!" And then he wrapped an arm around me and led me towards the ballroom.

"Breathe, Astrid," he whispered against my ear just as we were about to enter the ballroom. "We're going on a rollercoaster ride."

6.
PLACE CARD HOLDER:
Use a place card holder in line with your motif or theme to ensure that your guests will be seated according to your preference (not theirs!)

I fought hard to hold the tears that threatened to spill from my eyes when I saw the whole ballroom. It was exactly as I had imagined it would be. The colors, the hues, the lilies. Everything was perfect.

"Welcome to my dream wedding," I murmured to myself, but Ryder heard me.

"Welcome to the wedding that you're going to best—a hundred times over," Ryder whispered against my ear.

I looked up at him and he gave me an encouraging smile. Then he leaned his forehead against mine and he said to me, "Relax, Astrid. You have to remember, it's me you're in love with now."

And then he leaned forward and gave me a butter soft kiss. "And I love you more than your ex ever did," he murmured.

When I opened my eyes, I saw his handsome face, flushed with our kiss, his eyes sparkling. I found strength inside me. *He's really going to help me pull this off.*

"We can do this," I breathed.

He smiled. "We are doing this." He leaned forward against my ear. "Forget that we're pretending. Tonight, I really am your boyfriend. And you are mine, Astrid. I only have eyes for you."

If a guy as handsome as Ryder told you that he had eyes only for you, you should feel like you just won the lottery. I felt like I won a once in a lifetime chance to be with the prince I only see in my dreams. I thought I melted then and there.

It took me a while to realize that I did almost fall on my butt. My knees turned into jelly with the look that Ryder gave me and the words he'd spoken to me. He had his arms wrapped all around me, keeping me steady.

"Easy, love," he said in a low voice that seemed so familiar, so warm, so sincere.

I smiled up at him and then I kept myself steady.

We walked hand in hand into the ballroom. And we were just in time. Bryan and Geena were just settling into their seats after their dance.

Nicole led us to our seats and I could hear people murmuring from all over. I could feel hundreds of eyes on Ryder and me.

"What an entrance, Ash," Nicole whispered and I smiled nervously.

Ryder pulled a chair out for me, quite the perfect gentleman. I found that Nicole sat me with Adam and herself and some people I hadn't seen before in my life.

I smiled at them shyly and then I gave Adam a peck on the cheek.

"Sorry, we're late," I said to him.

"Oh, dear cousin. Don't worry about it. You had perfect timing," Adam said in a slightly higher pitched voice and I had to bite my lips to keep from laughing.

"You remember Ryder?" I asked him.

Adam nodded. "Of course, I do." He extended his hand to him and Ryder shook it.

"Nice to see you again," Ryder said politely.

"Where are my parents?" I asked Adam.

"They're over with Dad. They didn't know you were coming, did they?"

I shook my head. "I only told your dad I was coming."

"It looks like it." Adam grinned. He leaned forward to whisper in my ear, "Even the bride and groom didn't seem to know."

He excused himself from our table.

"Why aren't you making rounds to see your relatives?" Ryder whispered against my ear.

"Because I'm too nervous to stand on my own two feet." I smiled sweetly at him.

He laughed throatily, then leaned forward and gave my bare shoulder a gentle kiss.

"Come on, love. Maybe it's time you introduce me to your parents," he said.

I took a deep breath as Ryder stood up from his seat and pulled me to my feet.

I nervously made my way across the dance floor, towards the front tables where my parents were seated. Couples who were dancing stared at Ryder and me. Many of them were distant relatives who probably knew the real story and didn't really expect that I would show up tonight.

I found my parents sitting with Uncle Jack and his new wife, as well as some of my other distant aunts and uncles.

"Oh my God! What a lovely surprise!" My mother beamed as she gave me a hug.

As I hugged my father, I felt like crying again. However much I hurt, I needed to keep up appearances. I gave Uncle Jack a kiss on the cheek, and then I introduced Ryder.

"Mom, Dad, this is Ryder, my boyfriend."

"How do you do, Sir? Ma'am?" Ryder shook their hands politely.

Uncle Jack also extended his hand.

"Jack Ackers. I'm glad there's a certain someone who's making my girl blush," he said teasingly, and I could feel my face heat up. I could tell that he was relieved to see me with Ryder.

After finishing the rest of the introductions, they invited us to sit with them for a while. I turned nervously to Ryder, but his eyes sparkled as he pulled a chair out for me. He seemed so relaxed and confident. I squeezed his hand as he sat beside me and I felt him squeeze it back.

"What did you say your surname was?" Uncle Reynolds asked.

"Van Woodsen, Sir," Ryder replied politely.

"And where are you from?"

"Manhattan, Sir."

Uncle Reynolds seemed taken aback and then he gave Ryder an impressed smile.

"You're from New York?" Uncle Jack's new wife, Lilie, asked. "How did you and Astrid meet?"

"Well, I'm in town for business, Ma'am. We met through a mutual friend, whom I will always be thankful to for introducing her to me."

"What do you do, Ryder?" my father asked. Somehow, I knew his question was loaded; he was judging if Ryder was capable of taking care of me.

I was about to say something when Ryder squeezed my hand.

"I'm an entrepreneur, Sir," he replied. "I have... a couple of businesses in Manhattan and now, here in Malibu."

"What businesses?" my mother asked.

Ryder grinned at her. "I have a chain of music bars and restaurants, Ma'am."

"You know the Van Woodsens. That's what they do," Uncle Reynolds smiled. "Hey, some of your restaurants in New York take reservations as far as a month in advance. You don't suppose you can bump us in quickly if we're in town?" He chuckled.

"Uncle!" I hissed.

Oh my God! I did not think this through! I thought to myself. Why did Ryder's surname have to be or sound the same as a famous family? And worse, how could my uncle know them?

But Ryder squeezed my hand calmly.

"It's okay, love," he said to me, and then he turned to Uncle Reynolds. "Sure, Sir. Anytime. Give me a call whenever you're in the city."

"Perfect," Uncle Reynolds said happily.

"How about you, Astrid? What do you do nowadays?" Aunt Lilie asked.

"Um... I... ah..." I stammered. I felt Ryder squeeze my hand gently again, giving me the courage to... *lie.* Or dream out loud. "I'm thinking about starting up my own business."

"Really?" my mother asked, quite ecstatically. I could tell that she was worried about my answer.

I nodded nervously. "Well, it'll still be something like what I used to do before. Weddings. But this time... I'd like to do it on my own."

"That's great! Where are you going to get the capital? You know that's a great risk. A lot of money is involved," Aunt Lilie said.

"Yes, I realize that. But…"

"But I believe in her," Ryder interrupted. "I'm willing to bet my money on her. I know she'll be great."

"Oh, how wonderful!" my mother said beaming at Ryder.

"You mean, you're investing in her business venture?" my father asked, looking at Ryder.

Ryder nodded. "Yes, Sir. Your daughter is brilliant. It only took one look at this perfect setting to convince me that she's a genius."

"Oh, yes. I remember. Geena said she approached your old company to set this all up. You mean this was your concept?" Aunt Lilie asked, quite surprised.

Ryder answered for me. "Yes, Ma'am. Every single bit of it."

"Wow, you're good," Aunt Betty, Uncle Reynolds's wife said.

"Thanks," I said shyly.

I looked up at Ryder and found him staring at me with sincere admiration in his eyes and my eyes blurred with tears, because I realized who I am… who I was before Geena and Bryan destroyed me.

I stared across the table and found Uncle Jack looking at me, his eyes shining with tears. I wanted to cry more because I knew that he was genuinely happy for me. I realized that he felt guilty about what Bryan and Geena did. Now he seemed so relieved to see me evidently happier with a much better man.

"Your Dad and I might go to New York next month. Maybe you and Ryder can come with us. Ryder can take us on a tour in the city," my mother said excitedly.

Ryder looked at me and asked, "Would you like that, love?"

His voice sounded so sincere, I couldn't say no or think of anything to say, so I nodded slightly.

"Very well. It would be an honor to have you in my city, Ma'am," Ryder said to my mother.

We chatted for a while and I felt more relaxed as the following conversations dealt with topics other than Ryder's personal background.

Ryder put an arm around my shoulder and gave me a gentle squeeze. "Would you like to dance, love?"

I simply nodded, and smiled as graciously as I could. We excused ourselves from our company and Ryder led me to the dance floor.

A slow song played from the center stage as I stepped into Ryder's welcoming arms. I was so relieved that we were finally alone… well, almost alone and close enough to whisper to each other. I leaned my head on his chest and closed my eyes.

I felt a surge of excitement shoot through me again and then a sense of comfort… just when I needed it most. Like this is where I wanted to be… in Ryder's comforting, protective and passionate embrace. A tear rolled down my cheek.

"Why are you crying?" he whispered against my ear.

I didn't open my eyes. Instead, I snuggled closer and buried my cheek deeper into his chest.

"I'm just thinking that I feel … so safe here."

"Must you always be crying when you're in my arms?" he asked teasingly, but I could detect a note of concern beneath his light-hearted tone.

I pulled away to look up at him. "This is the first time I cried in your arms," I said, a slight frown wrinkling my brow.

He smiled and shook his head. He slowly leaned forward and gave me a light kiss, a simple brush of lips against lips. "This is the second time, love."

I was confused. I distinctly remember not crying in the lobby when he was hugging me, mainly because I was fighting the urge.

"When was the first?" I asked.

"That day in front of the jewelry store, you collided straight into me and instead of pulling away, you buried your face in my chest and I knew you were crying," he said gently.

I remembered that day. It was the day when I thought Bryan had already done enough to destroy my life. Ryder had already been there for me… and I didn't even know him. He gave me comfort at the exact moment I needed it the most.

"Oh my God!" I breathed. "I knew you looked familiar!"

He chuckled. "I knew you were crying for a good reason that day."

"When did you realize it was me?"

He pushed back a lock of hair behind my ear. "From the moment I took your order at the bar. I knew you looked familiar. Those eyes are… not easy to forget. I remembered you from that day. After all, who forgets a beautiful stranger who suddenly comes rushing into your arms, sobbing like a baby?"

I had to giggle at that.

"What were you doing in that jewelry shop?" I asked him.

He poked at his left ear, which had a pierce in it, but no stud.

"Oh."

I felt him pull me closer to him.

"Ryder?"

"Hmmm?"

"I think my Uncle Reynolds got you confused with some famous people in New York. You didn't correct him."

"But isn't that the point of all this?" he whispered against my ear.

"They believed you."

"That's the point too," he said.

"What are you going to do when my uncle makes good on your promise to get him into one of those restaurant chains that you don't own?"

He chuckled. "I'm a bartender, remember? I've been in the business long enough to know people. I'm sure I can make good on that promise."

"And my parents going with us to New York? This is a one-day event. I can't afford to write you a check the next time around."

He laughed. "You don't have to. You have my number. You can call me anytime you need me again. Consider the next one a favor."

I leaned closer to him and I felt him tighten his arms around me.

"I'm so glad you're with me, Ryder," I said to him. "I wouldn't be able to do this alone."

He kissed my forehead. "And I'm really glad you're mine tonight, Astrid."

After our dance, we went back to our seats, hand in hand, where we enjoyed dinner.

"Did you choose the food too?" he asked. I stared at the salmon fillet on my plate.

"In my head, I pictured a buffet for the guests," I replied.

"I know you weren't the cheapskate in your relationship," he teased.

I had to laugh at that because I knew it was at Bryan's expense.

After dinner, Ryder and I danced once again. He would give me occasional kisses that I didn't mind anymore. For the first time in months I felt that I was actually having fun with another man. A man who made me feel that I matter more than anyone. That I was the only woman in the room. That I was the only woman in the world for him.

I had a chat with former acquaintances I met through Geena and Bryan. I introduced Ryder to them. Some seemed genuinely happy for me and yet, there were some girls who looked at me like they couldn't believe I had caught a guy like this.

There were some girls hanging around us making goo goo eyes at Ryder already, hoping to catch his eye so they could send him some signal. I guess Geena's friends weren't very much different from her. Ryder didn't give them a chance. He showed everybody that he would only look at me.

When we were on the dance floor, I felt people staring at me more than they should. I'm sure I was the topic of most conversations at the tables. 'Operation: Revenge' was going exactly as planned.

It seemed I was the last person people thought would come to this wedding. They couldn't believe I was actually having fun.

In the middle of our dance, my Uncle Jack asked to cut in.

Ryder nodded graciously at him and stood by the side of the dance floor while we danced.

"I am so happy, Ash," Uncle Jack said to me.

"You should be. Your little girl got married today," I said.

"Not only that. You're here. I'm glad to see you're happy, and taken care of." He smiled.

I smiled back at him, trying to hold back tears. I was just a basket case today, it seemed.

"Ryder is quite a catch," he said. "He seems like a decent man, well-bred and he looks besotted with you."

He looks besotted with me, because he's a great actor, I thought guiltily.

My eyes drifted off to where Ryder was standing, but suddenly I couldn't find him. My eyes searched the ballroom until finally, I spotted him, holding his hand out to my mom and asking her to dance. My heart warmed at the sight and I could see my father laughing as my mother headed to the dance floor hand in hand with Ryder.

"He's a charming man. He's a hundred times better than Bryan, Ash."

"Uncle!" I couldn't believe what I just heard. "He's your son-in-law!"

"I know, sweetheart. I accepted him for my daughter's sake. However, I still can't forgive him for what he did to you and Geena. You two... are like sisters. Bryan drove a wedge between the two of you, and despite what your mother hopes, I know your relationship will never be the same."

I leaned forward and gave my uncle a hug. "Don't think about that, Uncle. Geena and I have a long... history together. Time heals all wounds."

"That's why I'm happy to see you here. It's a good start. And I'm so... so happy to see you with someone who... can heal you. Then hopefully, someday, you may forgive what Geena did to you, so you two can start all over again."

This time, I couldn't help tears from rolling down my cheeks. Uncle Jack had to wipe them away with his thumb.

"Now, now dear. You don't want to ruin your makeup."

We had a fat laugh as we headed off the dance floor. I danced with my father next. He too expressed his glee at seeing me on my feet.

"You're all radiant and happy. I don't think I've ever seen you this happy! That man makes you giddier than Bryan ever did."

"Dad!" I laughed. "Let's not throw stones."

He laughed too. "I'm really glad you found him."

"I'm glad I found him too, Dad." Out of all the lies I told that night, I know that one had truth in it. I was so glad I found Ryder... but not for the same reasons my father thought.

I danced with almost all my uncles and Ryder danced with almost all my aunts. There were a couple of cousins and bridesmaids hoping to get a dance from him, but Ryder danced only with the elder women in the room, all of whom were relatives of mine. They were all quite infatuated with him by the end of each dance.

After my dance with Uncle Reynolds, Adam surprised me by cutting in.

I had a laugh as soon as I looked into his mischievous eyes. He chuckled too.

"Is it worth your tens?" I asked him teasingly.

"So much worth it," he whispered against my ear. "You're a star, Ash."

"Thank you, but I can't take all the credit for it. I couldn't have done it without Ryder."

He nodded. "So, what do *you* think of him?"

"Hot!" I answered truthfully.

Adam raised a brow. "Well, he is a fine piece of art, but you have to remember why he's here with you, Ash. I don't want you to get your heart broken twice in the space of three months."

"I know you're worried about me, Adam. Don't worry, I'll be fine. A little flirtation with Ryder here and there won't hurt," I whispered to him.

"I'm just warning you, it's not hard to get your heart lost along the way with a devil like that."

I laughed. "You worry too much about me. I'll be fine. He's a great guy. I know why he's here with me, acting all lovey-dovey. Ten grand is worth it for him."

Adam sucked in a deep breath, as if he was bracing himself, and then he raised a brow. "How well do you know this guy?"

I shook my head. "Other than the fact that he's providing a face for the Alpha Male imaginary boyfriend that I'm showing off to everybody tonight, I know that he works as a bartender. Although I have to tell you, he's really smart. Apart from that, I don't know him at all."

"Will you spend the night with him?"

"Yes. Doing nothing, Adam. Maybe just talking."

"You're not afraid that he might be hiding a secret identity that you should be aware of?"

I laughed. "Seriously, Adam. Too much CSI."

He arched a brow at me.

I sighed. "I'll be fine. I don't think he'll rob me. I already told him that I couldn't afford his services again. You were the one who paid him. I doubt that he'll violate me in some way. A guy as hot as that could have his pick of any girl, any time, so I don't think he'll even entertain the thought of taking advantage of me. He's not a serial killer of some sort. We haven't heard of serial killings in the last decade in this city or in nearby states." The last sentences were meant to be a joke. Adam really was being too overprotective.

64

Adam sighed and shook his head. "I'm not worried about any of that. I'm worried about you falling for him for real."

"I gotta tell you, Adam, it is easy. He's… a wonderful guy. He's smart, funny, charming. But I just met him, and I doubt he'll want to see me again after this."

Adam nodded. "Just be careful, okay? He's probably the best guy to replace Bryan with, but only if he's willing to share a piece of his heart with you."

I laughed. "Now, that's new!" Somehow, I couldn't believe the same ruthless Adam could say something like that to me. "Who are you and what have you done with my brutal cousin?"

Adam laughed and then he leaned forward and gave me a kiss on the forehead. "I love you, Ash. Even if sometimes I have a weird way of showing it. I am so happy to see you laughing tonight. You sparkle like a diamond that even the bride herself is feeling like she is no longer the center of attention."

I stared back at Adam. "What? Did she say that?"

Adam shrugged. "Well, I danced with her and she basically asked me why you had to come. I told her that family sticks together. And besides, she sent you an invitation."

"What else did she say?"

"I think she's more irritated with the fact that people here are talking more about you, admiring your courage, and being happy for your newfound love."

"What did she say about Ryder?"

Adam sighed. "She was asking where you met him and how you met him. I said I don't know. She's keeping tabs on you and Ryder *at her own wedding*. This was a wicked plan, Ash."

I couldn't help laughing. "And it's working."

Adam nodded. "He's already won the hearts of our aunts. You might be up for competition. They already fancy themselves twenty-five years younger and in love with him." My eyes drifted off to where Ryder was, dancing with one of our young nieces. "And some of our nieces fancy themselves fifteen years older and in love with him."

Adam nodded. "I gotta hand it to the guy, when it comes to charming his lady's relatives, he's got a PhD."

I smiled. "Yes, he does. But I hope they won't remember him soon enough."

"Why?"

"Well, his name is Ryder Woodson. Somehow, our relatives mistook him as Ryder Van Woodsen. Apparently, the Van Woodsens are famous in New York."

"Oh. Is that so?"

I nodded. "I mean, it's brilliant! That name tells the tale itself. But Uncle Reynolds already asked him if he could get a reservation into one of the restaurants that the Van Woodsens own. Ryder had to coolly say yes. But what if Uncle Reynolds goes to New York next week? What am I going to do?"

"What did Ryder say?" Adam asked with narrowed eyes.

"He said he knows the crew of some restaurants in New York. He'll be able to pull it off."

"Then maybe he'll be able to," Adam said icily. Somehow, something in his voice told me that he was also worried.

"He should have corrected Uncle Reynolds when he had him confused with someone else!" I groaned silently.

"Yeah. He should have," Adam said disapprovingly. His gaze drifted to where Ryder was now, dancing with Nicole. "He really does know the way to your heart, doesn't he?"

I had to laugh, because I thought it was actually cute of Ryder to dance with my best friend. He and Nicole inched their way towards us.

"Hey, Nic!" I smiled at Nicole. "Great party!"

Nicole laughed. "Thanks to the brilliant wedding planner!"

"Yeah. Wedding of my dreams!" I groaned.

"You're going to top this, sweetie!" Nicole said to me positively. "A few years, maybe months from now, you are going to do a lot better than this!"

Standing there, hearing those words from Nicole, seeing Adam nod in agreement and Ryder smile in encouragement, I felt I found a new hope in me. The hope to rise above it all. To rise and triumph above Bryan and Geena. I knew that the time to start pulling my act together was *now*. Here, with the three people who stood as my allies.

7.
WEDDING GARTER
Worn by brides above the knee. Nowadays, wedding garters can come in different materials, and colors.

After dancing with Adam, Nicole and I switched and I was back in Ryder's arms once again.

"Hmmm… I thought you weren't going to dance with any other lady aside from me," I said, faking a cross expression on my face.

He chuckled. "Well, I figured, I needed to score with the women in your life, starting with your mother. I danced with the rest because I didn't want them to think I was only impressing your mother. Then I danced with your nieces and the little girls because I thought you'd think that was sweet. I danced with your best friend because I needed her approval, too."

"What's the verdict?"

He leaned closer to me and said, "Your soul is sold, love. I'm afraid I am the highest bidder."

I laughed as I stared up at him. He leaned down and gave me a soft kiss on my nose before leaning his head to the side to gently kiss my neck. Then he sighed and pulled me closer towards him. I rested my head on his shoulder.

"Can you just be real?" I whispered.

"You mean… can I just be rich, famous, and all these things I was pretending I am?" he whispered in my ear. I couldn't recognize the emotion in his voice. For the first time tonight, he seemed uncertain. It was as if he was afraid of my answer.

I shook my head. "No. Not that. I wish you could really be the wonderful, funny guy who only has eyes for me, and would dance with my mother, my aunts, my nieces, and my best friend to gain their approval… for my sake. Not for the sake of the fake rebound story of the year."

It took him a while to say something. I felt his arms tighten around me and his breath blew in my ears, making my knees feel weaker than they already were. "Even if I'm just your bartender, I am that man tonight, Astrid."

I hugged him back and I sighed. "I know, Ryder. I hope you know you're not just a bartender to me. You're my knight in shining armor."

"I'm not pretending, love," he whispered gently. "I told you… I am yours tonight. And you are mine."

I sighed. "Yes. I am yours, Ryder."

And somehow, I found myself fantasizing that it was true. That he would want me to be his. Not just because I asked him to. But I remembered what Adam said. It would be easy enough to lose my heart along the way. Especially, with a guy like Ryder. He didn't have to be the rich guy he was pretending to be. He's smart and ambitious, sweet and charming, yet, somehow, we... click.

Good thing I only have this night to be with him. Only this night to have him exist in my life. This night to believe that I am the apple of this wonderful man's eyes... the love of his life!

Ryder pulled away from me slightly. He had a mischievous smile on his face when he leaned forward and gave me a kiss on the lips. I indulged in his kisses. How often would a god like this want to kiss me anyway?

Well, in real life, I prefer to keep it real. I always thought a relationship with rich guys would be complicated. I wanted to be the center of my man's world. It's impossible to do that with a man who has the whole world in his hands. But tonight... I was making fantasies come true. Even though they weren't really my own. But it seemed to be everybody else's. And it seemed Ryder just stepped out of the pages of a fairy tale. So tonight, I got to have him. He was my knight... regardless of how much money he had in his pocket.

And the more I kissed him, the more convincing we were to the rest of my relatives, and to Bryan and Geena.

We were interrupted by an announcement by the host asking all the single ladies to line up in the dance floor.

I rolled my eyes. "Do I really have to go?" I asked Ryder.

He laughed and gave me a kiss on the lips again. "Of course! You're the fairest of all the single ladies here. You should go."

I watched with a bored expression as Geena giggled and the guests cheered, then she threw her bouquet with such force that it missed the eager bridesmaids behind her and landed directly in front of me.

My initial reaction when I saw the bouquet headed towards me was, *I paid for those! I paid for those!* Maybe that's what made me catch it.

Geena rolled her eyes when she saw her bouquet in my arms. The crowd cheered. I smiled widely, pretending that I was ecstatic about catching it.

It was the guys' turn to catch the garter. I saw that Ryder was one of them. He winked at me just as Bryan made the toss and I saw him fight his way to catch it. He almost landed on one of the other guys, but he triumphantly held the garter in his hand.

Soon, I was sitting on a chair and nervously watching as Ryder took my leg and slipped the garter on. He was told by the host to use his teeth to raise the garter up my knees.

I knew I had a violet blush on me. I could only squeal and cover my mouth with my hands. After all, I had to pretend that this wasn't the first time Ryder's lips were touching my legs.

The crowd cheered, *'Higher!' 'Higher!'*

My heart pounded in my ribcage.

Ryder laughed. He held the lace in his mouth this time. His eyes sparkled as he slowly raised the garter higher above my knees.

'Higher!'

'Higher!'

He continued to raise the garter, watching the blush on my face spread to my neck, then further down my chest.

I wanted to tell him to stop but then I looked up and saw the frown on Bryan's face and the irritated look on Geena's. So I looked back at Ryder and laughed instead. He raised the garter higher towards my thigh and stopped regardless of the cheers of the crowd. Then he bent down to kiss my knee gently. He stood up, took my hand and pulled me towards him.

We heard the people bang their spoons against the crystal glasses, asking the bride and the groom to kiss.

Before I could steal a glance towards Bryan and Geena, I felt Ryder pull my chin towards him.

"I don't think they just meant the bride and the groom, love." His eyes twinkled.

I giggled and stared up at him as he bent his face towards mine and gave me one head-spinning kiss. People cheered on and I think they were cheering for Ryder and me louder than they were for the newlyweds.

Slow music played from the surrounding speakers and I felt Ryder wrap his arms around my waist. I rested my head on his shoulder. He kissed my forehead and then he rested his chin at the top of my head. I knew we were the picture of bliss. The perfect, happy couple.

How I wished it were true. How I wished that I was totally over Bryan, that the impact of this wedding didn't hurt me a bit, that I could not care less that it was him and Geena who would be sleeping in the matrimonial bed I booked a couple of months ago. I wished that Ryder was really here for me, that he was here…because he wanted to be, and not because I paid him to be, but rather because he really did belong to me.

"Would you like to join me outside?" I heard him say.

I stared up at him. His handsome face was peaceful and at ease. I nodded. Hand in hand, he led me towards the veranda. I was happy to finally be alone with Ryder, to finally get away from prying eyes.

I was thankful for the cool air and the privacy. Although there was not much of it, since there were other people in the veranda too. I could even see some of Geena's bridesmaids flirting with some guys somewhere in the corner.

I stared at the lake view in front of us. I was content to stand close to Ryder quietly. It was comfortable.

I realized that I was more aware of Ryder's presence than I was aware of Bryan and Geena being in the same room as I was. I smiled to myself. More and more, I felt positive that I would get over them.

How pathetic am I? If Ryder weren't here with me, people would not think the same! Now only I knew just how painful it still was, and how sad I was.

I felt Ryder pull me closer to him. I felt his breath on my bare shoulder and then I felt his lips on my neck.

"Because it's just the two of us here, I need not make up an unforgettable line to propose," he whispered.

I laughed and faced him. His eyes were sparkling. I took in a deep breath.

God, I wish I had his spirit!

He took my hand in his and he kissed it gently.

"Astrid Ysabelle Jacobson…" he started and I was surprised that he knew my full name. "You are the epitome of beauty and strength. You are smart and creative… you have a brilliant mind. Being here shows just how courageous you are. Putting on a brave face and making your aunts and uncles think that everything is fine with you, even though you still ache, shows just how much respect and love you have for your family… seeing that you have not even thrown the bride and groom any antagonistic look or sarcastic remark, shows what a classy woman you are. You are a goddess, Astrid. Any man would be lucky to have you… any man would want to make you his bride. Someday, your *real* ever after will find you. Then you will understand that everything happened for a reason… you will learn to appreciate this pain… because if it weren't for this, you wouldn't find your way to the arms of your real soul mate, your real prince."

I couldn't help crying at those words. His face was so sober, his expression was so genuine.

"I've known you for a short time, Astrid. I consider myself lucky to have met you. Torn as you may be now, I know you, of all people, will rise above this. To tell you the truth, they say that the bride is the most beautiful woman at the wedding." He shook his head. "She's not. You are. Trust me. I'm not saying this because you asked me to. I'm saying this because… I look at your innocent beauty… and I know I'm incapable of lying to you."

He reached forward and wiped my tears with his fingers.

"Will you promise me some things?"

Because I couldn't say anything, I merely nodded.

"Will you promise me that you will allow healing to come? That you will rise above Bryan and Geena?"

I bit my lip and whispered tremulously, "Yes."

"Will you promise me that you will learn to love yourself beyond your love for anyone else?"

I let out a little giggle.

He took a deep breath. "And will you promise to find your way to me again… when the time is right? Maybe we can meet under different circumstances?"

This question took me aback a little bit.

"Why?"

"We belong to each other tonight, Astrid. But after this night… it's over." He took a deep breath. "Someday, I would like to see what you have become… after you rise above it all. I want to see that you have kept your promises. I'd like to see the real you. The you that is buried underneath the smile that you put on. The you that Bryan and Geena attempted to bury in pain. And… I would like you to see me, the real me. The guy behind the mask I put on the day I met you."

I stared up at him and realized what a sincere person Ryder was. He may not be the rich guy he pretended to be tonight, but the rest of him was genuine. The type that you rip right out of a romance novel.

"Will you promise to come find me again someday?" he asked solemnly.

I stared up at him, tears still streaming from my eyes.

"Yes." The word was a mere burst of air from my throat.

He smiled and then he took something from his pocket.

It was the ring. He slid it on my ring finger. My breath caught in my throat. It was ten times more beautiful than the ring Bryan had given me. The stone in the center was probably at least two carats.

It was lovely and as it sparkled in the light, I thought I was going to go blind.

"It's beautiful," I whispered.

"I'm glad you like it," he said. "It's not a rental."

I smiled at him. "It's lovely."

The stone could be cubic zirconia or probably moissanite. At least Ryder was honest about it; he didn't try to pass it off for a diamond when it wasn't. The beauty of the ring itself was so extraordinary that no one would mind what stone it was.

"A little reminder of your promises," he grinned.

I laughed and then I said, "Yes. I promise to heal, I promise to love myself, I promise to come find you when all this is behind me."

He grinned at me and then slowly his face descended towards mine and he kissed me. The kiss was deep, sincere… mind-blowing!

When the kiss ended, I couldn't bear to open my eyes. I was afraid that if I opened them, Ryder wouldn't be there. He'd be gone. Everything would be a dream.

Then I felt him kiss the tip of my nose. Finally, I opened my eyes and found him still staring at me.

"Are you for real?" I breathed.

He laughed. "I'm for real. At least for tonight." He released me and then he took my hand.

"Come. People will be wondering why you've gone missing," he said. "Plus, you've got another story to tell."

I giggled. "Yeah. Like what's the answer to 'when's the big date?'"

He smiled at me. "You can always say we haven't spoken about it yet. You've just said 'yes' to me tonight."

I sighed. "Oh, yeah. I'm still in heaven. This is all a dream to me."

When we rejoined the group once again, the first person I ran into was the very familiar groom.

"Astrid!" He beamed at me. "I am so glad you made it!"

Liar!

But I smiled at him. Ryder squeezed my hand encouragingly.

"I'm glad I made it too," I said bravely.

He stared at me for a while and then he looked over at Ryder.

I realized that I had to introduce them... and then kill myself later probably, but for now, formalities first.

"Am... swee... sweetheart, this is Bryan, the groom. Bryan... this is Ryder Woodson."

"Your date?" Bryan asked still looking at Ryder.

Ryder extended his hand to him. "Ryder Van Woodsen," Ryder corrected me. "Her... fiancé," he said.

In spite of my surprise that Ryder changed his surname, I didn't miss the shocked expression on Bryan's face.

"Wh... what?" he stuttered, not comprehending.

"That's right, Bryan," I said, keeping my voice steady.

"Wow! That was fast," he murmured under his breath, looking at me grudgingly.

"Apparently, still a lot slower than you," I said to him.

It didn't take long before Geena came up behind Bryan.

"There you are!" she said hugging her husband from behind, pretending to be oblivious of us... well of me, because I already saw her looking at Ryder as she approached us.

"Honey," Bryan said putting an arm around her.

"This is Ryder Van Woodsen. Apparently, he's Astrid's fiancé."

Geena looked at me for the first time. The insulting shock on her face made me want to slap her in front of her husband. Did she think I couldn't score a guy like Ryder?

Well, they both know me too well. They know I thought rich, cute boys were given fortune and good looks because they were lacking in the IQ department. Maybe Geena and Bryan couldn't believe I somehow chose to conjure a Ken doll to life and brought him to their wedding... and he brought his expensive, shiny car with him!

"How long have you known each other?" Geena asked.

"Two months," Ryder answered quickly. He pulled me closer to him, wrapping a possessive arm around my waist. He looked down at me with affection in his eyes. "I cannot wait to make her mine forever."

"Well, she's good at the waiting game," Bryan snorted quietly, but loud enough for Ryder and me to hear.

"I can wait as long as it takes," Ryder said. "She's definitely worth it."

Though Ryder didn't know what Bryan was getting at, I knew just exactly what he meant. I smiled bravely at Bryan. "I changed a lot since the day I found out you knocked up my cousin! I told myself that the next time I find a wonderful guy, I'm going to seize the day! No more waiting games," I said, trying to keep myself cool. Then I turned to Geena. "Congratulations on your wedding. I can't really say it's... original, but you pulled it off. You should be proud of yourselves. Now, if you'll excuse us, we need to retreat to our suite so we can celebrate our engagement privately."

I started pulling Ryder away.

"You rented a suite here?" Geena asked.

I turned back to her and nodded.

"Yes. The Paradise Suite. I was told it was the most romantic suite they have," Ryder replied.

Geena couldn't help giving Bryan a hard look that almost said, *Why didn't we get that instead?*

"We don't need the most romantic suite," Bryan said, as if reading Geena's mind. "My wife is pregnant. Nothing can be more joyous than that."

Somehow, I felt that that comment was for me. Bryan knew how much I adored babies and children! I smiled at them, refusing to be defeated. "Oh, is that why you got married so hastily?"

Geena blushed violently and I could tell there was some truth in my words at least.

"We got married because we're in love!" she hissed at me.

I smiled at them and I placed my left hand on my chest, so she won't miss the sparkle of my new ring.

"Oh!" I sighed sarcastically. "Well, I can say that's a relief!"

She stared at the ring on my finger and then raised a brow at me. I can almost see the lust in her eyes.

"It's lovely, isn't it?" I asked her. "Anyway, good luck with your life together. I think you're both going to need a lot of that! Ta-ta!"

I whirled around and pulled Ryder with me. We went straight for the exit without saying goodbye to my relatives.

I was holding Ryder's hand tightly, afraid that if I let go of him, I would not be able to support my own weight.

"Honey…" he started. I didn't respond. I kept on walking and dragging him with me. "Honey!" he called out louder this time around. He actually stopped walking and pulled me towards him.

I was afraid I was going to slip, but he caught me spot on, wrapping his arms around my waist and holding me against him.

I closed my eyes as I buried my face on his chest. I felt him hold me tightly. I cried silently in his arms, as he caressed my head gently, whispering soothing words in my ears.

"You're doing great," he whispered to me.

"I was, until I saw them." I snorted.

"Even when you saw them," he said. "He couldn't take his eyes off you."

I giggled humorlessly. "He couldn't believe I had the nerve to show up here tonight."

"He couldn't believe he let you go. That's what I see from the look on his face. Trust me, I'm good at reading people."

Tears rolled down my cheeks. "Did I do the right thing? Letting him go? He did try to explain himself and get me back, asking for another chance… but I shoved all the wedding details in his face. I didn't give him a second chance."

"He doesn't deserve a second chance. You deserved better," he said stiffly. I realized Bryan was somehow getting on Ryder's nerves.

I couldn't help feeling… flattered about that.

"I want to forget it all, Ryder," I whispered to him. "I want to forget them! I want to stop feeling the hurt and the pain."

He smiled and pinched my nose. "You can't cheat the healing process."

"Really? There's no bypassing this the fastest way possible? I mean, what can take the pain away?"

He sighed. "Time," he whispered softly, I could swear I heard notes of longing and regret in his dulcet tones.

"There's no way to fast forward it?"

He shook his head. "You can forget it tonight, but I can't promise you that you won't still feel heartbroken in the morning."

I smiled. "Okay. If only for tonight, Ryder. Help me forget."

He laughed and put an arm around my shoulders. "Come on then, we have an engagement to celebrate."

8.

THE WEDDING NIGHT: The first night as husband and wife.

If torn between the much-needed sleep and passionate lovemaking, keep this in mind: You only have ONE wedding night! Make it memorable. Make it count!

*E*verything was dark and hazy. I opened my eyes and the first thing I felt was the severe pain in my head.

I opened my eyes and saw light peeking through the curtains. I didn't feel cold like I usually do when I wake up in the mornings. Normally, an image of Bryan popped up in my head when I woke up, reminding me of my broken heart.

This time it was different. This time, the first image that popped up in my head was that of a much more handsome guy. His eyes were deep ocean green, his hair raven black. He looked like a wonderful Adonis drawn out from the pages of a historical novel. His face was perfect. His body... his abs were perfect, his muscles well-toned, his skin flawless.

Hey! Go back one second! I thought to myself. How did I know how perfect and well-toned his muscles were? How did I know his skin was flawless?

I closed my eyes once again, trying to recollect the memories of last night.

I remembered that the room he rented for us was perfect. It was twice the size of the room I booked for Bryan and myself, which was now being occupied by Bryan and Geena a floor below us. There were roses everywhere and we celebrated my victorious show with a bottle of wine. Then I remember all the crying and whining. I had a physical yearning to forget everything, and the only way to do that was to drink and drink, and drink some more. I don't think I've ever had so much alcohol in my entire life!

There were flashes of ... images in my head. But they were blurry and they were coming back to me very slowly.

I had felt as if all my nerves had come to life. I remember feeling bolder than I've ever felt. I remembered flirting with him, within the confines of our room, not caring what he would say or think. I remember letting go of everything I was holding on to, everything that I had been afraid of.

I remember touching him... in places I hadn't touched Bryan. I remember letting him touch me, in places no one has ever touched me before. Then I remember... the ripping pain, and the pleasure that came afterward.

I opened my eyes. My heart pounded wildly in my ribcage.
Did I just dream it all?

Slowly, I peeked under the sheets and I realized in horror that... everything I remembered were not just figments of my imaginative mind. I am not that creative in that department!

I turned my head to my left side and found Ryder lying flat on his tummy. His eyes were open and he was watching me carefully.

He smiled at me lazily. "You weren't dreaming," he whispered, as if he read my thoughts.

I sighed. "I was afraid of that."

He bit his lip. I guess he wanted to say something, but decided against it.

He reached forward and caressed my chin gently.

"Do you still hurt?" he asked very softly.

I shook my head and I knew I turned the deepest shade of red.

"Now you probably think Bryan was right to cheat on me," I muttered.

"No," he whispered. There was a sense of tenderness in his voice.

I was still skeptical. "What do you think then?"

He took a deep breath and said, "I think he was foolish not to wait."

I rolled my eyes. "Thanks. That makes me feel better!"

He propped up on one elbow and then he said, "It should make you feel better, because it's the truth, Astrid."

"Easy for you to say, Ryder. I avoided all advances from him, but I easily threw myself at you last night!"

He didn't say anything. He just kept staring at me.

It was true. I did throw myself at him last night. I was the one who began touching him provocatively. I remember he was trying to avoid some of my earlier advances. He was trying to be a gentleman, but I was persistent.

I threw my hands over my face. I felt so ashamed of myself.

"God, what have I done?" I whispered.

I heard him sigh and then I felt him take me in his arms.

"You made love to me, and it was amazing, Astrid! I refuse to regret it no matter what you say or do now! I will not feel sorry about last night. There is nothing to be ashamed of."

I pulled away from him. Then I turned my back on him. I didn't have the courage to look at him yet.

"We better go," I said curtly.

I heard him sigh, but he didn't say anything more.

I went to the shower and had a long bath. I wanted to cry, but the tears just wouldn't come. I wanted to remember my dream of giving myself to Bryan months ago. But all I could think of was Ryder; touching me, loving me, making love to me... I remember his fleeting, feather-light touches around my face and neck, his eyes staring into mine, the incredulous look on his face when he had felt the barrier of my innocence. I remember screaming his name over and over as I reached the realms of pleasure. He brought me to heaven twice and I clung to him with all that I had. I didn't even know I was capable of feeling all those things. I didn't know I could be sexual. I didn't know I could want a man the way I wanted him last night… or the way I think I still wanted him now.

When I got out of the shower, I was dressed in a long robe, fully covered.

Ryder came past me on his way to the bathroom. He was wearing only a towel wrapped around his waist, his abs in full view, and I couldn't help the desire that reeled through me again.

He stopped and stared at me for a long moment. I couldn't move as I stared back at him. He raised a brow at me. Somehow, he looked irritated, like he was stopping himself from saying or doing something.

Great! The first guy I ever made love to is irritated with me already… after just one night! I thought glumly.

He narrowed his eyes, as if he was trying to decipher something in my expression. Then he shook his head slightly and went into the bathroom.

I felt frustrated. Last night, he was the perfect knight in shining armor. He came to my rescue graciously, and absorbed every shock, every pain for me. Somehow all that changed this morning. Somehow, I see something in his eyes that resembles cold fury, as if I said or did something that offended him.

I have no way of knowing if Ryder slept with me because he wanted me for real. If I weren't writing him a check, I'd probably believe he did. And Adam was right. I didn't know Ryder at all. He looks like a god and he knows it. I don't know how often he has sex with a woman who throws herself at him. He probably made love to me because he thought it was part of our bargain.

I quickly dressed and then I placed his final check on the table.

I laughed humorlessly because right now, I felt like an old, lonely matron, paying for a younger, handsome guy to pleasure her!

Tears rolled down my cheeks and I knew I couldn't bear to face Ryder like that. *He'll try to make me feel better again, and I have had enough pretensions to last me a lifetime.* All the pretenses we put up with last night were enough, thank you very much! I couldn't bear to have him look at me with sincere, admiring eyes, knowing I paid him to do that. I came here on a mission and he helped me accomplish it. But it was over now.

He came out of the bathroom.

"Here's the rest of your payment," I said to him. I placed a pair of sunglasses over my eyes. I didn't want him to see just how painful this was all for me. "I'll meet you at the lobby. I'll see Nicole and probably say goodbye to my parents."

He didn't say anything. He just stared at me. His face was cold. Other than that, I couldn't make out the expression on his face.

"Will you ask the bellboy to bring my bag downstairs?"

He nodded once. Still he didn't say anything.

"Okay, I'll see you later." I hesitated, but when he made no move to stop me, I left the room.

I dialed Nicole's number. I hoped she didn't go home last night. I desperately needed someone to talk to.

"It's too early!" she groaned.

"Where are you?" I asked.

She gave me her room number and I rushed to it. Within a few minutes, I was banging on her door.

"What is wrong with you?" she asked angrily.

"Nothing," I replied coming into the room. Somehow, her room seemed small, compared to the room I shared with Ryder.

"Where's Ryder?" she asked.

"In our room," I replied.

Her eyes widened. "You spent the night in one room?"

I nodded. "He rented the Paradise Suite," I said.

"That's expensive."

"I know. But I think the ten grand should cover it."

I made a cup of coffee and then we sat on her balcony.

"You guys were great last night, Ash," Nicole said smiling. "You really did look genuinely in love with each other. You were every girl's envy last night."

I sighed. "I envy myself last night," I murmured.

Nicole laughed. "I know. You couldn't help wishing it were true. That you really are in that... state already. Except that you still hurt."

I sighed. Hurt? Somehow, a different kind of pain was bothering me now. I had not thought of Bryan all morning. All I could think about was Ryder and the pleasures we shared last night... and then the cold look he gave me this morning.

"You did go overboard on the kissing, you know." Nicole teased. "I don't think you were pretending."

"Maybe we're not," I said, sighing.

"Excuse me?"

"Well... he said to me that we weren't pretending. That last night, we really did belong to each other." I sighed glumly. "Only... I got carried away."

Nicole stared at me for a moment and then she asked, "Got carried away how?"

I sighed. I contemplated on telling her what really happened, but then I decided against it. I didn't think she'd understand. Somehow, I couldn't bear for anyone to think that I paid to have my virginity taken away from me. How pathetic could I be?

"I forgot that my life still sucked when I woke up today," I said.

"Oh God, Ash! Please!" She rolled her eyes. "I hope you saw the beautiful girl I saw last night. She was radiant, she was confident! Your life does not suck! Bryan was stealing glances at you the whole time. Trust me! I was looking at him. He couldn't get his eyes off you and he was throwing daggers at Ryder whenever he could. Trust me, that guy was chewing his nails last night! He wanted you more than he wanted his bride. And the fact that Ryder was all over you was driving him crazy."

I stared at Nicole. I tried to feel sorry for Bryan, but the only thing I felt now was... I don't know... a sense of vindication. But a bigger part of me still thought about all the things that happened between Ryder and me last night. Somehow, in the middle of the charade, something changed. Something in me. I couldn't pinpoint what it was. And the look he gave me before I left was still playing over and over in my head. He looked really pissed with me.

"Everybody was looking at you, Ash. They admired your courage. They thought you and Ryder are just the perfect couple. You are. You really are," she said. "He's a sweet guy."

I sighed. "Too sweet."

Nicole stared at me. "You like him, don't you?"

I stared at her and immediately I knew my cheeks burned.

"Oh my God, you like him! For real! You weren't pretending!" Nicole accused.

I rolled my eyes. "Nicole, please! Ryder could have had his pick of any woman last night. But he was mine. Because I paid him to be. It was a gig for him. And he did well."

"Come on, Ash. You should give yourself more credit than that! You're beautiful, for crying out loud! Don't let what Geena and Bryan did to you make you feel any less about yourself. You deserve better than that. A lot better."

I tried to understand what Nicole was saying to me. But being dumped and cheated on by the two people you thought admired you the most can really take a toll on your self-respect and confidence. And right now, I still couldn't move past that. I still thought I must be the most unattractive and unlovable person on earth for them to do what they did to me.

Nicole finished packing and then we went to the lobby.

"Do you have a ride?" I asked her.

She nodded. "Yes. I'll go with the rest of the crew. We have a van. You know how it works."

I nodded. "I'll see you later."

Nicole smiled at someone behind me. Then she waved goodbye to me.

I turned around and saw Ryder approaching me, my bag in his hand.

"Ready to go?" he asked. His voice was still a bit cold. I couldn't see his eyes; they were hidden beneath his dark sports sunglasses.

"Have you checked out?" I asked.

He nodded.

"Well, then let me say goodbye to Mom and Dad."

He went with me, like a true gentleman, as I said goodbye to my parents, my aunts and uncles.

Once we were alone in the car, we both fell silent. For the first time, I didn't know what to say to him. Now, we didn't need to pretend. No more need for formalities, or to start feeling at ease with each other.

It was a very long ride and it seemed that Ryder was also lost in his own thoughts. I reclined in my seat and then I closed my eyes and fell asleep.

In my dreams, I remembered touching Ryder; I remembered hugging him and I remembered the heat of his body against mine... and I felt love. I wanted to linger in his arms forever. I wanted to stay there and continue feeling loved, continue feeling desired.

I felt a tap on my cheek. It was so light, I could barely feel it. When I opened my eyes, I found Ryder staring down at me.

I stared back at him, not knowing what to say. I couldn't help thinking how beautiful he was. And that last night, he really did belong to me. But it was... over... too soon!

"I'm sorry," I whispered. I sat up straight on my seat and found that we were already in front of Adam's house. I sighed. "So, this is it."

He nodded.

I smiled at him. "Thank you, Ryder," I said quietly. "For a job well done."

He didn't say anything. He just continued staring at me.

I stared at the ring on my finger. I began to take it off, but then I felt his hand close in against mine.

He shook his head. "Keep it," he said. "You have promises you need to keep. This should remind you of them."

I bit my lip. I wanted to cry. How could he be so perfect? How could he be so wonderful? And how could the sincere look on his face be just a charade? Part of the act?

He pushed a stray lock of hair behind my ear.

"See you, Astrid," he said to me. But I knew he was saying goodbye for real. His job was done.

"Goodbye, Ryder," I whispered.

"I wish you all the best," he added.

"You too." I wondered whether he changed his mind about the third promise he asked of me. Perhaps after last night, he didn't want to see me anymore. Perhaps, he changed his mind about me. After all, I'm the type of girl who pays to have a guy to take her to bed. "Thank you. For a wonderful night."

His eyes narrowed. He took a deep breath and then instead of saying something, he simply nodded.

We stared at each other for a long while. My heart was pounding wildly inside my chest. It seems that we both wanted to say something to each other, but we couldn't bring ourselves to do so. It made me wonder if it was sex that changed and ruined the magic we shared last night.

"G-goodbye," I said, finally, cutting through the silence.

He nodded. I took my bag and then I got out of the car. As soon as I stepped out and closed the door behind me, Ryder sped off without another word or a backward glance. A tear rolled down my cheek. Ryder had been wonderful. I knew at that instant that he left a mark in my heart. And I couldn't help feeling empty now that I may never see him again.

I noticed that Adam wasn't home yet. I went inside the house. I placed my bag in my room and then I went to get a beer from Adam's fridge and sat on his deck to stare at the waves in the ocean, and the surfers dancing with them.

I tried to recollect everything that happened last night. The way that Ryder rescued me from every single embarrassment that could have happened to me, the way he made me feel that I was the queen in the room and he answered to my every whim, the way that he kissed me that made me feel I deserved every bit of it, the way that he touched me that made me feel like a precious fragile crystal.

I thought about Bryan and the irritated look he threw at Ryder. For the first time in months I was able to smile. Smile at the thought of Bryan, because I know now that I wouldn't always be crying over him. I wouldn't always be the one feeling sorry for myself. I know there is hope. Someday, I'd find someone who would look at me the way that Ryder looked at me last night. Now, I know that things happened for a reason, and knowing that I could wantonly lose control with a man like Ryder made me think I was meant to be passionate... more than I ever was for Bryan.

I felt Adam sit beside me. "Hey, cuz." He greeted me warmly. I gave him a warm smile. "Wow! You look better than you did the last time you sat in that chair."

I sighed and looked at the beach. "Maybe I am better."

"I see Van Woodsen had some positive effect on you," he said sarcastically.

"His real name is Ryder Woodson, Adam," I said.

He shrugged, but didn't say anything.

"Not to be confused with some rich people in New York," I said. "But our uncles and aunts, even Mom and Dad think that now."

"He pulled it off, didn't he?"

I nodded. "Very well. I can say that he is smart. He even sounded like he went to college."

"Maybe he did," Adam said.

"If he did then why does he make a living getting people drunk?"

Adam shook his head. "Maybe he just has a passion for… mixing drinks."

I shrugged. "He's a people person. He can listen to you whine over and over. Comes with the job description, I guess," I said.

"How was your night?" Adam asked.

I took a gulp of my beer because remembering all the things that Ryder and I did in the hotel room would surely make me blush all over again and I didn't want Adam to see that.

"It was… spectacular!" I replied. "Bryan and Geena thought I was engaged!"

"Yeah and she hated you more for that," Adam said.

I raised a brow at him. "Hate me? What right does she have to hate me for being engaged? I *was* engaged before she slept with my fiancé behind my back!" I said crossly.

Adam shrugged. "Geena knew the game, Ash. She knew the real reason why Bryan married her. It was the baby… and also because previous wedding arrangements had already been made. She knew that. She knows that her husband still harbors feelings for you. And she can't believe that in spite of all these, you appeared at that wedding reception with your head held high, all happy and in love… with an even better man. And you got engaged again! For real!"

"Not for real!" I rolled my eyes.

"But she didn't know that!" Adam said. "Somehow, she was wondering how it was possible you managed to get marriage proposals… while she had to steal fiancés and dream weddings. And of course… you stole her thunder on her wedding day!"

"I think it's only fair, since she robbed *me* of my wedding day!" I said sarcastically.

"Well, I just hope that you're happy, Ash," Adam said.

I remembered last night again and I knew that I had already started the healing process. I was happy because I conquered all my fears of facing my relatives and because I didn't look like the fool anymore. Then I remembered the passionate night that followed after. I sighed. The healing process had started before I knew it had already begun. I didn't need to be afraid to accept change anymore. I need not be stubborn anymore.

"I'll get there, Adam," I said to him. "Thanks to you, I know I'll get there."

He ruffled my hair and then left me alone in the deck.

My thoughts drifted off to Ryder again.

What was that look on his face? What changed him this morning? He said to me that he did not regret what happened to us last night, but then why did it look like he was mad at me afterward? What was going on in his mind?

I stared at the ring on my finger. It was lovely beyond words; it was hard to believe that it wasn't a real diamond.

Somehow, I wished we weren't mad at each other when we parted ways. I wished we gave each other one last kiss and then said our goodbyes.

Maybe because we slept together, it changed the agenda. It made him feel like if he continued being sweet in the morning, I would hope it was all real and he didn't want to give me any false hopes. He was just being true and honest. He was being a gentleman.

After I finished my beer, I went to take a shower. Then I dressed into my pajamas and unpacked my bags. It was still early, but already I felt exhausted, I just want to sleep.

I placed my dirty clothes in my hamper and all the unused clothes back in the closet. Seeing the gown I wore last night made me think of Ryder again, and how wonderful he had been.

It was all a scam… part of the charade, Ash! I scolded myself. Ryder was a figment of my imagination. I created him. With ten grand, I created a guy who only existed in dreams.

Handsome as hell, sweet as heaven.

I may be stupid enough to get too drunk and sleep with him, wishing he were real, but I knew I was not stupid enough to fall in love with a dream.

With a frown on my face, I placed my gown in my hamper.

I placed my wallet in my dresser. Making sure that the bag was empty, I opened all the pockets. I felt an envelope inside one of them.

I fished it out and found two envelopes folded together. I looked inside and found Adam's checks in both of them. The whole ten grand.

My heart pounded in my chest. These were Ryder's checks. He hadn't cashed the first one. Nor did he accept the second one that I left in the table for him.

One of the envelopes had something written in it in his neat script:

Astrid,
Remember your promises.
All three of them.
Love,
Ryder

I touched the words with my hand. Tears rolled down my cheeks. It confused me more to wonder how it was that my heart felt broken at this moment. Like I knew I wouldn't be seeing Ryder again in my life and a part of me did not like that. Like I wanted to take it all back and wished that I had been much kinder to him this morning. That I was able to thank him enough for what he did for me.

Lying down on my bed, I hugged the envelopes to my chest and I cried my heart out.

9.

HONEYMOON:

A passionate period following a newfound love or relationship.
A period of harmony.

*I*t was Bryan and Geena's first month anniversary. I know not because I was keeping tabs, or because I received an invitation for another celebration. I doubt they'll be inviting me to any special occasions in their lives anymore. I could care less. I know it's their first month anniversary because that's how long I have been smiling for real.

I had successfully stopped myself from thinking about Bryan and the *what ifs* and *what could have beens*. I knew things happen for a reason and someday, I would be thankful that they happened that way.

I was beginning to smile more… and for real. Especially when I looked at the ring on my finger and remembered that I made one wonderful guy a promise that I would allow myself to be healed. That I would believe in *'ever after's* again.

Whenever my mother called she asked about Ryder. I had to indulge her with made-up stories. And then when she made an attempt to see the two of us together, I said that Ryder was quite busy with a new bar that he's putting up and he may not be available any time soon. It always seemed to work… so far.

I didn't see Ryder again, but I wanted to. I was hanging out at Oil Rig with my friends, always on the lookout for him.

"He really got under your skin, didn't he?" John asked me once.

"No. I just wanted to see him and ask him how he is," I lied. In truth, I think Ryder really did get under my skin that night I got under the sheets with him. Well, of course, who forgets their first? Maybe the types like Geena do, but I'm nothing like her. I had a momentary lapse of values; I gave in to one night of wonderful passion with my knight in shining Armani. How is that easy to forget?

"Why don't you call him then?" he asked.

I did try to call Ryder. Once a day, I would stare at his number on my phone, make up a conversation in my head. I thought I would start by asking if he's on duty at Oil Rig tonight and then conveniently plan a night out there with my friends so I could run into him. But I always chickened out. And so far, once a week, I have been with my friends at Oil Rig, and he was never there. It made me wonder if he still worked there. But I was too afraid to ask his fellow bartenders.

"I can't believe he refused to accept the ten grand," Dannie said. "He could use it." I wondered the same thing too. "Unless, you slept with him and he felt guilty about taking the money."

Somehow, that comment irritated me so much that I wanted to slap Dannie across the face. But I prevented myself from doing so because I knew that it bothered me because... it was the truth. Sometimes, I think that maybe he didn't take the money because he already took so much from me.

He may not be rich, but Ryder was a stand-up guy. He was a gentleman and that made me admire him all the more. So much more that it made *me* feel guilty about sleeping with him. If it weren't for that, he would have taken the money, and there was no reason for him not to. He needed it as much as I did. Especially after renting an expensive suit, an expensive car, and a luxury hotel room.

I stared at the ring on my finger again. Well, at least the ring didn't cost him much. Still, I knew it cost him a couple of bucks, while he got nothing from me. Well, just my virginity.

I had been trying to look for a new job, but somehow, the job market was not hiring people with my skills. I was already beginning to feel restless. Pretty soon, all the money I had set aside would be gone.

"You can always come back and ask Fiona to give you your job back," Nicole said to me.

"I made her a millionaire, Nic. And she treated me like crap, not even giving me some consideration since she knew what I have been going through anyway!" I said.

"Pride!" Dannie rolled his eyes. "Are you happy to live off Adam's charity for the rest of your life?"

I sighed. "I'll find something soon."

When I got home that night though, I realized I was not as confident as I thought I was. Moreover, I realized that I was slowly getting scared. Weddings had been my life and if I didn't believe in dreams coming true or in *ever afters*, I don't have anything.

I was sitting at Adam's deck, drinking light beer when he joined me.

"How's my favorite cousin doing?"

I groaned. "I'm still a bum as you can see. Nothing seems to be available in the market. I mean, weddings are lucrative, but these companies are not hiring at the moment. One wanted me so much, but felt I was overqualified. I told them I'm fine with starting at the bottom; they said they couldn't do that to me. Sure! They would rather have me living in the streets!"

He took a deep breath. Then he said to me, "I have a client..."

"Sure you do! Congratulations," I said dryly.

He snorted. "Listen before you comment please."

I giggled. "Alright, fine. Attorney Adam Ackers, you have a client, and so?"

"He wanted to invest in something," Adam said. And for the first time, I thought he was having some difficulty in composing his sentences.

86

"If you want my advice, Adam... I can't give you any. I'm struggling with my own life as it is."

"What happened to listen first before you comment?" he asked in an irritated tone.

"Alright, fine!" I giggled.

Adam took a deep breath and then he said. "He... has some extra cash, and he didn't want to put it in a bank or on time deposit. He wanted to invest in a business venture, which he thinks is lucrative, but he doesn't have any idea about it. He asked me if I knew someone who knows how to manage the business."

I stared blankly at Adam, waiting for him to finish his story. He stared back at me.

"Now, what?" I asked.

He sighed. "It's wedding planning."

"Oh!" I said, realizing now why he is telling me all this.

"Interested?"

"To work for him? Yes!" I said excitedly.

"Not just work for him, Astrid," Adam said. "He wants no part in managing it. He's just the capitalist. He needs a partner who will start the business, manage it, and work on it. An industrial partner. He will be the main owner, but he needs someone to do the dirty work. And he needs someone who has a lot of experience in this industry; who knows this business from top to bottom. Who already has contacts out there, and possibly who has a good track record in this type of business."

I couldn't feel my legs, literally. My hands were shaking and I could actually hear my heart pounding against my chest.

"Adam, Adam! Are you kidding me?"

Adam took a gulp of his beer. "I wish I was," he murmured.

"Oh, my God! But that is huge!"

Adam nodded. "You're not scared, are you? I mean, I thought you were pretty good."

"I think I am! But I haven't managed a firm before!"

"But you did do weddings before."

"It's my life, Adam. I made Fiona rich!"

"Well then now, make somebody else rich! Including yourself."

My hands went to my face and I could feel how hot my face was.

"I don't know if I can do it! I don't know if I can make it that big!"

Adam reached for my hand and squeezed it.

"You have nothing to lose, Astrid."

"Except your investor's money," I said nervously.

"In that case, you should be glad I'm your lawyer," he grinned.

I sighed. It was a lot to think about. "Can I sleep on it first?"

Adam looked at me as if I was out of my mind. "This is a golden opportunity, Astrid. What is there to think about?" he asked.

I sighed. "This is too huge, Adam! I know I can do all the wedding stuff, but I don't know if I can do all the managing! It's just a lot."

Adam reached out for my hand and gave it a gentle squeeze. "I believe in you, Ash. I've seen Geena's wedding. It was lovely. You have what it takes. I just wish you'd had more courage to step up, take some risks. Explore the world, Ash. It's big enough."

"I'll let you know tomorrow morning."

I couldn't sleep that night. Yesterday, I would have taken any job! Didn't matter if it was making tea for the office secretary. Now, I was being offered the chance of a lifetime! And I didn't know what I was going to do about it! It was as exhilarating as it was terrifying!

I remembered Ryder. He did encourage this dream. He told me that I had the experience; I had the contacts, the skills, and the knowledge. I didn't have the capital then. But now an opportunity just presented itself. Could I let it pass? Was I strong enough? Was I mature enough for that kind of responsibility?

When I fell asleep that night, I pictured a wedding, one in the middle of a resort. Lighted balloons were floating on the shore, giving the entire shoreline a bright light. Guests were gathered in the middle of the venue. There was so much merriment; the place looked magical. There were flowers everywhere.

I saw myself in the corner. I was wearing a peach dress. I was looking at the place contentedly. I heard the bride and the groom say their *thank yous* to the guests.

"And to Astrid… thank you. For making the beginning of our 'ever after' so magical and wonderful," they said to me.

I woke up from that dream with a big smile on my face. I knew that in spite of the pain I still somehow felt when I thought about Bryan and Geena, I was not the type of girl who refused to believe in ever afters. I will always believe in that. And I will always come up with magical ideas to make dream weddings come true.

I stood up from my bed with renewed energy. I took a quick shower, had my breakfast and then gave Adam a call at his office.

"He's in a meeting. Can I ask him to call you back?" his secretary asked.

"Alright."

I paced the living room back and forth. I went to the deck, holding the cordless phone in my hand. I anxiously looked at my cell to see if Adam opted to call me there instead.

After fifteen minutes and I had not heard from Adam yet, I dialed his cell number from my cellphone.

It took four rings before he finally answered.

"Have you decided yet?" he asked.

"You didn't call me back!" I said in a demanding tone.

"Oh, I am sorry, Ma'am, but some of us have to make a living so we can keep the apartment that you are living in."

I groaned. "Okay, fine." I took a deep breath. "So, what are the terms of this... offer? Do I get to meet this guy? Do I give him my CV? Will he interview me first?"

"Well, I have already given him your CV."

"How did you get a copy of my CV?"

"You used my laptop and printer, didn't you?"

"Oh, right," I grunted. "So, what did he say?"

"Well, as his executor, I have the power to hire and fire people for him. So basically, he's leaving the decision up to me. But I need to submit reports to him on a monthly basis. We need to hire a good accountant for this. He is just interested in your expenses and your revenue. The only two figures he will look at."

"B—but Adam... you know that we might spend a lot at first to put up the business, do the registrations, rent out an office, buy some furniture, hire one or two assistants just to get the operation going. The business will not start making money until after six months or maybe even a year."

"He understands that. That is also up to me to justify," Adam said. "Don't mess this up, Astrid! Or we're both going to be fired! I'm handling so many of this guy's investments, I can't afford to lose my biggest client."

I giggled nervously. "I know, I know! Too much pressure already, Adam!"

"I believe in you, Ash," he said quietly. Then he sighed. "Anyway, the funds will be transferred to my account next week. You can start planning. I'll take a look at it and see what you're missing. I'll take care of setting up the business name and getting the business licenses. For the first twelve months of your job, you'll be getting a fixed fee although you will own thirty percent of the company. After twelve months, you'll have the right to forty percent of the company's profit." Then he gave me the amount of my monthly allowance. "Good enough for you?"

I couldn't breathe. It was... fifty percent more than what I used to earn with Fiona. Next year, I'd have the same amount plus forty percent of the total profits? So it all depended on how big I could make it in one year.

"Are you still there, Astrid?"

"Yeah, yeah." I breathed. "That's perfect, Adam!"

"Good. And you'll have full hiring and firing powers. I'm the only one who has the right to fire you though."

I laughed. "I won't let you down, Adam."

He chuckled, "I'll draw up the papers so you can sign them when I get home."

Because I still couldn't believe it was all happening, I stood up from my seat and I let out a loud shriek.

***

It had been a busy week for me. I spent most of my time at home, drawing up the proposal to submit to Adam. I hadn't done a whole organizational chart before, but I was glad to learn new things.

At the beginning, I intended to have one assistant. I could train her. We would put up our own website to give information about our company and our services. It was going to be difficult not having a gallery of previous jobs, but I knew we'd get there soon.

I needed to reestablish my ties with suppliers, photographers, videographers, couture, caterers, hotel managers, and resort owners. I didn't have bad blood with any of them so I figured that would be easy.

The toughest job would be finding the right place. Fiona's office was in a small building downtown. I had never liked the location because the streets around that area were crowded. It's tough to find parking and the office was not conducive for planning weddings.

I wanted a place somewhere in a quiet neighborhood that was easier to locate, with plenty of parking space, with a peaceful atmosphere.

By the end of the week, I was done with my initial proposal to Adam. He asked me to have dinner with him and we discussed the details in the restaurant. I was nervous as he was going through my notes.

Then he looked at me for a moment.

"What?" I asked nervously.

"You don't need to buy a van?" he asked.

"Later. Not now. Not when I don't have my first client yet. Too huge of an investment," I replied. "I can always rent transportation while I am getting established."

"You have a portfolio before in your previous jobs, couldn't you use that?"

I shook my head. "Don't you remember that when you sign an employment contract, it states that as long as you are an employee of that company, all your works belong to them?"

Adam chuckled. "Silly me! And I'm the lawyer!"

"Besides, let's leave Fiona Reeds alone. I have talent. I can do this. I don't have to use her," I said.

Adam nodded. "What about the location?"

"Will you come with me tomorrow? There's a property ten blocks from your place that I want to look at," I said.

"You're going to put up your business in our neighborhood?" he asked.

I nodded. "I want a serene, peaceful place, Adam. I don't want busy streets and crowded buildings. Besides, couples that hire a wedding planner will go anywhere if they believe she's good. I want my office to be comfortable for couples that are starting their lives together."

Adam. "Okay. But I have veto powers on this."

I nodded. He looked at my notes again.

"Just two employees?" he asked.

I nodded. "For now. Remember, we need to build my client portfolio first. I'll be willing to do that first job for free even. Well, the services will be free. They just need to pay for the expenses. I just need the shots that I can put up on my website and then the word of mouth. When things go well, I will hire another employee or two. I might even hire Nicole. And then we'll see if we can afford to invest in our own vehicle and driver." I sighed dreamily. "All that for later."

Adam nodded. "What are you going to call it?" he asked.

I smiled at him. I knew exactly what I would name this company. And this time, Adam would not have veto powers. That morning I woke up with a firm decision to go with this name.

"Ever After Concept Weddings," I smiled at him.

He raised brow. "Isn't that a little bit too cheesy?"

I laughed. "Apparently, you're someone who does not date or does not wish to settle down at all. You couldn't understand the phrase 'ever after' even if you tried, Adam. Leave it to me. If I was the bride and I heard that phrase, it would give me a sense of security that… this wedding will happen and my groom will not knock up my maid of honor first!"

Adam laughed. "Are you over them, Ash?"

"I'm smiling," I said. "There's still a bit of pain. But with all the excitement that is going on with my life, it is quite difficult to feel any angst or even remember that I am holding any grudge for anybody."

Adam smiled at me. "Then I'm happy for you, Astrid."

I smiled at him. "I'm happy for me too, Adam."

"Wh-what happened to your… bartender?"

If I was genuinely smiling when I remembered Bryan and Geena, somehow there was a pinch in my heart when I remembered … Ryder. With him, I remember a night of unforgettable passion.

He was a wonderful guy. He was probably the sweetest guy I've ever met. I wished I could just see him again, even just once.

I shrugged. "He… disappeared. I didn't see him again."

I looked down at my food and started fiddling with my ravioli.

I felt Adam tilt my chin so I could face him. He studied my expression. His eyes narrowed. "I… told you not to fall for him, Ash," he said soberly.

I rolled my eyes. "I did not fall for him, Adam!"

"Then why are you so glum?"

I shrugged. "I don't know… he… we developed some sort of friendship that night. He's… a great guy! I can't help but wonder where he is now, that's all."

Adam sighed. "Easy to fall in love with devils like that."

"Trust me, Adam. I did not fall for him that night. I just… wish I could thank him. Because if it weren't for him, I wouldn't be where I am now. I wouldn't look at myself so positively now. He was the first step to my… 'getting better' therapy." Then I looked at Adam. "Well, you are too. Because if you didn't loan me the ten grand, I would not be able to afford such an expensive date."

He chuckled. "No worries. None wasted anyway, right?"

I nodded. "Yeah. He didn't take a dime from you, but still… if you didn't open me up to the idea, I wouldn't have come across him in the first place."

Adam smiled. "I'm not saying that he wasn't good for you. I'm just saying that you shouldn't fall prey to the charms of a… stranger."

I smiled at him. "That's how you start, Adam. Fall for the charms of a stranger. Flirt. Bond. Date. And then… take it from there."

Adam nodded. "Yes. But like I said, don't fall in love with a stranger."

I smiled. "Bryan was my best friend even before he was my boyfriend and yet he cheated on me. I think I've known Geena all my life and yet she lied to me. They stole the things that I thought mattered most to me then."

"Then you didn't know them very well," Adam said.

I sighed. "Yeah, and they didn't know me very well either. More than that, I don't think they respected me."

"You know, Ash, you'll hate me for saying this, but I honestly think that you are better off without Bryan," Adam said. "I mean… if you didn't find out about the affair, you'd probably be married by now. That wouldn't have guaranteed that he and Geena would have stopped seeing each other behind your back. You would have found out about it eventually. And that would break your heart even more. At least now, you're halfway over them."

I smiled at him. "And I wouldn't be able to do this without you, Adam."

He rolled his eyes. "Yeah, yeah. I'm not a saint. I had to choose between you and my half-sister."

"Why did you choose me?"

"Because I love you both, and I had to choose between who was right and who had crossed the line."

"Fair enough. If I steal Bryan away from Geena now, you'd probably kick me out of the house."

"After I give you a good beating." He nodded.

I laughed. Then I shivered. "I couldn't imagine myself being with Bryan now. It feels… weird now. I think I'm happier if I don't think about him… them at all."

"Then you're over him."

"I'm still mad at them. I don't think that means I've fully recovered."

"Then use that anger to keep yourself from backsliding. To keep moving on… keep moving forward," Adam said.

I looked at the ring on my finger. I knew I was closer to keeping my promises to Ryder. I had healed… halfway. I was learning to love myself again. I was starting to feel good about myself and this business venture was slowly making me believe in 'ever after' again."

"Did he give you that ring?" Adam asked.

I smiled. "Ryder? Yes."

"Very nice for a bartender… who didn't take a dime of my money," he said coolly.

I laughed. "Why don't you like him? He's a wonderful guy, Adam. And he's smart. He's funny. He's romantic."

"See? And you said you didn't fall prey to his charms! You don't know him, Ash. Are you not afraid of someone who could spin a tale like that so perfectly? Could look at your parents straight in the eye and tell them he owned a couple of restaurants in New York when… as far as you know… he makes his living getting people drunk!"

"He lied for me, Adam," I said. "He carried it out so well for my sake."

Adam sighed. "Just… be careful okay?"

The cynical Adam; well, the last time he warned me about something, it turned out that my world was about to be ripped to pieces. But I knew he'd seen how broken I was the last time. He just didn't want me to go back to that hellhole again.

"You worry too much, Adam. I'll be okay. Bryan and Geena taught me well."

It was probably the first time in months that I really enjoyed going to dinner again. I was laughing so much and I was excited more than ever about the new things that were happening in my life.

Adam seemed to agree with my proposal so far. The next day, we drew up a contract. He'd been given special powers by his client to deal on his behalf so I signed the contract with him. It'd be just like working for Adam. Thank God, we managed to fix our differences; otherwise, I may not have been able to stand his sarcasm.

After signing the contract, he went with me to see the place I was talking about. It was a villa, a little smaller than his home. It also has a deck overlooking the beach.

"We could convert the whole floor into an office. I don't think the landlord would mind," I said. Adam still looked a little bit hesitant about the place. "This is going to be cheaper than a commercial space, Adam. We're just starting. I think this is better for us."

We went up the mezzanine floor. It had two rooms.

"And I can pay part of the rent because I can stay here," I said.

"Really? You're moving out of my place?" he asked.

I nodded. "It's about time, don't you think?"

"Then let's sign the lease!" he teased.

I laughed. "Come on! You really hated living with me?"

He shook his head. "No. I just felt weird living with a girl. You know… panties and bras in the bathroom!" He shivered and I laughed.

"So, are you okay with this?" I asked him.

He sighed and then he nodded. "I think you're on the right track saving as much as you can first."

Although some renovations would be needed, I was excited about the place. Adam signed the lease and issued the checks for the rent.

While they were doing the construction, I kept myself busy with posting for job openings and buying furniture. It was tough to find the best bargains that would also fit the whole idea in my head.

Days and weeks zoomed by. I did not have time to think about anything else but my new job and my new life.

After three weeks, the website was done and I was quite happy with the results. The office space was also done.

I had one huge space where I would be putting three tables and laptops. I placed little panels to segregate one area to make it a working space. Then I had one whole area enclosed in glass for the meeting room. The front of the house had a little garden. The front had a window display, which I would decorate later. In the reception area, I placed comfortable white couches where guests could wait.

I was satisfied with the way things had gone. It was an office, and yet, it still gave off a touch of home. I wanted my guests to be comfortable as soon as they walk in.

I hired a girl named Leilani. She didn't have any experience with weddings, but she worked for a PR company before. She had done parties, product launches and other big events. She needed a change and thought the wedding industry was growing with rocket speed.

I hired another lady, Rose, a new graduate who wanted experience in telemarketing and administration. She would be my receptionist and my telemarketer. Website inquiries were also her responsibility.

"I am so mad at you!" Nicole said to me while we were having dinner at Oil Rig one night.

I hadn't been hanging out with them much since I was so busy with the business.

"Why?"

"Why do you have to hire another girl? I'm here!"

I raised a brow. "I can't afford you yet Nic. The risks are high at the moment. I don't want you to lose your living if my business doesn't make it long term."

"I might as well lose it once you enter the picture!" she said crossly.

"Don't worry, Nic. As soon as I get this going and business picks up, I'll hire you." I smiled at her.

"Why not hire me now?"

I laughed. "Hey, stay put. We'll get there. I can't afford your salary yet."

She raised a brow at me. "You have to have more faith in yourself, Ash. Why can't you do this? This is your life, your soul. In fact, you were my company's soul! All we do now is recycle your ideas! It's getting old. I miss working with you! New ideas, new concepts. I don't mind taking a pay cut!"

I laughed. "No way, Nic! Give me a few months and I'll offer you the job. Right now, I just need my first five projects so I will have a portfolio."

"Hmmm… can't you use the old ones you used to work on with Fiona?"

"Do I want a law suit as early as now?" I asked matter-of-factly.

"Well, you're probably right. I'll bet Fiona will be so threatened by you that those pictures would not get past her," Nicole agreed.

"Guys, if you know anyone who's getting married, let me know. I don't care if I don't make money. I just need to build up my portfolio first," I said.

"Sure, sure. Are you willing to do gay weddings?" Dannie asked sarcastically.

I raised a brow at him. "Of course."

John wrinkled his nose. "Don't expect anything from me, Ash. I love you and all that, but I'm staying clear of friends who are settling down. Honestly, it gives me the creeps."

Now all of us raised a brow at John.

"What? I love being a bachelor!" he said. "Weddings are…" He shivered. "Excuse me, why is it a lucrative business again?"

"Because there are still guys in the world who aren't like you and thank God for that!" Nicole said crossly.

"Well, if you find that guy for yourself, let me know." John raised his brow at her.

Dannie and I exchanged knowing looks. Nicole and John didn't usually get along with each other well. However, sometimes, we both felt that it's not because they did not like each other at all, but maybe because it's more of the opposite. I'd like to do *that wedding!*

We all left the bar around midnight. John was going to take me home. Nicole was catching a ride with Dannie.

"I'll refer some clients to you, Ash," Nicole promised.

"Your boss won't like that!" I scolded her.

"Then let her fire me! All the more reason for you to hire me then!" She winked and then she got into Dannie's car.

As we waited for John's car to arrive with the valet, I noticed a familiar car parked in front of the bar. My breath caught in my throat and my heart pounded inside my chest.

It looked like the car that Ryder rented. Same make... an SLR McLaren. Same color. Again, it made me wonder how he got that car for that day. It must have been very expensive to rent it. Unless he knew some rich friends who owned a car like that and they let him take it for a spin for free.

I sighed. I remembered the day that I was with him in that car. It was my first step to recovery. And I was okay. Because of Ryder... I was okay.

"Do you miss the car?" John asked in a teasing tone.

I shook my head. There was a pinch in my heart. "No. Just the guy who drove it."

10.
ARRHAE: Wedding coins.
Given by the groom to the bride to signify his trustworthiness, that he is symbolically giving his material possessions or earthly wealth to the care of his bride.

Nicole referred some of her clients to me. She said that apparently, they were under budget constraints and the revised professional fees that Fiona had been charging made them lose interest.

They were very happy to meet with me. More so when I told them that since they were my first clients, I would waive all the professional fees. They just need to pay for the expenses for the wedding. But of course, nothing would happen without their approval first. I told them that I was building up my portfolio and thus, I didn't mind doing this for free.

"Are you sure?" the bride, Angela, asked.

I nodded. "Positive!"

The groom looked a little suspicious. I smiled at him.

"This is not my first time doing this. I used to work for Fiona. In fact, I was one of their pioneers," I assured them.

"Really? Why'd you leave?"

I sighed. "Long story. But… to cut it short, let's just say that my own engagement went down the drain and for a while, I was… socially dead. Now, I'm resurrected. What can I say? No heartbreak can make me stay away from making 'ever afters' come true."

The bride bit her lip and then she smiled at me. "I admire your courage! My sister-in-law just got dumped too. Maybe you have advice for her on how to get better. You don't look heartbroken at all!"

I shook my head. "I'm not! Not anymore!"

Her glance drifted off to my ring and her eyes widened.

"Oh my God!" she breathed.

"What?"

"A… are you still wearing your engagement ring?" she asked.

I looked at my ring and then I laughed. "No, no. This wasn't my engagement ring. This is…" I sighed, smiling at the thought of Ryder again. "This is some sort of a promise ring. I made some guy a promise and he… gave me this so I won't forget it."

"Sounds like a very expensive promise," Jacob, the groom to be, said.

"Oh no. I don't think so."

"We wanted that ring," Angela said, still looking longingly at my ring.

"I told you, you could have it," Jacob told her.

"No! Twenty-five grand? Are you out of your mind?" she said. "I'd rather we spend that money on our honeymoon," she said smiling at her fiancé. She glanced at my ring again. "You must admit, Harry Winston did great on that ring!"

"This… this isn't… a Harry Winston," I said.

Angela laughed. "Right." She rolled her eyes.

"Oh, she stares at that ring in a magazine every day. She knows," Jacob told me.

"I do not!" Angela punched him playfully in the arm.

I still didn't know what they were talking about, but I didn't want to talk about my ring anymore. First, because they'd already mistaken it to be a real Harry Winston and also because I didn't want them to start arguing over a ring that she was never going to have.

"Well, you were right to spend the money on your honeymoon," I told them cheerfully. "Have you already made plans with your travel agent?"

It took me half a day to finish my meeting with Angela and Jacob. When they left my office, they were much more excited about their wedding than they were before they met me. I was extremely pleased with myself.

As I sat on the deck outside my office, sipping a glass of pineapple juice, I smiled. I tried imagining where I would be had I married Bryan.

I'd probably be still with Fiona, answering to her every whim, watching her take all the credit and all the money for my brilliant and unique wedding ideas, and getting paid almost minimum wage for all the hard work that I put in. Then I'd come home, cook, and wait for Bryan to come back from work. We'd talk about our day, like good friends. He'd probably be too tired to make love to me, and since I never knew wanton desire at all, I wouldn't mind. I'd contentedly read a romance novel until I fall asleep.

And what would have happened if Ryder and I continued seeing each other after the wedding? I'd still be here, cooking a special meal for him probably, hoping to seduce him so he would stay the night with me. We'd probably have made love in every corner of this office already.

I bit my lip at the thought. *Damn!* How could the mere thought of Ryder arouse… unknown feelings in me? How could the memory of that night make me want to relive it over and over again?

Bryan never made me feel sexual. Ryder brought all my nerves to life and turned my world upside down.

Ryder asked me to come and find him again. When I am ready. Right now… I'm halfway there. I want my next relationship to last forever. I don't think I can stand to go over another heartbreak ever again. That is why I had to be careful. God knows I needed to see Ryder again. I could tell that he was a good man. He awakened my senses. But I need more time.

I stared at my ring again and smiled. *Harry Winston!* Well, it does look like one, but it can't be. Though, this ring is a hundred times more beautiful than the ring that I actually got from Bryan. Ryder has great taste! I wonder where he found this. Maybe when I see him again, I can ask him to show me.

I kept myself busy for the next few weeks. Angela and Jacob were going to have a beach wedding and I had to handle all the arrangements for them. They were going to say their vows along the shore and the reception was going to be themed paradise on the beach. I had it all figured out. I drew concepts for them to look at, so they could picture the idea that I had in mind. When Angela saw my storyboard, she almost cried. She was so ecstatic about the whole thing.

It took me more than a month to finish the concept, find the right materials, book the venue, photographers, videographers and make all the other necessary arrangements.

One week before the wedding, I was able to rest although not completely because I still had so much pressure before the show. This was the first wedding on my own. And this was going to be the start of things for my new company and I wanted it to be perfect.

Dannie asked me to go shopping with him. There's a new Technodiamond watch that he was itching to buy and we went around from store to store, trying to find a good deal.

I was looking at the diamond watches with lust in my eyes. I sighed. Someday. My time will come. I will be able to afford these.

The fourth store that we went to was the store that brought me so many memories. Except now, I no longer felt the pain when I thought about that fake ring—only embarrassment and anger. And then I remembered that this is actually where I first met Ryder and I cried in his arms.

Ryder. I smiled at the thought of him. I miss him! It's a wonder how I can miss him so much over these months when I'd only been with him for a day.

I wanted to see him again. So I could remember once more that he was real. That I didn't just invent him. He really existed. And for one night, he was mine.

"Oh my God, Ash! That looks exactly like your ring!" Dannie said breaking into my thoughts, pointing at the poster of a beautiful Harry Winston advertisement.

There was no mistake. It did look exactly like the ring Ryder gave me. The stone in the middle, the cut… the similarity was unmistakable.

"I know! But we both know this ring is a fake!" I whispered to him.

"Good morning, Ma'am, Sir, how can I help you?" the guy at the counter asked us. He was the same guy who had examined my engagement ring.

"Well, I'm actually waiting for the other sales guy to come back to me with the availability of the watch I asked for," Dannie said.

The guy nodded politely. "And you, Ma'am?" His eyes drifted off to my finger. I immediately took my hand off the counter.

He stared at me with a weird look on his face, as if he was trying to remember something.

I laughed. "You must probably be wondering where you met me, right? Actually, I came here before, I asked you to look at my engagement ring, and you told me it was a fake."

He nodded. "Oh, yes," he smiled sheepishly. "I remember. Well, I can see your fiancé was quick to make amends." He looked at my ring.

"Oh, no. No." I shook my head. "We… didn't get back together." I showed him my ring. "This… came from somebody else."

He smiled. "Then I suggest you marry this one before he gets away!" Something about his voice told me that he was gay. I could see Dannie staring at him with interest now.

"Well, thanks, sweetie," I smiled at him. "Actually, I dumped my fiancé before I even found out that the ring was fake! At least this new guy didn't pass *this* ring off as a diamond."

He stared at me with narrowed eyes. "But that *is* a diamond. And it's a Harry Winston." He said pointing at the Harry Winston poster of the ring that looks like mine, only it was in gold. Mine was in silver.

"No, no. This is just a good imitation. Besides, that's in gold. Unless they make this ring in silver or white gold too." I laughed nervously.

The guy shook his head. "No, but they make in platinum."

I stared back at him, completely dumbfounded. Then I insisted. "Sweetheart, you don't understand. There is no way the guy who gave this to me can afford a real Harry Winston. This is a fake! Probably a cubic zirconia or a moissanite. And it can't be platinum."

He shrugged. "Well, the inside should say PT 950, if it's the real thing."

I sighed, getting a little irritated now. This guy was so meticulous and so nosy that I wanted to prove him wrong now. "Alright, I'll prove it to you," I said, taking off my ring and looking at the inside of the band. There was no inscription. I turned it around and then suddenly, my heart actually dropped to my toes, when I saw *PT 950* inscribed on it. I swallowed hard.

"This… this can't be right," I whispered.

Dannie took the ring from me and had a look.

"Oh my God!" he breathed.

We both stared at the guy at the counter who was beaming a big *I-told-you-so* at us.

"Would you like to have the rest checked for its authenticity?" he asked although I think he already knew our answer.

I nodded silently and gave him the ring.

We waited for him impatiently. My heart was pounding inside my ribcage, I could feel my temperature rising.

I stared at Dannie.

"Well, if it's real then you can pawn it!" he teased.

I shook my head. "If it's real, I'm going to hunt Ryder Woodson down and shove it down his throat!" I muttered.

The guy came back. I raised a brow at him. "Well?"

He smiled at me widely. "It's the real thing. Harry Winston, emerald cut diamond, two carats on a genuine platinum band."

I swallowed hard.

"Doesn't this ring cost about twenty grand?" Dannie asked.

The guy shook his head. "The one on the poster does. It's twenty-two carat gold. This is platinum. This one actually retails for more than thirty."

I felt my knees turn to jelly at that instant.

"You can trust me on this. I heard you mention Mr. Van Woodsen? He's been buying jewelry from us at least once a month. I heard his mother is quite a collector of diamonds." He winked and something in his look made me feel like he thought I was damn lucky to be receiving a ring from Mr. Van Woodsen.

I shook my head, taking my ring back from him. "No. You misheard me. I don't know Mr. Van Woodsen. But I do know a certain *Mr. Woodson* who I will hunt down and kill," I said in such a serious tone that the guy actually stopped smiling.

"Thank you for your time and your... assessment of my friend's ring. If I can just get your calling card, we'll give you a call once we have some... requirements for jewelry," Dannie said. The guy couldn't help smiling and immediately handed him a calling card.

"Thank you, Garrie," Dannie said reading his name out loud.

Then he dragged me out of the place before I start hyperventilating.

"Oh my God!" I breathed. "I cannot believe this!"

"Yes! You're wearing a thirty thousand dollar engagement ring!"

"How? I don't know how Ryder could have afforded it!" I asked. Somehow things do not make sense. "God, I hope he didn't steal this or something."

Dannie raised a brow. "God, I hope not! With his looks... he'll be a hit in prison!"

"Even if he did... acquire this in illegal ways... why would he give it to me? Why not pawn it and take the money?"

"Only one way to find out," Dannie said as he headed towards his car.

Thirty minutes later, we were at Oil Rig. I kept staring at the bar, keeping an eye out for Ryder. John and Nicole joined us a couple of minutes later.

"What?" Nicole asked, grabbing my hand and examining my ring. "I knew this couldn't have been a fake! It's too beautiful!"

"How could he afford it?" I asked. "And why would he give it to me?"

Did he pity me because for my first engagement I had been given a fake ring? Did he feel sorry for me? But still… no one can be *that* sorry! Thirty grand! Maybe even more!

What could I have done to him that would make me deserve to keep this ring?

I snorted to myself. I did give him my virginity. And I wanted to laugh at myself for that until I realized…

I hope he didn't mean this as payment for going to bed with him. Because that would make me a…

"Shit!" I muttered under my breath. I won't rest until I find him! Until I talk to him again.

I dialed his number. His phone was off. I tried again. Still off. I stood up from my seat and marched to the counter.

"Where are you going?" Dannie asked.

"Ending this mystery!" I murmured.

There was a bald bartender who saw me approaching.

"How can I help you, Madam?" he asked.

"I'm looking for a co-worker of yours. Ryder Woodson?"

He gave me a confused look and then he shook his head, "I don't think I remember working with anyone that goes by that name, Ma'am."

I shook my head. "Maybe you're new. I met him here at this exact counter, a couple of months ago."

He smiled at me. "Sorry, ma'am. I've been here since opening. I'm telling you, there is no bartender by that name here. Never been."

"Maybe… maybe he was a temp or something and you were off the night he was on duty," I insisted. John came up beside me.

The guy shook his head. "I'm sorry, Ma'am. We have a strict policy here. No one temps for us. The owner has very… distinct policies. Everybody must be trained for months before facing a customer. So, no temps."

I sighed. "It… it can't be."

"I wish I could help you, Ma'am," he said apologetically.

I thanked him quietly. And then I turned my back on him, still confused.

Just then, I remembered what Garrie from the jewelry shop said. I turned back to the bartender.

"How about Ryder *Van Woodsen?*" I asked him.

He stared back at me for a while and then he said, "I'll call the manager, Ma'am. He can help you with that."

I watched him walk away. And then I stared back at John, who just raised a brow at me.

A minute later, a tall blond guy dressed in an expensive suit joined us.

"Yes, Ma'am. How can I help?"

I took a deep breath and said, "I... I'm looking for a guy who works here. Ryder."

"Mr. Van Woodsen is out of the country right now. May I ask what this is about? Maybe I can help."

"Does he work here?" I asked.

The guy shook his head. "No, Ma'am. May I ask what this is about? Maybe I can help you out," he repeated.

"If... if he doesn't work here, then how can you help me?" I asked a little impatiently.

He raised a brow at me but he didn't say anything. I realized he wasn't going to give me any information.

"Mr. Van Woodsen..." I started. "This guy that we're talking about... *Ryder* Van Woodsen?"

The guy nodded. "Yes, Ma'am."

I already felt like I was about to hyperventilate any minute.

"You see... I met a guy a couple of months ago... he introduced himself as Ryder. We had a little arrangement... I've been trying to call him today, but got his voicemail."

"I see. As I said, he is out of the country. Maybe he's on board a flight right now," the guy said politely.

"Okay." I took a deep breath. "But really? Ryder Van Woodsen? That's his real name? Are we talking about the same guy? Black hair, riveting green eyes?"

The guy smiled. "I think we are talking about the same guy. But really, Ma'am? How can I help you?"

I shook my head. "I... guess you can't," I said to him. "Do you know when he's coming back?"

The guy shook his head. "He comes and goes. He has other branches to look after. We do not know when he'll be in Malibu again."

I nodded. "Okay. When he does come back, can you please tell him that Astrid Jacobson is looking for him?"

The guy nodded. "I will pass that message along."

I nodded at him and smiled. Then I turned my back on him and started to go, but then I changed my mind. I turned back to him again. "And can you also tell him that when I do find him, I intend to personally kick his ass?"

The guy looked startled but he quickly composed himself. "I'll... I'll make sure he gets the message."

I nodded again and then quickly dashed back to our table.

I was quiet. My friends were waiting for me to say something. When Nicole and Dannie finally figured out that I might not speak for a while, they turned to John.

John sighed. "Apparently, a certain Ryder Woodson does not work here. Never has. No one knew him."

"So, what was he doing behind the bar then?"

"No one knew Ryder Woodson. However, a certain *Ryder Van Woodsen* seems to be so important around here, only the manager can talk to you once you mention his name," John replied.

"How could it be the same guy?" I asked in disbelief.

"He did say that Mr. Van Woodsen's name is also *Ryder.* And he also has black hair and green eyes," John said. He chuckled. "Wow! He must have been so taken with you to agree to pretend to be your date that night. No wonder he didn't take a penny from your ten grand!"

I stared at John. "It can't be!"

"Ash, wasn't he introducing himself at that party as Ryder Van Woodsen?" Nicole asked.

I nodded.

"He what?" John asked.

"He was telling everybody that his name was Ryder Van Woodsen. So much so, that whenever Ash introduced him as Ryder Woodson, he corrected her every time," Nicole said.

"If that guy you introduced to us really is Ryder Van Woodsen, then he isn't just a bartender here, sweetheart," John said. "He doesn't work here. Apparently, he owns this place."

I knew it by then.

It was the only explanation for everything. From the checks that he returned to me, to the car that he was driving, to the ease and grace that he had when he was talking to my relatives about business and assuring them that he could get them a table at a famous Manhattan restaurant, to the very expensive room that he rented that night, to the ring on my finger.

He must have thought this was a joke! He introduced himself to everybody except me! He gave his real name to everybody, but to me he gave a fake name!

"I... can't believe this!"

"Wow!" Dannie breathed. "You didn't make up the perfect guy that night. You really had him. He was the real deal."

"So, the story that you thought was real was the actual sham? And the fake story that you were telling your relatives that night was really the truth?"

"Apparently so. Except for us. We were a sham."

"No you weren't," Nicole said. "You said you didn't pretend right? He said that too. Just think that you had a one day relationship with Ryder Van Woodsen."

"Yeah. And having this ring makes me feel like a... prostitute. Like *he* paid for my company!"

"You should only feel that way if you went to bed with him." Dannie muttered.

I made a big mistake after that! I blushed to the roots of my hair so fast that I had no time to pretend otherwise.

"Oh my God!" Nicole breathed.

"Oh my God!" Dannie almost shrieked.

John looked away and took a gulp of his beer.

I covered my face with my hands. "Shit! I'm going to kill him when I see him again!"

"Why? I thought you said..." Nicole started.

"I said a lot of things, I believed a lot of things!" I muttered. "That didn't stop Bryan and Geena from hurting me beyond belief!"

Dannie and Nicole fell silent.

"No one is judging you, Ash," John said gently. "It was about time you gave it up anyway."

"Thanks John!" I said.

"Well, at least you gave it up to someone more gorgeous than Bryan!" Dannie said, trying to make the mood light again.

"And I got a thirty thousand dollar ring in return! What a high class whore I am!" I muttered.

"It's not that, Ash! Maybe he was just... gallant!"

"I told him to buy a ring that was fake, but would pass as being the real thing. Or he could rent the real thing and return it later. He didn't do either! And he only told me to keep the ring after all had been done! What else was this ring for? He doesn't know me. I don't know him."

"He's rich. Something to remember him by?" Nicole suggested.

I shook my head. "No. If he thought he could buy me, he's dead wrong!"

"And what are you going to tell him when you see him? That sleeping with him was actually for free?" Dannie asked in an irritated tone.

"Well..." Actually, I didn't know what I was going to say to him. "I'll tell him that... that he can take his ring back and shove it down his throat!"

"What good would that do?" John asked.

"I don't like owing people favors. Especially those with a huge financial value attached to it," I replied.

"Fair enough," Nicole said. She stared at my ring once again. "But still, very pretty!"

"He must have thought I was a joke, huh!" I whispered.

"Come on! You don't know that!" John said. "For all you know, you got under his skin the minute he laid eyes on you."

"If he really is who we think he is, then he's got a long line of mistresses pining for his attention. I just feel that he... bought himself a weekend entertainment and... I was it."

"Hunt him down, sweetie. So you can ask him why he did it. Why he spared you even a minute of his time," Nicole said, smiling at me. "Who knows? If John's right and you did get under his skin, then... Bryan would be eating *his* heart out at your wedding."

I glared at Nicole. Because even though I had been thinking about Ryder constantly over these past few months, I was thinking about Ryder Woodson, the bartender, who was sweet and kind, smart and funny, who steals lines from his sister's romance novels. The warm, gentle guy who made me feel like I was the queen of the world, that I deserved a prince like him instead of a loser like Bryan. Ryder, the simple guy with a great mind and a big heart.

Ryder Van Woodsen, on the other hand... I didn't know him at all. For all I know, he could be a fierce, manipulating, cold-hearted bastard who doesn't mind paying thirty thousand dollars to pretend to be somebody he isn't... and to take advantage of a desperate, pathetic, heartbroken girl like me.

If he really was all the things he said he was at that wedding then he was the epitome of what I swore never to date ever since I was a teenager.

I went home with a heavy heart because I knew, every day since the wedding, I'd been looking forward to seeing Ryder again. I thought that, given the chance, when I got my act together that I'd show him the real me; he might actually get to like me. For real.

But now... I doubt that *I* would get to like *him*.

11.

GUEST BOOK:

Your guests can write special messages on your wedding day. You'll want to remember who was at your party. Some opt to have a photo book printed with their prenuptial pictures and empty fields and spaces where guests can write their messages. It's a photo book and guest book in one!

*J*acob and Angela's big day was also a big day for me. It was my debut. A coming out… a vindication… a resurrection… a rebirth.

I worked tirelessly for the entire day, tying up loose ends, making last minute confirmations, making sure that nothing would go wrong.

The ceremony by the beach was perfect. The way we arranged the place made it look like they were not in the beach at all. Instead, they were in paradise. We had the reception in an open area, facing the beach where huge lanterns glowed along the shore and some in the sea itself. At least four bubble machines were blowing bubbles in the air. The ground of the reception had rose petals scattered around. All the guests were wearing flower garlands. Torches were lit around the area of the reception to give a little beach bonfire atmosphere. The whole setting was a combination of beach paradise and elegant wedding bliss. I was so proud of the results.

"I am so… so happy!" Angela said to me just before dinner started. "You are a genius, Astrid! I would recommend you to all my friends!" She beamed.

Jacob was so happy that his bride was positively glowing on their wedding day.

"Thank you," he said to me and I knew he really meant it.

I was looking contentedly at the guests. It was after dinner and the bride and groom were dancing along with the other guests. Just then, I heard somebody speak behind me.

"So, I see you are back in business."

I spun around and faced the source of the familiar voice. Bryan was staring back at me with a surprised expression.

I simply nodded at him, biting back a curse. Well, barely.

"Are… are you one of the guests?" I asked him.

He nodded. "Angela and Jacob were patients of mine."

"Oh. Do they still have all their teeth accounted for?" I asked in a sarcastic tone.

He chuckled. "God, I miss your sense of humor!"

"I don't miss yours though. Apparently, your idea of a joke involves getting my cousin knocked up behind my back," I muttered.

"I miss your feistiness, too," he said sadly.

He stared at me for a while and then he sighed. "You look really good, Ash." Something in his voice told me that he was not very happy about it. Not one bit.

Then his eyes drifted off to my finger.

"I see you're still engaged to Van Woodsen."

I raised a brow. "Of course I am! What did you expect? I don't change fiancés as quickly as you do, Bryan."

He sucked in a hard breath. "I gotta hand it to you, Ash. What a rebound relationship! Apparently, he was quite a guy. All your relatives are in love with him." Then he narrowed his eyes at me. "I don't think you love him, though. I know you," he said.

"You don't know what you're saying."

He shook his head. "I know exactly what I'm saying. You don't love him. I think you were just using him to get back at me. Does he know? Does he know that you don't feel for him half of what you felt for me?"

"Back down there one second, Mister!" I said, quite irritated with him now. "You don't know me, Bryan. Not even a bit. I'm happy now! Ten times more than when I was with you! He makes all my dreams come true."

"Really? You were never a mercenary."

"I didn't want his money."

"I heard the Van Woodsens' pockets run very deep. Especially, your fiancé's. Owning a string of exclusive bars in his own name already. Plus, those he will soon inherit from his parents. I thought you were different. I thought you *hated* rich guys whose worlds revolved more on their money than on their girlfriends. Rich guys who could easily replace you... or buy somebody else the way they bought you."

God! Why did I even fall in love with a bitter, accusing, self-centered bastard like this? I thought to myself angrily.

"You may be a guest here, Bryan, but excuse me for this!" I said and without warning, I gave him one sharp slap on the face.

I quickly turned on my heel before I could burst into very unhappy tears in front of him. I wasn't looking. I ran straight into a hard wall as I turned around. And because tears were already sliding down my cheeks, I refused to look back at Bryan.

I felt warm and comfortable at that very instant. I felt strong arms wrap around me in one comforting hug. I was too afraid to look. I just wanted to run away from Bryan.

"I see you haven't lost your touch, Bryan," a familiar voice said, which made my heart beat ten times faster. "It seems you still want the things you do not have."

There was a long pause. And then Bryan retaliated, "Are you really sure you have her? You don't know her as well as I do."

"I think I know her now more than any man does." And I knew there was a subliminal message hidden in that statement.

"I doubt she loves you that much!" Bryan said tirelessly.

"It doesn't matter. I love her more than enough for the both of us. Now, if you'll excuse us, I need to take my fiancée away."

I felt his arms come tighter around me as he whirled me away from Bryan. I followed his lead, but I refused to look up at him. I was afraid that he'd disappear... again. That he wouldn't be real.

He brought me to a secluded corner. Then his other hand came around me and he continued hugging me. I cried silently in his arms. I was so mad at Bryan right now. It was hard for me to believe that I wasted three years of my life with a loser like him.

I felt him pull away from me gently. Then he tilted my chin up so I could look at him.

Our eyes met and a mix of emotions surged through me. Happiness because I missed that friendly face, the face of an ally. Excitement, as I remembered the last night we spent together. Warmth, as I realized how cold I had been over these last few months. Caution, because I realized I did not know him at all. Fear, because I knew I could fall for him in an instant, but I knew I couldn't trust him the way I trusted him before.

"I was told that you were looking for me," he whispered softly. "I was also told that you couldn't wait to kick my ass." Although his voice sounded subdued, I could see that his eyes were dancing.

Realization of the truth dawned on me instantly.

Ryder *Van Woodsen*.

It was all true then. The message made it to him. I was hoping it wouldn't. Because that would mean he wasn't the owner of Oil Rig. That he was just a mere bartender. So I could feel free to fall for him. Because he would be more real to me than some rich guy.

I pushed him away, but his grip on my waist was tighter than I thought.

He raised a brow at me, challenging me. But his eyes were still dancing.

I remembered why I was looking for him in the first place. His ring! His payment for my virginity.

Anger surged through me again as I felt so embarrassed and so... low. I wasn't able to stop myself. He deserved the same thing I gave Bryan.

"Ouch!" he said gently as his left palm caressed his cheek. Then he took a deep breath. "I can't say I don't deserve that. Anything else?" His eyes were still dancing, one arm still wrapped around my waist.

"Damn it! Who are you?" I asked, pushing him away from me with all my might.

Finally, he let me go. I stood a good two feet away from him, holding my hands in front of me, warning him not to come near me.

"*Who are you?*" I repeated. "I don't know you."

He took a deep breath. "Yes, you do, Ash," he replied. "You know me. Maybe even better than anyone else."

"I don't even know your name."

"It's just a name! What difference does it make?"

"A lot!" I muttered.

He took a deep breath again and then he said, "Ryder... Ryder Anthony Van Woodsen."

"See? If you could lie about your name, you could lie about anything else!" I snapped.

"Wasn't it all supposed to be a lie, Astrid?" he asked me. "Wasn't it all supposed to be a sham? Wasn't that what you hired me for?"

"Because I thought you were real... before all that!"

He took a step towards me. "I am real, Ash!" he argued. "Every word I said at that party was true! About who I am. What I do. About my family. It was all me. I wasn't pretending to be someone else."

"But you allowed *me* to think you were someone else! Why, Ryder? Why would you agree to that deal? Why would you agree to be paid ten grand to pretend to be in love with me?"

He didn't answer. He took a deep breath and then he said, "I don't have an answer to that. Sometimes, I still ask myself the same question."

"God, I'm such a fool! You must have been having the laugh of your life behind my back!" I said angrily.

He shook his head. "I was having the time of my life. For the first time, I was sure that a woman enjoyed my company because of who I really am beneath my nametag."

"I wouldn't care, Ryder!" I said to him.

"I know," he said. "And I liked that. It shouldn't change anything between us, Ash."

I shook my head. "It does," I said to him. "I can't look at you the same way now."

Tears rolled down my cheeks. I started to take off the ring he gave me, but he was quick to close his palms over my hands.

"Don't!" he said. I stared up at him. His face was serious. His eyes were no longer playful and dancing. *Is this the real Ryder Van Woodsen?* I asked myself.

My phone rang that instant. I took a deep breath and answered it.

"Astrid, where are you? The party's about to end and I need you here," Leilani said to me.

"I'm coming," I replied.

I stared up at Ryder again. "I... I have to go to work."

He nodded. "I'll wait for you up front. I'll drive you home."

"There is no need for that..." I started protesting.

"I'll take you home," he said in a strident, demanding tone.

I didn't answer. Instead, I turned my back on him and walked back to the party.

I kept myself preoccupied. It was too confusing to think about Ryder.

Who did he think he was? The king of the world? Can I just easily forgive him for making a fool out of me? Does he think he can give a very expensive ring and expect me to shrug everything off?

I said goodbye to the guests. I made sure everything was in order.

Finally, I said goodbye to Angela and Jacob. Angela was in tears when she hugged me.

"Bless you, Astrid! Bless you!" she said to me, in between tears.

"Thank you very much, Astrid. It was a job brilliantly done," Jacob said, shaking my hand.

I said goodbye to my assistant and then I went down the front steps. True enough, a familiar McLaren was parked in front of the hotel. As soon as he saw me approaching, Ryder got out of the car and opened the car door for me.

We drove in silence. I didn't know what to say to him. I would have babbled endlessly with Ryder Woodson, the bartender, but I was seriously tongue-tied now, in front of Ryder Van Woodsen... apparently the richest bachelor in town!

I remember when I asked him to pose as my boyfriend he was reluctant at first. He said that I might not be able to afford him! Well, that was *so* true!

He parked in front of Adam's house.

I didn't live here anymore, but he didn't have to know that. I hadn't spoken to Adam in a while, I still had his keys and some of my clothes were still here, so I figured it might be a good idea for me to sleepover. I could use a little chat with my lawyer.

"I can't accept this ring, Ryder," I whispered.

He stared at me, raising his brow. "You accepted it before."

"I didn't know it was real then! Haven't you forgotten? I was the girl who couldn't tell the difference between cubic zirconia and diamond!"

"What does it matter if it's real?" he asked.

I took a deep breath. "I don't want to owe you anything, Ryder."

"You don't," he replied.

"With this ring on me, I feel like I do! And worse... it made me feel like... you paid me because of that night," I said quietly.

He sucked in a deep breath. "Whoa!" He stared at me with a hard expression on his face. "That was never my intention!"

"Then what was your intention, Ryder? Because the last time I checked, it is not normal to give thirty thousand dollar diamond rings to near strangers!" I snapped.

"You asked for a ring!"

"I asked for a fake ring! Or a rental!"

"The last guy who gave you a ring gave you a fake one already! I wanted to be original!" he snapped back.

111

I took the ring off my finger and I placed it in his palm.

"Here's your ring!" I muttered. "Until you give me a better excuse as to why you gave it to me, I can't accept it because every time I look at it and every time I remember what happened between us, I will always feel like... a first-class whore!" I opened the car door, stepped out and slammed the door behind me.

I walked towards Adam's house without a backward glance at Ryder.

I found Adam on the deck, drinking beer and enjoying a cigar.

"Oh, since when did you fancy a Monte Cristo?" I asked behind him.

He almost jumped up from his seat; I couldn't help laughing.

"Jesus Christ, Astrid!" he groaned. "I want my key back!"

I laughed and sat beside him.

"Relax, cousin." I took a beer from the cooler beside him. "If it makes you feel better, I missed you."

"It made me feel better! Loads!" he said sarcastically.

We sat there for a while, listening to the gentle breeze and the sound of the waves.

"What did I do to deserve this visit?" he asked.

I sighed and took a gulp of my beer.

"Funny thing happened recently," I said to him. "Do you remember that I was sporting a very lovely ring?"

"The one that was meant to blind the person unfortunate enough to stare at it for more than a minute?"

I giggled and then I nodded.

"So? What about it?"

"Apparently, it was a thirty-thousand grand Harry Winston."

Adam took a gulp of his beer.

"Only thirty?"

I raised a brow at him. "You knew!"

He sighed. "I can tell the difference from cubic zirconia and diamond, thank you very much."

"Why didn't you tell me, Adam?"

He shrugged. "You didn't ask."

I groaned. Then I said, "Don't tell me you also knew that the date I brought with me was a fake! He wasn't really a bartender!"

He was silent for a long while. I stared at him, unable to believe that Adam could hide the truth from me.

"Oh my God, Adam! How could you?" I groaned.

"Hey, Ash. It wasn't my position to tell, and he asked me not to."

"What? When?"

"Well, I got the door for you, remember?" he said. "I recognized him at first glance. Ryder Van Woodsen is a prominent guy in some cities. He was new here. But in Manhattan, he has face value."

"A-list?"

Adam nodded. "Sort of. Their family is not exactly unpopular. They're quite rich and they own a chain of restaurants on three continents. When I saw him, I told him immediately that I was expecting to meet a bartender. He asked me not to say anything to you. But he was willing to help you out in your own little game."

"Why?"

Adam shook his head. "I don't know. He didn't say."

I sighed. "That was why you were looking at him funny all evening. That was why you were constantly warning me not to fall for him."

He nodded. "I was not really happy that day, you know. Or maybe a little." He smiled. "Because I knew I would be getting my ten grand back. But other than that, I was worried."

I sighed. "He must have been having the laugh of his life that night!"

"Who knows? Maybe he was bored with his life," Adam said. "The ring was gorgeous though."

"I returned it," I whispered.

"Good for you," he said. "Show him you're not one of the material girls he knows."

I took a gulp of my beer. "I didn't know until the guy in the jewelry shop told me I was wearing an authentic Harry Winston. That's when I looked for him again. True enough, he wasn't known in Oil Rig as the bartender."

"He owns the place," Adam whispered.

"I've been duped twice in a row, Adam!" I muttered.

Adam smiled. "But if it's any consolation, I did a little research on him. He doesn't seem so bad. He was just too much into his work, but the good news is… he was never rumored to be a womanizer."

"I don't care about Ryder Van Woodsen, Adam," I said. But I knew something inside me was deeply broken. I don't know why. But I felt really sad to see him again today and find out that he really is Ryder Van Woodsen, and not the Ryder Woodson I was looking forward to seeing again."

"Then why do you sound so sad?" Adam asked wearily.

It took me a while to answer. "Because I was disappointed. Because, for a while, I was hoping to meet him again. To show him the side of me that isn't… you know… *cuckoo!*" I sighed again. "I really liked him. The guy who went with me to the wedding. He was funny and smart. Down to earth and… romantic. He inspired me to be better. And now, I think I am. I was hoping to find him again so I could see what… lies ahead of us."

"You found him again, Astrid. This could be the beginning of something great."

I shook my head. "I will never see him again." I stared at Adam sadly. "I will never see Ryder Woodson again. Because he doesn't exist. He never did."

"What about Ryder Van Woodsen?"

I shook my head. "I don't know him," I replied. "I never did."

"Well, don't you want to get to know the guy?"

I laughed humorlessly. "Come on, Adam! That guy is way out of my league! There is no way I'll fit into his world. It won't last. And you know, if I start believing in 'ever after' again, I need to find a man who can lead me to that. Not a playmate for a while who will ditch me later on. I don't want to live like that."

Adam narrowed his eyes. "Live like what? Like a queen? With a guy who can give you everything your heart desires?"

I shook my head. "I'm not asking for much. I never did. I like the simpler things. I just wanted a stand up guy, who can grow old with me, respect me, and won't look down on me. And I don't want to live like… a bomb is about to fall on my head any day. That he might tire of me because he lived in an exciting world full of glamorous women who would do anything and everything to take him away from me."

"You're a very complicated woman, Ash." Adam shook his head. "Now, I understand. Even a guy like Ryder Van Woodsen would be crazy about you!"

"I've been through a lot. And now that I'm almost out of that zone, out of danger, I… wanted to make sure I won't head down the same path again."

"I don't think you would head down the same path, Ash," Adam said reassuringly. "Bryan is… one of a kind!" he added sarcastically.

"He's a classic, isn't he?" I said shaking my head. "You know I saw him tonight. At the wedding."

"Oh? And how did that turn out?"

"Really bad. I slapped him," I said.

"Finally!" Adam threw his hands up in the air triumphantly, as if he had been hoping for that to happen for a long time. "Now, do tell!"

"Well, he came up to me and congratulated me for getting back in business. Then he said that he didn't think I really loved Ryder, that he thought I was just using Ryder to spite him. Then he told me that Ryder bought me. I couldn't take it. I slapped him."

"Still couldn't accept the fact that he lost you. And he lost you to a better man. And then what happened?"

"I turned away from him, and ran straight into Ryder. I don't know what he was doing at that party… but he was there at the right time. Bryan told him that he didn't think that Ryder really had me."

"What did Ryder say?"

"He doesn't give a damn," I replied. "He said he loved me enough for both of us and that's all that matters."

Adam snorted and then took a gulp of his beer. "Van Woodsen reads a lot of cheesy novels!"

"Sometimes I don't know if he's for real," I admitted. Ryder just blows me away. But then again, I really didn't know him.

12.
WEDDING FAVORS:
There are plenty of choices for wedding favors. You can choose from figurines, candles or mints. Just make sure that whatever you choose, it's not out of your theme and your budget. Plus, it should be something that you yourself would be glad to receive.

I made myself busy the next week. I got the early shots of Angela and Jacob's wedding. I asked permission for those to be uploaded onto my site. I also asked for some early video clips that showed most of the venue, the arrangements, and the highlights of the party.

I was very happy with the results. Rose was getting a lot of inquiries for our services.

I met with my friends at a new bar called Rig Style. I didn't want to risk meeting Ryder at Oil Rig. I promised to stay away from that place since I found out he owned it.

"So when will you treat us for a round of beers?" Dannie asked me.

"Once I start making money. Right now, it's still at take off stage. But I'm happy with how popular we're getting," I said with all smiles.

"You've always been great, Ash. This is you. This is who you are, and what you're made of," Nicole said. "And I won't forget what you promised me. You'll hire me as soon as the cash comes pouring in, okay?"

I nodded. "I promise."

When we took our bill, the waiter told us it has been taken care of.

"By who?"

The waiter stared at me. I raised a questioning brow at him.

"My boss said you'd know," he said. "He was hoping you would come up to his office."

At first, I didn't get what he meant. Then it dawned on me, and my heart pounded inside my ribcage.

"Oh, you've got to be kidding me!" I groaned. *How rich could he be?*

My friends looked at me curiously.

"Any chance this bar has the same management as Oil Rig?" I asked the waiter.

The waiter smiled and then he said, "Then I trust you understand what I meant."

I groaned and then I turned to my friends who were smiling now.

"Wow!" Dannie couldn't help saying.

"Okay, where's his office?" I asked the waiter.

I told my friends I wouldn't be long. I just need to tell Ryder that next time he wants to see me, he must make the effort to ask me himself.

I was led to the office upstairs. When I opened the door, I found Ryder standing on one side, looking through the glass wall, his back turned on me. I knew that he knew I was standing behind him, but I made no effort to call his name or to make any sound to indicate my presence.

"Can you do me a favor?" he finally asked.

I sighed. "What?"

He turned to face me. "Will you have dinner with me?"

"I already had dinner," I said, although it was more a snack than dinner. I intended to make some pasta when I got home.

"Would you humor me then?" he asked.

"What for?" I asked back.

He smiled and he stepped closer to me. "We... got off on the wrong foot the last time. I'd like to make up for it."

I rolled my eyes. "Ryder, what do you want from me? I know I owe you a favor. But can you tell me what you want in return so we can go on our separate lives?"

"That's the thing. I can't seem to decide what I want in return," he said, his eyes twinkling. I almost forgot how to breathe. He was so handsome and the look he gave me just blew me away.

I sighed and then I nodded. "Okay. I just need to tell my friends."

I dialed Dannie's number and told him that they could go ahead since Ryder and I had some business to talk about.

"Would you like to have dinner here then?" I asked Ryder after my phone call.

He shook his head. "No. I've got something else in mind."

He grabbed his car keys and then he took my hand. I tried to pull it away, but he only gripped it tighter, refusing to let me go. Then he turned to me and winked.

I heaved a sigh. I wished he would just tell me what the hell he wanted so I could start moving on with my life!

We drove quietly for a while. He parked in front of a hotel and then he got out of the car and opened the door for me.

"Mademoiselle," he said.

I stared at him and found that his eyes were twinkling, like he was suppressing a laugh or something. I didn't know what to say so I rolled my eyes and stuck my tongue out at him for a moment and then I walked past him. I heard him chuckle behind me.

We walked into a restaurant. He chose a spot outside where we had a lovely view of the beach.

The waiter handed us a menu. Although I said I already had dinner, I still ordered pasta. Ryder was suppressing a smile when he heard me order something from the waiter.

When the waiter left, we stared at each other blankly. Then Ryder chuckled.

"What?" I asked in an irritated tone.

He shook his head. "You're cute."

I knew I blushed at that. But I raised my brow at him instead of turning away.

"What do you want from me, Ryder?" I asked.

"Come on, Ash. You were not this grumpy at the wedding. What happened to that girl?"

I sighed. "That girl was desperate and broken. This girl is nearly fixed now and she's mad at you for lying to her, and making her feel like a first class..."

"Stop!" he cut me off. Something in his voice scared me. He took a deep breath. It was evident that he was trying to control his temper.

I was afraid to utter a word. I bit my lip, while I waited for him to say something.

He took a deep breath. "I never meant to make you feel that, Astrid," he said in a low voice. "In fact, I never planned to... I didn't plan the things that happened that night."

"I know. I threw myself at you. And you're just a man," I said.

His eyes narrowed. "Do you think I would take any woman who throws herself at me?"

I shrugged. "I don't know you."

"Exactly. You don't know me. So don't judge me, Ash." His words were bitter, but his voice was gentle. Like he'd been hurt by my words but he was trying to understand me.

"Then why did you do it, Ryder?" I asked him. "Why did you agree to pretend to be my boyfriend? You didn't need the money."

"Sometime, you don't need to have a reason for doing something. Sometimes, you just... want to," he said.

"It must have insulted you that I thought you were just a mere bartender."

He shook his head. "Not really. Would you have spoken to me if you knew I owned the place?"

I shook my head. "I wouldn't even look at you."

He smiled. "I was at the right place at the right time, Astrid. You needed me. Call it a favor."

Our food was served. We ate in silence for about five minutes. And then I couldn't help asking him, "What about the events that followed after? Was that a favor too?"

He stared at me for a while. He knew I was talking about the night we spent together. He shook his head, "That... that I did for my own benefit."

I blushed again and this time, I did look away from him.

The he reached forward and pulled my chin so I could look at him. "The ring was not a payment, Astrid. It was yours the moment I bought it. I never intended to just lend it to you… or to give it to you only after what happened between us. So… please… do not think otherwise."

"Why, Ryder? Why would you give me that ring in the first place? I know you're rich and you could afford it. But you don't just give out expensive rings to people you don't know."

"I know you, Astrid," he said softly. "And I know you deserved it."

"It's not enough," I whispered. "Your reason is not enough."

He smiled. "If I find a reason that seems 'enough' for you, will you wear the ring again?"

I raised a brow. "I gave it back to you already."

"It's still yours. I'm not going to send it back to the store," he said. "So? Will you?"

I sighed. I didn't know what that meant, or why he was so persistent, but what could it hurt if I accepted his gift? As long as he finds a good enough reason as to why he was giving it to me, then I guess it was fine.

"Only if your reason is good enough," I said.

He nodded. "Then we have another deal." He smiled.

"I'll get to be the judge, so don't keep your hopes up," I said seriously.

He laughed. "We'll see about that, won't we?"

* * *

It's Kaycee and Michael's wedding day. They were childhood sweethearts, and they wanted their wedding to be a feast of flowers. The place where the ceremony was held was covered in lilies. The reception had roses in shades of red, orange, and pink.

The floor was covered with rose petals. I mixed the artificial ones with the real ones to save on cost. Balls of roses hung from the ceiling in different heights. It looked like a classy fairy, flower land.

"I told you, you should hire me now," Nicole said. "You really could use some help."

I smiled at her. "I know, but not yet. I can't afford you yet."

After my success with Kaycee and Michael, Peter and Lyn, a referral that came from Angela and Jacob, hired me. And soon, inquiries just kept pouring in.

I built up my portfolio. Our gallery was filled with amazing shots of the weddings that we had done so far. I had strengthened my relationships with my suppliers. Even photographers and videographers loved working with me that they all promised to give me top priority and better prices. Since my concepts looked unique and brilliant, they also look good on their portfolio.

One Friday night, one of the rare weekends I knew I would not be working, I got an unexpected call.

"Miss me?" Ryder teased.

It must have been weeks since I last spoke to him. But I must admit that he crossed my mind... more than once a day... particularly before I go to sleep. But I shook off that thought and instead I pretended to be oblivious of who he was. "Oh, who is this again?"

"Oh, I'm so hurt," he chuckled.

"You can't be. Compared to you, I'm practically a nobody. I'm sure you have more people pining for your attention, my indifference is quite insignificant to you," I said.

"But you see that's what a normal human being actually craves. The attention that he can't seem to get," he countered.

"Hmmm... we are insatiable by nature. But my dreams are simple, Mr. Van Woodsen. I want not what I do not have."

This time he laughed. "And that ladies and gentlemen is our winner!" he said and somehow that statement confused me. "I'll pick you up tomorrow morning, seven sharp. Pack a weekend's worth of clothing, will you?"

"Excuse me?"

"I know you're not working this weekend, Astrid," he said. "Don't ask me how I found out. If you're not out of bed by seven A.M., I will haul you out of it. And something tells me that you may not like the methods I will use to wake you up. Although, I find it very, *very* tempting."

"Ryder, what game are you playing?"

"I'm not playing games, but I do remember that you owe me a favor. And this time I need you to do one for me," he replied.

I sighed. *Do it and get it over with.* I thought to myself.

"Do you know where I live now?" I asked him.

"I'm sure I can find it," he replied. "See you tomorrow." And he hung up, not giving me another chance to think it through.

I sighed in frustration. "What weird things am I constantly getting myself into?" I muttered under my breath.

Nevertheless, I packed a weekend's worth of clothing, not only that, I think I packed some of my best casual clothes, nightgowns I've only worn once, and underwear that I bought some time ago, thinking I would be using them when I got married.

Damn! I cursed to myself. *You're not thinking of sleeping with him again, are you?*

I stared at myself crossly in the mirror. I remembered the last night I was with him and how reason had abandoned me.

No! I will not allow myself to drown like that again! I will not sleep with Ryder Van Woodsen the second time around!

Firmly deciding this, I threw out the nightgowns and kinky undies from my bag and instead, I packed new sets of bikini panties and bras. The bikini underwear was low cut, but still very decent. I put two pairs of pajamas in my bag. Pastel-colored in candy-like designs. The kind that a sweet, innocent college girl wears on slumber parties.

I smiled to myself. I am not planning on sleeping with Ryder Van Woodsen! Who knows? He might even use that as another reason for me to accept the ring from him! Not only am I a whore for one night, I'd be a damn mistress!

The next day, ten minutes before seven, I was dressed in a pair of jeans and a violet blouse. I was fresh from my bath. I was confident I smelled and looked fresh. I was sipping coffee in my office reception, waiting for Ryder to ring the bell... if he could find my place, that is.

6:59, the doorbell rang. I was shocked! *How could he know these things?*

I opened the door ready to demand an answer from Ryder, but my breath caught in my throat at the sight of him.

His hair was still a little damp from the shower. He was wearing a beige turtleneck shirt under a white hooded jacket. He looked boyishly handsome; I almost forgot how to breathe.

"Good morning." He greeted me with a grin.

I finally composed myself and managed to raise a brow at him.

"What is it this time, Ryder?" I asked him.

"Relax," he replied. "I promise you'll have a lovely weekend."

I grabbed my bag and closed the door behind me. He took my bag from me as soon as I stepped out of the house.

"Hmmm... Manners. Impressive," I muttered sarcastically.

He chuckled. "Oh, there are some things you should know about me."

He put my bag on the backseat and held the passenger door open for me.

"Where are we going?" I asked as soon as he got inside the car.

He smiled at me shortly and then he said, "Do you remember you asked me a favor a couple of months ago?"

"Uh-huh," I said.

"Well... I kinda need the same thing from you."

I raised a brow. My heart pounded in my ribcage. "Wh... what do you mean?"

He sighed. "Well, we're going to a weekend get-together of sorts. With... old friends of mine. Two of my best friends are celebrating their anniversary. Last year, they made a wager that I wouldn't have a steady girlfriend before I turn thirty-one."

"How much is the wager for? Why don't you just pawn my ring and pay up?"

"There's no price for pride and dignity, love." He smiled.

"And I have to be the steady girlfriend?" I asked.

He nodded. "If it's not too much to ask?"

I heaved a sigh. "How could I say no? I asked you the very same thing."

"Thank you very much." He smiled and then he reached for my hand and squeezed it. "To make it easier, we can continue the same story that we told your relatives. We met a couple of months ago, couldn't take my eyes off you, went after you for a month until you finally agreed to go on a date with me."

"Okay. Well, you know my background pretty much. You know my friends and many of my relatives now. You know I just came from a bad breakup. You know what I do for a living."

"And you know about me too."

I shook my head. "No, I don't," I muttered under my breath.

He took a deep breath. "Okay, I'm from Manhattan originally. My family owns the Van Woodsen Restaurant Chains, which include the restaurants Rollo's, Mi Casa, Sugu, The Cellar, and some other smaller chains. We have these restaurants in New York, L.A., Miami, Chicago, Beverly Hills, Hollywood, Denver, and in other states. We have branches in Paris, Rome, Milan, Florence, Vienna, Berlin, Barcelona and Sydney. My grandfather started the business, and as early as now, I'm starting to learn the ropes, although I have Oil Rig, The Rig, and Rig Style as my own. I started them in Manhattan, and now, I'm branching out in Malibu. I only have one sister, Paris... who was born and raised in Paris 'til she was a teenager. She's got a bit of a French accent. She and my mother are the only two women that I've ever loved."

I stared at him and raised a brow. "You want me to tell your friends that?"

He laughed. "Okay, for the purpose of our little masquerade, let's say that Paris, my mom and now you are the only *three* women I have loved in my life."

"You don't have to say you love me, you know," I suggested. "We could be a couple that was once serious, but is now slowly drifting apart. We've just met a couple of months ago, you're too busy with your work, you barely have time for me, and we don't even have sex anymore!"

I turned red the minute I said the last phrase. I regretted that.

"Hey, hey!" he said. "I'm sure we will not be having those problems this early in our relationship. And besides... I'll never be too busy with work when it comes to my girlfriend. And the sex part... I'm sure I won't be able to get enough of my girl."

I sighed. "Seriously, you want your friends to think that this relationship is going somewhere?"

"Of course!"

"Do I have to get them to like me too, like what you did with my family?"

"Well, you don't have to try. I'm sure they'll like you just as you are," he replied.

"Obviously, you expect me to tell them I'm not interested in your money, right? Can't I just play the mercenary little girl who couldn't care less about your heart? So they'll hate me immediately and they'll beg you to break up with me? And then we don't have to lie to them anymore?"

He chuckled. "No," he replied. "My friends have been pestering to see me happy with a woman for years. It's been driving me crazy how hard they try to fix me up once in a while. They've got to stop! And you're here to do that for them!"

"I can't be myself then," I said.

"Why?"

"Because it won't be believable," I replied.

"Why won't it be believable?"

"First, the likes of me won't have the same friends as you. There's no chance that we'd ever meet."

"You're in the wedding industry, love," he reminded me. "There are plenty of chances for us to meet."

I sighed. "I'm not sure I'd even talk to you."

"Why is that? Do I look hideous or something?"

I shook my head. "You're just too flashy, too rich, too famous. I wouldn't want to be a part of your league."

He laughed. Then he reached out for my hand and squeezed it. "Then I found the perfect girl that my friends would love for me."

"I'll try my best, Ryder. But I'm not making any promises. I don't even know if I can pull this off."

He laughed again. "I won't leave your side."

"Oh, don't bother yourself too much," I said sarcastically.

"You weren't this sarcastic the first time I met you, you know." Although his tone was light, I know he meant what he said.

I sighed. "It's not me, Ryder. It's you."

"What about me?"

"I do not understand why you even… want to be friends with me. Why you are so nice to me? Guys like you are usually too busy to care about girls like me."

"Is that all?" he asked after a moment of silence.

I shook my head. "No." I took a deep breath. "I owe you the first steps of my recovery. I will forever be thankful for that. For months I've thought of you as a dear friend… an ally. I fixed my life, hoping that someday I'd see you again, and show you that I did keep my promises to you that night. But then when I found out who you were… I couldn't think of a reason why we could even be friends! I don't move in your circle and you don't move in mine. When you gave me that ring… I still couldn't help thinking that I was… just an entertainment to you. Maybe you were bored with your life and you needed someone to amuse you. I was… desperate and unfortunate enough to venture your way."

Ryder didn't say anything for a long time. I was afraid that I had offended him with my monologue. When I stared at him, he was concentrating on the road, his face restrained. I sighed and turned away from him.

We didn't speak for a while. Before I knew it, he was parking on a slot in the airport. He took a deep breath and then he turned to me. He looked at me for a while and then he said softly, "You're wrong, you know."

"What?"

"You're wrong about me," he said.

"I wouldn't know that," I said quietly.

"You will… by the end of this weekend. You will change your opinion of me," he said, his voice was so serious, it made my knees shake.

13.

THE MAID OF HONOR AND THE BEST MAN:

The Maid of Honor has to be unmarried. The Best Man can be a married man, or a bachelor. You can choose from your closest friends, you can choose from your family. But always keep this in mind: Make sure you choose one whose relationship with you runs deep and goes far back.

We flew business class to Miami. It was a first for me. I always thought business class flights were a waste of money. But Ryder had a lot of money to burn.

He checked us into a suite in a five star resort. When I stepped into the room and realized that there was only one bed, I instantly became nervous.

He must have sensed my discomfort because he looked at me wearily and said, "It's only right that we stay in the same room if we want to make this believable. But I'll stay on the couch, don't worry."

"I can stay on the couch, Ryder," I said. "I'm smaller. I'd be more comfortable sleeping on it."

"I'll be damned if I let a woman take the couch while I sleep comfortably in the bed," he said evenly.

"Okay. Whatever you say," I murmured.

He turned away from me and headed towards the door.

"We have two hours before we meet Janis and Jake. I will come back for you. Meanwhile, you can sleep if you want to."

He stalked out of the room. As much as I hated to admit it, I felt guilty. Ryder had been trying his best to be nice to me. To make the mood lighter. All I did was throw sarcastic remarks his way, and made the morning miserable for him. He was wonderful when *I* asked *him* to pretend to be besotted with me. He played his part wonderfully. Maybe I should do the same.

I rested on the luxurious bed. I only had a couple of hours sleep last night and now I was really sleepy.

I slept for about an hour and a half. I was still alone in the room when I woke up. I took a shower and prepared for the whole masquerade. I decided to do this for Ryder. I'd be everything he needed me to be and then my debt would be paid. I would not owe him anything anymore.

I slipped into a floral printed white sleeveless dress. It was simple and chic. I tied my hair in a bun and left some strands to curl on either sides of my face. I put on powder and lip-gloss. Then I put on my favorite perfume.

When I came out of the bathroom, Ryder was already waiting at the balcony.

"Should we go?" I asked behind him.

He turned around. He looked at me for a full minute, until I was blushing to the roots of my hair and then he smiled. He stepped closer towards me. "You're beautiful." I realized that if he was angry when he left me, he had somehow decided not to ruin his plans, as I had decided to do my part in this charade as well as I can.

I smiled. "Wouldn't want your friends to worry about your... taste."

"I'm sure they will be fairly happy."

Ryder took my hand in his and led me out of the suite and into the restaurant on the ground floor.

We approached a table where a beautiful blonde woman and a handsome guy with blond hair were having their lunch. The minute they saw us walking towards them, they froze. They stared at us with shocked expressions on their faces and it was obvious that they could not believe what they were seeing.

I instantly realized who they were. Janis and Jake... Ryder's best friends.

I squeezed Ryder's hand, hoping to get some courage. He looked at me and smiled reassuringly. Then he released my hand and put an arm around my shoulder. He leaned forward and gave me a kiss on the forehead.

"You look beautiful, love," he whispered to me. "You can do this."

I smiled at him. "I will do this, Ryder. For you," I whispered back before we reached Janis and Jake.

He smiled back at me. In his eyes, I could see sincere gratitude. I knew he was happy and somehow, my heart warmed and I knew it was not going to be difficult to pretend to feel affectionate for him.

His friends were still dumbfounded when I was introduced to them.

It took a minute for Jake to recover and longer for Janis.

"I'm sorry," Jake said. "We don't mean to freak you out. It's just that... this is a surprise! Right, honey?"

Jake had to pat Janis lightly on the back to bring her back to Earth.

"Oh, yeah. Yeah. Quite a surprise! We... didn't expect Ryder to have a... guest. You know... he... he usually comes alone." Janis smiled. Then she took a deep breath and leaned forward to give me a hug. "It's lovely to meet you. I hope we didn't freak you out."

"It's okay." I hugged her back and then I smiled at her. "It's actually... good to know that he rarely brings girls to your gatherings."

Ryder chuckled, "Oh, sweetheart! You have nothing to worry about, you were the first!" He stared at me with dancing eyes and I knew that the charade had begun. Ryder was not a stranger to me from now on. It's time to resume the play we started at Bryan's and Geena's wedding.

I smiled at Janis and Jake shyly. I knew I was blushing. Ryder put an arm around my shoulders and gave me a kiss on the temple. Then he pulled out a chair for me.

"So, how did you two meet?" Janis asked.

We spun the same tale. I met Ryder through a common friend and he fell in love with me at first sight, as if love at first sight were possible at all. He pursued me, but I was careful since I just came out of a serious relationship and so on and so forth.

His friends were amazed, but I could tell that Janis was sizing me up. Trying to see if I genuinely liked her friend and not his money. Jake was trying to measure Ryder's reactions to me. Maybe trying to determine if Ryder was not just after the sex.

It was easy to smile and look in love with Ryder. He was sweet and funny. I could almost tell what his punch line was going to be before the words were out of his mouth, and so I found myself giggling ahead of Janis and Jake.

By the end of lunch, I think I almost had Janis convinced that I didn't want Ryder's money. She was surprised that I didn't know all the names of Ryder's businesses and I didn't really show interest. Instead, I was genuinely concerned about how he was going to fit me in his busy life.

Janis was fascinated about what I did. I told her about the concepts I did for the weddings and she was impressed. I knew from the look on Jake's face that he was going to propose to her soon... give it a year or less. I might have a potential customer here. Although, I don't know if they will hire me if they find out that I was just pretending to be Ryder's girlfriend just so he'd win his wager with them.

We spent the whole afternoon together, all four of us. I discovered that Janis and Jake, although both coming from rich, powerful families were both down to earth. They did not have that heir or heiress syndrome, they didn't feel that everybody should bow down to them.

It was easy enough to laugh with them and joke with them. They felt like... normal people, and so did Ryder.

I realized that for the whole afternoon that we were together, I forgot that I didn't know him. He felt like the Ryder I was with at the wedding. I felt like I didn't know he was filthy rich. Like I thought he was just the bartender that I could laugh with and talk to. Like he was not out of my league at all.

We decided to swim. Ryder had a mischievous grin on his face; I instantly knew he was planning something.

I started running away from him, but he was too fast for me. He caught up with me after barely five steps. He carried me in his arms towards the water until we landed with a splash.

I was shrieking. When we emerged from the water together, he was roaring in laughter and I was punching him about the shoulders with a pout on my face.

Then his face descended towards mine and he gave me a thorough kiss on the lips, which I welcomed... and enjoyed.

That evening we played charades. Janis and Jake, who claimed they'd been together for almost all of their lives, couldn't get each other's clues.

Ryder and I on the other hand, just had this connection... like we could read each other's minds. He would give me a simple clue, a simple gesture, and the right word would come to my mind.

One time, Ryder acted out a clue. He pointed a finger at himself, and then gestured an imaginary cap being put on his head.

"Bartender?" I guessed.

He nodded. I shouted and jumped for joy. He came to take me in his arms, and lifted me off my feet. I gave a little hop in the air and wrapped both my legs around his waist. We were both laughing, then I leaned forward and gave him a kiss.

We were still laughing when he put me back on my feet.

They decided to kick it up a notch by moving on to phrases.

"Are you sure, guys?" Ryder asked them teasingly. "You can't even get the words 'pancakes' and 'lions'."

We annihilated them. It was like Ryder and I had known each other for a long time and our minds were totally connected.

The last word we had was the most difficult one and Janis and Jake were quite confident that we wouldn't be able to get it.

I stood in front of Ryder and showed my ring finger.

"Ring?" he asked.

I nodded. I pointed at myself and then at him, I made a hugging gesture, and I ran my finger from my eyes down my cheeks.

"A fake diamond ring!" he guessed.

I shrieked and ran to him again. He caught me in his arms and spun me around. He was laughing. I felt like crying, remembering my fake engagement ring for the first time in months. I stared up at Ryder and he was smiling apologetically at me. But I felt like it all happened in another lifetime.

Ryder leaned forward and kissed me passionately. I wrapped my arms around his neck and kissed him back. We only stopped kissing when Jake not-so-subtly coughed at us.

Ryder chuckled and kissed my forehead before finally releasing me.

"How long have you guys really known each other?" Janis asked in amazement. "I wouldn't make that one out for a *fake diamond ring*!"

"Neither would I if it didn't have a story behind it," Ryder said.

"Okay, tell us the story," Janis said.

We sat on the benches. Ryder pulled me over so I could sit on his lap. He wound his arms around me.

"The very first time I saw her was when she was walking out of a jewelry shop," Ryder said. "I was picking up a bracelet for my mother. As I walked into the shop, she ran into me. She wasn't looking where she was going. Her eyes were... blinded by tears." I leaned my head against Ryder's shoulder as I listened to his story. "We collided with each other and I had to hold her steady to prevent her from falling on her butt...

"But instead of pulling away from me, she held on to me and leaned her cheek on my shoulder and she... cried. She wept in my arms, without looking up to see whom I was. It was as if she had received such terrible news and she was desperate for some comfort. When she ran into me, she took her chance. She held on to me. I didn't know why she was crying, but somehow, I felt for her. So I held her for a while. I... provided the comfort that she needed at the time. And she... smelled so good, and felt so soft in my arms, I couldn't help it either."

"Why were you crying?" Janis asked curiously.

I took a deep breath. And then, with courage, I said quietly, "The guy at the jewelry shop told me that my ex-fiancé gave me a fake diamond ring."

There was silence. I stared at Janis and Jake and they were looking at me apologetically.

"I'm sorry," Janis said.

I smiled at them. "It's okay now, guys. I'm over it. I'm lucky I ran into Ryder that day. And I'm lucky to find him again shortly after that."

It's true. I was lucky I ran into him that day. I was also lucky that I found him again—at the time when I needed him the most. And it didn't matter whether he was the bartender or the owner of the bar... he was my savior. My knight in shining armor. When I looked into Ryder's eyes, I knew he knew that I meant those words too. He gently leaned forward and gave me a kiss on the lips. And then he leaned his head towards mine and breathed in the scent of me.

I sighed. I wanted to cry. I realized that he *was* the same Ryder that was with me at Bryan and Geena's wedding, back when I thought he was just a mere bartender. Nothing changed except for the fact that I knew who he really was now. But other than the rich birthright, he seemed like the same amazing guy who helped me show Bryan and Geena that I was better off without both of them! The same guy who helped me get over my broken engagement with flair. It wasn't until that moment that I realized how much I missed him. Just how much I had wanted to be with him without the pain I felt about Bryan and Geena.

As I leaned into his shoulder, I realized I was completely over Bryan and Geena. I was still angry with them, but I guess that will not change for a long time. Now, I have Ryder with me again. He's just so sweet and perfect. But I knew his life was complicated and I may not be able to keep up with it. And besides, being over your previous relationship doesn't mean you have to jump into a new one immediately.

But I had this weekend. He was mine again.

After this... I'm just not yet ready to be heartbroken again. I could have fun. But I couldn't hope for forever. Not yet. I'm still too vulnerable.

So maybe for now, I should just enjoy the moment while it lasts. For this weekend only.... Ryder Van Woodsen was mine.

***

The minute I stopped pretending, I started welcoming all his gestures. I started responding positively and that encouraged him to do more. I didn't care. I only had this weekend. Outside of this time and place, this fairy tale couldn't be real. I was not yet ready for a relationship. And I doubted I'd ever be ready to have a relationship with Ryder Van Woodsen.

We partied after dinner and a bonfire by the beach. Janis and I were becoming more comfortable with each other.

"So you were engaged once?" she asked when Jake and Ryder went to get our drinks.

I nodded. "He was my best friend for years before we started dating."

"Why did it end? Because he gave you a fake engagement ring?"

I shook my head. "No. It was over long before that." I sighed. "I was planning our wedding when I caught him having an argument with my cousin over whether or not they should keep their baby."

Janis's eyes widened. "You did not!" Her tone was abhorred, as if she couldn't believe what she was hearing.

"Did too." I giggled humorlessly.

"And you called off the whole wedding?"

I nodded. "But I made the big mistake of not canceling all the arrangements myself. I threw all the contacts and receipts in his face and asked him to make the cancellations himself, if he wanted his money back."

"And then?"

I sighed. "He didn't cancel. Probably figured it would be easier and much cheaper for him to push through with the wedding than call it off. So... my dream wedding happened. From the invitations, down to the honeymoon suite! It happened exactly how I wanted it to be. The only difference was, I wasn't the bride anymore!"

"He didn't!" Janis had her hands on her mouth. "That is disgusting! How... how could your cousin do that to you?"

I shrugged. "Beats me. But I think I've had a bit of my revenge already."

"How?"

"I attended the wedding."

Janis's jaw dropped and I had to smile at that.

"I went there with Ryder. I showed all my relatives how better off I was! I looked pretty and sexy, with an even sexier man in my arms!"

Janis laughed. "I'll bet Ryder tried his best to impress your relatives!"

I nodded. "He wasn't able to resist. He knew everybody was going to feel sorry for me because… I was supposed to be the bride that day. He tried his best to help me keep my head up high." I stared over at Ryder who was approaching me with my drink in his hand. "A pretty thing like that? Even the bride wished she was me."

Janis laughed again. "How wonderful! What a great way to get even! But still… what they did to you was… unthinkable."

"Well, heartbreak went even further. I lost my job after that because I didn't believe in *'ever afters'* anymore. I was telling brides-to-be that green was the color of vomit, instead of the color of fresh harmony."

"Wow! That's severe bitterness."

I nodded. "That was before Ryder came into my life." By that time, Ryder sat beside me and handed me my drink.

"What about me?" he asked.

I smiled up at him. "I was just telling Janis how much you helped me get over my breakup. Well, you helped me get even with my ex-fiancé and my cousin first. I don't think I would have done it if it weren't for you."

"When did you find out that your engagement ring was a fake?" Janis asked.

"After I received their invitation and found that everything was how I planned it for myself. I thought I should cash in on my bad luck. I was broke then anyway. I didn't have a job and was living with my cousin's half brother. At the jewelry shop, the guy told me that he wouldn't even pay a hundred dollars for my ring."

"That's cheap!" Jake said shaking his head.

"Yeah. He's cheap." I smiled. "But I'm over it now. That whole chapter of my life is over." I looked up at Ryder. "I'm so much better now," I said.

I wanted him to know that had he not been *the* Ryder Van Woodsen, I would have kept my promise to him… that I would have come to him when I finally got better. So he could get to know the real me. I knew that although I looked happy in front of Janis and Jake, I couldn't hide the trace of regret in my expression… and I'm afraid Ryder could see through me.

He stared back at me evenly, raising a brow. As if he knew… that I'd kept two of my promises already. But I didn't have any intention of keeping the third.

I looked away, not able to bear the weight of his stare. I knew I was blushing when I looked back at Janis, who mistook the meaning of my blush for something else.

Janis beamed at me. "I'm happy for both of you," she said. "I think you are what each other needs."

Jake nodded beside her in agreement. He raised his bottle to us for a toast.

I was still thinking about the look on Ryder's face when I went to the ladies' room with Janis. She was still beaming at me.

"I am so happy Ryder found you," she said.

"Why?"

"He's happy," she replied. "You make him happy. You two are like... soul mates. You have this connection that looks cosmic in some way. You... complete each other's sentences; you fit together like pieces of a puzzle. I couldn't believe that Ryder finally found his match!"

"Come on! His match?"

"You are. You're the one for him, I can tell," she said. "Jake, Ryder and I... we grew up together. And in high school, Jake and I started hooking up. We felt guilty that we left Ryder behind. We started getting serious when we were in college. And somehow we felt that Ryder felt out of place with us, especially if we planned our future or if we became affectionate with each other. We... wanted Ryder to find his girl. So we're sure that he'll be as happy as we are."

"And you believe he's happy with me?"

Janis nodded. "Yes. Ryder didn't seem interested in women, or dating. He didn't care much about romance. We thought he was not interested in having a relationship at all. We tried hooking him up with women before. He's just not interested. He was always busy with work. We didn't think he was ready to commit to any woman. We didn't even think he was capable of being romantic. He didn't show previous signs. That is why I was dumbfounded when he introduced you to us this morning. I was not expecting you."

"I hope... I didn't disappoint you," I said shyly.

"Are you kidding me? You're absolutely perfect!" She laughed. "You're absolutely gorgeous. I can see why he's taken with you, and I can tell you are not interested in his..." She trailed off, and then she turned red. I can tell she was embarrassed about what she was about to say next that she stopped herself.

"It's okay. I know what you mean. I'm not interested in his money." I giggled. "When I first... eh... started dating him, I didn't know he was rich! I mistook him to be something else."

"Oh my God!" she said. "You were the girl who thought he was a bartender?"

I stared back at her. How did she know *that*? "You know?"

She giggled. "I received a weird call from him one day. And he asked me, *do I look like a damned bartender?* I told him that technically, he is. He just owns his own bar. He said he met a girl, and she had mistaken him to be a bartender and she... liked him nevertheless."

I blushed. That was true. I liked him better when I thought he was… normal like the rest of us.

"So when he finally came clean about owning the bar, what did you do?"

"I slapped him."

Janis laughed. "Oh my God! No wonder he's so enchanted with you! Jake thought that Ryder had always been afraid women would only want him because he's rich. We thought maybe that was the reason why he was so aloof with women, and why he wasn't interested. He was too cautious. He's allergic to girls who want his money more than him."

I smiled at Janis. As we approached our table and I looked into Ryder's eyes, I realized glumly that I liked everything about him… *except* for his money.

"Something wrong?" he asked me.

I shook my head as I sat beside him. Janis took out her camera and placed it on a tripod. Then she and Jake went closer to us and told us to smile. Ryder laughed and squeezed me tightly. I leaned my head on his shoulder and I smiled happily.

I only had forty-eight hours. During that time, Ryder seemed to want me as much as I wanted him. We belonged together and the issue of his A-list status seemed far away. I felt like I was ready to be in a relationship again, and Ryder was not a complicated man.

We sat by the bonfire as we watched Janis and Jake dance.

"She's buying it," I told Ryder.

"Buying what?"

"Us," I replied. "She didn't think we were pretending."

Ryder raised a brow. He pulled me to him so I could sit on his lap. Then he gave me a tight hug.

"Is that what we're doing, love?" he whispered.

I stared back at him, my heart pounding hard in my chest.

"None of this is real, Ryder," I reminded him.

He smiled before leaning forward to kiss me on the lips. "But it looks real. It *feels* real."

I blushed. How could I be that transparent?

I looked at him seriously. "It's all for the show. This doesn't change anything, Ryder," I told him. "I'm only doing this because I owe you."

He narrowed his eyes. He looked like he wanted to say something, but choose not to. Instead he leaned forward and gave me a gentle kiss on the lips and said, "But here, we belong together."

I nodded. "Only this weekend."

He took a deep breath. "Then let's make the most of it, shall we?" And he kissed me thoroughly.

I felt wanted. The kiss that Ryder gave me made me feel a myriad of sensations all rolled into one. Heat emanated from his skin to mine. I didn't want him to stop. But we had to stop. Because we were sitting by the fire on the beach with people dancing and partying all around us.

He stared back at me. His eyes filled with desire. My heart kept pounding in my chest as I struggled to catch my breath. I wanted him. I knew from the look on his face that he wanted me too. I tried to think of reasons to stop falling into the edge of passion, but I could feel reason drifting away.

Finally, he stopped kissing me. He stared at me deeply. His eyes were drunk with passion. We both knew where this was leading to, and it was not part of the deal. We only needed to put on a show in front of Janis and Jake. But inside our hotel suite, we'd be two strangers who happened to share the same room and some acquaintance.

"Let's dance, shall we?" he asked.

I nodded. We both know that dancing would distract us.

When we got to the dance floor, Janis was beaming at me. A slow love song played. Ryder took me in his arms. I leaned my head on his shoulder. He wound his arms around me and enclosed me in a hug.

"Janis said you were afraid of relationships, because you were afraid women will only want you for what you're worth," I said.

He sighed. "It's only partly that. The bigger part of it is that I have been focused with my goals all my life. I didn't really have time to stop and commit to get to know one girl."

"You didn't believe in 'ever after' either."

He didn't say anything for a while. I felt a kiss on my temple. "Do you believe in 'ever after' now?"

I sighed. "I have to. It's what I do, but I believe that 'ever after' may be subjective. It can happen to a whole bunch of my clients. It doesn't have to happen to me. Maybe it doesn't happen to everybody."

"It should happen to you," he said. "You deserve it, Astrid."

"You don't believe in it," I said looking up at him. "Why do you wish it for me?"

"Because I know that *you* believed in it, and you make it happen for everybody else. You deserve it more than anyone."

I giggled. "Yeah! I wonder how I'll top Bryan and Geena's wedding."

He gave me a crooked smile. "You can. As long as you open up your heart again and find a man who can share with you what Bryan has with Geena."

I laughed. "Then I can marry you in the simplest Vegas ceremony and I would still top that! Because honestly, I have more affection for you than Bryan has for Geena!"

"Seriously?" he asked chuckling.

"And I don't think I like you all that much, Ryder Van Woodsen," I teased.

136

He laughed. "Let me change your mind about that, Astrid Jacobson." And he leaned forward and gave me a thorough kiss on the lips.

I don't remember how long that kiss lasted, but I knew that somehow it started a whole rollercoaster ride. We couldn't get our hands off each other. I think we were still kissing even when we went up to our suite. We couldn't wait to get inside. We were at it even in the corridors.

When he closed the door behind us and we were finally alone in our room, we both knew it was time for us to stop pretending. No need to convince anyone within the confines of this room.

He stared back at me and smiled sheepishly. I smiled back at him shyly. He reached forward and pushed a lock of stray hair away from my face.

"Jake told me that I was a lucky bastard!"

"Why?"

"Because you're very beautiful, and you're smart, funny, and you're grounded. You seem aware of the people around you, and you... care about what they say, how they feel. You're sensitive to others, keen on making others feel good. He said you're an angel and the devil that I am, I'm lucky to have you."

I laughed. "How could he say all that?"

"Because Jake is a shrink," he replied. "He makes thousands of dollars reading people's personalities, deciphering the messages they do not say verbally."

My eyes widened. "And you had the nerve to ask me to pretend I was your girlfriend? Didn't you think he would be able to guess that?"

He laughed. "That's why I didn't tell you what he was. So you wouldn't feel self-conscious or scared. But you're a natural."

"We're both naturals," I said. "I guess we both have a knack for acting."

"We both have talents for acting in love with each other," He whispered. Then he stared at me deeply, which made my knees go weak. "I wasn't acting all the time, Astrid." He leaned his face slowly towards mine. "A lot of the things I did today were actually... real." And he brushed his lips to mine gently.

Instantly, my blood stirred. Desire flooded through my veins. I couldn't help myself. I couldn't help showing him that I wasn't acting all the time, too. I kissed him back. Fiercely. I kissed him more passionately than he was kissing me. He lifted me off my feet. I wrapped my arms around his neck and wound both my legs around his waist.

He kissed me back, hungrily, passionately. He started walking towards the bed. I landed on my back and he landed on top of me. I was matching his kisses. I was as hungry as he was. It was like I'd been set on fire. Had I been like this the night of Geena's wedding? No wonder I lost my virginity by the end of the night!

I didn't know I was capable of feeling all these emotions... all this passion. Heat radiated from my skin. I couldn't stop kissing Ryder. I wanted to give him everything that I could.

However, suddenly I could feel him slowly putting his guard up. He was controlling his kisses. He was trying to put out the fire within him. But I didn't want him to. I wanted him to devour me. I wanted him to give in to the passion. I needed him to take what I was offering him.

"Ryder!" I screamed his name and I kissed him hungrily again.

He kissed me passionately, but then he began to pull away.

"No!" I begged in a low, hoarse voice, and then I pulled him by the neck and kissed him again.

"Stop it, Astrid," he whispered softly, but he kissed me again.

"No," I whispered.

He pulled away from me gently. "I'm on the edge, Astrid! Don't push me!" he warned me.

Ahhh! So I wasn't the only one on the edge. But he was trying to get a grip of himself. Trying to be a gentleman.

I smiled at him mischievously, and I pulled his head to me again. I kissed him hungrily... jumping to the brink of passion and pulling him with me.

I heard him curse softly. "Damn it!" Then he became completely unrestrained. He let go of my lips only to nuzzle my neck.

"Ryder..." I whispered.

"Astrid..." he whispered back. And he kissed me on the lips again hungrily.

I felt his hands all over me. I felt myself slowly losing consciousness, giving in to the tide of passion. Ryder was not thinking any more than I was. He was touching me in places I wouldn't let anyone touch me before. He removed my clothes and kissed every bit of skin he exposed.

I was matching his passion with mine. I showed him that he was not the only one lost in desire. I was there too! I was with him. Because I knew I only had this weekend, this place, where we belonged together, where I could fantasize that he could belong to me forever, where I could believe that forever exists.

"I want this, Astrid," he said to me.

I smiled at him and kissed him.

"I want to be sure that you want it too," he whispered hoarsely.

He sat up from the bed and pulled me with him, so that I was on top of him, mounting him.

I wrapped my arms around his neck, aware that we were both completely naked now.

"Ryder!" I screamed. Desire enveloped me in magnitudes I couldn't describe. He wrapped his arms around my waist.

He kissed me thoroughly.

"Ryder, please," I silently begged. I was inexperienced in this. I don't know what I wanted.

"How could you be like this with me and then completely ignore me in the morning?" he asked suddenly.

I pulled away from him. "What do you mean?"

"You were like this the last time. You wanted me like this. Yet when you woke up in the morning and realized what we did, you felt ashamed of yourself. That... pissed me off," he said.

I laughed. I realized now what he meant. I was a completely different person in bed with him. But that was the last time. I didn't know what I wanted then. I knew that I wanted him now... without the hope of forever.

I leaned down and kissed him again. I smiled. "I'm sure now, Ryder," I said to him. "I want this... but only tonight."

He shook his head. "What if I want this beyond tonight?"

I shook my head. "I can't," I said.

"Why?" he asked.

"Because you're *the* Ryder Van Woodsen," I replied. "You're far too complex, too complicated. I know you won't fall in love with me. And I'm not ready to have a relationship yet either. You're being cautious about your status. I'm being cautious with my heart. We're both guarded. So this won't work. But... I want you."

"And God knows I want you, Astrid!" he whispered and kissed me passionately.

"Then we have this night, Ryder," I said. "It can't go beyond this."

He shook his head. "Give me this weekend, at least," he said.

I stared back at him. He was devilishly handsome. He was everything I would want and more. But he was also everything I knew I wouldn't have... forever. But the thought of the weekend sounded good. Very good.

I smiled at him. I nodded. "Deal," I whispered and then I kissed him hungrily again. He didn't break the kiss, but I felt him reach for the drawer of the bedside table.

I felt his hands trembling, fumbling with something behind my back. He cursed breathily as he struggled with the unseen obstacle. Pretty soon, I heard the ripping sound of plastic. I smiled to myself as I realized what he was doing.

Ryder held me by the waist and slowly guided my movements above him. He thrust his hips upward and guided my waist so I could meet his thrust. My arms and legs wrapped around him, I wanted to consume him! I wanted to feel as if we were one and nothing could separate us. Ryder's hot hands framed my face and he stared into my eyes with an intensity bordering on painful. Our movements were synchronized, fluid and graceful.

The pleasure stung me in little sparks throughout my body, a kind of indescribable sensation. My breath shook and faltered, little gasps catching my throat. Ryder panted roughly; his breath caressed my lips and chin. My hair fell about us like a curtain, and we were in our own world.

There was nothing else that existed except for Ryder and me. His pupils were contracted with desire, the green of the iris swirling in tiny whirlpools of lust. With each of our movements his eyes got darker and darker, until they were a dark forest green.

"Ryder…" I whispered. "Ryder… Ryder…" His name echoed in time with our movements.

His eyes fluttered closed, and his head tilted back. The muscles in his neck were tense and bulging. Through his parted lips I could see him gritting his teeth; straining for control. Sweet feeling enveloped me, and I sobbed his named. Just like that, reason completely abandoned me and I let myself be drowned in the ocean of our passion.

When I woke up in the morning, the first streaks of sunlight were just appearing. I could hear the sound of the ocean. I knew I was in paradise. It was peaceful here. No boundaries. No limits. I was aware that I was completely naked in bed and Ryder's arms were around me. His naked body was touching mine. I smiled to myself. I felt good. This feels right.

I wound my hand over his and intertwined our fingers. I felt him shift behind me and I felt a kiss on my back. He nuzzled my shoulders. I giggled. I could feel the shadow of his beard tickling my shoulder blades.

He pulled me so I could lie on my back and face him. He looked down at me, stared at me deeply. And then he leaned down and gave me a deep kiss on the lips. There was no need for words after that.

When I woke up again, it was already ten in the morning. I was enclosed in Ryder's tight embrace. I looked up at his handsome face. I looked at his chiseled features, his long lashes, his strong jaw, the cleft on his chin, his perfect nose. I bit my lip. He really was handsome. Very handsome, I still couldn't believe I was lying in bed naked with him.

He slowly opened his eyes. The minute he saw me, he smiled. He pulled me by the neck and gave me a kiss.

"Good morning," he said.

"Good morning," I replied.

He smiled. "Now, that's a better response than last time."

I remembered the last time we slept together; I was so confused about what happened between us. He was so pissed with me. He didn't speak much.

"The last time you weren't so great either," I grunted.

He raised a brow. "That's because you made it look like sleeping with me was the biggest mistake you'd made in your life."

"Just in case you've forgotten, it was my... first time. And you were a stranger. A stranger I paid to pretend to be in love with me. I didn't know whether you slept with me because you wanted me or because it... came with the job. And I felt... ashamed," I said ruefully.

He stared at me for a moment and then he pulled me towards him. "It was never a job, you know. None of the things that I did for you that night was because it came with the job. I did all that because I wanted to. I wanted you. I pretended to be a bartender because I wanted to help you out. And I enjoyed every minute of it."

"But you did make an effort to resist my efforts to flirt with you that night."

"And you knew that every effort was futile." He sighed. "I resisted not because I didn't want you. But because I felt I would be taking advantage of your... grief, your frustration. That night was supposed to be your wedding night. And I knew that you were not completely over Bryan then. It was wrong to take you when I knew you wanted to be with someone else."

I shook my head. "I didn't want to be with Bryan that time. I knew I was better off. But... I went into an episode of self-pity. That somehow, nobody wanted me. I had to pay somebody to sleep with me."

"You didn't pay me," he said softly.

I nodded. "I knew that after. But then I found out who you really were. And then I felt like *you* paid *me*."

He sighed. "You read me all wrong," he said. "And sometimes, I think you're still reading me all wrong."

I didn't answer. We stared at each other for a while. No one said a word. And then Ryder sighed again.

"Now, do you believe that I wanted you?" he asked.

"It doesn't matter," I replied. "This weekend... is a dream I will soon wake up from."

"Because I don't belong in your world?"

I shook my head. "Because I don't belong in yours."

"If... if I was just Ryder, the bartender... would you want to be part of my world?"

"I'm not ready to be part of anybody's world. I was burned too much to start over."

I was not ready for hopes of 'ever after' just yet. The healing had to be complete for me. I didn't hurt at the thought of Bryan and Geena anymore. I may hate them forever, but I'm not affected with what they do with their lives. I didn't even think about them anymore.

I still cringed at the thought of entering into a serious relationship or going steady with another guy. To trust that one man would only have eyes for me... for all eternity? I was not yet ready to risk that. I couldn't go through the hell of heartbreak again.

"How long do you think this will take?" he asked.

I reached out and touched his cheek. "I don't know. I'm not in a hurry."

He smiled, but that smile did not touch his eyes. "Like I said, I want you to have your 'ever after'. You deserve it more than anybody else."

I smiled back at him. Tears threatened to peek from my eyes. I knew Ryder was sincere. I knew that he meant every word that he said.

"Thank you," I whispered.

I snuggled closer to him and he gave me a tight hug. And as I lie there in his arms, feeling safe, comforted, and wanted, I realized just how sad it was that Ryder and I came from different worlds. It was a pity because he was everything I could ever ask for if I were to believe in 'ever after' again.

***

It had been a wonderful dream. For the whole second day, there were no pretensions between Ryder and me. I wanted him. He wanted me. I was his girlfriend and he was my boyfriend. I was free to express the way I felt without thinking of the complications of a relationship... and certainly not the complications of having a relationship with a tycoon like him.

It was physical. It was bliss. It was a dream and soon enough, it was over. We were both quiet when he was driving me back to my place. Both of us were lost in our own thoughts.

I looked back at the magical two days when I existed in Ryder's world. He was mine. He gave me his full, undivided attention, like I was the only woman that mattered in the world. I lived the dream of blissfully being with someone. Someone who couldn't get enough of me.

When we boarded the plane, I had to resist the temptation of reaching out for his hand or leaning my head against his shoulder. I had to stop myself from tiptoeing and giving him a kiss on the lips. The show was over. Our agreement was only for the weekend. I helped him win his bet with his friends. In the process, we gave in to whatever magnet that pulled us together. But that was it. And it was over.

He opened the car door for me in front of my house. He walked me to my front door. My heart felt so heavy. It was as if I missed him already. But I had to remind myself that I couldn't fall for him. I couldn't fall for anyone yet. I have to protect my heart. And Ryder was capable of hurting me ten times more than Bryan ever did.

I looked up at him. He was staring at me and somehow I couldn't read his expression. He smiled and then he took a deep breath. He reached out to push a lock of stray hair away from my face.

"Astrid… I know you don't want anything to do with me," he said. "But… I sincerely hope we can be friends."

I stared at him. I could tell that he was serious. And that made my heart feel lighter. And I knew that I couldn't deny him that. Ryder was one of the most wonderful people I'd met. I may not believe he and I could genuinely be involved with each other, but yeah, friendship works. I nodded.

"I mean it," he continued. "I hope we can be friends. Friends that get in touch with each other regularly… call each other when they're in each other's cities. Maybe even grab some dinner or lunch some time. Not the *I-knew-you-from-somewhere-sometime* kind of friends."

I giggled. Then I nodded again. "Okay. Sounds easy enough."

He stared at me for a while. And then he smiled slowly. "Thank you… It has been… a… surreal weekend."

"Surreal? Even for you?" I teased.

He stared at me seriously. "Even for me, Astrid."

My heart pounded inside my ribcage. But then I had to remind myself that even if Ryder and I were attracted to each other, I was not ready yet. Even if I were, he's a complicated man. A relationship would be too demanding. He'd be too busy for me, and I'd crave too much of his time.

I wanted my next relationship to be nothing like my relationship with Bryan, where both of us were caught up with our own stuff. I was too busy with my job to notice the looks and the secret smiles that he shared with Geena.

Now, if I were to have a relationship again—if I would allow myself to believe in 'ever after' again, I'd want to give my boyfriend time every day. And I'd want the same from him. Like what Ryder and I shared this weekend. I wanted it to last for more than a weekend. I would want my boyfriend to be truly mine… and mine alone.

"Now my debt is repaid," I told him.

He nodded slightly. Then he took my hand in his and he slowly brought it to his lips.

"Until we meet again," he said.

I smiled and then I turned away and closed the door behind me. My heart felt heavy. I don't know why. But somehow, a part of me felt so lonely.

14.

BRIDESMAIDS AND GROOMSMEN:

Forms part of your entourage. They must be of assistance when required at any given time during the wedding.

*T*uesday night, I met up with my friends. "So, what happened to you last weekend? You don't just take off to Neverland and not tell us!" Nicole scolded me.

"I went to Miami," I told them. "Something I needed to do to repay my debt."

Dannie raised a brow. "Who were you with?"

I took a deep breath before I answered. "Ryder Van Woodsen."

"Holy crap!" Nicole wailed. "Do tell!"

"There's nothing to tell!" I told them.

"You don't spend a whole weekend with a god and say that there's nothing to tell!" Dannie scolded me.

I sighed. "I met up with his best friends. He had a bet with them. He had to introduce a girlfriend to them before his next birthday. He asked me to pretend to be his girlfriend. Same thing I asked of him at the wedding. Since he didn't accept my check, I thought I would repay him this way."

"Didn't he accept your virginity before?" John laughed. I threw a ball of tissue at him.

"So? Nothing happened?" Nicole asked. I turned red, and unfortunately, my friends could read me like a book.

"So you're hooking up with this guy! Finally! Next time you meet with your family, you won't be lying anymore! The charade has turned real," Dannie said.

"Of course not!" I snorted. "I made a mistake that night of the wedding. Okay, let's say I repeated that mistake—a lot—this weekend. That doesn't mean it's for real. Ryder Van Woodsen? Come on, guys! Do you think guys like him stick to a monogamous relationship that leads to the altar? Besides, I'm not ready for a real relationship yet."

"Then why did you have sex—a lot—this weekend?" Nicole asked raising her brow.

"It wasn't part of the deal. We tried to stop it from happening, but the pull was stronger than either of us could fight. We gave in. But we made it clear to each other that it was just for the weekend."

"Then ... you agreed to not see each other anymore?"

"We agreed to be friends. But nope, we're not going out on dates. No hope of a commitment in the future. Ryder is a complicated man. He is too busy with work and too guarded about his... status in life. I'm sure he'd be a great friend... even a friend with benefits. But after Bryan, I don't need that, guys. I need to believe that I *could* get married again. That 'ever after' is still possible in my future. I'm not looking for a temporary fix or a playmate."

"Wow! Ryder is a lucky man!" John said shaking his head.

"Just exactly what do you mean by that?" I asked.

John shrugged. "I mean… you're not exactly a wallflower, Ash! If you weren't my best friend, I'd be hitting on you right now!"

I rolled my eyes. "And your point is?"

"Within twenty-four hours of meeting you, you gave him what Bryan was coveting for years. And then you spent a hot weekend together, and *you* told *him* you don't want anything to do with him. Wow! I must get pointers from this guy!"

I threw another ball of tissue at him. But even though I didn't want to admit it, I knew that John had a point. Usually, girls spend a steamy weekend with guys and ask for more. I can't say I was not tempted. But what for?

I don't think Ryder is a relationship kind of guy. If he were, then he would have found himself a real girlfriend instead of asking me to pretend in front of his best friends. I was in a relationship that I thought would last forever. It didn't. Why would I risk entering a relationship that didn't spell forever from the beginning?

But Ryder and I have this… physical connection. We gave in to that thirst. I had to walk away quickly… while I was still unscathed.

"I'm not ready to have a relationship just yet. Ryder… well, there was a physical thing between us. I gave in to that. But that's all. No expectations. No commitments. No strings attached!"

I knew that I'd rather be sad about the fact that Ryder and I could never be than heartbroken for trying and then seeing that it was never going to work.

Friday night, I worked late. It was already eight in the evening when I decided to call it a day. My phone rang. My friends could be in one of the bars already, asking me to follow them there.

"Hello," I answered without looking at the caller ID, expecting it to be Nicole, Dannie or John.

"Ash…" That familiar voice did not belong to any of my three best friends.

My heart pounded inside my ribcage. It took me a couple of seconds to find my voice.

"Hi," I said almost in a squeak.

"I'm in town," Ryder said. "I've just gotten off a long meeting and I'm starving."

I smiled to myself. "So, what does that have to do with me?"

"Because I happened to drive by your block and I was thinking maybe you're hungry too."

I giggled. I didn't have dinner yet and I was starving.

"So what do you have in mind?"

"Japanese, or Chinese. Something Asian," he replied.

There's nothing wrong with dinner. We did agree to be friends. Have some dinner some time. Not exactly a date. And I was hungry. I didn't see anything wrong with this picture.

"Alright," I said quietly. I could barely breathe.

"Okay. Come out of your house anytime you're ready."

I laughed. "You're here already?"

"A few seconds away."

"Then what would you have done if I said no?"

"I'd… be eating alone." He chuckled.

"Okay, give me fifteen minutes."

When I hung up, I raced to my room. I hopped in the shower quickly and then I dressed in a white floral dress. I only put on lip-gloss. No time for make-up. Didn't really want Ryder to think I was trying to look good for him. That is just completely the opposite of what I was standing up for. We slept together in the past, and now we're just friends. I didn't need to impress him.

When he saw me come out of the house, he got out of his car and opened the passenger door for me. I looked up at him before I got inside. He had a crooked smile on his face.

"Hi," he whispered softly.

I smiled back at him. "Hey." His smile was about to melt my knees and I was blushing already so I quickly hopped inside his car. I took deep breaths as he rounded his car to get into the driver's seat.

We didn't speak to each other for the next five minutes. It's as if we both didn't know what to say.

I stared over at the car window. *Stop this, Astrid! You have to stop feeling all giddy and weird! You're friends who are going to dinner! Treat him the way you'd treat John!*

"So, how are you?" he finally asked, breaking the silence.

"Busy. Business is picking up," I replied. "I'm going to do three weddings this month."

"That's great!"

"Yes. Especially since we're just a startup company."

"You're not exactly new to the business. And you have it in you. I knew you could do this," he said to me, smiling.

I felt warm. I sincerely felt that Ryder meant that. This is one guy who believes in me.

I smiled back at him. "Thank you, Ryder. You have… faith in me."

He didn't say anything. He just smiled that crooked smile again.

Damn! This guy is just too handsome for my 'just friends' scheme!

"How… how about you? How are you doing?"

"Not bad," he replied. "Janis is asking for your number."

My eyes went wide. "Oh my God!" I breathed. "Did you give it to her?"

He shook his head. "I keep on conveniently forgetting to text it to her. But I must warn you. I may not be able to hold her off forever. She will get your number and give you a call."

"What do I do?"

He chuckled. "Talk to her. She's not that bad."

"That's not what I meant, Ryder. She'll ask about you. About us."

"Tell her that you have not seen me in days. But we keep in touch by calling and texting each other. I don't talk to them every day for them to know exactly where I am and what I've been doing. I think you'll be fine."

I sat back on my seat. "That's easy enough. She knows you're a busy man. You'd be too busy to see me at least five times a week."

He raised a brow at me. "Wanna bet?" he asked in challenge.

My heart pounded inside my chest. I bit my lip. He continued staring at me seriously and it was getting more and more difficult to breathe. I turned away from him. "Eyes on the road, mister," I said instead.

He went quiet for a while and then he said, "I'll never be too busy to see my girl, you know."

I smiled. "You're too busy to find a girlfriend. You had to ask me at the last minute."

He shrugged. "What if I wasn't really looking?"

"What if you were too busy to realize she'd already passed you by?"

He shook his head. "Nope. My girl will sparkle so bright it will be hard for me not to notice her."

I stared at him and somehow he was staring at me deeply. Part of me was flattered. I looked away from him, unable to bear the weight of his stare. I looked out the window.

"I thought you didn't believe in 'ever afters', Ryder Van Woodsen," I said.

He heaved a sigh. "I don't know what to believe anymore," he said. "I've been cynical about dating and going on relationships because of... who I am. I was afraid the girl I'd meet would only be interested in my money... my financial status."

Now there's the reason why Ryder and I could never be! I couldn't stand him thinking I was only interested in his money. The thing with Ryder was... I think I like everything about him! *Except* for his financial status. So he and I... we could never be more than what we were now. Friends pretending to be lovers when the occasion calls for it. Friends who slept with each other at some point in their lives.

"How did you get to be that cynical?"

He shrugged. "My dad is not exactly a saint," he said. "He... well, he's been through marriages and divorces. Some are with younger women, who left him too soon... taking some fortune with them."

"Oh... you mean your parents are not together anymore?"

He shook his head. "They divorced when I was younger. Then they got together again and had Paris. Then they divorced again when Paris was about five. Now, they're just business partners. My mom tolerates my dad's marriages as long as he just spends his share of the family money and he leaves my mom's, mine, and Paris's alone."

"And so he's been through a series of failed marriages with... gold-diggers?"

He chuckled humorlessly. "All six of them."

"S-six?!" I asked, astounded.

He nodded. "All loveless. All failures. All for the money."

"Whew! That's... tough. You know to not even have a successful marriage out of all those six."

"Yeah. He's a player anyway. I don't think he's heartbroken when the marriage is over. Some of those divorces, he initiated."

"Wow! I should meet your father," I said.

He raised an eyebrow at me.

"He sounds like a great potential customer. You know... lots of repeat business," I said, laughing.

Ryder laughed. "Yeah. You should. By the time he's seventy, he'll probably give you at least five successful transactions."

"How old is he now?"

"Sixty."

"And he's been married seven times?"

Ryder nodded. "Actually, eight times if you count my mother twice."

"But he and your mother are still on good terms?"

Ryder nodded. "They're business partners who used to be married to each other and have two kids."

Ryder took me to a famous Japanese restaurant close to the beach.

We talked more about each other's families. I told him about Adam and how he grew up with Geena and me. I told him how Geena had been like a sister to me, and how Uncle Jack had been like my second father.

When the bill came, I took out my wallet. Ryder handed the waiter his platinum card.

"How much was mine?" I asked.

"Nothing," he replied.

I raised a brow at him. "That's not fair! This is not..."

"I know," he replied cutting me off mid-sentence. "But I dragged you out of the house so I could have the pleasure of your company. I owe you. It's only fair that I pay for your dinner."

"I was gonna go out to dinner, too, Ryder."

"Yeah and you could be with your friends. Instead, you accompanied me."

"You're not convincing me."

149

He chuckled. "Alright, then you owe me. I'm going to have to ask you for a favor someday."

"You have a habit of hanging a bomb over my head, you know," I groaned.

He laughed. "I promise this payback will not have you boarding a plane."

"Yeah, right!" I rolled my eyes.

When we drove around my block, it was eleven in the evening.

"Where do you stay here? A hotel?" I asked.

He shook his head. "I have a house here."

"Oh. That's good. You've got business here. Only makes sense for you to own a property here too."

"Yeah, but then sometimes I don't come here for more than a week. The house is left alone with no one maintaining it or overseeing it."

"You're rich, hire a maid."

"I have one. She cleans when I'm here. But it's not the same, you know. I want things to be spic and span all the time, and when I'm not here, I want to make sure that... my furniture is tended to, my plants are watered regularly... you know those things."

"Get a roommate."

"I don't know many people in this city," he said.

"I can tell. Otherwise, you'd have better company for dinner tonight. I guess I was your only choice, huh."

"Well, what do you know? Sometimes it's good to pull your hair out or hit your head with a sledgehammer," he teased.

I reached out and pinched him on the arm.

"Ouch!" he complained, laughing.

"Where do you live here?"

He stared at me for a while and then he gave me that crooked smile. "Actually, a few blocks from you."

I raised a brow at him.

"Come, I'll take you to my place," he said. "I've been coming and going in this city for a year now and that house never had a visitor."

"Seriously? Never?"

He shook his head.

He parked in front of that huge house a couple of blocks away from where I live.

I stared at the gate for a while and then I laughed. "It *is* your house."

"What?"

"Remember that day at the wedding... We agreed to tell people that you lived in this house and I was afraid that one of the guests would actually be the owner of the house and we would be caught. You... must have been laughing at me a lot that night."

He smiled. "I admit that part amused me. But I was not laughing at you. For all it's worth, I was… happy that night. For a change, I figured someone likes *me* even though I was just a poor bartender."

I blushed and looked away from him. I didn't say anything.

Ryder whispered, "Funny how all that changed the minute she realized who I really was."

I stared up at him, thinking that he was teasing me, but the look on his face was sober. He was serious. Somehow, something in his eyes told me that he was hurt or insulted or somehow annoyed that I liked him better when I thought he was poor, and I liked him less now.

I smiled at him. "At least we both know we could never be… more than friends. You can't marry beneath your rank in the society, Ryder. You've gotten too cynical for that. You need to find an heiress. Then you'll know she wants you for you. Not for your financial status."

He narrowed his eyes at me, as if he wanted to say something, but chose not to. Instead, he turned to open the front door.

When I stepped into his house, I felt a sense of coziness. His living room was huge. He had a massive set of couches. There was a fireplace and a huge serenity fountain. His LCD was at least sixty inches, and beside it was a wall containing a huge DVD and Blu-ray collection. The whole living room had hues of beige, brown, yellow, and green. It opened into a huge deck facing the ocean. He had a bar on his deck with a separate fridge for liquors and drinks. His house spelled luxury and comfort at the same time. And I thought Adam's house was already too luxurious!

"What do you think?" he asked.

"Wow!" I said. "And you almost don't live here?"

He shrugged. Then he led me to the deck. We sat on the chairs and he handed me a beer from the fridge.

"It's just a shame that I don't get to visit and check up on this house at least once a week. Just to make sure that the maid has done her job. Restocking the fridge with food is a problem, too."

"Why?"

He shrugged. "Because my schedule has been erratic, I can't stock up much on milk, veggies, or fruits. They'll just go bad and it's not nice if they spoil in the fridge."

"Can't your maids throw out spoiled foods?"

He shook his head. "They can't always judge which ones need to go."

"Well then just stock up on liquids and go for long-life milks," I suggested.

He nodded. "Believe me, I'm trying."

We stayed there on his deck, chatting. He took out a blanket so I could wrap it around me to keep me warm. We were laughing and talking about almost anything under the sun.

When I glanced at my watch, it was already four in the morning.

"Oh my God!" I breathed. "It's already four!"

Ryder smiled. "Time flies."

I stood up from my seat. "Well, I have to go."

"I'll take you home."

"No worries. It's only a few houses away, Ryder. No point taking your car out from the garage."

"I'll be damned if I let you go home alone, love," he said, and somehow, I knew that I would not be able to change his mind no matter how much I argued with him.

"It's just a short walk, Ryder." I tried one last time.

"Then I'll walk you," he said.

I admitted defeat. We took our coats and then we went out of his house.

"When are you going back to New York?" I asked him.

"At nine in the morning."

"That soon? How long have you been here?"

"One day."

"Wow!" I breathed. "Your life must be quite toxic."

He shook his head. "Not really. I've just started Rig Style Malibu. I check on it once in a while. Once it's established, I can conduct my business over the phone. On the other hand, my family is opening a new restaurant in Manhattan. That's my project, too. It's like taking care of two babies in two different cities, but once they can stand on their own, I'll have air to breathe. A lot of it."

We reached my house. I took out my keys and then I looked up at him. He smiled slowly.

"Thank you for your company," he said. "It's been a pleasure."

I smiled back at him. "Likewise."

"Well, I'll be off now," he said. "I'll see you when I get back."

"See you when I see you."

He smiled again and then he took a step back.

"You know my number," he said. "Call me... when you need me. Any more events in your life that I can be of service with... or if you just feel like a chat. It would really be nice to have *you* calling me for a change," he said with a chuckle.

I giggled. "Okay. I'll remember that."

He nodded. "Good night, Astrid. Sweet dreams."

Then it was over. I felt a sense of loneliness as soon as he was gone. Like I'd been so used to the cold, then he came and I felt warm and I was hoping it would not end, but it was over too soon.

I thought about Ryder when I went to bed. His smile. His handsome face. When we're together it was hard to believe that he was *the* Ryder Van Woodsen... rising tycoon... heir of the rich Van Woodsen clan.

15.

HEIRLOOM:

Something of special value handed on from one generation to another.

*T*he next Friday, I had a surprise visit from my mother. She was with Uncle Reynolds and his wife.

"We won't be long. We just want you and Adam to come with us to Manhattan," my mother said.

"What? Why didn't you tell me immediately?" I protested.

"It was a spur of the moment thing for us. Your uncle has a meeting in Manhattan. We decided to come with him," Aunt Betty said. But there's a look on her face that I cannot decipher.

"Where's Dad?"

There was silence. Then Uncle Reynolds said, "He's busy. He's meeting up with some of his associates for the weekend."

I was not convinced by my uncle's reply. I immediately felt that something was up. The look on Aunt Betty's face is far too intriguing. I didn't ask, though... not yet.

"Alright. I'll pack a few clothes," I said.

Adam wouldn't be able to make it. He had a court hearing in the afternoon. He promised to follow if he could, but I seriously doubted that.

At the airport, I was watching Aunt Betty carefully. I thought she was whispering too many things to my mother that they both did not want me to hear.

"Which hotel are we going to stay in?" I turned to Uncle Reynolds.

"Where does Ryder live? We figured we'd stay at a hotel close to his apartment. You might want to stay with him while we're there."

Shit! Ryder! I didn't see this one coming!

"Oh, I'm not really sure if he's available on such short notice. He's busy putting up another branch of his family's... restaurant."

"What? He's too busy to see you? Is that what you mean?" my mother asked. And somehow, I know that question was loaded.

I shook my head. "No, no. He was just here last week. One day. You know... because he... misses me."

"If you ever marry a man, Astrid, just make sure he'll always have time for you... and that you know where he is all the time," my mother said. She sounded like she was talking to a five-year-old child. Her eyes drifted off to my finger. "Geena was telling us that you got engaged. When were you planning to tell us? And where's the ring?"

Shit! Shit! Shit!

I took a deep breath. "Mom, relax. Ryder and I are not really planning to get married too soon! He... did ask me to marry him. I

153

did… say yes, but with conditions. You know… it's more like a promise to marry each other… if the right time comes. Which is not *today*!"

"What are you waiting for?" Aunt Betty asked.

I shrugged. "Well… if the time is right, we'll both know it."

"I think he's a good man. He can provide you with the best things in life," Uncle Reynolds said. "And he looks genuinely in love with you."

I laughed nervously. "Well, I am… genuinely in love with him too."

"So?" my mother asked me.

"So what?" I asked her back. I honestly didn't know what she was demanding of me.

"So where are we staying? And will Ryder have time to meet up with us?"

I smiled at my mother. "Mom, you took me by surprise. I didn't know you were coming. He doesn't know I'm off to New York with you. It could be a long shot. When we get to Manhattan, I'll try to ask him to see us… but if he can't, we really cannot blame him."

"Well, call him now so you'll know," Aunt Betty insisted.

Damn! I tried to think of other ways to get out of this. But as I stared at three pairs of eyes looking at me expectantly, I knew that my only way was to give Ryder a call. So I dialed his number.

Please be in Greece or Paris! I silently prayed.

One ring.

"That's a number I didn't expect to show up on my phone," he greeted me cheerily.

"Hey…" I trailed off as the three pairs of eyes are still staring back at me, studying me. I took a deep breath. "Hey, *honey*," I said with an emphasis on the '*honey*'. "Guess where I am?"

It took a moment for Ryder to answer. "Hmmm… New York? Or on your way to me?"

Now I was the one surprised. "How… how did you know that?"

"Intelligent guess, judging by your voice and your unusually sweet greeting." He chuckled.

"Yeah… I'll be on board a plane to New York in thirty minutes. With my mother and Uncle Reynolds and Aunt Betty."

"Let me guess," he said. "I'm Ryder, the fiancé again?"

"Uh-huh," I replied curtly. "But… aren't you out of town or out of the country?" I asked him. Ryder could just say he was and the worse thing I could ask him to do was to give me a call every two hours to check up on me so we could still make a bit of a show. He didn't need to make an appearance.

"Nope," he replied quickly.

I took a deep breath. I refused to be discouraged by Ryder's attempt to be… *funny!* "I know this is so last minute of us! Perhaps, honey, you can just tell me which places we need to visit."

"Not a problem. I'll take you on a tour, myself," he said.

I was getting irritated. I tried to smile sweetly in front of my family. "We should have told you earlier so you were able to tweak your schedule."

"Astrid..." he said on the other line. "If I make an appearance, I'm expected to deliver an outstanding performance as your devoted fiancé, right?"

"Uh-huh," I replied curtly then proceeded with my alibi. "It sucks! I was really hoping to see you! But I know... we should have scheduled this at least a day before!" I gave a pout, which I hope looked really genuine. "I'll pretend you're with me, though."

Ryder didn't say anything. "Hey are you still there?" I asked.

"Yes," he replied quietly. I felt really stupid for calling him like this. I know I sounded like an idiot.

I took a deep breath. "I'll call you later... you know... for a chat," I said. I hope he realizes that I mean it this time. When he didn't answer, I said quietly. "I miss you." It was a whisper. I didn't know if he heard it. But I meant it. One week had passed since the last time we saw each other. I made no effort to call him or text him. That didn't mean I didn't want to. For days, I had been staring at his phone number on my cell, but I was too scared to make the call. Besides, he didn't call me either.

I heard his sharp intake of breath. "Do you mean that?" he asked.

My heart pounded inside my ribcage. I was scared to answer, but I still decided to answer with the truth. "Well... yes. Of course," I said very, very quietly, I was not even sure he heard me. My aunt smiled at me. I guess, I was blushing like hell!

Ryder didn't say anything on the other line, much to my disappointment. I took a deep breath. "We need to go. We're boarding in like... fifteen minutes," I said. "I'll give you a call... if I get lost... you can be my personal GPS." I giggled nervously. Still there was silence so I decided to hang up.

I was irritated, embarrassed, and angry at myself. When I raised my chin up, I found the three pairs of eyes still eyeing me curiously.

I sighed. "He's... on a business trip. He would love to see you, but he said... if only we told him two hours ago, he could have canceled his... trip."

"We'll just stay in Astoria when we get there," my uncle said.

I was still scolding myself all throughout the flight. I was being silly! What was I thinking phoning Ryder in front of my family? I could have just told them straight that he was in Paris! I could have texted him later to tell him that I told my family that he was in Paris because they expected to see him in Manhattan.

When we landed in New York and left the airport, all ready to get into the next available cab, I was shocked to find a familiar figure approaching us.

"Oh my God!" I breathed as I watch Ryder walking towards me.

155

He had a twinkle in his eye and then he pulled me to him and bent down to give me a kiss on the lips. It was a soft, undemanding kiss... almost yearning, almost begging, and it left me almost begging for more.

"How's my girl?" he asked me.

I looked up at him, I whispered, "Wonderful." I couldn't find my voice. Too many questions were racing in my head. He smiled at me, and then gave me a kiss on the forehead before he turned to my family.

"Good afternoon, Ma'am," he nodded at both my mother and my aunt. Then he turned to Uncle Reynolds. "Good afternoon, Sir."

"Lovely to see you again, Ryder!" Aunt Betty said. "Astrid said you were out of town!"

Ryder nodded. "I was just about to go to Chicago for a meeting when she called me. It's not every day I get a call from her telling me that she's on her way to me. So... I canceled everything else."

My mother and Aunt Betty looked like they were about to cry after hearing that. "It's good to know that she's on your priority list," my mother said.

"She's number one, Ma'am," Ryder said smiling. Then he motioned to the parking lot. "Let me take you to your hotel." Ryder led us to a black Porsche Cayenne. He drove us to Waldorf-Astoria.

"I hope you don't mind, when Astrid said you were going to visit, I took the liberty of booking a suite for you," he told Uncle Reynolds at the front desk.

"Lovely," my uncle said and he took out his credit card.

Ryder held his hand up. "No worries, Sir. My city, my treat." He smiled at them.

"That's very generous of you," my mother said beaming.

The bellman took our bags. "This way, Mr. Van Woodsen."

As we made our way to the elevator doors, employees of the hotel were smiling at us, greeting Ryder all the way. The room that Ryder booked for us was massive. It was probably the most expensive suite in the hotel.

We took the room with a very good view of Manhattan. "Mom and I will take this one," I said.

My aunt stared at me. "Aren't you going to stay with Ryder, dear? I mean, you don't see each other every day. You may have a lot of catching up to do."

I shook my head, "No..." I started.

"Actually, if it's okay with you, Ma'am, I would rather Astrid stays with me in my apartment. It's only a few blocks away and you're welcome to visit anytime," he asked my mother without looking at me.

"Not a problem. I'm sure you two lovebirds missed each other over the week."

"Very much," Ryder said.

Damn it! Why is he doing this? I asked myself helplessly.

"I'll give you time to settle in," Ryder said. "Freshen up. Do you have any particular agenda for the day?"

My uncle shook his head. "We just want to go around the city. Have dinner. Hey, maybe I can finally eat in one of your restaurants. It was very hard to get a booking."

Ryder smiled. "Certainly. Where do you prefer?"

"Hmmm… I've always tried to reserve at Sugu, but they're always fully booked."

Ryder chuckled. "Yes. Business is good. Japanese food is a seller. I will make the necessary arrangements. Meanwhile, Astrid and I will go to my place first. We will see you after two hours? We can probably have some snack and then I'll take you wherever you want to go."

I stared at Ryder. He was not even looking at me. It was as if he wasn't giving me a chance to say no to his plans. I looked at my mother and my aunt and they were quite excited. *Damn! I think they're in love with the guy!* He was such a charmer. Even my uncle seemed to approve of him very much. Now, how can my next real boyfriend compete with my current fake fiancé?

As we set out to go, Aunt Betty called to me, "Astrid, I heard your ring was huge! When will we get to see it?"

I stared at Ryder nervously. He chuckled. "Today. I took it from her last week to have it polished. I was planning to give it back to her when I saw her this weekend. It's wonderful that you decided to go to New York and drag her along with you. It's been a miserable few days for me."

"Wow! You're so sweet, aren't you?" my mother sighed and she looked like she was on the brink of crying again.

"Now, off you go, lovebirds! We'll see you after two hours," my aunt said, shooing us away, as if she was afraid my mother would say something that I wouldn't like or would embarrass me in front of Ryder.

I didn't talk to Ryder on the way to his apartment. I was mad at him. He ruined my alibi! He was playing his part *too* well… It was not just a job well done—it was overkill! It was almost as if he was really trying to gain my family's approval! And he was not afraid to use his charms and his… privileges to achieve that!

He took me to a penthouse apartment. All throughout the ride, he also didn't attempt to talk to me. He swiped his access card and the elevator opened up to a huge apartment, much bigger than the suite that he rented for my family. It had a huge fireplace, a billiards table, and a huge plasma television and entertainment system. He had a sofa set and a massive rug in front of the fireplace. Towards the center, beside the door leading to the balcony that had a wonderful view of the Empire State Building, was a huge king-sized bed. The apartment was one massive space, no separate bedroom.

I turned to him. He put my bags down on the floor. He raised a brow at me and asked, "Do you think you can talk to me now?"

I remembered that I was mad at him. I was so irritated, I didn't want to speak, and so I just started hitting him mildly on his arms.

"Wait! Wait!" He caught my wrists to prevent me from hitting him again. I glared at him.

He laughed. Then he leaned forward and kissed my forehead. He pulled me to him and wrapped him arms around my waist.

"Boy, am I glad you're here!" he whispered against my hair.

Suddenly he was hugging me and I knew he meant what he said... He was glad that I was here with him.

I stared up at him and I could see the circles under his eyes.

"What's wrong?" I asked.

He shook his head. "I'm just tired. It's been a long week." Ryder pulled me to him again and rested his chin against my head.

"Ryder... you didn't have to do this!" I said. "You could've just stayed away. Even my mother would understand why you wouldn't be able to see us. You didn't have to... go against my plan!"

"And what? Have your mother think that I can only give you a fraction of my time?" he asked. "I told you I'm never too busy to see my girl."

"And I told you this is a fake engagement!" I muttered under my breath.

"I think you also told me you miss me," he countered.

I pulled away from him. I knew I was blushing from head to toe. I was so embarrassed. I knew I did say that. And I did mean it. But when I said that to him, I thought I wouldn't have to face him for at least another week!

He brushed his fingers against my burning cheek. "God, I missed that blush!" he said, adding to my embarrassment. He stared at me deeply. "And I missed you too," he said. "And I will never pass up the chance to play your fiancé again. So... just... humor me for a while."

"Ryder... I know you're busy. This is too many favors already," I said.

I felt him shake his head. "I'm really glad you came," he said. "I could use some time to unwind."

"And you need me to do that?" I asked.

He hugged me again and then he took a deep breath. He didn't say anything. Somehow, I knew that he'd been stressed out and he was glad to see an ally... a friendly face, someone on his side who wouldn't put any pressures on him, would instead attempt to take that pressure away. I wanted to help him, too... in what little ways I could. So I wound my arms around his waist and hugged him back.

"Thank you, Ryder," I said quietly. "I don't think my family will be doubting that this... relationship isn't real. You're not some random guy

I picked to pretend to be in love with me so I could escape the embarrassment of a broken engagement." I sighed. "You're doing more than you should. You didn't have to pay for their hotel rooms. I have to pay you back."

"Shhh," he said. "My city, my treat. Besides, it's the first time you visited me here. It's my treat to you."

"It's an expensive treat! Ryder, you have to stop spoiling me!" I groaned.

He laughed. Then he pulled away from me and to my surprise he bent down and swept me off my feet and carried me towards the bed.

"Hey!" I complained. But I don't really know what I was complaining about. I stared at Ryder and he looked tired, as if he hadn't slept in days. "Are you okay?" I asked him.

He stared at me and then he smiled. "I didn't sleep last night."

"Why?"

"I've just opened Rig Style Manhattan," he replied. "Two bartenders didn't show up. I had to fill in. And then by the time I closed at six in the morning, I had to fill in for my dad in meeting his accountant who just flew in from L.A. The meeting just finished when you gave me a call."

He settled me on the bed. I kicked off my sandals. Ryder took off his jacket and his shoes. He eased down on the bed beside me. He looked really tired.

"I really shouldn't have imposed on you," I said guiltily.

He smiled. "I just need one hour to recharge," he said.

I stared at him. He looked like he hadn't slept for days. He was stressed. But he still had a smile on his face. His eyes still had that glitter. He looked like a happy man, albeit, really tired. And saying he just needed one hour and he'd be able to entertain my family again was too endearing for me.

I reached and touched his cheek with my hand.

He smiled at me and then he reached forward and pulled me to him. My heart pounded in my chest. *Is he going to kiss me?*

But he didn't kiss me. Instead he pulled me to lie down next to him, making me rest my head on his shoulder, enclosing me in a hug.

"Lie with me for a while?" he whispered.

How could I say no to that? It was too sweet! And because I thought I would scream the minute I open my mouth, I just nodded.

I felt him kiss the top of my head. Then he drifted off to sleep with me locked in his arms.

I didn't know how I was going to feel. I knew I was attracted to Ryder. I meant, physically attracted. But this... this was not the same. This isn't sexiness or physical attraction. This was... warmth and comfort.

As much as I would like to deny it, because I knew I was not ready for a relationship just yet, this… felt wonderful. I felt comfortable, and warm. As if there was no place I would rather be. As if he really did belong to me.

I fell asleep myself and my dreams were filled with warmth and laughter. I woke up after an hour and a half. I was still locked in Ryder's arms, my head comfortably rested on his shoulder. He smelled of faint aftershave--fresh and masculine.

He tightened his hug on me and then I felt him kiss the top of my head again.

"Astrid," he whispered.

I thought he was calling me, waking me up. However, when I looked up at him, I realized he was still sleeping. Instantly, I felt warm. He whispered my name in his sleep! I smiled to myself, unable to believe that it could be real. I buried my head deeper into his shoulder and I closed my eyes.

I woke up after another thirty minutes. I stared up at Ryder. He opened his eyes lazily and he stared back at me. He smiled.

"Ready to go?" he asked.

"Up to you. Are you sure you don't need any more sleep?"

He smiled. "I said one hour. I think I had two. I should be fine."

"Alright," I said. I slowly pulled away from him and sat up from the bed. I looked around his apartment.

"Ultimate bachelor's pad," I whispered.

"I've lived here since I was twenty-five," he said. "The house in Malibu is more like… entering into adulthood."

I giggled. "Yeah. And you stay here a lot don't you?"

He shrugged. "I travel at least six times a month. I stay in Malibu about two nights a week. I can't really say I stay here a lot."

"Must be tough being you, Ryder," I whispered. "You have the world in your hands. It's… hard to keep up with you. No wonder you couldn't find a steady girl to introduce to your friends."

"I introduced you," he said.

I laughed. "Not the sham relationship, you know. A real one."

He stood up from the bed. "Well, as far as your family and my friends are concerned, I have a real, happy relationship. And we need to go so I can make an impression on my future mother-in-law."

I laughed. "I think they're already in love with you, Ryder."

"I seem to be winning every one of your relative's approval, except yours."

"That's because I was the only one who knew you were acting." I giggled.

He stared at me for a while and then he turned away and opened the drawer on his bedside table. He took a box out and then opened it. It was my ring… I mean, the ring he gave me. He took the ring from the box and held his hand out to me.

"What? I said I will not wear that ring again… unless you find a good reason why I should," I said.

"Your mother expects to see it on your finger tonight. How about that?" he asked, his eyes filled with challenge.

I raised a brow at him, but I knew he was right. My mother and my aunt would be looking for this ring.

I held my hand out to take the ring from him. He raised a brow at me and then he took my hand and placed the ring on my finger instead.

"You know I will be returning the ring before I go."

"I'll find a reason soon enough. And after that, who knows? You won't be taking that ring off your finger ever," he said and I think I forgot to breathe for a whole minute.

I sighed and stared at the gorgeous ring on my finger. And somehow, I had to remind myself that it all was a sham.

"It will break their hearts if they find out we aren't for real," I said.

"They don't have to find out, you know," he said.

I sighed. "Yeah. But we'll have to invent the breakup story of the century." I smiled at him. "Don't worry. It will be my fault. Let's blame it all on me."

"You don't have to break their hearts," he said. "At least not yet."

I nodded. "Works either way, Ryder. Let me know anytime you can't pretend to be my perfect fiancé anymore."

And somehow that thought pinched my heart.

16.

BELLS:

One of the most common symbols of marriage and weddings.

The minute I entered my mother's hotel room, they noticed my ring.

"Oh my God, this is just too gorgeous!" my mother said, pulling my hand.

"This is expensive!" my aunt breathed. "It's a Harry Winston!"

"You're embarrassing me!" I hissed at them.

Ryder just chuckled.

"You spoil her too much, young man," my mother said, but I could tell that she was very happy for me.

"She deserves it, Mrs. Jacobson," he said. "Astrid deserves to wear a ring as beautiful as she is."

Ryder was the epitome of grace and gallantry. He was everything a girl could ask for in a boyfriend! It's like he was ripped right out of the pages of a romance novel. Sweet, funny, he treated my mother and my aunt like they were queens. He kept up with Uncle Reynolds' endless chatter about the stocks, business and Forex. Ryder could handle it all. Looking at him, I wouldn't even know he was the same man who slept beside me an hour ago. It's like he had tons of energy saved up somewhere.

He took us around the city. We went to Bloomingdale's. I tried on a couple of dresses. Ryder patiently sat on the couch, playing judge. He told me whether or not the dress I put on looked good on me. He was an even better shopping companion than Nicole was. He paid attention to me.

I settled for three dresses. I took them to the counter to pay for them, but Ryder was quick to hand over his platinum card.

"No!" I said sharply. I raised a brow at him.

He just laughed and then to my surprise, he leaned forward to give me a quick kiss on the lips.

I glared at him. "What was that for? They're not even around!" I hissed at him.

"Oh, I'm sorry, Ma'am. I guess I got carried away," he whispered teasingly.

The cashier handed him his credit card bill and he signed for it. I smiled at the cashier, but when we turned away, I gave Ryder a pinch on the arm.

He laughed. Then he put an arm around my shoulders and gave me a squeeze. "You're too cute."

When we went out of the store, we heard a woman's voice call behind us.

"Ryder!"

We turned around and I saw a stunning blonde with long legs approach us. She was tall, but her mini skirt was very short. She could pull it off though. She looked more like she was walking on the runway than Bloomingdales.

"Alizia." Ryder nodded at her.

She lunged forward and gave Ryder a hug.

"How have you been? It's been ages!" she said.

Ryder gently pulled away from her. "I've been good," he said. "Busy."

"When were you not busy?" The girl giggled and rolled her eyes. "You might as well marry your restaurant chains!" She giggled again.

Obviously, she was flirting with him. And I didn't know why, but somehow, that really annoyed me.

I stared at the girl. She was gorgeous. Like she was Hollywood celebrity! I could tell that she was wearing expensive clothes. Her bangles were adorned with diamonds, as well as the sunglasses perched up her head. Right away, I knew this was the type that vied for Ryder's attention. This was his world—where he could have the pick of girls as rich and as beautiful as this. And I felt as annoyed as I was insecure. I looked away from them.

Suddenly I felt Ryder pull me towards him.

"Alizia, I'd like you to meet Astrid," he said. He looked at me. "Alizia and I shared a few classes in Harvard."

And she's smart too! I thought glumly.

"Alizia, this is Astrid, my… fiancée," he said.

The statement raised brows! Including *mine*!

It took me a moment to recover. I extended my hand to Alizia, who still looked dumbfounded.

When I extended my hand, her eyes drifted off directly to my fingers to see if I was sporting an engagement ring, the sort Ryder Van Woodsen can afford.

And voila! I was! I smiled at her cheerily.

"Wow! I am honored to meet the girl that finally tied Ryder Van Woodsen down!" she said to me, smiling.

"It took some work," I said. "But I was successful."

Ryder chuckled. "That's not true! You got under my skin the minute I saw you," he said.

"So when's the big day?" Alizia asked.

"Well, we haven't set the date yet," I said.

"Oh, better hold on to him until then. Your man is a slippery catch," she said. Then she turned to Ryder. "Congratulations! I'll see you around." With one final wave, she went off.

I raised my brow at Ryder. "Old flame? Someone you charmed during one of your bartender episodes? Speaking of bartender episodes, you filled in as a bartender last night, didn't you? You must have gotten a dozen phone numbers." I didn't know what just came over me. But somehow, the idea of Ryder charming another woman as he pretended to be a bartender, the way he flirted with me the night I met him really irritated me! Plus, women… looking like Alizia! Supermodel that fits an heir like Ryder.

I turned away from him so he could not see the frown on my face. It took him a few seconds to catch up with me.

"Oh, okay, so we're playing the part of *jealous fiancée* now," he said in an amused tone.

"I'm not jealous!" I snapped. I glared at him and then I walked away.

After a few seconds, I felt him tug at my hand. He pulled me to him and to my surprise, he gave me a hug.

He was chuckling. I tried to pull away, but he refused to let me go.

"It's not my thing to flirt with my customers," he whispered. "As far as Alizia goes, we went out twice in college. Two dates. Nothing happened. She tried initiating a third date… plenty of times… but let's just say she's not my type."

I pulled away from him, relief washing over me. "You didn't have to explain that to me. I wasn't jealous! You can fake an engagement, but you can't fake jealousy." I started walking away. He caught up with me.

I was silent for a while, and finally, just to break the ice, I said, "Really, Ryder? Alizia? Tall, blonde, legs that go on forever? Not your type? Even I find that hard to believe."

"Nope." He said with a popping "P."

"If she's not your type then I don't know what is."

He chuckled. "Well, recently I discovered I have a certain weakness for petite, strawberry blondes with rare violet eyes."

Is he mocking me because I showed a hint of jealousy?

I glared at him. "Well, too bad there's very few of them!" I snapped and increased my pace.

"There's only *one* actually."

My heart pounded in my chest. I stopped walking and faced him. I raised my brow, frowned, but didn't say anything.

"I made a mistake when I said it's not my thing to flirt with my customers. I actually did that… *only once*. Because I couldn't resist." There was laughter in his eyes. That embarrassed me more.

"Stop that, Ryder!" I said in an irritated tone.

He raised a brow and feigned innocence. "Stop what?"

"Stop… making me blush!" I said and started to walk away.

I heard a low chuckle and then I felt him take my hand. He pulled me towards him and gave me a hug again. "But you're perfect with your blush, love," he whispered.

"But you shouldn't be making me!" I said, burying my face in his chest. I shouldn't be showing this much emotion for Ryder. At least not when we're not in front of my family.

"But I like seeing you blush, love," he said quietly. "Let it be my prize for a job well done."

I stared up at him and I could see that his eyes were dancing. I raised a brow. "Who said it was a job well done?"

He laughed. "I think they're pretty convinced," he said. He looked behind me and then he said, "But if not, maybe this will change their minds." Before I knew it, I was being kissed thoroughly. Instantly, my heart melted, my knees turned to jelly and I forgot how to breathe. The butterflies were running wildly inside my stomach. Electricity flowed from Ryder's lips to mine. I wanted... to linger there forever, in his arms... with his lips on mine.

"Oh you two lovebirds." I heard my Aunt say behind me.

Ryder stopped kissing me, and acted as if he had not seen my aunt and mother coming.

He stared at me, and as if he was contended that I had blushed enough, his lips curved into a crooked smile and then he released me gently.

Damn! I looked away from him. I turned to my mother who was staring at me lovingly. Her eyes were almost wet, as if she were so happy to see me being thoroughly kissed in public.

"Are you okay, mother?" I asked her.

"Oh she's just feeling nostalgic," my aunt replied quickly. "You know... she misses your dad."

My mother looked like she was about to say something, but chose not to. Then she reached out and touched my cheek. She smiled at me and whispered, "He loves you a lot. You're lucky. Even if he isn't rich... you're lucky because he's crazy about you."

Then before she could say more, my aunt pulled her away into a nearby jewelry shop.

I was still staring after them. I felt Ryder standing beside me. When I looked up at him, he was staring at me wearily.

"Something's wrong," I said.

He nodded slightly. "But it doesn't look like she's ready to talk about it yet."

"I'm worried."

"And yet you're going to have to give her time, until she's ready to let it out. But you have to make her feel that you're there for her. Even though she's not telling you that she needs you."

I stared up at him. Hearing him say those words made me wonder if he was The Ryder Van Woodsen, heir of a multi-million dollar family empire. Sometimes, it was hard to believe who he was.

"Why did you have to be *the* Ryder Van Woodsen?" I said under my breath. I knew I said it to myself, but I knew he heard it too.

I started walking, leaving him to tail behind me. He didn't make an effort to catch up with me. I didn't slow my pace down.

And I meant what I said. No matter how wonderful Ryder was as a friend, I was afraid he'd be just as complicated as a boyfriend. Besides, I was not ready for a relationship just yet. And when I was… I wanted more than a man who wanted to share his bed with me. I wanted a guy who would give me his heart and soul and put me in the center of his world.

I followed my mother to the jewelry shop. She and my aunt were looking at some rings. I looked over at some bracelets. I saw a white gold necklace with a huge amethyst pendant surrounded by diamonds. It was absolutely stunning. I looked at the tag price. It was expensive, but I figured I could afford it by the end of the month after I got paid for the two weddings I had booked for the week. Adam paid me on a monthly basis. I could afford the necklace at once, but I wanted to show him profit by the end of the month. I didn't want the investors to pull out too early in the game.

"That will bring out the hue in your eyes." I heard Ryder say behind me.

"It's beautiful." I smiled. "Something to look forward to when I get my paycheck at the end of the month."

He nodded. "How's the wedding business doing by the way? You always seem busy."

I smiled at him widely.

"It's great! I've been getting a lot of inquiries. I do an average of two weddings a month now. I plan to increase that average to about four by the end of next month."

He smiled. "See? You've come a long way from the girl that whined about being jobless at that wedding."

I took a deep breath and looked at the necklace. A couple of months ago, buying jewelry was the least of my worries. Now, I was looking at a fine gem and dreaming of making it mine soon.

I looked briefly at Ryder. I knew I wouldn't be where I was now without him if he hadn't encouraged me or given me a push. Adam and my friends had been telling me that there was a silver lining in the mass of dark nimbus cloud at the top of my head. It was Ryder who showed me not only the silver lining, but also the colorful rainbow over the horizon.

Even if there was no hope of a real relationship between the two of us, I knew that I would never be where I am now, if it wasn't for him. And I will hold him dearly in my heart… for the rest of my life.

I reached out and gave him a gentle kiss, smiling against his velvet lips. If he was surprised when I pulled away, he didn't show it. Instead

167

he smiled back at me and reached out to push a lock of stray hair away from my face.

"Thank you, Ryder," I whispered.

"You're welcome, love," he whispered back, and I just knew it was one of those moments when we just connected. We knew exactly what the other was thinking.

Until, we were interrupted by my aunt.

"Astrid, could you come here for a second?" my aunt called. I reluctantly left Ryder's side and went to the counter where my aunt and mother were looking at a beautiful diamond studded ring.

"Pretty?" my aunt asked.

It was beautiful, but without a doubt, very expensive.

"Very," I replied. "What for?"

"Nothing. Your mother is thinking of buying it."

"Yes. Using your father's credit card!" my mother grunted.

"Mom, did you and Dad have a fight?" I couldn't help asking now.

She shook her head immediately. "No. Of course not!"

"She's just not happy that your father was not able to come with us on this trip," my aunt butted in.

"And to get back at him for that, I am going to buy myself a treat," my mother muttered.

"That's an expensive treat!" I said.

"He can afford it."

I didn't know why my mother was acting so weird. I knew that something was up. Maybe Ryder was right. I just needed to give her time. I might as well call my father tonight, too.

All of a sudden, I felt someone come up behind me. Before I could turn around, a pair of hands shoved something over me from behind.

"Oh my God, that is absolutely beautiful!" my aunt and my mother breathed, looking at the necklace that Ryder put on me.

My hand went to necklace and even without looking at it in the mirror, I know what it is. My heart pounded in my chest.

"Ryder..." I started to protest, but I felt a kiss at the base of my neck.

"A guy can give anything to his fiancée," he whispered. "Your family expects that."

That frustrated me. I couldn't refuse the necklace in front of my mother and my aunt.

I turned to face him. His eyes were dancing.

"Doesn't it bring out the violet hue in her eyes?" he asked my aunt and my mother.

"It absolutely does," my mother said. "It looks lovely on you."

"Mrs. Jacobson, please make sure that she wears this necklace to every gathering that you have, especially when I'm not with her," he said to my mom. "Something to remember me by."

My mother laughed. "You're so sweet, Ryder. Yes, I will remind her to wear that necklace every time she comes to see us."

I glared at Ryder. He laughed and then pulled me to him and gave me a hug.

"I'm still going to give you back the ring," I whispered when I buried my face against his chest.

"The necklace will do for now." He chuckled.

And because I knew he had defeated me, I slid my hand inside his jacket and gave him a hard pinch on his side.

He laughed and he gave me a kiss on the forehead. Then he took my hand and we all went out of the jewelry shop.

When my mother and my aunt were far ahead of us to hear what we were talking about, I turned to him.

"Why did you do that?" I demanded.

"Because I knew it will look lovely on you."

"Ryder, this is not part of the deal! This is expensive!"

"But the glare you're giving me right now, and the blush on your face? Priceless!" he teased.

"Don't do this!" I told him. "I feel so… indebted to you already."

"Don't. I'm just playing my part well."

"Too well!" I said.

He sighed, then pulled me to him again and gave me a hug. "Come on, Ash. I'm tired. I don't want to argue with you. Just… accept the necklace. I want to give it to you. I don't know why. But I do. And… well, I was hoping to see delight in your eyes when I put it on you, actually. Not… anger bordering on wrath."

Now, I felt guilty! He went out of his way to give me an expensive necklace so he could see delight in my eyes? That's too sweet! And I refused him that reaction?

Honestly, I was delighted with the necklace. I just didn't know why Ryder had to give it to me.

I stared up at him, and sighed. He would have been the perfect fiancé. But he isn't really mine.

"Thank you," I whispered quietly. Then I tiptoed and gave him a kiss on the cheek. I smiled beatifically at Ryder, because I *was* delighted. Because I knew that deep inside my heart, I did want him… even though he was too complicated for me.

***

We went to Sugu for dinner. There were people lined up, all in cocktail dresses and nice expensive suits. They didn't look like ordinary people at all.

Uncle Reynolds bumped into a man about the same age. He was with his wife and a guy just about Ryder's age. He had dark blond hair and startling blue eyes. He was eyeing me curiously and when I looked up, he smiled. I nodded and gave him a slight smile.

"I didn't know you were going to New York!" my uncle said, shaking the man's hand.

"Only for the weekend," the man said.

"Did you have dinner already?"

"We were hoping to. This looks like a nice place, but I didn't realize you needed to book one month in advance," the man said. "Are you going in? Did you have a reservation?"

"Yes, we're going in. We've made arrangements."

"You're lucky! We'll go find some other place. Try the *Yakizakana.* This place is quite famous for it," the man said.

"If I knew you were here as well, we could have called earlier to make arrangements."

"I don't think you can do that. Not in this place. I don't think even celebrities can get a table here at the last minute."

"Well, I'm sure we can make last minute arrangements," Ryder interrupted. He looked at my uncle, as if asking him if he would like to invite his friends to join us.

"Of course," Uncle Reynolds said. "If it's not too much to ask, Ryder."

"It's fine, Sir," Ryder replied. He turned to the man. "There are three of you?"

The man nodded, and he looked a little confused.

Ryder went ahead of us, and the lady at the reception immediately smiled at him. "Good evening, Boss." She greeted warmly. "Your table is ready."

"Can you please tell Jason to add three more? I have three more guests."

"Certainly, Sir," the lady said and she immediately spoke to someone on her headset.

The man turned to Uncle Reynolds. "Wow." He breathed. "You know some people."

My uncle laughed. He turned to introduce us to his friend, his wife and his son, who I learned is named, Daniel.

"Dan, for short," he said extending his hand to me. When I shook it, he gave it a squeeze.

I heard somebody clear his throat behind Dan. Dan turned towards Ryder.

"Daniel Hughes," he said extending his hand to Ryder.

Ryder shook it, but the expression on his face was cold. "Ryder Van Woodsen."

I didn't know what was going on, but somehow, I was afraid of the cold look both men exchanged with each other.

"The table is ready," he said to my uncle.

"Wonderful!"

Ryder turned to me and took my hand in his. I saw Dan look at us before he followed his parents inside.

We were seated in a secluded VIP room. I sat between Ryder and my mother. Across the table sat Dan who was eyeing me curiously. And somehow, I didn't know why I felt self-conscious. He was cute! Maybe not as cute as Ryder, but definitely way better looking than Bryan.

Ryder was sitting quietly beside me. When I think of him, I feel like I shouldn't even be looking at Dan, who was eyeing me with interest. I stared up at Ryder and I could see he had an irritated look on his face.

"Are you okay?" I whispered to him.

He wound an arm at the back of my chair and I felt him trace circles on my shoulder, but he didn't answer. He was looking at me, and I couldn't read the expression on his face. He was fine before we stepped in the restaurant, and now he looked a little pissed. Was it because of Dan?

I smiled at him. I would rather spend time comforting Ryder with whatever it was that made him angry than make flirty eyes with Dan.

"Thank you," I whispered to him. "Uncle Reynolds seemed very pleased."

He smiled at me crookedly. "You're welcome."

"Is there something I can do in return?" I asked. "You don't look too pleased."

He shook his head. "I'm okay. I don't know what has come over me," he whispered against my ear. "But I don't think I like the way that guy is staring at you."

I laughed. I didn't know what to feel. Confused, excited, thrilled, scared. All emotions enveloped me at once. But somehow, that made my heart jump in delight. Was he jealous?

"Are we playing the part of jealous fiancé now?" I whispered to him.

"If I am, will you do something about it?" he asked evenly.

I smiled at him. "Yes. Maybe I'll play the part of comforting, loving, overly sweet fiancée."

His eyes finally glittered and then he replied, "Then yes. Hell yes!"

I giggled. I inched closer to him and gave him a kiss on the cheek. Then I leaned my head on his shoulder. I felt him put an around me and then he gave me a kiss on the forehead.

"So, Ryder, how did you manage to squeeze us in at the last minute?" Mr. Hughes asked. "I thought that was impossible."

My uncle replied for him. "It is impossible. But you know Chuck, he owns the place. So nothing is impossible for him."

Mr. Hughes was taken aback. "Oh. Really? But you're so... young!"

Ryder smiled. "Actually Sir, my parents own this place. I will not take ownership until next year."

171

"It's the same thing!" Mr. Hughes laughed. "How did you get to know Reynolds?"

"I'm marrying his niece here." I think that reply was directed more to Dan than his father.

"Oh, you're family now," Mr. Hughes said.

Ryder nodded. "More or less. I'm working my way in."

Dinner was nice. I could understand why people actually lined up to dine here. The food was absolutely superb! The servings were big compared to other fine dining restaurants. The place was neat and cozy. The ambience was lovely. The menu had lots of variety.

"How do you find the food?" Ryder asked me.

I smiled at him. "Wonderful!" I said. "You have a Japanese cook?"

He nodded. "The best in the city."

"I wonder how much you pay him."

When he gave me a ballpark figure, I almost choked. His chef was being paid about five times the salary that Adam gave me.

"That much?"

"Well, we're generous with our employees. Without them, our business would not be this good."

"That's a great business practice," Mr. Hughes said. "I wish all companies were like that."

"No wonder everybody who served our table looks genuinely happy!"

"My great grandfather started as a waiter. He taught my grandfather, who taught my father, the value of the people who face your customers."

"Then your business will have a lot more years to go."

"That's the plan." Ryder smiled.

Ryder would give me occasional kisses and would constantly hold my hand. I enjoyed it. He was sweet, as always, and I felt like I was stealing a few moments of heaven.

My uncle asked for the bill, and so did Mr. Hughes. Ryder shook his head. "No bill. My treat."

"Come on, getting us reservations is enough!" my uncle insisted.

Ryder chuckled. "It's okay, Sir. Astrid, or Astrid's family and friends, don't pay here."

"Well, then thank you."

We parted ways with the Hughes. Dan came up to me and shook my hand. "It was lovely meeting you, Astrid. Not really… lovely to know you're already engaged."

I giggled nervously. "It was nice to meet you, too and your family."

"Well, take care. And tell Van Woodsen to take care of you."

"Don't worry, I will," Ryder said coming up behind me.

"Thank you for dinner." Dan offered his hand to him and in spite of himself, Ryder shook it.

When Dan walked away, I stared up at Ryder.

"With all due respect, you play the part of jealous, possessive fiancé quite well," I teased.

He raised a brow. "And you, my love, are not playing the part of comforting, loving, overly sweet fiancée well enough."

I pouted. "What? I was being sweet," I protested.

He shook his head. "Not good enough. I'm still pissed. You promised to comfort me, ease my anger."

"It's not my fault if you are so difficult to please!" I argued.

He shook his head. "On the contrary, I am one of the easiest people to please... and you... can please me the easiest."

I looked up at him nervously.

"One kiss?" he asked.

I tiptoed and gave him a kiss on the lips.

He laughed. "Still not good enough. You ought to give me a real kiss, love."

I pouted and was about to kiss him again when my uncle called us.

"Shall we go back to the hotel? We can rest now and have an early start tomorrow. I'm sure Ryder needs his rest too."

I stared at Ryder. "I guess I was saved by the bell."

He laughed. "That's what you think. But you ought to give me that kiss by the end of this night."

"Ryder! Why are you doing this?"

Before he could answer, my aunt called us to go.

He laughed. "That is what you call '*saved by the bell*.'" Then he advanced towards where my aunt and mother were. He led them to his car leaving me dumbfounded, nervous, and excited all at the same time.

17.

CONTRACEPTION:

Part of the honeymoon checklist, if the couple is not yet planning on having babies immediately after the wedding.

We dropped off my family at the Waldorf Astoria. Then, Ryder and I drove back to his apartment in silence.

We were playing a dangerous game. In truth, no guy would put up with this. Why Ryder was doing so, I didn't know. And he was doing it so well, and so nicely, it was getting more and more difficult for me not to feel something for him.

Damn! Already physically attracted to him; I didn't want to wish this was all real. I couldn't take that risk.

When he closed the door of his apartment, I turned to him nervously. He was smiling at me mischievously.

"Ryder, I can't really kiss you here. No one is here to see us. No need to put on a show," I said.

He stepped closer to me and tilted my chin gently so he could look into my eyes. "Who said I wanted it for the show?"

Without giving me a chance or warning, he bent down and gave me a thorough kiss on the lips. That kiss swept me off my feet. Once it started, it was so hard to stop.

He ignited the fire that had been threatening to light since this morning when I first saw him. I kissed him back, with just the same passion. He nuzzled my neck, and I pulled him to me.

"Ryder, please stop!" I begged him. "We shouldn't be doing this." I said, but I couldn't make the effort to push him away.

"I know," he whispered. "But I can't seem to help myself."

He went back to my lips and kissed me savagely. I couldn't help responding the same way. I was hungry for him. I wanted him with every bit of my feminine being. At the back of my mind, I couldn't help thinking how complicated we were making things. We'd already slept with each other on two separate occasions. Could we really afford to make it a third?

He wound his arms around my waist and lifted me off my feet. I clung to him, neither one of us dared to break the kiss. I landed on his soft mattress. He landed on top of me.

"Ryder..." I took a deep breath. "We have to stop..."

He kept kissing me. "Good luck with that," he said in a low chuckle, and then he nuzzled my neck again.

"Damn it!" I cursed and pulled his neck and kissed him on the lips.

I started pulling his jacket off him. I didn't care anymore. All I cared about was how good I felt whenever Ryder's lips landed on any part of my body. I wanted him. I knew I couldn't afford to keep him for good, but it didn't matter. What mattered was now.

He took his shirt off, then I took off mine. He nuzzled his way down from my lips to my chest. I couldn't contain it anymore. I felt thirsty and hungry and I wanted Ryder at that very instant.

But then he stopped. He stared at me and then kissed me gently on the lips. He smiled. "This has nothing to do with the necklace I gave you, Ash. Before you put any more ideas in your head."

I laughed. Then I pulled him to me and gave him a gentle kiss on the lips.

"I know. I won't return the necklace in the morning."

"Good." And he started kissing me again. I lost all my clothes save for the black bikini panties I was wearing. Ryder was only in his boxers.

He kissed me again. I couldn't contain the fire threatening to consume me anymore. Ryder was teasing me, prolonging my agony.

Finally, I couldn't take it anymore, I said to him, "Ryder, please… just put the rubber on and take me!"

He stopped kissing me all of a sudden. I opened my eyes, worried about what made him stop. He was staring at me curiously.

"What? Why?" I asked.

He shook his head. "I don't… I don't have… protection here, Ash."

"What? You don't keep any in your apartment?"

He shook his head. "I don't bring women here. What would I need it for?"

"Don't you have one in your wallet?"

"Now you know not all guys keep condoms in their wallets." He chuckled.

"Then what are we going to do?"

"If you're worried about pregnancy, then I can withdraw," he suggested.

"But pregnancy isn't the only thing you worry about when you have sex, is it?"

He laughed. "You read a lot of Cosmo magazines!" he said. "In a polygamous relationship yes. But… we are monogamous, aren't we?"

I stared back at him. "What… do you mean?"

"I mean I haven't shared a bed with another woman since I met you, and as long as there's a chance that we're going to do this, I'm not going to."

I smiled back at him. I didn't know what to feel. I just thought that right then and there, I had died and gone to heaven. I was not expecting Ryder to make that commitment. I thought it was a physical thing for him, but he was willing to make it exclusive between us. And somehow, that thought was as breathtaking as it was scary and confusing for me.

My desire for Ryder prevented me from thinking far beyond and ahead. I'd deal with that thought in the morning.

"Well... you know I haven't... before you. And I haven't..." I stammered.

A glitter lit in his eyes and he gave me a kiss on the lips. "You mean to say you haven't been with any guy but me?"

I nodded shyly.

"Then we both have nothing to worry about," he said. He leaned forward and gave me a kiss on the lips. Then he nuzzled my neck again.

"Why are we doing this, Ryder?" I whispered.

He stared at me. "Because I want you, Astrid. Not in the make-believe games that we play. I want you... for real."

I kissed his jaw. "And everything Ryder Van Woodsen wants, Ryder Van Woodsen gets."

He stared at me deeply. And I thought I saw a shadow behind his eyes. He shook his head. "Not everything..." And then without another word, he lost himself in me.

***

When I woke up that morning, I was naked and wrapped in Ryder's arms. I felt comfortable and safe, adored and protected.

I heaved a sigh. It had been exhausting night of lovemaking. I was almost afraid it would consume all of me. I lost myself to Ryder. All of me. I didn't think, I didn't speak, I just... felt. I felt him inside me. And now, it made me want to stay locked in his arms forever.

I stared up at him. He was still sleeping. I knew he had a long day yesterday. He might want to sleep most of the day today. I'd imposed too much on him. But he was brilliant! He was the perfect fiancé and I'm sure my family did not have a doubt in their minds that I was okay now. That the Bryan-Geena episode no longer bothered me. That my engagement with this wonderful, sweet guy was real.

I propped up on my elbow and watched him sleep. He had a handsome face: his chiseled features, his perfect nose, the slight cleft on his chin, his long lashes. He was perfect.

Ryder and I, when we're together on equal footing, felt like two pieces of a puzzle. We complimented each other, we read each other's thoughts, and we finished each other's sentences. We made a great team. He made me laugh. He saved me from hell. He encouraged me to be better. He would have been the perfect boyfriend, perfect fiancé. But he was still a complicated man, with a complicated life.

When this was all over, he would still be the heir of the Van Woodsen Empire. He was everything I tried to avoid since Kevin Moore and his mother insulted me over dinner many years ago. And Ryder's family was probably a hundred times richer than they were.

I didn't think I could afford to break my heart again. And not with Ryder. He was ten times the man that Bryan or Kevin was. Ten times the man I wanted! And I was afraid I would hurt ten times more if he broke my heart. And my heart… was the one thing I had left to protect.

I reached forward and gave him a kiss on the lips. Suddenly, his arms tightened around me, he kissed me back. He laid me on the bed and kissed me thoroughly.

"Good morning," he said.

I smiled. I touched his cheek with my palm. "Good morning."

He smiled at me mischievously and then all of a sudden he was on top of me and he was kissing me hungrily. The fire inside me ignited again and soon, I was screaming his name at the gates of Nirvana.

When we woke up again, it was already nine in the morning.

"I'm going to the hotel," I told him. "What are you up to today?"

"I'm coming with you," he replied.

"Don't you have work to do?" I asked.

He shook his head. "When my fiancée is in the city, I'm all hers."

I giggled. "You are too sweet! But I'm not really your fiancée, so you don't have to go to hell and back for me."

"As far as your family and my friends know, you are my fiancée. I'm not going to go down in history as being the first unromantic Van Woodsen."

"Really? Your family has that tradition?"

He nodded. "Well, save for my father, who's too romantic. Apparently, he forgot that the tradition meant he's only supposed to be romantic to *one*."

"You're not like him?"

He shook his head.

"I thought heirs and tycoons like you always have a line of women waiting for them?"

"There may be a line, but that doesn't mean I have to take my pick every single time."

"Why is that? You said to me last night that you don't bring women here. You don't have condoms in your wallet. Why?"

"Why not?"

"You're not gay."

"Hell no!" He said. "You, of all people, should be able to tell that."

I laughed. "Why don't you have sex all the time like guys of your age and privilege do?"

He shrugged. "I don't pick sexual partners overnight like some men do. I've always been pretty cautious. And besides… why would you share your bed with someone you can't bear to look at in the morning?"

"Supermodels and girls who look like Alizia are running after you. They're beautiful! Why can't you bear to look at them in the morning?"

"Because it's all clothes and makeup," he replied. "Nothing much underneath."

"And you don't like women who wear nice clothes and makeup?"

"I want one who looks more beautiful without makeup and wearing the simplest of clothes. Someone who looks prettier in the morning, with her skin so fresh and her hair disheveled against the pillows. Someone whose smile in the morning is brighter than the sunshine," he said solemnly looking at me deeply.

I stared back at him, not knowing what to say. I knew I was blushing.

"Someone whose cheeks turn the darkest shade of pink at a mere compliment I throw her way."

I turned away from him. Instantly, I felt him tilt my chin so I could look into his eyes.

"Yes, Astrid. Just in case you were wondering. I was talking about you."

I sighed. "You're still Ryder Van Woodsen."

"So?"

"So we will never work," I said to him. "Someday we'll drift apart from each other and I will lose you... and I don't want that, Ryder. I would rather have you as a friend and know that I can call you or see you once in a while than lose you forever. You've... grown too dear to me. So we cannot insist on making this real. And besides... I'm not ready to commit myself just yet."

He sighed and somehow, I detected a hint of frustration in him. He stared at me and said, "So until then we'll just be friends?"

"We will always be... just friends."

"For your information, friends don't do what we did last night and this morning," he argued.

"That was a slip," I said, turning red again. "We really have to stop, Ryder."

He leaned forward and gave me a kiss on the lips. I kissed him back. When he pulled away from me, he said, "Yeah, good luck with that."

I reached out and pinched him in his arm as hard as I could.

"Ouch!" he yelped.

He took both my hands and pinned them at the top of my head. I struggled to get away from him but he was too strong for me. Then he leaned forward and kissed me again thoroughly. And then we were both lost again after that.

When it was over, we both stared at each other thoughtfully.

"I'm serious, Ryder. We have to stop."

"Hmmm..." was all he said.

I took a deep breath. "I'll make you a deal. New York," I said. I couldn't believe I was going to do this again, but somehow, with Ryder, I just couldn't seem to help myself. I didn't want to want him, but damn, I did! I couldn't help but give in to him… at least one more time. For the *last time,* I promised myself.

"I'm listening," he said.

"It ends when I leave New York."

He took a minute and then he answered, "Okay. I won't make advances on you when we get back to Malibu. But until then, I have a whole weekend to do whatever I want with you."

"Can you do me a favor?" I asked.

"Anything for you, Ash."

"Can you stop being Ryder Van Woodsen for a day?"

"What do you mean?"

"I mean no expensive cars, no platinum credit cards, no high-class restaurants, no expensive presents. I want you to be you. Just you." I stared at him. "Like the bartender I met that night." And I knew I asked him this because that bartender seemed more real to me. That guy seemed more like the guy I dreamed of.

He smiled, and this smile really touched his eyes. He leaned forward and gave me a kiss on the lips. "Yes. And you, my love, are officially mine today."

I didn't know how long we made out in bed. We were laughing, tickling each other and chatting. Then we took a shower together. It felt good to be free to express what I felt for Ryder.

He put on a pair of jeans and a white hooded sweater. I smiled because he looked like the boy next door… a beautiful boy next door.

"You can't take your car," I reminded him when we were out of his building.

He smiled. Then he pulled me to him and gave me a kiss on the lips. "I know the rules, love."

We took a cab to the hotel. I told my family that Ryder's car needed to go for service and thus we have to commute or take a taxi today. My family didn't mind. The weather was perfect. And besides, it was nice to experience being a first-hand New Yorker.

To my surprise, Ryder knew how to take a bus and the train. He knew the city quite well, and he looked comfortable commuting like… an ordinary person. When we were walking down Sixth Avenue, I was looking at him thoughtfully. It dawned on me that I really, really liked him. Ryder fit in this world too… my world.

He stared at me and smiled and then he put an arm around me and kissed my forehead. I put an arm around his waist and I leaned my head on his shoulder. I knew that right then, in that moment, we were a picture of bliss.

He told my aunt, uncle, and mother that we would go somewhere and we'd meet them back at Macy's after an hour. Then he took my hand in his and led me out into the streets.

"Where are we going?" I asked.

"I want to show you something," he said.

We walked a couple of blocks and then he led me to a lane where there were bridal shops, stores that sell wedding favors, and then florists.

"Wow!" I beamed as I went inside one bridal shop to study the quality of their wedding gowns.

I was delighted to go to the wedding favors' shop and saw a variety of materials that I could use for the weddings that I plan.

Ryder was staring at me seriously.

"What?" I asked.

"Weddings happen in New York almost every hour," he said. "You'll get plenty of supplies here. And with your ideas, you'd be a hit here."

I raised a brow.

"Did you not consider branching out?"

"In Manhattan?"

He nodded.

"I'm fairly new. I haven't even shown profits."

"But you're growing at a record rate."

I shook my head. "I'm merely an employee there. It's not my decision to make."

He took a deep breath. "I'm sure you can convince your investor."

"Maybe. But I want to show income first."

He nodded. Then he took my hand and pulled me out of the shop.

"If I branch out here, then I'd be like you. Half here, half in Malibu."

He stared at me and his eyes glittered. "Exactly!" And without giving me time to react, he leaned forward and kissed me thoroughly.

18.
FLOWERS:
An important element that makes up the whole wedding. Flowers must go with the theme, and must always match or compliment the motif.

I found my mother in deep conversation with my aunt. When she saw us coming, she turned away, but not before I saw that her eyes were glistening with tears.

I raised a brow at my aunt, but she merely shrugged.

We went back to the hotel. Uncle Reynolds and Ryder had coffee in the living room and I figured it was time to speak to my mom and aunt privately.

"What's going on, Mom?"

She shook her head.

"Mother, I'm not a child anymore. Tell me what's wrong."

All of a sudden she launched into a fit.

"Oh my God, Mom!" I said, hugging her.

"Your... father is having an affair!" she burst out.

"What? When?"

"It's been going on for a while now!" she cried.

"How can you be so sure? Did he confess?"

She shook her head. "But I know... I just know."

"Mom, you can't accuse Dad without proof! How can you tell?"

"He's always away... he's talking to someone secretly on the phone... I know he's having an affair!"

"Mother, come on. You can't be sure so don't stress yourself out. Dad is innocent until proven guilty."

I tried to console my mother. I knew my dad. He couldn't be having an affair. He was too sweet for that. He was a responsible guy.

Ryder didn't say much to me on our way back to his apartment. But he held my hand. I was happy about the silence and the comfort he provided.

When we reached his apartment, I picked up my phone and gave my father a call. He wasn't answering. I tried about ten times, no success.

I stared over at the wonderful New York view from Ryder's balcony. Tears threatened to pour down. How could my mother think that my dad was cheating? Maybe Mom was just being paranoid about the whole thing.

Suddenly, I felt arms wrap around me from behind. Ryder kissed my neck gently.

"Are you ready to talk?" he asked.

I sighed. "I don't even know what to say," I said. "My mother thinks my father is cheating. I tried calling my dad, but he wasn't picking up."

"How do you feel about it?"

"Confused. I love them both. But if Dad really is cheating, I don't think I'll be able to forgive him either. I know what it's like to be cheated on. It's ugly and it hurts."

"But you're better off now, aren't you?" he asked.

I turned around to face him so I could look into his eyes. "Which Ryder are you now? Ryder, the multi-millionaire, or Ryder, the substitute bartender who saved me from hell?"

"I'm Ryder Van Woodsen, the guy who would go to hell and back for you," he whispered. "Doesn't matter whether I'm rich or poor."

I smiled at him. "Then yes. I'm definitely better off now," I whispered.

He leaned down and kissed me gently. After the kiss, I sighed and gave him a hug. I leaned my head on his shoulder.

I closed my eyes and inhaled his sweet masculine scent. Ryder, whether rich or poor, was my solid rock. And he'd become more precious to me each second. I wished I were ready to jump into a new relationship. I wished Kevin Moore hadn't made me feel I would never be good enough to date a filthy rich guy. I wished Bryan hadn't taught me to protect my heart with my life. I wished Ryder was just a simple guy who would rather hold my heart in his hands than the world full of power and privilege. I wished things were just as easy as ABC or 123. I wished this moment with Ryder would be frozen for eternity. Right here. Right now. Where I was not afraid to open up my heart again. And Ryder wasn't cynical about women dating him for his money. Here, where we were on equal footing. So I wouldn't have to worry about broken hearts or shattered dreams.

"Can you stay like this forever?" I whispered.

He tightened his arms around me. He sighed. "Can *you* stay like this forever?" he asked back.

"We're complicated, Ryder."

He shook his head. "No. *You* are complicated, Astrid. Me, I know what I want. It's you who has to figure out what *you* want."

I whispered, "You can't really want me."

He took a deep breath. "But I do! God, I want you... *so much!*" There was frustration in his voice.

I stared up at him. "Ryder, I'm not ready for a relationship yet. And even if I were, I'm afraid you are more than I can handle."

"I want to kill whoever made you like this!" he whispered.

I shook my head. "It's not just that, Ryder. I don't want to get heartbroken again... especially not by you. I don't want to lose you, Ryder. So let's just... stay as we are. Uncomplicated. Friends."

He took a deep breath. When he looked back at me, I think I saw defeat in his eyes. Then finally he said, "You're still in New York. And we still have a deal." He bent to give me a thorough kiss on the lips. Then he swung me up in his arms bridal style and carried me to bed.

***

When we reached Malibu and I said goodbye to my family, I didn't feel like going home just yet.

"Wanna grab a bite?" Ryder asked.

I smiled at him and squeezed his hand. It was like he could read my thoughts loud and clear.

I nodded. He smiled at me. Then he drove to Oil Rig. The place was packed, but he led me to a reserved VIP area. He asked what I wanted to eat.

"Boy, I could really eat some steak, huh!"

He laughed. "Alright. You deserve some comfort food. Steak it is!"

My phone rang. It was Dannie. "Are you still in New York?"

"Nope. Just got back to Malibu," I replied.

"Where are you?"

"Just got to Oil Rig."

"We were there a couple of minutes ago. It's packed! Did you get a table?"

"Yeah. I'm having dinner here!"

"How did you manage that? The line was too damn long!"

"I'm with... Ryder."

"Well, of course!" I didn't miss the sarcasm in his voice.

I sighed. "I don't have time for this Dannie. My parents are having a big fight! I just want to forget about them for a while."

"Oh shoot! I'm sorry!" he said apologetically. "Can we join you there?"

I looked at Ryder and he knew what I was about to ask him before I opened my mouth. "Three?"

I nodded.

"Send them in, I'll give instructions at the reception," he said.

I smiled at him. "Thanks."

In a few minutes, Nicole, Dannie and John joined us.

I told them about New York and how my mother went there to get her mind off her fight with my father. Ryder dined with us and then he excused himself for a while to check up on his staff.

"Oh my God!" Nicole beamed looking at me. "I'm dying to ask! What is that on your neck?"

"Um... a necklace?"

"Did you buy that or did you get that as a present from your very rich boyfriend?" Dannie asked.

185

"He's not my boyfriend!" I protested.

"But he gave you that?" Dannie asked.

I sighed. They knew I couldn't afford the necklace yet, so there's no point in lying to them.

"Yeah, he did. And don't ask me why," I said.

"And you're wearing your engagement ring again!" Nicole said surveying my finger.

"I had to. My mother knew about the engagement. They were looking for a ring. Ryder had to give it back to me."

"So he never returned the ring after you returned it to him?" John asked.

I shook my head.

"What's this? He's got a standby engagement ring handy?" John teased.

I glared at John before Ryder returned to our table. Then Nicole and Dannie asked me to dance.

"He's watching you," Dannie whispered against my ear.

"Who?"

"Who else?" Dannie said looking over at our table. I turned around and saw Ryder with John. He was looking at me. When our eyes met, he winked.

"I think he really likes you," Nicole said.

"He plays his part very well!" I said. "Too well, I'm afraid my family will be heartbroken if we break this thing off. It's not real. You guys have to remember that."

"Well, tell that to *him* not us!" Nicole said evenly.

"Do you like him?" Dannie asked.

I sighed. "Yes. But do I want my heart to be broken again? No."

"But you want him."

"I've wanted him from the moment I met him. But it's... complicated. And I don't want to risk my heart or my friendship with him for something that might not last forever."

"Why do you keep saying that?"

"Because I've been there before. Guys like Ryder have fun with girls like me, but at the end of the day, their families expect them to marry within their own circle."

"Ash, one rich guy shot you down. Who knows? Maybe Ryder is different!" Nicole said.

"Do I really want to risk everything we have just to prove myself wrong?" I asked.

"Don't you think he's worth the shot?" Dannie asked.

"Guys, I came here to have a bit of fun so I could forget that my parents' marriage may be on the rocks. Leave Ryder and I alone for a while, okay?"

The two finally let it go, but I knew the looks on their faces. Someday, if I regret my decision not to go after Ryder, I had two best friends who would tell me, "*I told you so.*"

It was one in the morning when we decided to go home. I'd had six bottles of alcohol and was feeling tipsy.

"I'll take you home," Ryder offered. I said goodbye to my friends and let Ryder lead me to his car.

"When will you be back to Manhattan?" I asked him.

"Tomorrow, six a.m.," he replied. He looked at me wearily. "Are you sure you want to be alone?" he asked reaching out for my hand.

I intertwined our fingers. It felt warm and I instantly felt comforted. I didn't answer, but tears were rolling down my cheeks.

He knew the answer even though I didn't say anything. The next thing I knew, he was parking his car in front of his house.

He opened the car door for me. I'm not sure what I was doing here, but I was sure it was a lot better than whining inside my room alone.

He lit the fireplace in his living room. Then he pulled me to sit beside him on the couch. My heart pounded in my chest. He promised not to make any move on me. The deal we had expired the minute we left New York.

He put his arms around me and held me.

"It's okay, love. You can cry if you want to. For now, that's all you can do. At least it will make you feel better," he said gently.

I buried my face on his chest and let the tears fall again. But now, I knew I was not alone. I had Ryder with me... my savior, my rock.

I must have fallen asleep. When I opened my eyes, I was resting comfortably against soft mattresses. Light was seeping through the glass doors. I could hear the soothing sound of the waves on the ocean.

I propped up my elbows and found myself lying on Ryder's soft bed, with the comforters draped over me to keep me warm. There was no sign of Ryder. I looked at my wristwatch for the time. It was already nine in the morning. I sat up and found myself dressed in a big baggy shirt that I was sure was Ryder's.

I remembered that he had to take the six a.m. flight. Did he cancel his trip?

I stood up from the bed and went out of the bedroom.

"Ryder!" I called. No answer.

I went to his living room. There were keys on the table, and there was a note under them.

Ash,

I hope you'll be okay while I'm gone. There's a meeting in Manhattan that I can't miss. Otherwise, I would have stayed.

Keep the keys with you until I come back. You're welcome to stay here anytime you want... in fact, I would like it if you do.

Don't worry too much. Things will fall into place soon. And if they don't, you know I'll always be here for you. You just say the word...

Call me as soon as you wake up.

By the way, you can arm and disarm the alarm system. The passcode is 278743.

Love,

Ryder

I read the note a couple of times. Tears rolled down my eyes again. But this time, I wasn't crying because of my parents' problems. I was crying because I missed Ryder already.

He'd been the epitome of strength to me. He's been there in my darkest hours. He helped me get back on my feet. He'd been too sweet, too kind. And every day, I wished more and more that he was not a complicated man. That he was just the boy next door that I could hope to have an 'ever after' with. So I wouldn't be scared to take a chance with him.

I dialed his number. He answered in one ring. "Good morning, love," he greeted cheerily.

"Good morning."

"Do you feel better?"

"Yeah. Except I need coffee," I said.

He laughed. "I have a coffee maker in the kitchen. Water's in the fridge."

I walked over to his fridge. Its only contents were a box of milk, a pitcher of water, a box of orange juice and a pack of butter.

"Do you live in this place at all?" I asked giggling. "Your fridge is almost empty."

He sighed. "I can't really trust the maids to refill the fridge."

"So what do you do when you're here and you need to... eat?"

"I order out. Or I call the bar and have one of the guys bring me food. Or I just simply go out."

"Don't you want to stock up your fridge at all? I mean, you're here at least once a week."

"Well, I just don't have the time to do the grocery shopping."

"Oh well, would you have time for anything other than work?"

"I have time to be your fiancé, don't I?"

I felt guilty. That was true. No matter how busy he was, Ryder magically found the time to pose as my devoted fiancé in front of my family.

"I'm sorry I impose on you too much."

"Why are you sorry?" he asked. "I like being your fiancé."

I sighed. I wished it were true. That he really likes being my fiancé... and not just for the sake of the charade.

I broke the uncomfortable silence that followed. "I forgot to give you back your ring."

"It's your ring, Astrid," he said in a serious tone.

"Ryder... I don't want to have this argument anymore."

"Neither do I," he replied.

I held out my hand and looked at the beautiful ring on my finger.

"You don't give thirty thousand dollar diamond rings to strangers, Ryder."

"You're not a stranger, Astrid."

"You promised you'd find a good reason. Our engagement in New York was just make believe. So I'm compelled to give this back to you."

He laughed. "Alright. You win," he said. "Just hold on to it until I get back."

"Can't I leave it here?"

"No. Please. My safe will be installed next week. It's more secure on your finger. I promise I'll take it back when I see you."

"When are you coming back?"

"A couple of days."

"Alright. I'll have coffee and then I'll lock up," I said.

"Hold on to the key for me," he said. "Ash..."

"Yes?"

"You can go there anytime you want."

I laughed. "Ryder, you go to another person's house to visit them. Why will I go here if you're not here?"

"Well, just in case you need a change of scene." He chuckled.

I walked over to his living room. "Hmmm... that I can use." I looked at his movie collection. "Have you watched all these movies?"

"Some," he replied. "Some I'm finding time to watch."

I read some of the titles on his huge collection. "Let's see what sort of movies Ryder Van Woodsen fancies... *The Godfather, Scarface, The Godfather II, The Godfather III*... you're an Al Pacino fan." I went all the way to the other side. "There you go! *Notting Hill, My Best Friend's Wedding, Runaway Bride, Stepmom*... you're a fan of Julia Roberts, too. Hey, there's a movie I'd like to watch! *Pretty Woman!*"

"You haven't seen *Pretty Woman*?" he asked.

"In passing," I said. "My friends in college were watching it once, I was cramming for an exam the next day."

"Hmmm... you can watch it."

"One of these days, when I need to unwind, I just might treat myself to a pizza and a movie here at your place."

"You're welcome anytime. You have the keys," he said.

We chatted for another ten minutes and then I said goodbye to him. Then I finished my coffee and went off.

For the next few days, I kept my mind off my parents' problems by keeping myself busy. Ryder and I had been texting each other almost every hour. He narrated what happened each day to me. I did the same. Every night, he would call me and we would talk until one of us would fall asleep. It was like he was not in Manhattan at all. Like, he was just right there beside me.

19.

USHERETTES:

Their role is to make sure that your guests do not lose their way on your wedding party.

One night, Ryder called me to ask a favor.

"The maid will come tomorrow. Usually I'm there when she does. But I won't make it this week. Can you stop by my house? She doesn't have a key. Just let her in and stay there while she does her stuff."

"You want me to supervise your maid?"

"Not really. Just be there to make sure that everything's in order."

"Alright. I think I can handle that."

The next day, I went to Ryder's house. His maid was a woman in her forties named Zara. She didn't look like a maid at first, more like a diner waitress. She was chewing gum and was wearing a skirt way above her knees.

"Where is Mr. Ryder?" she asked me.

"He's in Manhattan," I replied. It looked to me that she was disappointed that the boss was not in. Judging by her makeup and her short skirt, this woman had another agenda in mind in cleaning Ryder's house. I didn't like that idea.

"Are you one of his employees in the bar?" she asked.

I shook my head. "No."

"Relative?" she asked again.

I shook my head.

"Employee in Manhattan?" she insisted.

I turned to her. In a very controlled voice, I said, "No. I'm his... fiancée."

She was taken aback. Then she looked at me from head to feet, sort of measuring me. "Sorry. It's just that the boss never brought any woman in this house. You were the first."

"That's very comforting to know," I said to her. Then I took my Chinese takeout to the deck and ate.

Zara finished her chores after two hours. Before she left, I checked if everything was in order. I checked the plants, the rooms, the bathrooms, and the kitchen. I must admit, she did a very good job. She was very thorough. Even though I was irritated with her for attempting to seduce Ryder, her great job in the house deserved a tip. And so I gave her a generous one.

She smiled at me. "Well, I guess you and the boss are two of a kind. Congratulations on your engagement."

I smiled at her. "Thank you, Zara. Have a nice day."

When she was gone, I called Ryder.

"Did you sleep with your maid?" I asked him.

"Hell no!" he replied. "Why? What's wrong?"

"Oh my God! Didn't you notice that she was trying to… make you notice her or something?"

"I'm not naïve, Ash. But I'm also not interested."

"Really? Short skirt, bulging neckline?"

"Nope," he said. "But it is uncomfortable for me to be in the same room with her."

"Why? Difficult trying to keep yourself cool?" I joked.

"No. More like… difficult trying to keep myself from throwing her out of the house! Just so you know, I don't like aggressive women."

"Ryder, she asked me who I was."

"You should have told her you're my fiancée," he said.

"I did actually," I said shyly.

"That should stop her from going to work in… shrunken clothing!" He chuckled.

"Wow! Cleaning day must be difficult for you, huh."

"Not my favorite part of the week. However, she does a very good job. As much as I don't trust her, I am happy that she keeps the place dust-free. If I could only just leave her alone in the house and just wire her the money… if that would work, that would be heaven for me."

I don't know why I volunteered for the job, but the next thing I knew, I was offering to watch the house whenever Zara was around to clean up.

"That would be great, Ash! You can schedule it at a time convenient for you."

"Not a problem," I said. "You do me all sorts of favors anyway. It's time I make it up to you. We're friends, remember?"

"With benefits?" he teased.

"Before. But that ship has sailed." I giggled. "Now, let's try to be normal friends. I never was a friend-with-benefit type of girl before I met you."

"You were innocent when you met me, Astrid," he said. "I shouldn't have touched you."

That stung. "Thanks!" I said sarcastically.

"Don't get me wrong!" he said quickly. "What I meant was… the most amazing night of my life would be the end of me." I heard his sharp intake of breath. "I shouldn't have started what I couldn't finish. I shouldn't want what I cannot have." There was sadness in his voice. For a while, I thought my heart was going to break.

"Ryder…"

"I know!" he interrupted. "I'm Ryder Van Woodsen, right?"

"You're my knight in shining armor, Ryder. But I don't believe in fairy tales anymore. I don't want to wake up one day and find myself shattering to pieces again. Bryan broke me, and you fixed me. If I break because of you, I don't think I can be fixed again. So please, I would rather have you in my life, as a dear friend. And I will love you forever."

He didn't say anything for a whole minute. Then he sighed. "Whatever makes you happy, Ash," he said in a broken voice. "I gotta go. I have a meeting in five minutes."

"Bye." I hung up.

My heart felt heavy. I couldn't help the tears from rolling down my face. *Damn!* He's not even my boyfriend, and I'm sad and heartbroken already!

I was protecting my heart. I didn't think I could take the pressure of being Ryder Van Woodsen's girlfriend. It would be too demanding and I would want from him more than phone calls, more than a few dates. I would want more. I would want him to love me... not just *want* me.

I would want an ever after with him, but this was not a fairy tale where Prince Charming meets Cinderella and *boom*! He wants to marry her that very instant.

Ryder's life was too complicated for me. Plus he lived in Manhattan most of the time. I didn't want a relationship that was technically long-distance. Bryan was right under my nose and he screwed me big time!

I knew I made him sad with my decision to stay friends. Someday, he would understand. We both had to accept that this was the way we should be. Close friends that were there for each other and do each other crazy favors.

Since I was doing favors anyway, I decided to grab my bag, hopped into a cab and went to the grocery store. I bought boxes of milk, juices, beer, flavored vodka, ice cream, patties, hotdogs, eggs, and some microwaveable noodles and pasta. I also bought peeled, ready to eat carrots and some other veggies.

It was a lot to carry, but I was happy with what I was doing. I wanted to do Ryder a favor. It was nothing compared to the necklace that he gave me, but when I placed everything inside his fridge, I felt happy and excited. Now, the huge expansive fridge looked like a real fridge. It was such a small thing to do for him... in return for all the things he did for me.

***

Friday, I finished with a wedding before midnight. Ryder surprised me by picking me up at the hotel where the reception was held.

"I didn't know you were coming!" I said.

"Then it wouldn't be a surprise." He laughed. "You want to grab something to eat?"

I smiled. "I'm starving. But my feet are killing me!"

He drove to his place and called his staff to bring some food to us.

"Drinks?" he asked.

"Watermelon vodka would be nice," I replied.

"Ahh…" He hesitated and then he opened his fridge. I smiled to myself. I knew he noticed how it was now filled with all sorts of things. "Hmmm… looks like Santa did a stopover and filled my fridge."

After a few seconds, he was sitting on the sofa beside me. "That was sweet." He said looking at me deeply and then he handed me my vodka. "Thank you."

I smiled at him. "You're welcome. It's not much compared to the necklace, but I'm glad you liked it."

"I loved it," he whispered. He stared at me for a long while, his eyes holding emotions I couldn't understand.

I raised a brow at him in question. He sighed and then he smiled weakly. That smile seemed sad… frustrated even.

I looked away from him, unable to look at him looking like that. He was my rock. And I didn't want to see him breaking because of me. But I didn't want to break because of him, too. It did not matter what I wanted now. What mattered was what I didn't want to happen again in the future.

When he took me home, I took the ring off my finger and handed it to him. He raised a brow at me.

I laughed. "You're not tricking me into wearing this without a reason, Ryder. You promised."

He smiled and then took the ring from me. "Alright. A deal's a deal."

I nodded. "That's right." Then I fished his keys from my pocket. "And here are your keys."

"Keep it."

"Why?"

"You promised to watch the maid for me," he reminded. "And it's nice to have a restocked fridge when you get home."

I laughed. "Touché! Alright, I'll keep it."

"I'm serious, Ash. You can really go there and stay anytime you want. When it's late and you're still there, please don't go out alone. Stay the night."

"I'm not a kid, Ryder! Who will assault me?"

"But you, my love, possess something that appeals to some criminals, particularly men. And I'm afraid I'm not comfortable with the thought of you being on your own in the streets at night."

"I've lived in this neighborhood for months!" I rolled my eyes. "I know it's not Manhattan where you just go out of your apartment and people are everywhere. But sometimes, it's just your luck. You go, you go."

"Have you heard of something called, 'tempting fate'? What if you're not yet supposed to go, but you twisted your own fate?"

194

I laughed. "This argument will never finish! Okay, I'll take care of myself. I won't go down any dark alleys. I won't walk from your house to mine alone when it's dark."

Our conversation was interrupted by a phone call. It was my mother.

"Are you okay, Mom?" I asked.

"I'm perfect!" She sounded so happy. "Your father and I talked. He wasn't having an affair. He was planning a surprise for me actually. A little anniversary celebration. He'd like to reaffirm his love for me. He's been so secretive about it, that I thought he was having an affair! I'm so... stupid."

"Wow! That is great! But I'm hurt! Why didn't he tell me? I'm a wedding planner! I could have arranged everything for you!"

"He doesn't want to bother you, he knows you're too busy with work already because you've just started. Plus, it's a small event. You and Ryder are expected to be here next weekend for our family reunion. If you don't come, I will disown you."

I laughed. "Alright, mother. We'll be there," I said after my mother told me what day and time we are expected. After I hung up, I stared at Ryder. "Are you busy next weekend?"

"Your mother talks quite loudly, I heard half of your conversation already," he said chuckling. "I'm glad they're okay now. And yes, I will come to your family reunion... as your fiancé."

I smiled at him. "Thank you, Ryder. You've been... so patient with me. I don't even know why you're doing this."

He smiled at me. "Someday, I'll tell you."

I don't know what he meant by that, but I didn't insist.

"Okay, so pick me up at three on Friday? Is that okay with you?"

He nodded. "I'll be here. On the dot. Promise."

I smiled. Then I reached out for his hand and gave it a squeeze. "Thank you, Ryder."

"You're always welcome." He smiled.

20.
ARRANGED MARRIAGE:
A marriage born out of a business arrangement where both parties aim to benefit from the other.

Adam asked me to have dinner with him. But I knew my cousin better. He only invited me over for dinner to either drop a bomb on my head or he'd touch base on what's going on with the business. So even though it was casual, I was ready with the figures in my head, just in case he asks.

"Business is good?" he asked casually.

"I knew you took me to dinner for a reason!" I accused, pointing a finger at him.

He chuckled. "Just asking."

I smiled at him. "It's great!" I said. "In a few months, you'll see those figures going green."

"Maybe it's time to expand."

I stared at him. "What do you mean?"

He shrugged. "Well, my investor saw the last reports we gave and he… was impressed. He sees opportunities in bigger cities and asked if you were willing to take the business there."

"Adam, it's too soon." Although I admit I have been thinking about this.

He smiled. "And yet look how far you've gone! The numbers you're giving me plus the ones on your pipeline are pretty impressive."

"Wow!" I breathed. My heart jumped for joy. It's always good to be complimented for a job well done… especially by Adam. "Tell him, I'm flattered. It's good to know that your investor understands that businesses take time to earn profits, but we are going on an amazing rate."

"That's why he's serious about branching out," he said.

Talk about luck. It seems so timely for Adam's friends to think about branching out. Just a couple of weeks ago, Ryder was mentioning the same thing to me.

"I'm thrilled, Adam! But it's a huge step! I don't think I've even proven myself here."

He smiled. "I think you've proven yourself enough for him to believe that this idea will work if taken upscale, too."

"It will take a lot of money!" I said wearily.

"And my investor has deep pockets!" He grunted.

"How… soon?"

"As soon as you say yes, I guess. You can work out the proposal."

"What will happen to this branch? Will they close this down? I don't think I can bear that. This is my baby."

He laughed. "Relax. You can run two branches, can't you? This branch will still stay. You can hire someone to oversee everything so you don't need to be hands on, and then you can build the second branch."

We discussed the possibilities. By the end of dinner, he convinced me that this may be a big step, but it's a great opportunity for me. I told him I'd hire Nicole to manage the Malibu branch. Ryder crossed my mind, and I knew the first city I'll look into.

"Can I choose where to go?"

"My investor already has a city in mind."

My heart sank. What if I don't like the place they want to go to? I hope Adam doesn't say Timbuktu or anywhere outside the country.

"Wh-where?" I asked wearily.

"New York. Manhattan."

Wow! Talk about luck! Or... fate!

I did have my heart set on Manhattan; Ryder was there. I'd been there. Ryder already showed me the places where I could get supplies.

That was really good! But you know, if something sounds too good to be true, it probably is.

My hands started getting cold. A thought played in my mind and I didn't know what to do with it. I was afraid to ask Adam. I know I still had to, because if I didn't, that thought would not let me sleep at night.

When Adam took the check, I asked, "Adam... you have very rich friends don't you?"

"Well, yeah. It's good for my job."

"This investor or investors, aren't they asking to take some profits now?"

"The red figures on the report decreases every month. Now we're on breakeven. When you invest here and there, you know the rules. I'm sure the pressure to see the green will not come until after three months or more."

"How many investors were there?" I asked.

"One," he replied. Then he stood up. "Come, let's go."

While we're waiting for the valet to bring Adam's car, I asked, "Is there another investor who came up to you and suggested a branch in Manhattan would be a good potential? Or is this the same guy?"

He looked at me and drew his brows together. "Why are you asking these questions, Ash?"

I shrugged. "Putting up a new branch takes a lot of money. I just want to know if we'll answer to more than one guy if we branch out in Manhattan. Different people respond to different types of news."

"Same guy, Ash. Let *me* worry about that. You just do what you do best," Adam replied in an irritated tone.

The car came and Adam and I drove to my place. I was still lost in thought. Adam's news was great! But somehow, I found it too great. And just too much of a coincidence!

"Why so quiet?" Adam asked.

I took a deep breath. "I'm thinking, Adam."

"Hey, you can think!" Adam said with a feigned shocked expression on his face.

"Ha-ha! Very funny. And I'm usually smart too! That's why I feel compelled to ask... You have one investor. Is his name *Ryder Van Woodsen?*"

Adam didn't answer. I stared at him. He was staring ahead at the road. I counted. *One, two, three...* it seemed to go on forever. *Nine, Ten.* Still Adam didn't respond and that alone told me the answer I was waiting for.

"Oh my God!" I threw my hands up in the air. Adam bit his lip. It seems that for the first time in many years, he didn't know what to say.

"Why?"

"Why what?" he asked.

"Why did you do this?"

"Do what, Astrid?" he asked back. "Allow the guy to invest in your talent because he believes in you? Because he doesn't want you to waste your brilliance working for people who would only take advantage of you? Or allow him to help you get back on your feet and see yourself the way he sees you?"

I could tell that Adam was holding back his anger. But I couldn't do the same. I was humiliated. Was Ryder playing me all along? Was I... a business investment? He said he knew the reason why he was doing me all these favors... and now I do too! He's making sure he doesn't invest in a losing venture.

Adam and I started working on this business even before I found out that Ryder Woodson, my bartender, was really Ryder Van Woodsen, the heir born with a silver spoon! When I thought I would never see him again, he'd been there all along! Investing in me. Banking on my talents!

We stopped in front of my house.

"Look Ash... Ryder came to me and said he thought you were brilliant at what you do and didn't want your talents to go to waste. Plus, he thought that you working on what you do best, and what you love the most would restore your spirits, which he so adored from the moment he met you.

"He was looking at investing in something other than what his family's been doing for decades anyway. He thought it would be perfect if you started your own wedding planning company. He didn't want you to know it was him because he knew you would never agree. So he asked me to take over. But he wanted nothing to do with it. He's just a capitalist. He just wanted reports on a monthly basis to see the progress. He wanted you to have full control."

I couldn't believe what I was hearing. And worse, I didn't know how to feel! I'd always thanked Ryder for my recovery. My getting back on the wedding planning business was the only thing I thought I didn't owe him. But I was wrong. What was he trying to do? Was he buying me?

"How could you not tell me this, Adam? You know I've been torn by lies already. How can you not warn me?"

Adam took a deep breath and I can tell he felt guilty. "Ash... I wanted to. But back when we started all this, you didn't know that the date you brought to that wedding really was *the* Ryder Van Woodsen. I was right; you were hell bent on hating him when you found out. Then, when you finally found your common ground, I didn't know how to tell you anymore. And believe it or not, Ryder also didn't know how without losing you. For all it's worth, Ash, I think the guy's crazy about you. Give him some credit."

"What credit? For tricking me into managing his business venture?"

"For getting you back on your feet! For believing in you when you didn't believe in yourself anymore, and employing all means to make sure that you do again!" he said angrily.

I was upset because I felt manipulated and played. Ryder Van Woodsen, his money and his silly games!

I got out of Adam's car.

"Ash!" He ran after me. "Please be rational about the whole thing. Just think about how good Ryder had been for you."

"Maybe that's the problem, Adam. He's *too* good for me! And now, I found out that I was a business venture! Welcome to the lifestyle of the rich and the famous, right?"

Adam closed his eyes in dismay. Then he threw his hands in the air. "Alright, fine! I've told you everything I know. Maybe it's time you wake up from this dream and face reality Ash! It's time to break your fake relationship with Van Woodsen so you can finally see the difference between what's fake and what's real!"

"Well, Adam, I can't break up with Ryder if he wasn't really my boyfriend, can I?" I asked back angrily.

"Are you sure, he's not your boyfriend, Ash?"

He stared at me intensely. I opened my mouth to respond but surprisingly, no sound came out. I guess... I wasn't entirely sure what my answer would be.

Adam sighed. "And for your information, he's only willing to invest in Manhattan if you're a hundred percent sure you want to move there. Otherwise, he's willing to fly in and out of L.A. as frequently as it takes."

He gave me one hard look and then he was gone.

I was trying to sort out the way I felt. It's been a while since I felt heartbroken, and now, I'm feeling like that again. But why did I feel this way about something that wasn't really mine? Ryder and I were nothing, and we could never be anything!

So he was my boss. I worked for him. Now, it's even more complicated.

But shouldn't it be complicated only if I were dating him for real? We're friends! A couple of times, we did slip away from the boundaries of morality... but who doesn't sell herself to the devil for a few moments of heaven once in a while?

Maybe Adam's right. It was time to face reality. Because in reality, as I knew it, Ryder and I were nothing. No commitments. No strings attached.

He'd done me plenty of favors, I'd repaid my debt. He invested in my talents; I'd established his business. In a few months, I'd be able to show him profits, and then I would be free to go. It gave me time to look for something else, somewhere else. It wouldn't be a lost investment for him because I would hand it over to somebody capable... someone like Nicole.

It was time to wake up from this dream and start facing reality. I planned to tell my family that I broke up with Ryder. He was too serious about getting married, whereas, I had learned the value of not rushing into things when I broke up with Bryan. I wanted to enjoy single-hood, and he wanted to settle down right away. I'd tell them that as much as he was a good catch, I was not good enough for him now.

A huge part of me felt shattered. As if I really did break up with Ryder... as if the relationship were real.

I met up with my friends the next night and I told them the truth.

"What?" I asked. "Are you not going to say anything?"

Dannie sighed. "I would. But you're not going to like it."

I raised a brow at him. When did Dannie care about my feelings? When he opens his mouth and lets his brains spill out! "Say it!"

He shrugged. "Are you sure Ryder isn't your boyfriend?"

"He's a friend. Sometimes, he's a fling. Because I wasn't ready to date just yet."

"That's dense, Ash!" Nicole said crossly. "You were ready to date ages ago! You just didn't want to. You don't feel the need to because Ryder's there!"

"He's my rock!" I sighed. "But I knew from the start that we could never be! Whatever we had was temporary! We're like the best of friends. But beyond that... I'm scared it wouldn't last. So... I would rather have him as a friend forever."

"Then why aren't you dating anybody else? Not even *one* date, Ash! Your thoughts, your time, your days are pre-occupied by Ryder Van Woodsen and you don't mind. In fact, you love it! So he's not nothing to you!"

"He's not!" I said crossly. "He's… a dream. And it's time to wake up now."

They looked at each other wearily. Then Dannie said to me, "Okay. Try. One date. Go out with another guy. Maybe you'll be able to tell the difference."

"I'm not sure I'm ready." I sighed.

"You're ready to have a relationship, Ash! You're so over Bryan, which was the point of your whole charade with Ryder! But still you refused to date because you're not waking up from your dream, if that's what Ryder is! It's him you want!" Nicole said.

"It doesn't matter! Guys like Ryder want you for a while… but in the end, they are bound to marry their female counterparts. Rich. Privileged."

"Then try going out with somebody else. Maybe you don't need to move on from Bryan anymore. You need to move on from Ryder!"

That thought still echoed in my head until the next day. I wasn't myself when I met with the preferred photographer of one of my clients.

Ryder hadn't called me or texted me in days. Ten bucks says that he'd already spoken to Adam. Maybe even the great Ryder Van Woodsen needed time to make up excuses!

"You okay?" Tyler asked.

I shook myself back to reality. "I'm sorry. I just… didn't have much sleep last night. You were saying?"

He smiled. "I'll show you these styles in the coffee shop around the corner. I can use some caffeine as well."

I stretched out from my seat. "You're probably right."

We went to Starbucks. After getting our coffee, we discussed the shots that the bride would like to take specifically. I suggested places, and took down the list of establishments I have to contact to make the arrangements.

Afterwards, Tyler and I had a chat about the business. When we finished, I stood up and gathered my things.

"Tomorrow night," Tyler said. "I have a little get-together with some photographers I know. Do you want to come as my date?"

I shook my head. "I'm sorry."

If Tyler was surprised, he didn't show it. In fact, I think he was more amused when I turned him down.

"Boyfriend?"

"No."

"Just broken up?"

I didn't answer. I have gotten out of a bad relationship a long time ago. And yet… why am I turning down a date with Tyler?

"Okay. I'll change my answer. Yes, I'll come with you as your date."

There was nothing wrong with saying yes to Tyler. It was probably the first time I'd been formally asked out by a guy after Bryan. Not as a favor or as repayment of my debt.

I knew I should feel excited. Instead, I felt … really uncomfortable. The feelings were too strong; I wanted to call Tyler even at six o'clock the next evening to cancel.

Tyler was cute. An average guy with ambition; someone like me. I really didn't understand why I felt so heavy inside. Even when he picked me up from my place, my heart felt like it was going to break in half and shatter to the ground. Like I had to stop this whole thing and be somewhere else.

Most of the people in the party were photographers, and some of them were like me, brought in as dates. I should have been feeling happy to meet all these people. But the fact that we met up in Rig Style made it more difficult. The place had a way of reminding me of somebody I really didn't want to remember.

I belong in this world. I kept repeating to myself. Somehow, I felt silly because I didn't know why I felt so out of place. I wasn't even at ease talking to these people.

I stood in one corner while Tyler talked to one of his friends on the other table. Man, this date was the worst! And it was not because of Tyler!

"Still working?" I heard someone ask behind me. The hairs at the back of my neck rose as I felt his warm breath in my ear.

I was almost too afraid to turn around to face the owner of that very familiar voice.

I stared at Ryder blankly. The expression on his face was hard to describe. He looked sober and haggard, as if he hadn't slept in days. He looked… miserable.

When I looked into his eyes, a voice inside me was involuntarily saying, *This is where I belong. This is where I belong.* I wanted to hug and kiss him and lose myself in his masculine scent, his warm embrace.

Then all of a sudden, I felt Tyler put his arm around my shoulders.

Ryder threw him a cold, murderous look that I hadn't seen before.

But instead of being intimidated, Tyler held his ground and in that jolly expression he seemed to always have, he asked, "Is there a problem, mate?"

Ryder raised a brow at him and then he turned to me. I didn't know what to say to him. I wanted to remove Tyler's arm from around me, but I found that my limbs were frozen. Including my tongue!

In a voice colder than the look on his face, Ryder said, "Oh, I get it. You're on a *date!*" He made it sound like it is the most disgusting thing he's heard in his entire life.

"Excuse me, but I don't think I'll allow you to harass my date, mate. So back off before I call the bouncer on you."

Ha-ha! Ridiculous! If only Tyler knew who he was talking to.

"Is that all you got? *Call the bouncer on me?*" Ryder asked squarely. "I'd like to see you try, *mate.*"

Tyler removed his arm from my shoulders and started pushing Ryder.

Oh God! Kill me now!

"Stop!" I said to both men. I was doing this for Tyler. For his health and his pride. Ryder could doubtlessly strangle a man with his bare hands with all the martial arts training he had.

Ryder gave me a hard look. "Please?" I pleaded him.

He gave me one last stern look and then I saw defeat cross his face. "Fine!" Then he stared at Tyler one last time and then he walked away.

A part of me wanted to run after him. Another part of me kept scolding myself for feeling bad. Ryder was not my boyfriend. Yes, we did sleep with each other sometimes. Yes, we did go out... as a favor to each other. But other than that, there is nothing about us that is real. All of those kisses, all of those hugs were for the show and for the favors we did each other... there were some that were real, but we both decided on their expiry dates and they never happened again after the last time.

But why did I feel so guilty? Why did being there with Tyler feel so wrong? Was there a part of me that truly belonged to Ryder?

When Tyler took me home, I still was not in the mood to talk. When he walked me to my door, and leaned his face down to kiss me, I turned away. "I'm sorry," I said to him. I couldn't bear to kiss him.

"I thought so." He smiled. "I guess, you're not ready to go out with somebody else yet."

I stared up at him. "What do you mean?"

"Is that your ex? The guy in the bar?"

I didn't answer. Because I didn't know what Ryder was to me anymore.

"Seems that he's not over you yet either. Maybe you two just need to sort out your differences. He looked like he was about to murder me when I put an arm around you. And you... you look like you wanted to be with somebody else all evening."

Tyler smiled at me and then he leaned forward to kiss my forehead.

"I really did like you, Astrid," he said. "But perhaps in another lifetime..." He smiled.

He went to his car and before he drove off, he said to me, "See you at the photo shoot. Good luck with your guy."

Was Tyler right? Did I really want to be with somebody else? Did I feel wrong about going out with him because I really do belong with

Ryder already? And if he looked like he wanted to murder Tyler, did that mean he felt I belong to him too?

I didn't know what I was doing, or why, but the next thing I knew, I was sprinting towards Ryder's house. I didn't know what I would say to him, but maybe when I saw him, I would know. When I stared into his eyes at the bar, it seemed that some things made sense... especially about the way I felt about him. Maybe all I needed to do was talk to him once and for all. Maybe it was time to wake up from the dream and start facing reality.

Whatever came out of our conversation tonight, it seemed that I would have to break off my engagement with him tomorrow in front of my family. I need to stop living a lie. For both our sakes... I need to start moving on.

His car was parked in front of his house. *Great! He's home!*

I rang the bell twice. No answer.

Courage, Ash. Courage. I said to myself. *It's now or never.*

I heard movement from the other side of the door and I braced myself.

When the door opened, I was shocked. I guess the answer to my questions would be... *never!*

Long legs, light blonde hair, sparkling blue eyes.

"Oh my God!" Alizia breathed when she saw me. "I'm... I'm really sorry... I didn't mean to... Ryder is upstairs. I thought..." I saw shame cross her face as she trailed off.

Ryder came up behind her. "Who's that..." He trailed off when he saw me.

Not this again! When can my relationships not end with another woman on the background?

I composed myself and with all the courage I could muster, I said, "Just me. I just wanted to tell you that you don't need to come to my parents' thing tomorrow. It's better that way. I'll be the one to tell them that it's over." I stared up at Ryder.

I refused to let tears blind me. *I'm not crying over some guy who wasn't really mine!* At least not in front of him. "We're... over," I said and then I turned on my heel and left.

21.
WEDDING ANNIVERSARY:
A celebration of another year of marriage, no divorce, no separation. Whew!

*F*riday morning, I called up Adam. I wasn't really mad at him. I knew that he was only looking out for me. I told him that I would catch a ride with him, as I wouldn't be going with Ryder to my parents' party.

"And if they look for Ryder, what will you tell them?" Adam asked.

"That we're taking time off. That I wasn't ready. Ryder is a wonderful guy, but he was too serious about getting married and I'm not ready for that commitment yet. Plus, he's in Manhattan eighty percent of the time."

"And what will you *really* do about Ryder, Astrid?" he asked.

I took a deep breath. "He's not my boyfriend. He's... my boss apparently. I'll keep working on this, until the profits start coming in. And then I'll look for other opportunities. Don't worry; you can hire Nicole to take over. She's just as good as I am," I said. "Then give me a month or two, I'll move out of my room too."

"You didn't have to do that, Ash," Adam said. "Ryder has no intention of pulling out his investment."

"I don't want to owe him anything anymore, Adam."

He sighed. "Alright, whatever. I'll pick you up at two."

Ten minutes to two, I went out of the house to wait for Adam.

I almost choked when I saw Ryder's car outside. He was leaning on the passenger door.

"Wh-what are you doing here?" I asked him.

He was wearing a pair of pitch-dark shades, I couldn't see his eyes. The arctic look on his face matches the glacial tone of his voice. "If you want to end this, let's end it together."

"What do you mean? You're gonna come with me to my parents' anniversary so we can tell them that we're over?"

"Yeah, why not? That's what you wanted, right?" he said coolly.

I took a deep breath. "It's gonna be harder for me to tell them if you're there!"

"Then it's gonna be harder. I'm sorry, love, but if there's one thing I will not make easy for you, this is it," he said raising his brow.

"Adam is supposed to pick me up!" I said.

"No, he's not," he said. "He's probably on his way there." Then he motioned his hand for me to get into his car. "Ma'am?"

I groaned and then I got in. He rounded his car and hopped into the driver's seat. We drove off in silence. I looked out the window. My heart was hammering against my chest.

I wanted to touch Ryder. He looked even more handsome than he did the last time I saw him. Only then, his expression was warm and jolly, like I was perfect in his eyes. But now, the look on his face was serious and irritated.

The music inside his car was loud. He made no effort to lower the volume. It was as if he wanted me to know that he was in no mood to talk. And I was glad. I didn't know what to say to him either.

Finally, we arrived at my parents' house.

My family greeted us warmly. Ryder removed his sunglasses to reveal his eyes. He looked like he hadn't slept in days. When he smiled at my parents, that smile didn't touch his eyes. When his eyes met mine, his expression was dry and impassive.

Where is the Ryder Van Woodsen I've known and liked?

I felt like crying. I missed him—the Ryder that I fell asleep talking to over the phone and in bed; the Ryder who playfully gets carried away with hugging and kissing me.

We greeted our relatives. Ryder felt right at home with them. He played with my nieces. Many of them still remembered him from the wedding. We were with my family all day, but somehow, we avoided each other.

I was trying to find the right time to tell my parents that Ryder and I were over. I knew they would be very concerned. I'd tell them that we decided to remain friends and that is why he still came with me.

I found my mother in the kitchen. I helped her with the cupcakes she was preparing.

"You seemed very happy," I told her.

"How can I not be? Your father loves me the same way after all these years!" She beamed. Then she looked at me. "My only daughter is with a man who will take care of her better than I hoped."

I looked away from her guiltily. I took a deep breath. "Yeah, about Ryder and I..." I started. "We're not..."

Just then Ryder burst into the room with my eight-year-old niece Carol on his back. *Must he be such a pain?*

"I'm beat, little princess," He told her as he put her down. "Why don't you play with your brother outside while I catch my breath?"

Then he turned to us. My mother was smiling at him widely.

"You need help there, Mom?" he asked.

Mom? What the hell?

I narrowed my eyes. "Why are you calling her 'Mom'?" I demanded.

"I told him to. You'll be married in a year's time anyway," my mother said.

"Who said we're getting married in a year's time?" I asked.

"Ryder did. I asked him when the big date is and he said he's just given you a year to tie all the loose ends in your life and he'll keep the pressure on! But by the looks of it, maybe it's less than a year." My mother smiled.

I stared at Ryder. How could he tell my mother that? He knew I was going to tell them that we're over!

I glared at him. He gave me that crooked smile. And instead of being fazed by my anger, he winked at me and turned to my mother. "Yes. I can't wait for her to be Mrs. Astrid Van Woodsen."

My mother laughed. "We'll always be thankful for the day you met Astrid. When Bry…." my mother trailed off.

"It's okay," Ryder said. "I know everything about Bryan and what he did. In fact, it was during those difficult times that I met Ash. It was his loss, and my gain. Astrid is a gem."

"You're too sweet, Ryder. And you know we already consider you a part of this family."

Oh great! Just perfect!

Then my mother turned to me. "You were about to tell me something, dear?" my mother asked.

Ryder raised a brow at me. "Yes, love. What were you about to say to *Mom*?" He won this game and he knew it. There was no way I would tell my mother that Ryder and I were over after all *that*.

I was fuming. How could he make this so hard for me?

"Nothing," I said. "I'm going to get some air."

I went into the backyard and found my father sitting on one of the tables smoking a cigar.

"How are you Dad?" I asked.

He smiled. "I'm happy, sweetheart. Thirty years of marriage. And I'm still in love with your mother the same way."

"I envy you. You found your 'ever after'."

He laughed. "You found yours, too," he said motioning over to where Ryder was now, talking animatedly to Uncle Reynolds and two of my aunts. "You're very lucky. He didn't have to be rich as long as he's in love with you. Looks like you got lucky in both departments."

I took a deep breath. I opened my mouth to tell him that Ryder and I were over. Then I looked at Ryder. He looked genuinely amused when he laughed at Uncle Reynolds's joke.

"That's one man who will do anything for you, Ash," my father said. "I didn't really like Bryan that much, but you loved him and you were happy when you told us you were engaged. When he cheated on you, I wanted to shoot him between the eyes."

My eyes widened at my father's comment. I didn't know he felt that way when he found out about Bryan and Geena.

"Then you went to that wedding all happy and in love… with a man who is more in love with you than Bryan ever was… and Ryder is a more decent man. He makes an effort not only to impress you, but also your family. And I couldn't be any happier this day. I'm happy about my marriage to your mother, and I'm happier to see my one and only daughter being taken care of by a man who can give her a better life than I ever did."

I knew I should have spoken. I knew I should have ended it there. But instead, I stood there quietly, tears brimming in my eyes.

My father smiled at me. "Give me raven-haired, violet-eyed grandchildren," he teased.

I smiled. I didn't know what to say, but I knew what *not* to say. I knew that I just didn't have the heart to tell him that the only person taking care of his little girl was herself.

The day pulled through with me helping out my aunts with the preparations and Ryder charming my cousins, nieces, and aunts.

When I took a rest from putting icing on the cupcakes, I sat on one of the swings, thoughtfully watching my teenage cousins and nephews play the guitar on one corner.

Just then, Ryder joined them, sitting with the guys and singing along with them. He looked like a teenage boy, playfully changing the tones and lyrics of the songs and then laughing along.

He looked like he was genuinely enjoying himself. From where I sat, he looked like the playful Ryder once again. The Ryder that I missed. He looked so far from the cold, calculating tycoon who drove me here.

"He looks like he belongs there," a female voice said beside me.

I stared up and found myself staring at Geena's big blue eyes. Unlike the last time I saw her, I found that her eyes were dim and she has circles around them. She had just delivered her baby a couple of months ago, but she'd already lost so much weight.

Geena sat on the swing beside me. I remembered when we were kids; we would hang out on these swings a lot. Now, we'd been through a lot more in months than we had in twenty-five years.

"I'm glad that you are happy, Ash," she said quietly. I couldn't believe my ears. She took a deep breath. "At least it takes some of the guilt away. Bryan was not good enough for you."

I stared at her for a while. *Seriously?*

She smiled at me sadly. "I used to envy you a lot," she said. "I may have everything that my heart desires... materially, but I lack the attention, the adoration, and even the love that you have. Everything just seems to come so easily to you. The room just lights up when you enter it. I may be the white rose in the corner, but you... you're the sunflowers and daisies all over the place." She took a deep breath. Still I couldn't find my voice. I was afraid that if I opened my mouth, profanities would come flying out.

She continued, "I didn't like that at some point. My dad loves you like you were his own. Even my half-brother likes you better than me. And you're not even related to them by blood. I grew up envying you. And jealousy has an ugly head.

"I failed to see that all throughout these years, you were the one who stood up for me. You were always there to defend me, to point me to the right direction. You were my best friend, Ash. But…" Tears were rolling down her face now.

"I… betrayed you. I thought you were happy with Bryan and I wanted that relationship, too. You were dating each other for years and I couldn't even find a guy to date me for two straight weeks. He was cheating on you though. Not with me. There were others… I know because I went to bars almost every night. And Bryan and I started moving in the same circles, having the same crowd, without your knowledge…"

Okay that's it! I don't need to relive my nightmares. *I'm okay now.* "Geena, I don't want to hear this…"

"But you have to," she begged. "For my sake. Please? So I can finally get it off of my chest."

I closed my eyes for a moment. I bit my tongue. I decided to look over at Ryder, to calm myself, and get a little bit of courage to listen to Geena.

"Alright," I said without looking away from Ryder.

"Whenever Bryan took you home at night, he'd go to bars, meet girls, have one night stands. I thought, you couldn't really blame him because he wasn't getting any from you. But when it was getting to be too much already, I confronted him about it. And in one sudden, twisted moment, we just went at each other."

For a while there, I was afraid that she was going to go into details about how she and Bryan had sex for the first time. If she goes graphic, I promise I will kill myself!

"And then it happened again and again. We both knew we needed to stop. Because of you. But we couldn't. We didn't mean to betray you, Ash. It just… happened. But you have every right to curse us forever."

Oh, thank God she got that one right!

I stared at her. Tears were rolling down her cheeks. "What do you want from me, Geena? My forgiveness? My consent?"

She took a deep breath. "I want to know that you're happy. You don't have to be happy for me… for us. I just want to know if you truly are happy." She looked over where Ryder was. "At first, I was mad at you for beating me again. Sporting a guy who is a hundred times better than Bryan. Filthy rich. Handsome. Smart. I thought you did it to spite me, to make Bryan jealous. If those were your intentions, you won, Astrid. I was envious of you and Bryan was insanely jealous. You were all we talked about on our wedding night!" She took a deep breath again.

I let her go on. "We thought it wouldn't last. I thought you were doing all that for the show. But he's still here. You're still together. And the way he looks at you… there's so much tenderness in his eyes. It was even better than the way Bryan ever looked at you and I thought he was so in love with you! Ryder watches you all the time. And even though you're already together, he still cannot wipe that look of yearning on his face.

"Bryan broke your heart, but you found a man who loves you ten times more than he ever would have." Geena took a deep breath. "What we did to you may not have any excuse... but I want to know if you're really happy. With Ryder. That he makes you happier than Bryan ever did... so I can at least tell myself that even if I hurt you, it was some sort of blessing in disguise. That Heaven has used me to pave the way to your true happiness. I know it's a lousy excuse to make myself feel better... but it really would. So I need to know if you really love him, and that you're really happy," Geena said in an almost begging voice.

I looked at Ryder again. He was holding a guitar now and was playing it. And then he started singing. The kids around him listened intently. And somehow, so did I. He was good.

His voice was sincere and mesmerizing. He sang soulfully. I couldn't help being drawn to his voice.

I knew the song he was singing.

Picture, you're the queen of everything,
as far as the eye can see,
under your command...
I will be your guardian,
when all is crumbling,
to steady your hand...

As he sang, with head bowed down and his eyes closed, I couldn't help feeling all sorts of emotions. I felt as if there was something inside him that hurts and he's pouring it all out in a song.

Tears were rolling down my cheeks now, and I don't know why. He looked up and finally met my eyes.

"Don't let me go... don't let me go... don't let me go..."

The look he gave me was so intense; I couldn't bear the weight of it. It was as if he was making a plea... to me. I lost my breath. If only he meant that... if only I didn't find Alizia in his house last night...

I looked away from him and turned to Geena who was watching me carefully. Then she slowly smiled.

"I know you, Ash," she said. "Sometimes, even better than you know yourself." She took a deep breath again. "I think I know my answer too." She smiled. "And I feel better. I'll try to work it out with Bryan. I know he still loves you. But I will try... for our baby at least. If... we break up and he runs to you, please, Ash... don't take him back.

Not for me. But for yourself." Then she looked at Ryder and then back at me.

"You should recognize a good thing when it's in front of you. He genuinely loves you. More than you love him. I can tell that you've been avoiding each other all day. If something's wrong, try to work it out. He's good for you, Ash. And I want you to be happy. This guy will make you happy. Don't underestimate the intensity of your feelings for him. You love him… probably more than you loved Bryan. And if you choose to invite me to your wedding, I want you to know that I will be there. And for once, I will be genuinely happy for you."

Geena stood up. I was still speechless. I just didn't know what to say to her. Honestly, I loved Geena too. We grew up together and we'd had good times. She was jealous of me, but now she's terribly sorry for everything she did. I looked at Ryder again. He was strumming the last notes of his song. Tears continued to roll down my cheeks.

"Do you know that you never cried whenever you and Bryan were fighting?" Geena asked.

I stared at her. Was she right? I could hardly remember what it was like with Bryan now.

"You didn't care as much. Bryan was your friend, and the relationship was comfortable and easy. But relationships don't have to be easy all the time, Ash. What's more important is that it's… passionate, exciting, as much as it is comforting. The perfect thing is that you should marry your best friend, who you have the hots for… not some guy who's just practically your roommate.

"Ryder is perfect for you in all aspects. If you thought your relationship with Bryan was… sensible… what you have with Ryder is… magic. I hope you think about that." And when I stared up at her again, I saw that she has a genuinely happy smile on her face. "I'm okay now, Ash. Maybe forgiveness will come between us. Someday. But thank you for giving me the hope that it will."

When she left, I felt all sorts of emotions run over me. Relief, because I knew that somehow Geena meant every word she said. Guilt, because I'd cheated everyone by letting them think that I was okay. Confusion, because even though I was set to break my fake engagement to Ryder, my heart felt heavier than it did when I broke up with Bryan.

When Ryder came into my life, he picked me up from whatever hole I was in. He was the glue that put me back together. He knew wedding planning was my passion, so he invested in it and banked on my talents. Maybe he did it as a businessman. But he helped me up. Without telling me what he was doing.

He became a constant thing in my life. Time breezed through without me noticing that slowly, I was becoming my old self again, maybe even better and Ryder was becoming the pillar of my strength.

He could be so persistent; I couldn't shake him off. In bed, we're like a dormant volcano exploding. We shared a passion that sometimes seemed uncontainable, and yet we had this bond that seemed so comforting.

Now... we're approaching the end of our charade, I knew it was the right thing to do. But somehow, I couldn't bring myself to do it. It felt like the most difficult thing I ever had to do in my life. I couldn't tell my parents that we're over because then it would mean I was really letting him go.

And God knows I didn't want to! Because even though he was the epitome of the lifestyle I stayed away from since I was a teenager, I knew that he was also the epitome of the man I hoped to have an 'ever after' with.

Tears kept rolling down my cheeks. I'd reached the shoreline. I stood there staring at the ocean. When I was younger, I came to the beach a lot... to think... to tell my troubles to the waves and hope that they would take all of it away.

I thought about Geena. I knew she was not happy with Bryan. But the fact that she wanted to know if I was happy with Ryder told me that she was truly sorry for what she did. I searched my heart for any grudge for her or even for Bryan... I found that there was none. Not anymore. I just didn't care anymore.

And then Ryder... how could I bring myself to tell my parents that it's over? I'm not even wearing my engagement ring anymore, which surprisingly nobody noticed... not even Geena. When it's over, that will be it. Ryder will be out of my life. How can I bring myself to let him go... to wake up from the dream? To admit that he belongs to someone like Alizia after all. And all I had were a few moments of borrowed heaven.

Just then, I felt that I was no longer alone. I felt Ryder's presence behind me. Tears still kept rolling down my cheeks. I wanted so much to lose myself in his arms. To hold him, touch him and tell him that...

I love him... even though he was just a dream. Even though it was time to wake up now. Even though I was scared... of having a relationship... especially with a guy like him.

Even though he had Alizia now...

Could I blame him?

How many times did I turn him down? I never gave him a chance. How long did I make him wait? For nothing!

I should have taken a chance when he begged me to. And now... I was too late. I closed my eyes, and more tears came. I wrapped my arms around myself and I silently whimpered.

Just then, as if he couldn't take it anymore, I felt Ryder's hand on my shoulder, forcing me to turn around and then he crushed me into his arms. I buried my face on his shoulder and cried quietly.

He didn't really belong to me and yet, this heaven in his arms just felt so right! There in his arms, I felt like I could be whoever I wanted to be, and we'd hold each other this way just the same. But I knew.... I blew away all the chances I had.

Ryder didn't say a word. He just held me, the way I wanted... and needed to be held. He kept me warm, safe, and comforted. After a while, the tears stopped, but we still continued standing there, locked in each other's arms.

Then he took a deep breath and said, "You don't have to break this off to your family yet if you can't."

"You've made it difficult for me," I whispered quietly.

"I told you I would," he said. "It wasn't going to be easy."

"But why?"

He sighed. "Because I wanted you to be sure about what you're doing first before you tell your family that I'm not going to be around to take care of you anymore." And that just made me want to cry even more.

"Ash... I didn't mean to lie to you about the investment," he said. "I really was looking for something to invest in with the first profits I had from Oil Rig and Rig Style. I saw how lucrative your industry was and I saw how brilliant you were during that wedding. I knew you were looking for a job. It presented a great opportunity for me, so I took it. I didn't want to tell you yet because when I made the deal with Adam, you didn't know who I really was. I couldn't tell you, but I was planning to."

"When?"

He took a deep breath. "Every day, I wanted to tell you. It was hard to lie to you every single day. And I every time I tried... I just chickened out."

"So what do you want me to do with your business now?"

"Keep doing it. It's yours as much as it's mine. Your contract with Adam has always been that you're a partner. I'm just a capitalist, Ash. You own all the hard work," he said.

"You want me to be your business partner?"

"You already are. I want it to stay that way."

A mere business partner... but what could I expect? Him telling me that what we had during the past months was real?

"I'll think about it," I said to him. "About the fake... engagement... it's not fair to you if we keep doing this, Ryder. We both need to keep up with reality... and I can't come between you and Alizia. It's not fair. You've helped me more than enough."

He pulled back and stared down at me. His eyes narrowed.

"Alizia..." he started.

But then we were cut off by a voice calling us from a distance. I looked over Ryder's shoulder to see my niece, Cathy waving at us.

"Pictures!" she called to us. "Come!"

I stared up at Ryder. It looked like he wanted to say something, but then he took a deep breath and said, "We better get going."

I nodded. I was disappointed. I wanted to know what he had to say about Alizia. As much as the truth would hurt, I knew I would rather hear it from him straight. I knew I had no right to be angry or jealous anyway. And besides, I went out on a date with Tyler in the hopes of moving on. Ryder deserved to do the same. In fact, he deserved it more than I did. He was the one who was doing me a favor. I was the one with the heartache to get over and a face to save.

As we walked back to the house, Ryder suddenly took my hand and intertwined our fingers. I stared at him and raised a brow.

He smiled slowly and said, "You're still engaged to me here, remember?"

I nodded. "But keep a safe distance. I know what it's been like to be cheated on, and I don't want the same pain for any other woman... even though we're just pretending, Alizia doesn't know that, and she may not understand."

Ryder's face tightened, but he didn't say anything.

My heart felt heavier. It felt more torn than it was this morning. It was as if he was confirming what I feared... I had lost my chance... I had lost him.

22.
I DO:

Powerful two little words that actually mean, 'I will love you, take care of you, serve you, protect you, for better or worse, in sickness and in health, for as long as we both shall live.'

Before I joined my parents, I looked at Ryder and said, "Thank you, Ryder. You've been very kind to all of us. I guess this is the last, huh? I'll call my parents after a week to tell them that it's over. Don't worry. I'll make sure nobody blames you. I'll tell them that I want to stay single for a while. To… date around…"

"Do you?" he asked bitterly.

I raised a brow. "Do I what?"

"Want to date around?" he asked.

I laughed… to cover up the pain that I feel inside… and to hide the truth behind the lie that I'm about to say.

"It's been a while, hasn't it?" I turned away because I couldn't bear to lie to him anymore. I joined my family for the pictures. Ryder took a picture with us, too.

I tried to laugh, dance and chat with as many of my relatives as I could. I was avoiding Ryder. I didn't know what to say to him. More than anything, I didn't want to feel any more pain. I had gone from one major heartbreak to a love unrequited in less than one year.

In truth, when he asked me if I really wanted to date around, what I really wanted to tell him was… *No. I just want to date you… for real.*

The evening wore on. I hadn't spoken another word to Ryder again. I managed to evade him. We didn't even dance a song.

It was time to go. Most of my relatives had gone home. I said my goodbyes to my parents. Bryan had a smirk on his face in one corner. When I looked at Geena, she had a wistful smile on hers. I knew I couldn't stay mad at her forever. It was pointless. Bryan was nothing to me now anyway. So I gave her a slight nod… to give her hope that forgiveness would come… in time. She took a deep breath and it seemed to me like she was on the verge of crying.

I felt Ryder stand behind me. I finally turned around to face him. The look on his face was somber and cold, like he was bottling up all his anger, sadness, and frustration until he is in the clear to let hell break loose.

"You can't avoid me forever," he whispered.

"I wasn't…" I started. But what's the point of denying the obvious?

He raised a brow at me. I met his gaze evenly. "Let's go home. Say your goodbyes to my parents. It will be the last you'll see of them."

He narrowed his eyes. Then he walked towards where my family was. He shook my father's hand and he gave my mother a hug.

On our way to his car, my father called out to him, "I will hold on to your word, Ryder."

Ryder nodded. "Yes, Sir."

When we climbed into his car, I glared at Ryder. "What was that?"

"Nothing." He started the engine.

"You have to tell me!"

"No, I don't," he said.

"Why not?"

"Because it's just between your father and me," he replied.

I sat back on my seat, fuming by the second. How could Ryder make a private conversation with my father? What did he tell him? Why was my father asking him to keep his word? Was there a secret that my father told him that Ryder promised to keep? Was this about money or some investment that my father was going to make that Ryder agreed to help him with?

I'll call my parents to tell them that Ryder and I are over. I will have to break this fake engagement. It won't help if Ryder continued to rub elbows with my father. I already knew and admitted that I was in love with him. I wanted this engagement to be over and done with so I could begin another journey into the healing process. It may feel worse this time around, but I'd been here before and I survived it. I was a rock!

What do they say? *"Every day is a test. If you wake up alive today, it means that you got an "A" for yesterday!"* I got over Bryan. I would get over Ryder too.

Ryder didn't betray me when he slept with Alizia, or if he tried to start things with her. He's absolutely free to do whatever he wants with his life. He actually held up his own life in lieu of the big favors I asked of him.

I was so bent on thinking that he and I could never be that I didn't even notice what was happening to me… that I was falling in love with him for real. I was stealing moments of heaven with him thinking that they only happened in dreams, that I forgot the fact that you cannot cheat your heart and my heart didn't know it was just a game… my heart thought that we were for real… that I could have him for my 'ever after'.

Had I figured this out before, I would probably have tried to confront my feelings and see if I could try existing in Ryder's world… even though I was scared. Now that Alizia had officially entered the picture, it reminded me that if I really did love Ryder, I should let him be happy… with one who's fit to be the wife of a tycoon and can raise future tycoons in accordance with the norms of the upper class society. One whom his family would easily accept.

That's Alizia. Ryder deserved Alizia. For all the good things that he was, he deserved to have a perfect life, free of complications of geography or status in life.

We reached my home. I knew I couldn't force Ryder to tell me what his deal with my father was, but I could always pick up the phone and call my dad. When I tell them that Ryder and I are over, my father will tell me the deal with Ryder and hopefully not pursue it anymore. Ryder need not be tied down to do favors he shouldn't be obliged to do.

I turned to him. "Thank you, Ryder," I whispered. He was looking at the road, his expression cross. He didn't say anything. "For everything. From the beginning... you have done more than your part and you've done it beautifully well. It was... a great 'fake' relationship." I giggled humorlessly. "But you know... it has to end some time."

He sighed. "Yes. It has to end."

I bit my lip to prevent a whimper from escaping my lips. That hurt. I knew that it had to end, but hearing Ryder say it broke my heart ten times more. It was as if he just put out the last glimmer of hope that I had in my heart.

"I don't want to cause problems between you and... Alizia. I know she won't be happy about this, even if you tell her that you were just doing me a favor."

He didn't say anything. He continued to stare at the road aimlessly. After a full minute of silence, he got out of the car and opened my passenger door for me.

This is it! This is probably the last time I will see him. The last time that he will exist significantly in my life.

I got out of the car and we headed towards my door.

I turned to him and smiled. I knew that smile looked horrible. I was trying my best not to cry. I missed him like crazy already.

"Thank you for coming with me," I whispered. "And thank you for pretending to be my fiancé for... more than half a year. You were wonderful, Ryder. You're everything a girl could ever ask for. She's a very lucky girl." And then I tiptoed and gave him a kiss on the cheek.

He didn't say anything. He just stared down at me with that grave expression. I stared back at him and I knew he could see the tears in my eyes.

I turned my back on him and headed towards my front door. I knew I could only hold back the tears for less than a minute longer.

Then I heard him say, "Alizia and I are nothing."

I turned around to look at him. "What?"

He took a deep breath and took a step closer to me. "When you came to my house that night, she was there to use the bathroom. Said she can't use the toilet in the bar and she had to change her clothes or something. If it was a ploy to seduce me, I want you to know that she didn't succeed at it. Nothing happened. I took her back to her hotel just as soon as you walked out." When I looked up at him, I thought I saw a glimmer of light in his eyes. "You know I don't like aggressive women... and over the years, I've mastered the art of dodging them."

219

I took a deep breath. "It's actually none of my business. Why are you telling me this?"

"Because I want to know why you came to my house that night," he said. He was staring at me intensely. "The truth, Astrid. I think I at least deserve that!"

The intensity of his look and his voice almost scared me and made me want to run away. But I knew he was right. He deserved the truth. No matter what he decided to do with it.

"I wanted to get my answers…" I said. "I wanted to know what we are… what we could be…"

"You went out on a date," he said, a trace of annoyance still evident in his voice. "Are you opening yourself up to a possibility of a relationship?"

I shrugged. "I don't know," I whispered softly. "I guess I just wanted to prove to myself that… I was single."

"You weren't single, Astrid!" he said agitatedly. I stared up at him. "For months, you were in a relationship… *with me!*" His voice and his words made my mind go blank. "You were just too stubborn to admit it, Ash! And I put up with it! I waited! Until you'd finally be ready to admit it to yourself!"

I couldn't believe what I was hearing. It wasn't all fake for Ryder! It was easy enough for him to treat me like a princess, to answer to my whims… because for him it was all real.

Then his expression softened. "And I would never touch Alizia," he said. "Because I would never cheat on you, Ash."

Tears rolled down my cheeks. I was more confused now than a few moments ago. Now, more than ever, I did not know what Ryder and I were anymore. There was a thin line between pretending and reality.

"Maybe it's time we finally settle the score. Here. Now," he said sternly.

I stared up at him. He stepped closer to me and stared at me deeply.

"Are you ready to have a relationship, Astrid?" he asked seriously.

I took a deep breath. I nodded. Because, honestly, I thought I was.

"Are you ready to be with *me?*"

He asked me the question I wanted him to ask. I knew the answer to that question now more than ever. In spite of all my fears, all my insecurities, all my uncertainties, I knew what I wanted now. It may be a dream, but I wanted it. And I knew in my heart, that I had to fight for it. Because Ryder was *really* worth it!

But when I stared up at him and saw the cold expression on his face, I couldn't find my voice.

"Do you even *want* to be with me?" He rephrased his question. But still I couldn't answer.

Ryder narrowed his eyes. He looked angry, frustrated, and broken all at the same time. He shook his head in disbelief and then turned to walk away. I knew I should say something, or this moment would pass and I would regret it forever.

"I want to be with you," I croaked. "Only… you," I added quietly.

He turned back to me. Somehow, something in his expression changed. The cold and angry expression was fading from his face. He took a step towards me. He looked at me deeply, reading every emotion in my teary eyes.

I took a deep breath. "But I'm scared, Ryder…"

He drew a deep sigh of relief. "Oh, God, sweetheart…" he whispered and the next thing I knew, I was enclosed in his warm embrace. The embrace I missed so much. Tears kept rolling down my cheeks.

"I've been burned and deceived in the past. I was scared for that to happen again. I prevented myself from falling in love with you. Because I knew we didn't exist in the same world. I didn't want to lose you in my life. And I didn't want to get hurt anymore."

"Why would I hurt you? I, more than anyone, know the hell you have been through," he said.

"Why me, Ryder?" I reminded him. "I have nothing to give you in return."

"I already have everything," he said. "You're the only thing I want."

"I'm not glamorous, I'm not rich, and I'm not fit for someone like Ryder Van Woodsen. I'm not what your society or your family expects or wishes for you."

He laughed and hugged me tighter. "On the contrary, you're exactly what my family would wish for me. I think you will dazzle my society without even trying. And maybe you don't know that Ryder Van Woodsen didn't want a rich wife. He just wanted a woman who would love him even if he was poor." Then he pulled away from me so he could look into my eyes. "And that's you, love."

"You may want me now, Ryder. But for how long?" I asked.

He kissed my forehead. "How about forever and after that?"

I looked up at him. "How could you say that?"

He laughed and pulled me to him again. "Let me tell you a story that will perhaps ease your mind," he said. "I told you before that someday I'd tell you why I am doing you all those crazy favors… well, there's something I should have told you a long time ago." He took a deep breath.

"When I was a teenager, girls would come easily to me and Jake. We got chased, not because of who we were, but because we lived in mansions with limos, shiny cars, bottomless pockets. Plastic girls who wished to be a part of the big pie. Jake's been in love with Janis almost all of his life, and we've known each other since we were kids. Janis was just as rich as Jake so he's assured that she wasn't after his money. He was lucky. In that aspect, I envied him. Ever since I was young, I wasn't

221

into womanizing... I grew up thinking these girls only wanted my money. I wanted to find one like Janis, who loved Jake for who he really is. Not because he was an heir to a huge inheritance. And in this day and age, it is difficult to find someone like that. Who would like you for who you are inside?

"One day, I walked into a jewelry shop to buy my mother earrings. I accidentally bumped into some clumsy girl. Her scent filled my senses and to my greatest shock, she hugged me and cried in my arms, without even looking up to see who I was. It was the first time in my life I felt needed. Not for my money... but for the warmth, comfort, and protection I could provide.

"When I looked down at her, I saw a beautiful, but torn and broken soul. When I walked into that jewelry shop, I couldn't get her out of mind. She got under my skin the minute I saw her. I didn't complete my purchase. I ran out of the store to start looking for her. I went into my car and rounded those streets for like an hour searching for where she could have gone, afraid that I may never see her again.

"And then one night, when I was doing my rounds at Oil Rig, I saw her again, sitting alone in the bar, trying hard not to look miserable. I knew I had to meet her, but I wasn't used to picking up girls, or trying to start a conversation with one... so I took off my jacket, borrowed a cap from one of my bartenders and went to the counter to take her order.

"When she told me her story and told me she needed help, I just couldn't resist. It was the easiest way for me to see her again. At that point, it didn't matter what I was doing. All I knew was that I wanted to get to know her better and I'd like to see her again, so I agreed to help her. I saw her spirit and her will to survive through her pain and humiliation, and I admired her even more. And for the first time in my life, I felt like someone liked me for me... it didn't matter if I was poor. I felt lucky that night. For once, a woman enjoyed my company without knowing who I really was.

"The investment, I did it partly because I saw the potential in it. Another part wanted me to give her a fresh start. Because the sooner she gets over her past, the faster I can start to pursue her. But sooner or later, she had to find out who I really was. And she didn't like me anymore... didn't like me as much as she liked the bartender she met.

"And somehow, no matter what I did, the issue of my birthright got in the way. To make things worse, I go crazier and crazier about her every day. Believe me, I never hated being Ryder Van Woodsen in my entire life. But I did. Because I wanted her more!"

I listened carefully to his story. I couldn't help whimpering, crying rivers of tears silently in his arms.

"The bet that I had with Janis and Jake wasn't that serious. If I didn't have a girlfriend by then, I would just pay for their entire honeymoon when they get married. I was planning to give it to them anyway, as a wedding gift. So it didn't matter if I lost. But by then, I was already losing her... I needed to come up with a quick plan to keep seeing her. And when Janis reminded me about the bet, an idea crossed my mind. I took her to Miami, not just to win the bet, but also to make her fall for me. But this girl can be pretty stubborn sometimes. She was all bent up in her beliefs that no one could change her mind. But I put up with it. I was willing to wait for as long as it took because ever since I was a teenager; I was hoping to find a woman who would love me for who I am inside. And I know that the fact that I'm Ryder Van Woodsen prevented her from taking a chance on me."

He pulled away from me so he could look into my eyes. I stared up at him, not able to stop crying. It seemed like I could see Ryder's soul in his eyes... like he was baring it all for me.

"Every time we pretend we're together, that was the only time I could freely express what I really feel for you, Ash. I express how much I wanted to take care of you. How much I wanted to hold you in my arms, and make love to you. Whenever I was your fiancé, I picture how life would be like when we're truly together... and I know it would be perfect.

"When we stop, I had to pretend I don't feel anything for you, I held back every bit of emotion. For a while now, it seemed that whenever I pretend to be your fiancé, that's when reality starts for us... when we go back to being just... friends... that's when we start to pretend." He took a deep breath and leaned forward to kiss my forehead again.

"You were so convinced that you don't belong in my world... but you don't realize that I belong to you! For months now, Ash... you call me, I answer in one ring. Anything you want, doesn't matter what time or where I am... I pull it off for you. Didn't you ask yourself why I was going to hell and back for you?"

I giggled in spite of my tears. "I thought you were just crazy about saving poor damsels in distress."

"I was crazy about you," he said. "God! I'm still crazy about you!" Ryder pulled me to him again and locked me into a tight embrace.

"You said I was having a relationship with you..." I started.

"It felt that way to me," he said. "We're on the phone all the time, you have keys to my house, I'm at your beck and call... really, Ash? You didn't notice?"

"You tricked me!" I said giggling.

He shook his head. "I wanted you to realize that it didn't have to be complicated. I wanted you to get used to a life with me... and I was hoping you'd find it comforting... that you could handle it... that I was far from the rich assholes you met in your life. So when you're finally ready to admit to yourself that you're ready for a relationship, I would be the first on your list... regardless of whether I was Ryder Van Woodsen or not."

I closed my eyes and savored Ryder's scent, and his warm embrace. I realized that he was right. I'd been living in his world for months, and he never judged me, or disappointed me. He was the sweetest thing I knew. I don't know how his family would react to me... but I knew this guy would fight for me. And that's all that matters.

"I cannot help who I am, Ash," he said wistfully. "I cannot change who I am. I will always be Ryder Van Woodsen. But I want you in my life. I want you more than I've wanted anything in my life! I'm willing to wait for as long as it takes. I'm even willing to honor your 'no sex before marriage' policy, if that's what it takes, and I will do it better than Bryan ever did. I'll fly back to Malibu for you as often as you want. Just... trust me, take a chance on me. And I will do my best to make you happy."

I smiled at him. "I am happy, Ryder. With you... in this *fake relationship* we're in. What would it be like if we do it for real?"

He smiled back at me. "A hundred times better," he promised.

"Don't make any promises you can't keep," I warned him. "I've had my fair share of broken promises already."

"I know. I'm not making any promises I can't keep. I promise if you take a risk with me, it will be a hundred times better!" he said seriously.

I stared up at Ryder's eyes. The truth was I wanted to be with him as much as he wanted to be with me. I may be scared, but I wanted him more than anything in the world. He was right. It doesn't matter whether or not I was ready for a relationship with him. Sometimes, the only thing that mattered was the way we felt... what we wanted. After all the pains I'd been through with Bryan, maybe I really did deserve a life with Ryder. Maybe Geena was right. I had to feel the pain of a broken engagement with Bryan because he wasn't the one meant for me. Someone better was.

Finally, I smiled at Ryder. Then I tiptoed and gave him a kiss on the lips. He savored that kiss, as if he'd been dying to kiss me for days.

He took a deep breath. "I love you, Astrid Jacobson. More than I've ever loved anybody. You... are my life. I will take care of you, I will protect you. I love you! I love you! I love you!" he said. Then he leaned his forehead against mine. "Give me your answer, Ash. Will you risk being with me? For real?" he whispered against my lips.

I closed my eyes, tears rolled down my cheeks. I was so overwhelmed with what Ryder said. I could hardly believe my ears.

When I finally found my voice, I said. "I went out on a date just to prove to myself that I was ready... but when I was there with that guy, all I could think about was that something was wrong, like I was cheating. When I saw you, I felt so guilty and so scared. I couldn't even kiss the guy... I could not fall for any other guy or date anyone else.

That is why I came to your house that night." I took a deep breath. "I love you too, Ryder. I guess that gives you your answer."

He smiled, a genuinely happy smile. Then he leaned forward and kissed me very thoroughly. He kissed me with all his heart, all his soul. He kissed me like he couldn't believe he was kissing me for the very first time in his life, like he didn't want to let me go ever again.

When he pulled away he smiled at me and said, "It's good to kiss you like that and know that I wasn't doing it for the show... or that kiss didn't have to be over soon enough."

I knew exactly what he meant. That kiss felt like... unlocking all the chains I built around my heart. Then the intensity of my love for him swept through me in waves I could barely contain. Tears rolled down my cheeks and I realized how close I had come to losing him... to making the biggest mistake of life.

I tiptoed and kissed him again. He kissed me back as hungrily as I did. Then he leaned his forehead to mine and took a deep breath. When he pulled away, he picked me up on my feet and carried me in his arms, back towards his car.

"What are you doing?" I asked, giggling.

He smiled at me. "Taking you home."

He carried me to his car and settled me on the passenger seat. He drove to his house. When we reached the door, Ryder picked me up again and carried me inside his house.

"Welcome home, love," he said to me. "Your 'ever after' starts now." As I looked up his face, he was just as sincere as he was boyish. This was the Ryder that I missed. The real Ryder. And when he said that my 'ever after' started now, I wanted to cry again. I held on to him tighter and buried my face on his shoulder. I silently prayed that this wasn't all a dream because I didn't want to wake up from it.

He took me to his bedroom and laid me down on the bed. He took off his jacket and kicked off his shoes.

I laughed when he leaned down towards me with a mischievous smile on his face.

"Hey, didn't you say you were going to honor my *no sex before marriage* policy?" I asked.

He raised a brow. "I did? I don't remember!"

He leaned down to give me a kiss on the lips. He looked down at me and in a more serious tone he said, "Yes, I did. And I'll do it... all you need to do is ask."

I smiled at him. I was tempted to. But I'd been on that road before. What was the point of holding Ryder back when we'd already shared many nights of passion, and my body craved his helplessly?

I shook my head. "I'm not going to," I whispered to him.

He narrowed his eyes. "Are you sure?" he asked. "Because whatever you say now becomes your final answer. You can't change your decision half-way, love."

I laughed. I shook my head and then I pulled his face towards mine and gave him a kiss. "I'm sure."

He smiled at me and then he kissed me hungrily. I kissed him back, letting that familiar desire for him envelope me completely. He undressed me, kissing every bit of skin he exposed. I kissed him as hungrily as he kissed me. He looked at me in eyes dark with desire. Without taking his eyes off me, he claimed me, finally making us one. I let out a loud moan. Ryder swallowed them with his kisses. Then he leaned his forehead against mine and sucked in a deep breath. "I love you, Astrid! You have no idea how much!"

Panting, I leaned forward and kissed him back, saying, "I love you too, Ryder. Maybe just as much as you love me."

23.
BOND:
A connection that fastens things or people together.

The next morning, I woke up Ryder with kisses. He smiled at me and then he held me by the waist, pushed me on my back and pinned me between his body and the soft mattresses of his bed. There was no need for words after that.

It was almost noontime when we got up from bed. I knew that Ryder would leave soon and this made me want to cry already.

"What time's your flight?" I asked him.

He smiled and pulled me to him. "Tomorrow at ten."

"Why?" I asked in surprise.

"I canceled things today."

"Ryder... why did you do that?"

He kissed me. "I wanted to. A day won't hurt. It's our first day together... for real. The first day that didn't have to end."

I gave him a hug. "Geography's going to be a bummer, won't it?"

He chuckled. He pushed a lock of stray hair away from my face. "Let that be my problem."

I stared up at him. "That's not fair. I don't want you to stress yourself out too much traveling so often to Malibu. I know you live most of your life in Manhattan."

He smiled at me. "You know the solution to that problem, love. But until you're ready, I'll fly in as often as possible."

I hugged him. Tears brimmed in my eyes. I missed him already. If I wanted to solve this problem, I only needed to make a move to Manhattan myself so Ryder needed only to fly back to Malibu once a week.

I gathered my clothes on the floor. Ryder did the same to his. Just then I remembered one thing—Ryder and I hadn't used any protection. I sat back in bed quietly, thinking. In New York, Ryder didn't wear a condom either, but he withdrew. Now, I don't remember him doing so.

"Something wrong?" he asked.

I shook my head nervously and stood up to go to the bathroom. I was nervous. I wasn't counting the days of my period, because I wasn't sexually active. That was obviously before Ryder. I tried to remember the last time I had my period.

I felt Ryder pull my hand so I could sit back in bed. He tilted my chin up so I can look at him.

"Tell me," he said.

"I told you there's nothing."

He narrowed his eyes. "I know you well by now, Ash. For months, all we had were signals and moods, and I had to decipher every sign that you threw my way because I couldn't go ahead and demand my answers verbally. So now, I know that something's bothering you and please... I'd like to know."

I stared back at him. I took a deep breath. "You didn't... withdraw." I said quietly.

He was taken aback by what I said and then he laughed. He pulled me to him in a hug. Then he whispered, "Every queen needs a prince or princess in her ever after too, doesn't she?"

I pinched his arm. "Ryder!"

He laughed again. "Okay, so let's discuss this," he said. "I honestly don't mind. As long as it's with you, I'll be the happiest man on Earth, not that I'm not already."

"Ryder, we just officially got together last night. You haven't even told your mother about me."

"Of course I have," he said.

"What?" I asked nervously. I hadn't met Ryder's family. And I was so scared they would be against this... against me.

"My mother knows I'm helplessly in love with a beautiful wedding planner from Malibu named Astrid, who has dazzling violet eyes. She knows you were torn by a broken engagement thanks to your cousin. I was the rebound guy who was waiting patiently for you to realize that you're in love with me, too. And the fact that I have money in the banks made it more difficult for you to admit that I'm the right guy for you all along. And she couldn't wait to meet you, Ash. She admires your spirit in fighting back. Moreover, she likes the fact that you liked me more when I was just a bartender."

"Wh... when did you tell her?"

"I came clean with my family, and Janis and Jake, when Adam phoned to inform me you were fuming about the investment," he said. "Paris wants to meet you now more than ever. Janis was a little heartbroken to know you weren't really my girlfriend and asked me to swear to do whatever it takes to win you over. In my world, Ash, you're quite a rare find. Both my mom and my sister thought I was lucky to find you. They couldn't wait to meet you."

My eyes widened and I felt more nervous. He laughed. "Don't worry. They already like you. I know they'll like you even more when you meet."

"Do I have to meet them soon?"

"Of course!" he said. "Especially if you move to Manhattan."

I stared back at Ryder and I could see in his eyes that he really wanted me to move to New York. He was not pressuring me yet, but it was definitely something he wanted to happen. "I promise to think about it." I said to him.

He smiled. "That's good enough for now." He leaned and kissed me on the lips. Then he stared back at me for a while before saying, "So, you want to discuss contraceptives?"

I nodded shyly.

"I am only comfortable with two. Withdrawal and condoms. If you go on the pill, I want to make sure it's perfectly safe, no side effects. I don't want anything that could have any adverse effect on your health. I do want to have babies in the future, love. I don't want to decrease our chances of having one when you're ready."

I smiled back at him. "Okay. Withdrawal is probably the riskiest method there is, and condoms break."

He shrugged. "So what? Then we'll have a baby. Nothing would please my mother more!"

"Ryder, don't you think we're moving too fast?"

He laughed and pulled me into a hug. "Too fast? You have been practically engaged to me for months now, you know. But if you feel like I'm crowding you or something, let me know. I'll go slow."

I reached up and gave him a kiss. "No. I'm just a little overwhelmed. I still can't seem to believe that this is happening for real."

"Me too." He sighed. "Just yesterday, I was longing to hug you again and feel you hug me not for the sake of putting on a show in front of Geena."

Now, I remembered Geena and I smiled. "Geena may be right."

"What did you talk about?"

"She wanted to know if I was happy. She told me the story from the beginning. Apparently, Bryan was cheating on me long before he and Geena hooked up. Geena wanted to feel a little better by making sure that I'm happier than I've ever been. So she can feel better herself. She wants to make it work with Bryan. She wants my consent… she wanted to know if I was happy so she could at least tell herself that she was a blessing in disguise to me. That she paved a way for me to find a better, happier life with a much better man."

"Are you happier?"

I stared up at Ryder's handsome face and I smiled. "Yes. I am."

"I know you've been burned before, Ash. This may prevent you from trusting and giving yourself fully to your next relationship. Please don't hold back on me. I am not the man that Bryan was. I promise you, it will be different with me. Love me with all you have… because I love you with all I have."

I hugged him. I couldn't help crying. He smiled at me and gave me a quick kiss.

After a quick shower, I dressed in the pants I wore yesterday and one of Ryder's long-sleeved shirts.

"We need to go to my place. I need to change clothes."

He laughed. "My shirt looks sexy on you."

"But I'm not staying a minute longer in these pants!" I protested.

"Alright. You need to pack a couple of clothes anyway," he said. "My flight's tomorrow morning. I was hoping you'd stay one more night here."

I smiled at him, and reached up to give him a kiss. "Of course." I sighed. Even though I had him for the whole day today, the idea of him going back to Manhattan tomorrow, and not seeing him for about a week already broke my heart. I missed him already. This honeymoon state just ended too soon.

"Are you okay?"

"I miss you already," I whispered.

He chuckled and tightened his arms around me. "My normal schedule requires me to be in Manhattan for four days and two days in Malibu. The extra day is up to me, although by the looks of it, it seems Malibu is the place to be during my day off."

I reached up and kissed him on the jaw. "It's going to be crazy for you, traveling so much. But I can't ask you not to do it. I will miss you so much."

"I will miss you more," he said. "I've waited for this. I'll try my best not to mess it up. Just trust me, okay?"

I nodded.

We went to my house. I changed into a pair of jeans and a long-sleeved blouse. Then I packed a night's worth of clothes with me.

When I came out of the house, Ryder asked, "Do you know how to drive?"

I raised a brow at him. "Of course! Cars do not come cheap to us village people, but I learned some tricks."

Ryder laughed and tossed me his car keys. "Show me."

I laughed. "Alright. Mr. Van Woodsen just got himself a chauffeur."

"A beautiful one at that!" he laughed.

When I got into his car, I adjusted the seats and the side mirrors. His car was a little bit more complicated than the normal ones I'd driven before. Ryder had to give me a bit of orientation before I took his car for a spin. I liked the car. It was comfortable and it was fast. I felt good being able to drive again after more than a year.

We went to Oil Rig. I stood by the glass walls of Ryder's office to watch what's happening on the floors. All of Ryder's staff was well-coordinated, as if they were trained to work for the finest restaurants, instead of a bar. I could tell that Ryder really knew what he was doing.

He came behind me, put his arms around my waist and nuzzled my neck.

"Are you strict with your employees?" I asked.

"Why do you ask?"

I shrugged. "They all look coordinated."

He chuckled. "I hire the best, and I train them long. They're well-compensated. And they get all the tips and service charges. Once a week, they can bring their family here and dine for free. I know each and every one of them personally. They can come to me directly if they have a problem. I believe that if you motivate your people positively, you'll get better positive results."

"How are you going to manage all these when you finally become in charge of your entire empire?"

"I had a plan," he said. "I used to think I could take care of it all. Fly from one country to another."

"And now what happened to that plan?" I asked.

He stared at me for a while and then he said, "You changed it."

My eyes narrowed at him. "What did I do?"

He leaned forward and gave me a kiss on the lips. "I fell in love with you," he said. "You made me realize that there are more important things in life than money and success, and that one way or another, I would have to delegate. Find some free time for myself. Remember that day you came to New York? I had the longest day of my life. Working for twenty-four hours straight. And then you came. I was so glad you were there. When I slept with you in my arms, I knew there was no other place I would rather be. And that if I did have you in my life for real, I wouldn't miss the chance to come home to you."

"Now you have me in your life for real," I told him. "Geography is still a bummer."

He smiled. "I'll figure something out. If I can't fly to Malibu, I'd probably ask you to fly to New York."

I smiled at him. "I'd like that," I told him. "Honestly, I like Manhattan. I'd like to visit again."

"I hope you like it enough to move there," he whispered.

I laughed. "I said I'd think about it."

That night, Ryder and I made love slowly and passionately. It was amazing. I couldn't get enough of him. And it seemed that he couldn't get enough of me either. After making love, we stayed in bed, locked in each other's arms.

"I'll leave early tomorrow," he said. "I won't wake you up anymore. You still have my keys don't you?"

I nodded. "I'll give them back to you when you get back."

"Nope," he said. "They're your keys. Keep them. I want you to be here while I'm gone."

"Why?"

"For my peace of mind. I know you'll be safer here. You know this house has a central alarm system. You can enable it and it rings the police directly if something goes wrong."

"I am safer at my place when I work late. Remember you didn't want me to walk down the street?"

"You don't have to walk," he said. He kissed my forehead. "I'm leaving my car keys to you as well."

I laughed. "You're going to trust me with your car while you're not sitting in the passenger seat?"

"It has comprehensive insurance," he said. "Seriously, love. I want you to drive my car while I'm not here."

I stared back at him. "Ryder... that's an expensive car."

"You're more precious than the car, Ash," he argued. "Please. Think of it as my way of protecting you while I'm not physically with you. I would rather you drive the car than walk or take a cab." He looked at me in the eye. "Please, love. No arguments?"

I took a deep breath. I knew I couldn't argue with Ryder once he put his mind into something.

"This is the price to pay for being with you, isn't it?" I asked him. He narrowed his eyes. I took a deep breath. "I have to get used to expensive things and gadgets."

He laughed. "We need to find a balance," he said. "I'm just as comfortable with walking as I am with driving my cars. There's one thing I need to ask you." He tilted my chin up so I could look into his eyes. "I can't help who I am, Ash. I'll always be Ryder Van Woodsen. But that does not change the man you fell in love with."

"Now that we're on the topic, what else is there in Ryder Van Woodsen's world? Because I don't want to be taken by surprise."

He sighed. He held me tighter, as if he needed to secure his hold on me before he told me the real deal.

"I grew up in Manhattan... with my father. Paris lived in Paris with my mother. My parents separated when I was seventeen. Because of my father's womanizing activities, my mother thought it was the best idea to give us the first parts of our inheritance earlier, put it in a trust that we could access when we came of age. I had access to mine when I was eighteen." He looked at me seriously. "I'm not going to lie to you, Ash. It's huge."

"Must be. Your parents would probably leave at least a million or two in your trust."

He took a deep breath. "More than a hundred actually."

I stared up at him, my eyes wide. "Wow!" I breathed.

"I was investing since I was eighteen," he said. "I made my first million when I was twenty."

I listened quietly to Ryder. I knew he was rich. But until now, I didn't have an idea just how much.

"Soon, I'll be inheriting more when my father retires and finally gives me full reigns to the business. I will be the one to handle it full time. Paris will just be part of the board, with controlling shares. But she won't have hands-on management."

"Why not?"

"Because she doesn't want to. She would like to operate my bars more than our restaurants."

"She operates your bars?"

"Except the ones in Malibu."

"What else do I need to know about the man I'm sleeping with?" I asked.

He chuckled. "I'm practically debt-free," he said," he said. "I don't mortgage to invest. I owed my first investment to my trust fund. And I rolled the income into another investment. I'm practically made, Ash. Success came to me at an early age. I guess I was lucky. My parents made sure I had everything I needed and more."

"Yet you're grounded, Ryder," I said. "When we're together, I find it hard to believe you are *the* Ryder Van Woodsen."

"That's what I have been trying to tell you," he said," he said. "I don't exist in glamor, and my life isn't always in the limelight. I can be your ordinary guy… your normal bartender even. You don't have to be afraid with me, Ash. Just take a chance."

I nodded. "I already am."

He hugged me to him. "Please don't deny me the chance to spoil you… to make you feel like a queen. I like it. I used to hate girls who chased after me because of the material things I could give them. Now, the woman I want doesn't want anything from me at all. Maybe that's one of the reasons why I fell in love with you. But that doesn't take away the fact that I am who I am. And I want to shower you with everything, Ash. Please don't deny me that."

I laughed. "Okay. But don't squander your millions on me, Ryder. You have to remember, a bouquet of flowers and some diamond jewelry weighs just the same to me, as long as they came from you."

He chuckled. "I'll remember." He stared at me for a while and then he took a deep breath. "You're beautiful," he said," he said. "I love you."

I smiled. "I love you, too."

Ryder leaned forward and kissed me. That started a whole rollercoaster ride of passion again.

***

Ryder was gone when I woke up the next morning. He left me a note on the bedside table.

Love,
I mean it. I want you to stay here while I'm gone. I left the car keys here. You can arm and disarm the alarm with the password.

I'll be home sooner than you think. I'll just finish up with my meetings and I will come home to you. Until then, please be miserable without me. Because I am miserable without you.

The password is 278743. To make it easier for you to remember, spell your name on the keypad. :-)

I love you very much.

Ryder

I cried after reading his letter. I missed him so much already. It wasn't like this with Bryan. He could go to a convention for a week and I would still be my chirpy self at work. I was too busy with my job then, I didn't have time to miss him. But with Ryder, it was different. It seemed that no matter how busy I became, I'd still have a heavy lump in my heart.

When Bryan broke my heart, I was torn and broken. I thought the only way to take the pain away was to get back together with him, put it all behind us. Had I done that, I wouldn't be here in Ryder's bed, hugging my pillow and missing him like crazy.

Ryder is everything that I have ever dreamed of. He's everything that I was afraid to dream of. Who would have thought that a couple of months ago, I was whining and sulking about Bryan and Geena? Now, I'm having a fairy tale relationship with a Manhattan prince.

I guess I had to feel that pain in my past to journey towards Ryder. And I wouldn't want to have it any other way. I think I would go through a hundred more of the heartbreaks with Bryan, if it meant I would have Ryder to come home to at the end of it all.

My thoughts were interrupted when my phone rang.

"Where have you been hiding?" Dannie asked.

I had not spoken to my friends since the day I left for my parents' anniversary.

"Nowhere," I said. "How are you doing?"

"I'm good. Let's catch up. I want to hear all about your parents' anniversary and your date with that hot photographer," he said," he said.

"Where are you?"

"I'm still at home. Meet you at Starbucks?" he asked.

"Okay. Want me to pick you up and we'll go to Starbucks together?"

"Fine. I'll call Nicole and John. Hopefully, they have time off from work."

After I hung up, the landline rang.

"Hello," I answered.

"You don't know how that feels," Ryder said chuckling. "Calling home and the voice you'd like to hear the most answers your telephone."

"You're not shy with flattery, are you, Van Woodsen?"

He laughed. "Except it's not flattery. I'm just… telling you exactly what I feel," he said," he said. "Did you just wake up?"

"Yes," I replied quietly.

"Are you crying?"

Now, after hearing his voice, I couldn't help crying. "No." But I knew the tone of my voice betrayed me.

"What's wrong, love?" he asked.

I took a deep breath. "Will it drive you away if I tell you that I miss you already?"

"No," he replied seriously. "I miss you too."

"God, Ryder! I have to stop being silly!" I said more to myself.

"You're not silly," he said. "I like it that you miss me."

I took a deep breath. "You really did leave your car keys," I said.

"I told you I want you to use it," he said.

"How did you get to the airport?"

"The usual. I asked one of the guys from the bar to pick me up," he said," he said.

"Alright, I'll just arm your alarm when I leave," I said. "Speaking of your alarm, did you just change your password today?"

"No," he replied. "I've had the same password for months. Remember? I told you this before."

"Really, Ryder? My name?"

He laughed. "I've been crazy about you for months, love. I remembered changing the password after we got back from Miami. I knew then that I was in too deep and there is no way I could escape you."

"Ryder…"

"Hmmm…"

"Don't break my heart, okay?"

"I won't, sweetheart. I love you."

"By the way, I'm going out to meet Dannie," I said.

"Good. You know how to drive there?" he asked.

"I know how to walk there."

"Very funny, Ash. Whatever happened to letting me indulge you?"

"That's a flashy car, Ryder," I said.

"It's a safe car," he said.

"Alright." I sighed. "Are you sure you won't get mad if I bump it or something."

"No. But I will if something happens to you."

"Okay. Go back to work," I said to him giggling. "And Ryder…"

"Yes, love?"

"Keep your promise, okay? Be miserable without me," I said.

"I already am." Then he took a deep breath. "Astrid…"

"Yes?"

"Always remember that I love you, okay? I'll always be that guy who would do anything to protect you, make you happy. I want you to know that even before I met you, you were the woman I needed, the woman I had been looking for."

Tears rolled down my cheeks. "I'll remember that, Ryder. And I love you too. I didn't know you were what I needed until I met you. And thank you... for finding me too."

When we hung up, I had to take a couple of minutes to compose myself. There was a heavy lump on my chest and I couldn't help but cry again. I didn't know love could be this strong. It was amazing because I never felt half of these emotions when I was with Bryan and I was all set to marry him. Even if he didn't cheat on me, our marriage would have been a mistake. And what I had with Ryder was... a beautiful combination of all things that are right.

Dannie was already in front of his apartment when I arrived in his neighborhood. He was staring at the car in awe. When I let the window down on the passenger side and called out to him, "Hop in!" his jaw literally dropped. He didn't move until I blew the horn.

When he was inside he was looking at me in amazement.

"You're driving..." he said and trailed off.

"Ryder's car," I finished for him.

"But why?"

"Because he wants me to," I replied. "And he can be very persistent."

"So what is this? Like a company car? He owns your company doesn't he?"

I shook my head. "Yeah, he owns the company I am working for. But he didn't let me use this car because I am his employee."

"Okay. I'm lost."

I smiled at Dannie and then I bit my lip. I knew I was blushing.

"Oh my God!" Dannie covered his mouth with his hands. "Sweetheart! For real?"

I nodded.

I parked in front of Starbucks. As soon as I was out of the car, Dannie hugged me. He had tears in his eyes.

"Are you happy?" he asked.

"Very! I cannot believe just how much!" I said to him.

Nicole and John were already sitting inside when we walked in.

"Was that you who just arrived in Ryder Van Woodsen's McLaren?" John asked.

I nodded.

"Why are you driving his car? Is he here?" Nicole asked.

"He's in Manhattan," I said.

"Don't tell me you're car-sitting."

I laughed. "That's also one way to put it. The other way is that Ryder doesn't want me to take a cab from this point forward."

"Why?"

"He's overprotective. Not that I mind," I said happily.

John chuckled. "Looks like the fake relationship just became real."

Nicole's eyes widened. "And you didn't tell us?"

"We just got together the other night. And yesterday we couldn't take our hands off each other. I couldn't call you. I felt like I was running out of time. Ryder had to go back to Manhattan early this morning. He was supposed to be back yesterday. He just extended his stay."

"So unlike the other trysts you have, this one is a full blown relationship now?" Nicole asked.

I nodded. "I love him, guys!"

"We know!" John said. "I think even Van Woodsen knew that a long time ago. Only you didn't want to admit it because you were afraid that he's too... elite for your taste!"

"I know. But I'm not afraid anymore. I want him. It doesn't matter if he comes in a shiny gift wrap when he's delivered to me."

"You're very lucky, Ash. He really cares about you," John said. "Remember that night we were at Oil Rig and the three of you went to the dance floor? Van Woodsen was watching you. He couldn't take his eyes off you. I noticed and I told him that I could tell he really likes you. He looked frustrated, and said that 'like' was a huge understatement because he's crazy about you. I knew he meant it. He couldn't understand why you didn't want to be with him. I told him that you were like this ever since Kevin Moore."

My eyes widened. "You told him about Kevin?"

"Relax, Ash! The guy had to understand where you were coming from."

"I thought I couldn't handle his world. That I couldn't exist in the same places as him. But I don't care anymore. Ryder is different from Kevin. Kevin was an ass. Ryder is a beautiful soul. Nobody has made me this happy. I may not belong in Ryder's world, but I'm sure now, I belong to him. I took a chance. I know he will shield me from the pain. No one in his high profile world or family would judge me. And even if they did, who cares? Only Ryder's opinion matters to me."

"So he's going to fly in and out of Manhattan?"

I nodded. "Fridays, Saturdays and Sundays, I have him here. Mondays to Thursdays, he's in New York."

"Well, if you love each other that much, you should be able to figure it out," Nicole said. "You're still in the business, aren't you?"

I nodded. "Of course. Ryder and I found our common ground now. He's asking me to be a partner, not an employee."

They all beamed at me. "We're happy for you, Ash. You really deserve this after all you have been through."

"I know. And I am so happy," I said, tears brimming in my eyes.

My phone beeped. I read Ryder's text message: *I love you. I'll be home sooner than you think! Wait for me ok?*

I smiled dreamily. I knew it was too much to ask. But if I really knew Ryder, I had a feeling we would be making love tonight. He would find a way to come back to me before the day was over.

And I couldn't wait. I thought about cooking a nice meal for us. He was not the only one who was romantic and full of surprises.

When I looked up my friends, they were smiling happily for me. I know they waited a long time to see me as happy as I am now.

I stayed with my friends for a while longer. Just then, my phone rang. It was Janis.

I know I have some explaining to do, but I was really hoping she'd forgive me.

"Hey Janis," I greeted chirpily.

There was silence. Then Janis croaked, obviously trying her best not to cry.

"What's wrong, honey?" I asked her nervously.

"You have to come to Manhattan," she said.

"Why? What happened?" My heart hammered inside my chest.

"Ryder had a car accident."

My phone slipped from my hand and suddenly, I felt my world crashing down on me.

24.
VEIL:
Covers the bride's face to the groom until he has fully committed to her
after the wedding ceremony.

I am made of stone. I can do this. I am not giving up! I told myself over and over.

I was sitting on the deck of Ryder's Malibu home. After so many nights I still felt alone, my heart was still broken and every single minute, I ached for the man who swore he would make my 'ever after' come true.

But he was not here anymore... I never felt so alone in my life. The pain was ten times worse than what I felt when Bryan and Geena betrayed me.

I remembered his laughter, his smile. I remembered his arms around me and the way he would look at me. I remembered how he never gave up on me. How he waited for me to realize that he was the right one for me. How long he waited for me to realize that I was in love with him after all.

He told me he would never hurt me. He told me that he would never make me cry or miserable.

But why do I feel like shit now? Damn, I must also look like shit. I haven't had a proper night's sleep in four months. I haven't been eating well. My employees are taking a lot of the pressure from my business because they understood that I was not myself.

I try not to let any of it affect me. But the pain of losing Ryder was a hundred times worse than being cheated on by Bryan and Geena. At least I had the right to be angry with them. But not this time. I had no right to be angry with Ryder at all no matter how badly I was hurting.

Everybody was worrying about me. Everybody was making a fuss. Everybody was trying to do everything they could to cheer me up, to make me strong.

Jake and Janis visit me frequently. My friends plan parties and night outs just to cheer me up. Even Ryder's sister and mother tried their best to reach out to me. It was unfortunate that we met each other for the first time at the hospital the same day Ryder had a car crash.

They were all making sure I didn't lose it. Trying to make sure that I would not do anything stupid. Like jump off a cliff and kill myself.

But I knew I would never do that. Because I told Ryder that I would always remember that he loved me. That I would never forget that. I would never give up. I would wait.

Being in Ryder's home has been my refuge. Because here, I still felt that he was with me. I could still hope that the phone would ring any minute and I would hear his voice on the other line asking me to be miserable without him.

He got that one right. I was miserable. I had been miserable for four freaking months!

Because I knew that phone would not ring for me. My cellphone will not beep with a text message from him. The Ryder Van Woodsen who loved me for the past few months was gone.

As fast as he told me that he would love me forever and after that, he was gone. Ryder... my savior, my knight in shining armor, my rock... the man who went to hell and back for me.

And with that thought I looked up at the sky and shouted, "Why?!" And tears kept coming.

***

Whenever I dreamed, I dreamed of the darkest hour of my life. I wanted nothing more than to wake up from it all. Except... it wasn't really a dream or a nightmare. They were memories... memories that ended my time with Ryder so abruptly even before I fully embedded myself in his life.

I remembered after I received a call from Janis, I rushed to the airport and immediately rushed to the hospital. My hands were shaking. My heart was pumping loudly inside my ribcage. Tears continued to stream down my face, but I couldn't even whimper. I was too scared to even make a sound.

Please God! Save him! Let him live! And I won't ask you anything ever again! Let him survive this!

I never thought Ryder could get hurt. He was my knight, my rock. He was supposed to be the strong one. He was always the one saving me, catching me from the fall. But now, I would trade everything I had just to have him live.

Suddenly, long smooth fingers enveloped my hands. I stared over at the dazzling green eyes staring back at me.

She looked brazenly beautiful. An aristocratic face that is so much similar to Ryder's.

Paris gave me an encouraging smile.

"My brother will come back for you," she said. "I know it. He will live... even if only to see you smile again."

Those words were meant to encourage me, but instead it made me cry even more. Because I knew that she was right. If the choice were up to him, Ryder would definitely come back for me.

Another woman sat beside me. I stared up at her. She had a regal face, and an almost formidable stand. She was as graceful as she was strong. She wasn't crying. She smiled at me. Her name was Helen Thompson, Ryder's mother.

"We have the best surgeons in the room with my son," she said. "I told them to make sure they do everything they could to save him."

I nodded, in spite of my tears.

Ryder's mom held her hand out to me. "Come. Family should wait together," she said.

Paris put an arm around me and we all went into a lounge to wait for news of Ryder's surgery.

At first, I was scared to meet Ryder's family. I knew most rich people would prefer an equally rich woman for their heir.

But from the moment I arrived at the airport, Paris had arranged for a limousine to pick me up and take me to the hospital. As soon as she saw me, she recognized who I was and hugged me, as if she had known me for a long time.

The first thing that Ryder's mother said to me was, "I wish we had met under more fortunate circumstances, Astrid. But I am glad to finally meet the most important woman in my son's life."

They had been nothing but nice to me. And their calmer reaction towards Ryder's accident gave me a little strength that Ryder could survive this.

A man arrived at the waiting room.

"All those bastards are in jail now," he said to Helen. "And I will make sure they stay there."

I knew he was talking about the drunken teenage kids who hit Ryder. They were speeding and they almost totaled Ryder's Cayenne. The only things that saved him were the car's safety features. But still, he suffered from severe head trauma and a couple of broken bones.

I was looking down and didn't notice that Mr. Van Woodsen was looking at me.

"And who is this beautiful young woman?" he asked.

I stared up at him and thought I saw a ghost… only an older version of it. He had raven black hair and his piercing green eyes were similar to Ryder's.

"Before you get any ideas, Richard, I have to inform you that this beautiful girl already belongs to your son," Helen said matter-of-factly. And then she turned to me. "Sweetheart, this is Richard, Ryder's father." She leaned closer to me and in a lower voice she said, "Don't worry. Ryder is nothing like him." Then she turned to the man. "Richard, this is Astrid, your son's fiancée."

I stared back at Ryder's mother. "I'm sorry, Ma'am… I'm not his fiancée," I corrected her.

She stared at me and smiled. "I think you will be… once the doctors get him fixed."

I looked at Ryder's father and extended my hand. "It's nice to meet you, Mr. Van Woodsen."

He shook my hand. "It's nice to meet the woman who finally captured my son's heart. For a while I thought he would be like his mother. Cold and incapable of falling in love."

"I think my son is better off that way. Unlike you who falls in love with anything that wears a skirt," Helen retorted haughtily.

Clearly, even though Ryder's parents managed to be in the same room with each other, they both still had a lot of unresolved issues.

"Mom, Dad..." Paris interrupted. "If you keep on with the bickering, Astrid will probably turn down Ryder just so she won't be part of this family."

As if realizing the way that they were behaving, Ryder's mom smiled at me apologetically and Mr. Van Woodsen said, "I'm sorry, Astrid. I guess it's too early for you to witness that."

I forced a smile.

Paris took my arm and said, "Come, Astrid. I'm starving. You look like you need chocolate to cheer you up."

I was quiet all the way to the cafeteria. Paris ordered coffee and devil's chocolate cake for both of us. When I sat on the table opposite her, she was eyeing me wearily.

"I'm sorry," I said. "I can't help worrying."

She smiled. How could she be so calm?

"Ryder will get through this," she said.

"I really hope you're right." I stared back at her. She looked so much like Ryder, but she looked every bit feminine and beautiful. Her hair is perfectly tied in a pony. Her long delicate fingers ended with perfectly trimmed short nails. Her skin was creamy and flawless. She was every bit a princess with her calm demeanor, bright eyes, and haughty smile.

"My brother loves you, you know."

I nodded. "I love him too." Then tears brimmed in my eyes again. "God, I wish I could say that to him again."

"You will," she said encouragingly. "He's a fighter. He won't give you up so easily. Well... you know that by now, right?"

I nodded. I knew that. Ryder spent months waiting for me to realize that he was the right one for me. I only realized that two days ago. And two days is just too damn short for me to show him that I was worth the wait. I prayed that I had more time with him. And I would make up for all the months I resisted falling in love with him.

"I was so excited to meet you," Paris said. "I thought my brother cared for nothing but our businesses and his own self. But when he gave me Oil Rig Manhattan, I knew something was up. And then I realized it was you. He was ready to settle down and spend down time with the girl of his dreams."

"How do you know I was the girl of his dreams?"

"Because you made him fall in love," she replied. "And he seemed so incapable of doing that. He wanted a woman who would like him even if he wasn't who he was."

"The fact that he is Ryder Van Woodsen made me think twice or thrice about falling for him," I said. "I didn't want a complicated relationship."

"But he's so much worth it, sweetheart," Paris said. "Ryder is probably the sweetest guy I know. He just doesn't show it."

I smiled bitterly. "He showed me all the time. I was too stubborn to appreciate it. And then... two days ago, I gave in. I gave up fighting what I feel for him. I thought I'd take a risk. Because he was worth it. And now..." Tears rolled down my cheeks. "This can't be over!"

"Ssshhh..." Paris reached out and squeezed my hand. "A love story as beautiful as yours couldn't be over too soon, Astrid. You have so much more to go through together. You both deserve to be happy with each other."

Just then, her phone rang. It was her mother. My heart pounded in my ribcage.

God! Please!

Paris hung up and she stared at me. She smiled slowly. "Surgery is done," she said. "The doctors said he is stable, but still unconscious."

Relief washed through me. Tears streamed down my cheeks. I stood up and hugged Paris.

"See? I told you, your love story isn't over yet," she said as she hugged me back.

***

I stayed with Paris in Ryder's apartment. In the mornings, I relentlessly stayed on Ryder's side, waiting for him to open his eyes. His vitals were stable, but we couldn't be sure he was out of danger until he opened his eyes.

He had a broken wrist and a couple of broken ribs. His major injury was to his head. And that worried everyone the most.

Then finally, he opened his eyes. I hugged Janis in relief when we first heard him speak.

"Come on, guys," he said to them. "I'm slightly tougher than you give me credit for."

Then he whispered everybody's names, as he looked at us one by one. We were all laughing and crying at the same time. It was such a relief for us to see him get through a terrible accident.

Then finally, his eyes landed on me. I smiled at him with all the love I had in my heart.

A glitter lit in his eyes for a moment and then it died. He narrowed his eyes and continued staring at me.

Finally, he opened his mouth and asked, "Who the hell are you?"

Everybody in the room gasped, including myself.

"Ry... Ryder... you're kidding, right?" I whispered.

He raised a brow and stared at me haughtily. Then he stared at his father. "Dad, I told you I don't want a female secretary! We discussed this. The last thing I want is for one of our female employees to get too close to me and hope she could get her hands on my..."

"Ryder Anthony Van Woodsen!" his mother's voice boomed in the room getting everybody's attention, including Ryder's. "I didn't raise you to act so ungentlemanly towards a woman... especially if she is your girlfriend."

Ryder blinked back at his mother. "Girlfriend? The last time I checked, I was very... *very* single."

I lost my breath. How could this be?

"Wait..." Paris said. "You don't remember Astrid?"

"Is that her name?" Ryder asked. He looked back at me curiously. "I'm pretty sure I would remember having a girlfriend. But I don't. Sorry, sweetheart. Nice try, though." And he turned away from me.

My heart felt like it just shattered to pieces. How could he act like this towards me?

Jake came back with the doctor. We were asked to leave the room. Jake put an arm around my shoulder and escorted me outside the room.

"What's wrong with him, Jake?" I asked.

"I have a suspicion. But we need tests to confirm this," he said," he said. He squeezed my shoulder. "Ryder loves you, Ash. Trust me. I've known him since we were kids. No matter what happens, I want you to keep remembering that, okay?"

Then he went back into Ryder's room.

Tears streamed down my face. Paris and Janis both hugged me.

"It will be okay," Janis said.

I took a deep breath and hugged them back. "But at least, he's conscious now, right?"

Even if he was acting weird like he didn't know me, I was sincerely glad that he made it out of this accident alive.

We waited for a whole six hours. We were asked not to see Ryder while the tests were being done. Even Jake didn't want to say anything to us. The waiting was killing me. I was relieved that Ryder would make it. But I was so scared by the way he acted towards me when he woke up.

It was three in the morning when finally Jake came to the waiting room. He looked tired. But I could see that he didn't look devastated, and somehow that was comforting enough for me.

"He's stable," he said and everybody breathed in a sigh of relief. Then Jake took a deep breath and said, "But... he's suffering from retrograde amnesia."

"What?" Mr. Van Woodsen echoed.

"It's a form of amnesia where the patient loses some of his memories. But it could be temporary. It could heal by itself eventually."

"When?"

Jake shrugged. "We can't tell."

"What could be done?" Ryder's mom asked.

Jake shook his head. "Nothing much. Some therapies could help. But other than that, we just wait it out."

"How... how much of his memories did he lose?" I asked in a weak voice.

Jake had a hard expression on his face when he looked at me. I could immediately tell it was not good news for me.

"How much?" I repeated my question.

"A year, Astrid."

I gasped. *A year*. No wonder he didn't remember me.

An arm came around me. I realized it was Paris's. She gave me an encouraging squeeze. When I stared up at her, tears were brimming in my eyes.

Paris promised that Ryder would come back for me. He did come back alright. But not for me. He didn't even know me.

"Could we... see him?" Janis asked.

Jake stared at me for a while. Then he said, "It's not a good idea for Astrid to see him yet. He's not ready for you, honey. We have to take this slowly."

I whimpered. When I squeezed my eyes shut, tears slid down my cheeks. But I completely understood what Jake was saying. We all had to do our parts in getting Ryder through this. And right now, my part was... to stay away.

"I... I understand." I whispered.

"It's already late, child. You haven't had enough sleep. You could rest. I will ask the driver to take you back to Ryder's apartment."

I didn't argue. I nodded and gave Helen a weak smile. Then I looked at Jake. "When could I see him?"

"I will see how he improves in a couple of days," he replied.

I fought the tears and kept a calm façade in front of Ryder's family and friends. The last thing they needed was to see me devastated. They deserved to be happy that at least Ryder is out of danger now. That he would live through this.

But once I got inside the limousine that Helen sent for me, I broke down and cried my heart out.

25.

VELLUM:

A thin, transparent or semi-transparent type of paper the effect of which resembles a frosted glass, commonly used in wedding invitations.

Ryder.

When I woke up at the hospital, my first thought was that I was late for my meeting in Malibu. I just opened Oil Rig and would soon open another bar, Rig Style.

When I opened my eyes, my family and friends were staring back at me curiously, all with tears in their eyes.

That's when I realized that something must have happened to me. Judging from the throbbing pain I felt in my head, the fact that I could barely move my body due the tight bandages wrapped around me in the rib area, I guessed that I was in a car accident.

Damn! I wonder which of my cars I have to say goodbye to. I hope it's not my McLaren. I just bought it a month ago and the price was not sweet at all. I would hate to say goodbye to it so soon.

When I spoke, I told a joke and everybody around me laughed in relief. I called each of them by name. Then, my eyes landed on an unfamiliar face.

Strawberry blonde hair. Exotic, mesmerizing eyes. Legs that seemed to go forever. Curves that all seemed to be at the right places.

Who is she? What is she doing here with my family, looking torn and relieved at the same time?

In spite of myself, my heart hammered inside my ribcage and my pulse doubled its pace. I couldn't take my eyes off her. She was... enchanting. Beautiful. I studied her further. Her skin was flawless and creamy. Her eyelashes were long and even though she has circles around her eyes that seem to say that she hasn't slept in days, she still looked mesmerizing.

It took me a moment to realize that I was actually dazzled by her. I, Ryder Van Woodsen, cold and proud of being fully in control of my testosterone levels to prevent a woman from having power over me, am experiencing intense waves of *desire* for a woman I haven't seen before in my life.

She looked at me with hopeful, teary eyes.

What? Is she expecting me to know her name?

Is she one of Paris's friends? Or maybe Janis's? I didn't think I died, so how come I see an angel before me? I don't know her. But damn! I'm interested. I would definitely get to know her.

Her perfect lips were quivering, as if the suspense was killing her. She was expecting something from me. What?

Actually, she wasn't the only one expecting me to say something to her. Everybody in the room fell quiet, looking at me, waiting for me to say something... to this woman.

Well, right now, there are a hundred things I would like to say to her. But I would rather say them when we're alone... hopefully with a bed nearby. My mother would be scandalized if she knew my exact thoughts about their guest right now.

I opened my mouth, and the first thing that came out was, "Who the hell are you?"

Everybody gasped. And she looked devastated. Soon, I learned that her name was Astrid. And apparently, she introduced herself to my family as my girlfriend.

Damn! What does she think of me? Or my family? That we were a bunch of morons?

Nice try! The little chit thought she could cheat her way into my world. Where did she come from? How did she even know me? I was certain I haven't seen her before. I would have remembered.

I gave her one last look before they were all shoved outside the room. She was in shock, as if she didn't know what hit her. Funny because I thought I was the one who got into an accident.

For hours they ran their tests. My mind was floating. I was barely aware of the questions they asked me, which I answered absent-mindedly. About eighty percent of my consciousness now focused on the bombshell waiting outside with my family.

Why did she introduce herself as my girlfriend? Did she plot the whole thing, and think I wouldn't wake up to call her on her bluff? I wouldn't be surprised if her next trick included telling my family I got her knocked up. Gold-diggers these days are getting more and more creative. But this one... she looked so naïve, so innocent.

Ten bucks say she won't come back to see me again. She had been discovered. She would probably slip away slowly because the minute my father realized she was lying about being my girlfriend, he would call the police on her.

What a shame. She was so... beautiful. And just the mere thought of her had me reeling with desire.

Damn! Something must be seriously wrong with me. A potential crook or mercenary has gotten her hands into my family and all I could think about was getting under the sheets with her.

Finally, they finished the tests. The doctor was explaining to Jake and me some retrograde shit. I couldn't care less. As long as I was strong enough to stand up, I would be out of this place in no time.

When the door opened again, I watched the people coming in one by one. I scanned their faces, hoping to see her again. But just as I suspected, she was gone. She fled!

A lump formed in my throat and my heart felt like it had been twisted tightly. *Damn it!* I don't understand this. Why do I feel like this? All because I didn't see her again?

I was really disappointed. Something about her piques my interest to the highest level.

My family kept reassuring me that everything was going to be okay. They said therapies would be done and I should be all right. I don't know why they fuss so much. I'm okay. I feel fine. It's just a bunch of broken bones.

Everybody left after an hour. Only Jake and Janis lingered a while longer.

"We… thought it wasn't a good idea for you to see Astrid yet," Jake said.

I stared at him for a long while. "Where is she?"

"In your… she's home," Janis replied. But I didn't miss the first response she was supposed to say. Is she in my apartment? Well, that's fresh! Who the hell is this woman?

"Who is she?"

"She is… your girlfriend, Ry," Jake said. He took a deep breath. "But with your amnesia, unfortunately, you wouldn't remember her."

Amnesia. The word registered in my mind for the first time today.

"What?"

Jake blinked back at me. "Weren't you listening to the doctor, man?"

I shrugged. "I figured that's what you're there for," I replied.

"Shit!" Jake cursed. He stared back at me. "You have retrograde amnesia, Ryder. You lost a year of your memories."

If I was heating up with desire at the thought of Astrid a while ago, now I felt like ten buckets of ice have been poured over my head.

One year. I lost a year of my memory. I took a deep breath and stared at my best friends again.

"One year?"

Jake nodded.

I figured it shouldn't matter a lot. I could read about the current events on Google. I would ask for month per month reports on my businesses and I should get everything back on track. I would check all my bank accounts to make sure I didn't squander my money over the last year.

It doesn't matter, right? After all, nothing much could happen to me in a span of one year. *Right?*

I asked them about Oil Rig and Rig Style. Apparently, I have two bars in Malibu now, perfectly operating well. I just opened another branch in Manhattan and all my bars are doing perfectly well. Paris is managing all the ones in Manhattan. Why I allowed that, I don't know. Apparently, I invested in a wedding events business that just opened about six months ago and is now doing well, I was contemplating on branching it out in New York. Astrid is heading this company.

I pressed the skin between my eyes. My head suddenly hurt with all the information that I got from Jake and Janis. It was like looking at my life in full fast forward. Except that it doesn't feel like my life at all. I don't remember any of this.

And there were some that didn't seem right. Like why the hell would I trust Paris to handle my business? I'm quite territorial and meticulous with what I do, particularly with my ventures. And I don't invest in things I absolutely have no experience, knowledge, or interest in… like wedding planning. For starters, I don't even think I would be married at all. I don't believe in marriage. Can't really blame me for the ideal setup my parents have, right?

Did Astrid make me do all these things? How did she convince me to put up a business for her? How did she make me… weak? Gullible?

"Ryder… Astrid is your…" Janis started.

"Stop. I don't want to hear it," I cut her off.

"But you have to! You're in love with her!"

I raised a brow. *In love?* No. Ryder Van Woodsen is not capable of falling in love. Especially, with a woman he doesn't know or hasn't known for a long time. I've made sure of that. For years, I have mastered the art of dodging feminine charms for fear that they were just after my money. I learned well from my father's marriages, thank you very much!

"Ryder, Astrid is the woman you have been…" Jake started.

"Save it," I said. I shook my head. "I don't want to hear about it. Whatever she's done, it wasn't good. I know now I've made stupid decisions in the past year. I don't want to hear how I've been gullible enough to fall for her charms. So please, if you want this friendship to not end, spare me the details about Astrid. I don't want to hear them."

"She's hurting! She was worried sick that you wouldn't wake up from your coma. That you wouldn't survive this accident," Janis protested.

I laughed humorlessly. "Well, she shouldn't have been worried that I was in a coma. She should be scared now that I'm awake."

"What are you going to do?" Janis asked, fear evident in her eyes. Yeah, this is one girl who knows me too well.

"I will fix my life," I replied. "I will undo whatever stupid things I've done in the past. And I don't care who gets hurt in between. It's time to put a stop to this Astrid's manipulating spells. They won't work anymore."

Janis gave me a shocked look. She took a deep breath and then she balled her fists. For a moment, I thought she was going to attack me, broken ribs and all. But Jake held her firmly by the waist.

Jake gave me a look of disapproval. "Ryder... there's about eighty percent chance you're going to recover from this amnesia. And I guarantee you... you would regret it if you go down this path."

"Then I'll take full responsibility for all my actions," I said confidently. I've lived all my life without a woman and I was happy. Why would I regret it if I wake up from this, and Astrid was gone? Life goes on as usual.

Tears spilled from Janis's eyes. Damn! What has Astrid done to my best friend? Janis was tough and feisty. Why is she crying for a girl we didn't even know? A girl who doesn't even look like she was one of us. A girl who might have a hidden agenda underneath her innocent and sweet façade.

Janis stood up from her chair and headed for the door. She gave me one angry look and then she slammed the door behind her.

I stared at Jake, who looked like he was trying his best to understand me, but underneath that calm face of his, I know he was also raging mad.

"I won't regret this," I said to him. "You know me."

He smiled bitterly. "That's the problem, Ryder. I know you too well. And I know that when you do wake up from all this mess, you would wish you never survived this accident at all."

Then he stood up and left without another word.

Great! Now it's me against everybody. What has that woman done to everybody in my life?

I thought about her mesmerizing eyes, which were unique and interesting. Suddenly, I wanted to stand an inch away from her, just so I could tell what her exact eye color is. I know it isn't blue. It's something more beautiful and enchanting. And how she managed to enchant each and every one around me is beyond my understanding. But I intend to change that. Regardless of whether Jake was right or not. Regardless of who will be the casualty in the end.

***

I heard the sound of sweet laughter in my ears. I reached out for her and enveloped her in my arms. She stared up at me; her violet eyes were enchanting me. Wow! So violet eyes do exist. And the woman in my arms was beyond beautiful.

She wrapped her arms around my neck to pull me down for a passionate kiss. I completely drowned. I lost myself in her. My heart felt like it was bursting with emotions. Emotions I felt only for the first time in my life.

"I love you," she whispered to me.

I took a deep breath and took in her sweet familiar scent. *I love you too.* I wanted to say, but I when I opened my mouth, no words came out.

Then I saw tears in her eyes. Her soul was visible in them. She was sad. And I felt an unfamiliar feeling inside me like I wanted to comfort her and make everything right again, so she could smile that sweetest smile for me again. I felt like I wanted to kill anybody who would put tears to her eyes. She doesn't deserve to cry. She was too beautiful to be miserable. I felt like I would do anything to make her happy.

"Come back to me, Ryder." I heard her whisper. And I felt my heart shatter at that very instant. I wanted to tell her that I would come home soon. That she should wait for me. I wanted to wrap my arms around her again, see the love in her violet eyes shine for me. But when I reached out, there was only darkness. She was gone. But her scent lingers in my arms. Her memory faded into darkness. And all of a sudden, I feel empty and broken.

I opened my eyes. Light streamed from the window. And I realized that it was just a dream. I dreamt of a woman. Who she was, I wasn't sure. I couldn't remember her face, only her violet eyes and the memory of her scent still lingered with me. I remembered how I felt when I held her. It was like I was home. I haven't felt like that before. Weak and yet, it seemed like I was the strongest I could be. Different, and yet, complete. Lost and yet, there was nowhere else I wanted to be.

The door opened, bringing me back to reality. My sister was staring back at me with a hard look on her face. I took a deep breath. I realized that the scent of the woman in my dreams still lingered with me. I closed my eyes for a moment, and for a while, I thought I remembered that scent. It seems familiar to me. But I can't remember why. What does that scent remind me of? Or maybe I should ask, who?

"She was here," Paris said, walking towards the side of my bed. "We told her to stay away for a while, but she just couldn't help herself."

I stared back at her and her face was the same as it always was. Stoic. Paris is good at hiding her emotions. She's actually good at hiding many things. But she just doesn't know that I know almost all of the things she tries to keep to herself. She doesn't know that I know underneath her sweet, haughty princess façade, is a rebel on fire.

Like right now, I know she is raging with anger. She is just better at keeping her emotions in check than I am. And for a woman, that's a very admirable trait. I pity the guy who would one day try to win her heart. I pity the guys my father tried to set up to be her husband. They all fell to her feet and not one of them actually became successful at making her fall in love.

Paris is a hopeless romantic. Not many people know that. She's had boyfriends before and had fallen in love more than once, but after a heartbreak or two, it looked like she just gave up. Her more important mission now, it seems, is to prove to my father that he could never manipulate her into marrying a man he chose for her. And for years, she's always been successful. Until now, he worries for her future. He wasn't always there for her. And I think he feels guilty for that. He wanted the best for his daughter, and he wanted to make sure she would marry well. The last thing we want is a scumbag who would use her and squander the wealth that was hers from the moment she was born.

"Did you see her?" she asked.

I shook my head.

"Good." She murmured. Finally, someone who was on my side.

"It was right for you guys to tell her to stay away from me," I said. "Permanently."

Paris raised a brow at me. Anger flared in her beautiful green eyes again. "Oh, I'm sorry bro. I think you misunderstood me. I wasn't asking her to stay away from you for your own good. It's for her own."

I stared back at her, seriously confused. I thought this girl looked up to me like I was her hero.

"From the moment you woke up, all you did was crush that poor girl's spirit, Ryder! The old you wouldn't be so ruthless," she said. "I can't stand on the sidelines and watch you beat her over and over again. That's why I wanted her to stay away until… you're you again."

Oh great! So now Astrid got to my baby sister, too. What is it about that woman?

"Paris… there's no point fighting about this okay? Aren't you glad that at least you still have a brother?" I asked.

Guilt crossed her face. And then she sat down on the bed beside me. She sighed. "You're right. I'm sorry. I am glad that you're back. I just… hope you would be your old happy self again."

"I am happy," I said.

She shook her head. "No, you're not, Ry." She sighed. "I saw you that morning of the day of the accident. You were… in heaven. You talked like you couldn't believe what was happening to you. There was a permanent smile on your face, and your eyes were sparkling like you were mad." She smiled bitterly at the memory. "That's happiness, Ryder. When I saw you that morning, it made me wish…" She swallowed back a sob. "It made me wish I could fall in love again. That I could smile like an idiot like you were. The first time you saw me, you gave me a hug, lifted me off my feet and spun me around like I was still six years old. I knew that you really were happy."

I listened to her in shock. The person she described wasn't me at all. What did I smoke that day?

"Was I high?" I asked.

She giggled. "No, you idiot," she said. "You just came back from Malibu. And you told me you were actually thinking of flying back there in the evening. I thought you were crazy for even thinking you could go back and forth from Manhattan to Malibu every day!"

"Okay, I thought you said I wasn't stoned. Because that doesn't sound like something a sane person would do."

"Yes, you were crazy, Ryder. You were crazy in love with Ash," Paris said sadly.

I felt overwhelming sadness fill me all of a sudden. I can't understand it. But at that moment, I felt miserable. As if I remembered feeling all the things that Paris said, but even before I try to grasp on to that feeling, it was gone. And for that, I suddenly felt angry. I don't know why. I don't even know who I was mad at.

"Paris, please," I whispered. "Could you leave me be for a while?" I asked, turning away from her and closing my eyes.

I heard her deep sigh of frustration. And then she headed towards the door and closed it behind her.

There is no doubt in my mind that I wanted Astrid. I could feel desire reel through me at the mention of her name. But at the same time, I can't remember feeling all the things that my sister and my friends were saying to me. I can't feel the love they desperately wanted me to remember. Lust is different from love.

And the lunatic my sister described to me was not me at all. Did I become a whole different person because of her? I like being me. I'm happy being me. I'm contented with my life. I don't need to change for a woman. Moreover, I don't need to be weak because of her.

For years, I have been careful not to fall in love. Love means weakness. And I can't bear the thought of being weak... not even for one second. I can't bear to have another person have full control of my life, or my emotions. I built a Goddamn shield to keep feeling emotions that would lead to my fall someday.

I don't know the guy my friends and my sister kept describing me as. That was not me. That guy is an idiot! He sounded like he's ready to give up everything he worked hard for, his wealth and his life, and hand it to a woman on a silver platter.

There was only one woman I would have wished for if ever I would fall in love at all. A woman who would love me even if I weren't Ryder Van Woodsen. Somebody who wants *me* even if I don't have money in my pocket. But reality check! My family was too popular; my name always rang a bell. I was probably one of the most eligible bachelors in the city, even in the country; I was easily recognizable and wanted. By wanted I didn't mean, women really wanted me. They wanted the heir of the Van Woodsen multi-billion dollar empire.

No. It's impossible to find a woman who would really like me for who I am. She doesn't exist. I could only hope to marry well to ensure the family wealth stays intact and my wife does not use her status to extort me for all I was worth. That was the plan. I was okay with that. That was my reality.

But my friends were telling me differently. How the hell did I let go of all I believe in for a woman? How the hell did that woman get through my shield?

254

Maybe it's a good thing that I lost my memory. Because I have been given a chance to undo this foolishness without the complications of the so-called undying-love I apparently have for her.

26.
BRIDAL REGISTRY:
A log of the couple's gift preferences aimed at making it easier for wedding guests to shop for gifts for the couple.

Astrid.

I went to the hospital every single day. But I never got a chance to see Ryder. The doctors didn't encourage it until all the tests were done and they were sure about the gravity of his amnesia.

"You should go back to Malibu," Janis advised. "We'll keep you posted, when he's ready to see you."

I shook my head. "He should at least try to see me, Jan," I said hopefully. "Maybe if he sees me… it would trigger some memories to come back."

"We have to do this slowly, Ash," Jake said. "Only time can help Ryder now."

I think the sight of me was unsettling to Ryder and it didn't help his recovery to be emotionally aggravated. But I couldn't help myself. Once, when he was sound asleep, I went to his room. Tears welled up in my eyes as I saw him still in bandages. I was so happy that he made it. Even though he didn't remember me, I will still always be thankful that God heard my prayers. Ryder was alive.

I leaned forward and rested my head on his arm. I allowed tears to come. I wanted to feel his warmth. I wanted to feel his love again. But I guess I had to wait some more. I knew deep inside that mind of his were his memories of me. And he would fight for his way back.

I stared at his peaceful, handsome face. Ryder. My knight in shining armor. My rock. Now, I will have to be strong for our love. And I will wait for him, no matter how much it hurts.

"I love you," I whispered. Then I leaned forward and kissed his forehead gently, still careful not to wake him up. "Come back to me, Ryder."

I felt his fingers flinch a little. My heart pounded inside my chest. I knew he was not ready for me yet. And I didn't want to make things worse than they already were. So, slowly I backed down from the bed and tiptoed my way out of his room. I leaned on his door and took a deep breath.

When I opened my eyes, I found a pair of curious, beautiful green eyes staring back at me.

Paris smiled at me apologetically. "Did he see you?" she asked.

I shook my head.

"I know it hurts, sweetheart," she said. "But give it a little bit more time. He'll come around. And I'm sure he would ask for you." She gave my hand a squeeze and then finally, she went inside the room.

In spite of all their advice, I still went to the hospital every single day. Once in a while, when I knew he was sound asleep, I would go to his room. I would whisper, "*I love you*" as I kissed him goodnight before I went back to his apartment and cried my heart out.

A month had passed before he finally asked for me.

"Are you Astrid?" a nurse asked me while I was in my usual spot in the waiting room. I was alone, waiting for one of Ryder's friends or family to keep me company.

I nodded.

"Mr. Van Woodsen would like to see you," she smiled.

I felt a glimmer of hope that maybe he finally remembered me. I stood up from my seat and followed the nurse to his room. Ryder was sitting on the bed. He looked better than the last time I saw him. His stitches look like they were starting to heal now.

I stood at the foot of his bed. The nurse left us. Ryder stared at me for a long time. He was studying me. My heart pounded in my chest, and I realized that I wasn't breathing properly.

When I looked into his eyes, I couldn't see the usual emotion he used to have whenever he looked at me. His expression was void of love and tenderness. I bit my lip, hoping desperately that he would say something.

Then finally, he took a deep breath and said, "Well, at least you are pretty."

He didn't say that gently. I couldn't recognize the exact emotion in his voice. He sounded like he was angry, but he was also a little relieved. "You say you're my girlfriend?"

"Y-yes," I said weakly.

He raised a brow. "You lack conviction when you say that. It makes it harder for me to believe it."

I took a deep breath again and then repeated my answer, "Yes, Ryder. I am your girlfriend."

"How long have we been together?"

I didn't know how to explain this. Unofficially, we've been together for about ten months. But officially, it was a lot shorter than that. Yeah, like two days before he forgot about me.

"We've been together for less than a week before your accident... officially."

"*Officially?*"

I nodded. "We've been pretending to be engaged for about ten months now."

He narrowed his eyes. *"Pretending?"*

I nodded. "It's a long story."

"I'm sure! As you can see, I can't remember all the stupid things I did this year. So please... feel free to enlighten me!"

"Stupid?" I repeated. That felt like a slap in the face. Did he think having me, as a girlfriend, was stupid?

"Yes," he replied. "Why would I pretend to be somebody's fiancé? Do I look like I couldn't get a woman to marry me for *real?*"

I shook my head. "No."

"Then why, Ms. Jacobson, would I pretend to be your fiancé?"

I sighed. "Because I asked you to. My ex-fiancé cheated on me with my cousin and I attended their wedding with you. You helped me out, so I could save my pride and my dignity in front my family."

"Why would I do that?" he asked.

I shrugged. "Because... because you said you liked me. And that was your way to get to know me."

He raised a brow. "You mean I agreed to play along with your charade so I could get you to bed?" he asked blatantly.

My eyes widened. "No, Ryder," I said. "You would never do that. It was never about the sex for you. You're... for real. You really cared about me."

"I couldn't care about you on such a short notice, miss. I wonder what you did before that."

"You said... you said I got under your skin the first moment you laid eyes on me."

He stared at me. And then he laughed so hard it started to insult me. He shook his head. "Clearly, miss, you are mistaken. That does not sound like me at all." He swung his legs to the side of the bed and he stood up.

My heart pounded in my chest as he approached me. When he was close enough he looked down and studied my face. He looked into my eyes. Then I saw a glimmer of emotion there, some sort of recognition. But it was so short I thought I must have imagined it. "Are your eyes violet?" he asked.

I nodded. I couldn't breathe. He was standing too close. And it killed me to know that this was the same man I loved, my Ryder... and yet he was so different and because of that, I couldn't get through him at all.

"You sure you're not a witch?" he asked. "Because you must have put me under a spell or given me a love potion. That would be the only explanation for all my rash actions. The man you are telling me about now does not sound like me at all."

I closed my eyes in disbelief. Then I took a deep breath and reminded myself that it was not his fault there was a stupid cloud in his brain that veiled his memories of me.

"Ryder, I know this is too much to handle for now." I figured Jake was right to keep me away from him for the past month. "Let's... take this slow," I said to him.

"Well, you should have told me that ten months ago!" he said. "Apparently, this year I did everything in super-fast mode! If you really know me, Ms. Jacobson, you know I don't fall for a woman that fast. I am not rash. More importantly, I am not gullible."

I nodded. "I know that, Ryder."

"So can you just tell me what you want from me and we can end this charade now? My life is already complicated as it is."

"Ryder…" I started. What was he saying? Was he breaking up with me? Without him knowing me and everything that happened to us in the last year? So unfair!

"What did you really want, Miss Jacobson? Is it the money? How much?"

"What?" I asked back, totally appalled.

"Come on, miss. It's only the two of us in here. And I noticed that you have won over my mother, my sister, and my best friends. I want you to stay away from them, too. Could we stop all pretenses now and let's just go our separate ways and pretend nothing happened? I am willing to compensate you for your trouble."

My eyes widened. I swear, if Ryder didn't already have a brain injury, I was going to inflict one on him. I was seething with anger. *How dare he? What does he think of me?*

"I don't believe this!" I threw my hands in the air.

"I know, right? Me too!" He rolled his eyes sarcastically.

I stared back at him, tears starting to brim my eyes.

He stared back at me. He narrowed his eyes and I saw a glint of emotion there. Then his expression turned cold again.

"Please don't cry, Miss Jacobson," he said. "It won't work on me."

I blinked back the tears. How could this Ryder be so mean?

"Let's not beat around the bush. You probably came from a middle class family. You came here, no fancy clothes, no expensive jewelry. I was told you were a wedding planner. I think you are ambitious; you needed somebody to bring you to the world of the rich. Well, maybe it's a good thing that I lost a year of my memory, because I have time to undo what you are about to do to me."

"Ryder, don't say this," I begged him silently, tears rolling down my cheeks, in spite of him asking me not to cry.

He stood there watching me. I knew that he was only trying to be mean to me to shove me away. I could see a glimmer of emotion in his eyes, but he was fighting it.

"When was the last time I went to bed with you?" he asked.

I stared at him, confused with his question. "What…"

"Answer the question. When was the last time I had sex with you?" he asked bluntly.

"The day before your accident," I replied weakly.

"That would be over a month ago," he said," he said. "I want you to take a pregnancy test. I just want to make sure that you're not pregnant."

Every queen needs a prince or a princess in her Ever After too. And suddenly, remembering him say those words to me so tenderly made me cry even more. I wiped the tears on my cheeks and nodded.

"What would you do if I am?" I asked back.

He raised a brow at me. "Aren't you on the pill?"

I shook my head slowly.

He shrugged. "I'm sure I always used protection. I doubt that you are pregnant. But just in case, I want to be sure. And then we will talk about you staying out of my life so I can start fresh. As you can see, I lost a year of my life. That's a lot to catch up on."

"Why... why would you want to get rid of me?"

"Because I don't trust you," he said," he said. "How the hell you made me fall in love with you, I do not know. How you made me put my money on your business, I am also not sure. You must be really good in bed. I am usually not the type of man who would fall under a woman's spell. And I stay away from girls like you."

"Girls like me? What do you think I am?"

He shrugged. "I don't know you well enough to judge you. But the last thing I want is to end up with a mercenary slut who is only using me to gain access to my bank accounts!"

"Mercenary slut?" I echoed. Is this what Ryder was like before I met him? "You're calling me a mercenary slut?"

He shrugged. "I didn't say that you are. I don't know you well enough to judge you. I'm just saying that I'm trying to stay away from women who only wanted me for what I am worth."

I bit my lip and balled my fists inside my jeans' pockets to keep myself from swinging the metal food tray across his face.

"Maybe it's not a good idea for us to talk today. I'll see you some other time," I said to him.

I turned away from him. When I looked back, I found that his eyes were looking at my behind. He was totally checking me out. Finally, he looked at my face.

"Well, for what it's worth, I understand why I would have been attracted to you," he said. "But I still don't think you could trick me into marriage... or love."

I was so angry, hurt, and insulted, I didn't bother to retort back. I turned away from him and bumped into Jake who was just getting inside the room.

He stared down at me and saw the tears I was trying to hold back. His expression softened and he reached out to touch my shoulder.

"Astrid, are you okay?"

"I'll be fine, Jake. I'm a rock!" I said to him, mustering all the courage I could find.

Then I turned to leave the room. I heard Jake shout at Ryder, "Not cool, man! Totally not cool!"

I was so upset when I got back to Ryder's apartment. Ryder seems like a total stranger now. I never knew he could be this harsh, this mean. When I met him, he was a dream. He was a sweet guy who I thought only existed in romance novels and fairy tales. This Ryder also seemed unreal… but in a terrible way.

God, he was worse than Kevin Moore! And Kevin and his mother were the reasons why I vowed I would never date a filthy rich guy who was out of my league. I didn't want to be judged, to be measured whether or not I met the minimum acceptable standards. I didn't want my boyfriend and his family to question me, to doubt whether I really loved him or was in it for the status and the money.

It took me months to stop fighting what I feel for Ryder. He was so persistent, so sincere, so desperate; he did everything to make me believe him, trust in him. And now… he was an example of the very reason why I didn't want to fall for him in the first place.

Sometimes, I find my stupid situation so hilarious, I would actually roll on the floor laughing if I was not too busy bawling my eyes out.

That night I slept in one of his long-sleeved shirts again. And as I lay down on his bed and cried my heart out, I prayed for about the millionth time that this was just a bad dream that I would soon wake up from.

***

"You could keep staying in Ryder's apartment," Paris told me the day that Ryder would be going home from the hospital.

"No, it's okay. I know he's still not ready to see me," I said. "I could stay in a hotel."

"Nonsense," she said. "He will stay at my mother's house for a while. At least there, we have maids and butlers to attend to his needs while he is healing," Paris explained. "He won't come back to his apartment. Stay there."

I should be happy Ryder's physical wounds were healing. I would have been the happiest woman on earth if only his memories hadn't gotten messed up… if only he could remember even a second of our time together.

"Do you think I could see him again?" I asked.

Paris nodded. "Yes. He has to deal with you, no matter how hard he tries to run away from it."

"I don't understand that, actually."

262

"My brother didn't believe he could actually fall in love. You confuse him," Paris replied. "And he doesn't know what to do with you."

Oh, this Ryder Van Woodsen knows what to do with me all right! He wants to get rid of me so fast; he was even willing to pay me. But I didn't tell anybody that. I know Ryder didn't mean it. If he were himself, he would never say those words at all.

I went with Paris to her mother's house. Helen had a ten-bedroom mansion. The whole house was swarming with butlers and maids keeping it well taken care of.

Helen was ecstatic to see me. "Sweetheart." She gave me a hug. "I'm so glad to see you. I told one of the maids to call Ryder."

Helen and I chatted in the tea room, while Paris excused herself.

"That girl." Helen sighed.

Paris?

"You're family now, Astrid. I suppose I could tell you. I worry about her."

"She seems like a girl who could take care of herself," I said.

"Yes. Sometimes a little too much." Helen heaved a frustrated breath.

"I don't understand."

"Paris is sometimes too independent, too tough, and too smart for her own good. I worry about the guys she dates. I want her to marry well, you know."

My heart sank. Did all rich people have this unwritten rule to marry within their circle?

"It's different with Ryder, of course," Helen said, not even looking at me. "He could marry whoever he likes. He's going to be the head of this family. And he's practically made well for himself. His wife's job would be to keep him sane and happy. Paris's future husband, however, must make sure she continues living as comfortably as she is now. I would hate for her to end up with a good-for-nothing man who would not only mess up his life, but also exhaust all of Paris's share of the family's wealth."

She had a point. She's not judging people based on wealth. She just didn't want a douche to end up with her daughter. I guess, I could live with that.

"I'm sure Paris would be responsible enough to know that."

She sighed. "Yes. You know, her father always sets her up with a man?"

I raised a brow.

"Yes. She hates it. And she does everything she can do to defy him to the point that she embarrasses the guys he sets up for her. I guess he probably tried to fix her up with at least five guys and all of them don't even want to be the same room as Paris now."

I bit my lip to prevent myself from laughing. I couldn't believe that delicate, sweet, and innocent Paris had a naughty, feisty side. It was enlightening to hear, actually.

Just then, we were interrupted by their butler. He looked at Helen, but he refused to look at me.

"Mister... Mister Ryder said he... isn't feeling well," he said, but his voice lack the conviction, so I'm thinking that wasn't the real reason I couldn't see Ryder. And judging the Ryder I last spoke to, I'm sure his butler is finding it so hard to rephrase the words he said as to why he couldn't see me.

I fought back the tears that threatened to spill from my eyes. I couldn't show Helen how hurt I was. She would feel guilty, I know.

"That's... that's okay. I think he needs more time." I said quietly.

For the first time, the butler looked at me. He gave me an apologetic smile, which confirmed my earlier suspicion that Ryder didn't want to see me on purpose.

I nodded at him slightly.

Helen must have sensed this, too. And I know she felt sorry for me. "Well, since my son is unable to see you, I think you have some free time on your hands, right?"

I nodded.

"Come, sweetheart. I wanted to go shopping today and I needed better company than Paris. Her taste in clothes is sometimes too different from mine. Would you mind spending the afternoon at the mall with me?" Helen asked.

How could I say no? I know Helen would like to do something for me to make me feel better.

"Thank you, Helen," I said. "If you think I would be good company, then I would be happy to come with you."

Ryder's mother obviously likes shopping. And it's no surprise to me that almost all the sales staff of the luxurious brands knew her. I decided to relax and be myself. I did one of the things that I actually do best. I critiqued the clothes she chose as well as the bags and jewelry. I guess one of the perks of my job is learning what has class and screams elegance, whether in detail or in whole. I think I actually impressed Helen with my skills. She was complimenting me about it.

"Now, I know why you are good at what you do, dear," she said when we were having coffee.

"I guess I always had it in me," I said. "I love what I do. It's effortless for me."

Just then, Helen handed me a paper bag from Cartier.

"This is for you, dear."

I shook my head. "Helen, no," I said. "I couldn't accept this. It's not even my birthday."

She laughed. She took out a box from the bag. "I would like to thank you for your company."

"And you're welcome. I enjoyed myself. But you didn't have to give me something in return," I said.

She opened the box and I saw a beautiful platinum bracelet.

"It's my thank you gift, not just for today, dear," she said. "This is to thank you for loving my son patiently." She took the bracelet and locked it on my wrist. "And to remind you to always find the strength to fight for both of you."

Tears brimmed my eyes as I stared back at Ryder's mother.

"I'm so sorry, Astrid." When she looked at me, her eyes were welling up with tears, too. Helen hugged me. "I know that my son chose the right woman. I know how much he loves you! But he's always been like this. Thinking that every woman he finds is just after his money. I know that when he gets better, you will be the first person he will look for. If he only remembers that the reason why you two didn't happen quickly is because you didn't want him to be rich, that you were more thrilled with him when he was a bartender."

I wiped the tears from my cheeks. "I don't know how to make him find his way back to me. And I'm so scared that everyday, I lose him more and more."

"Just wait, my dear." His mother said. "He's still the same man. Somewhere in that stubborn mind of his, is the man who lives and dies for you."

She squeezed my hand. I touched the bracelet that she gave me and I smiled back at her.

"Thank you," I said. "And I hope you are right."

"He's my son. I know he will find a way back to you."

And I could only hope that it was still true. That the man I love will wake up from this trance and remember what a good thing we have. The good thing that is waiting for him.

27.
PRENUP:
A legal document filed before marriage that states what would happen to the couple when they get divorced, particularly in terms of their finances and property.

Ryder.

*F*our months since the accident, and I'm slowly returning to my old shape. My wounds have healed. Minor broken bones and stitches... nothing I cannot recover from.

Except for one—the wound in my brain. There is still this veil that keeps one year of my life from my consciousness.

One year. I thought, how significant could that year be? I can read year-end reports from my businesses and I should be fine. I can spend a day on the net and catch up on what happened to the world.

I can heal from this and still go on with my life. No hassles.

I feel normal. I feel like nothing happened at all. I still have the people I love around me. Paris has grown to be responsible, taking care of some of my branches. My mother is still doing a great job managing some of our businesses. Janis and Jake are still the same. Both are still pains in my ass sometimes. Still the same in love couple that cannot resist making out even when I'm around. My dad still has a fetish for marriage and divorce.

Everything is fine. Normal.

It's only when they bring up her name that things start to feel hazy. It feels like when I look back, a huge portion of my life is covered in thick black smoke. Something is there. But I don't know what it is. And she is a big part of that missing piece of the puzzle.

Who was she? How did I find her? How did I fall in love with her?

Everybody who is ever close to me told me that I was head over heels in love with her. But how could I be? I don't know her. I don't remember her. How could I love somebody that I barely know? How could I fall in love with somebody I met less than a year ago? It's just so... unlike me!

"Are you okay, man?" Jake asked behind me. I was staring at our estate through my balcony, doing my favorite pastime since the accident—thinking.

I shrugged.

"Astrid came yesterday. Did you see her?" he asked.

"Nope!" I replied curtly. "I told the butler to tell her that I am feigning a brain trauma, and thus I could not come down to see her."

"Shit man!" Jake cursed beside me. "Why are you purposely hurting Astrid?"

"I doubt that she was hurt. Remember, she's a rock!" I said.

I have to admit I admire her spirit. She doesn't give up. She keeps coming back here, flying from Malibu to New York every week, coming to my mother's house, asking to see me. And every time, she goes away with the same results. She ends up speaking to either Paris or my mother, but never did I come down to see her.

"Ryder, I know you were like this. You just didn't care much about women. You looked at them the same way. After your money, gold-diggers. You are too guarded! But Astrid is…"

"Shut up, Jake! You're supposed to be on my side. I don't want to hear about Astrid! If I hear any one of you tell me again how in love I was with her, I swear, I will kill myself!"

"But you are, asshole!" Jake snorted at me.

"I can't love somebody I do not know, genius! That's just the way I am. I will not fall for a woman that easily. She must have… I don't know… given me a love potion or something. I am telling you. That woman is no different from the rest. She's with me because she wants the life that I could give her. She's already manipulated me… and you."

Jake stared at me for a long while. Then he sighed. "Ryder, when that cloud in your brain goes away, I want you to repeat this conversation over and over in your head and you will realize just how much I wanted to punch you right now. In fact, I believe when you do get better, the first thing you would want to do is kill yourself!" And then he walked away from me.

So much for being a shrink! I thought to myself, shaking my head.

Great! Even my best friend is taking Astrid's side. What is it about her? What makes her so special that all the people close to me are practically worshipping the ground she walks on?

Ugh! I don't want to know. I specifically asked Janis, Paris, and Jake not to tell me about Astrid. I don't want any more pressure of remembering her. It's bad enough that she changed my life a lot in the past months. I know she's leading me on. For all I know, she must have slept with many different men just to get to their pockets.

I didn't date a lot. But when I did go out on a date, I made it a point to date a woman who had something to say for herself. I was too cautious that she would be like my father's mistresses and wives—only after the money. So as much as possible, I tread very carefully, making sure that the woman really wants me and not my money, or she doesn't care about what I could give her because she can very well provide for herself.

Somebody like my old friend, Alizia. I've gone out with her a couple of times. She is beautiful, smart, and came from a prominent family. She doesn't need a man to support her. She can very well fend for herself. That is why I tried to go out with her. She was safe. I was trying to see if something could ever happen between us. But over the years, we just didn't go beyond a date or two, but I don't remember why.

Recalling Alizia's strong, sharp features and supermodel looks, I found myself suddenly thinking about a strawberry blonde goddess, with rare, enchanting violet eyes. She was very much different from Alizia. And yet... I found myself more drawn to her.

Damn! I should really go out more. I can't keep thinking about the woman who was the end of me. Maybe I was given amnesia so I could have a second shot at fixing my life. But I can't keep feeling something for her. It will only distract me. I can't keep burning with desire with just a mere thought of her. I must focus on getting my life back on track.

I dialed a number and decided to just relax and maybe have a bit of fun tonight.

Two hours later, Alizia met me at a diner near my mother's place. We haven't seen each other in a while, and I don't know when I saw her last since I don't remember a year of my life.

She was still the same old, gorgeous, and glamorous Alizia I met in college.

"So, how's..." she started and then trailed off, unsure of whether she should continue. I could only guess what she was about to say.

"If you mention Astrid, I'm going to walk out now," I said to her.

Does anybody in my life not *know Astrid?*

She laughed. "You don't remember her, huh. Your fiancée."

I snorted. "I just said let's not talk about her."

"Okay, so what do you want to talk about?" She batted her lashes at me. Jesus! She's still a flirt.

And I still don't understand why I don't feel even a slight spark for this woman. She's gorgeous. But I don't know why I just don't feel my nerves jumping for her. Maybe that was the reason why we never became a couple. She may be a safe choice for me, but she just does not excite me. Unlike Astrid, who heats up my skin with just the mere mention of her name.

"Ryder?" a voice suddenly said behind me that caused my heart to jump and my breathing to stop.

That voice... for a moment, I thought I remembered something. So familiar, it almost felt like... home.

I turned around and found Astrid staring at me. She looked over at Alizia who seemed to have frozen in her seat.

I stood up and faced her. Her eyes were looking at me with wild curiosity, as if she was asking for an explanation for something. Oh right! I made excuses about not feeling well enough to see her. And here I am... on a date with another woman.

"What?"

For a few seconds, she looked away, trying to compose herself. And then she took a deep breath.

God, she is so beautiful. Now, I do get why I would fall for her charms. Just looking at her makes me want to do things to her... make her scream, forget everything else, except for my name.

"I went to your house. You... weren't... ready to see me," she said in a broken voice.

I sighed. I wanted her to give up. I don't enjoy hurting her over and over again. I was raised to be a gentleman. I was taught not to hurt a woman, physically or emotionally. And making the beautiful Astrid Jacobson cry is the last thing I wanted to do. I wanted to make her scream my name in bed, yes, but I don't enjoy seeing her eating her pride away for me every single day.

And I know better than take advantage of her, too. In fact, I know that if I haul her into my bedroom and make love to her, she will never even protest. She would welcome it. After all, she claimed herself to be my girlfriend.

But I don't want to give her false hope either. I don't know her. I don't trust her. And I don't want anything to do with her until I figure out what she did to make me do all the crazy things I did for the past year, knowing that I was too cautious, too guarded, and too careful. How did she pierce through my shield?

I took a deep breath. She has to face the truth. Even if I put it a little more bluntly for her. "Miss Jacobson, when will you get it?" I asked her. "I will never be ready to see you."

I saw anger flare in her eyes. And damn! I don't think I have seen anything sexier. This woman is as fiery as she is fragile. I can tell she has many levels, which makes her even more exciting... desirable. I wonder what it would be like to uncover all her layers.

Then her eyes brimmed with tears. "You know, this may not wake you up at all, but it's worth the shot!" She said angrily, and without warning, I felt her power slap on my face.

I froze for a while. I wasn't expecting the slap. Well, maybe a little. But what I wasn't expecting is that electricity that shot from her skin to mine. The touch of her skin burned me. And for a while, I thought I would not recover from it. A flicker of light went in my head. Like a window, slightly opening. My nerves seemed to jump back to life, just with the mere touch of her skin.

I stared back at her. Tears were streaming down her cheeks. Somehow, something inside me felt heavy. Very heavy. Seeing Astrid sad, I suddenly felt the urge to pull her into my arms and comfort her, protect her. I cannot bear to look at her beautiful face filled with sorrow. I don't know why. *I don't even know her!*

She stared at Alizia, who stood up from her seat. Then she gave me one last hard look and she turned away, tears still rolling down her cheeks.

The sight of her leaving made me want to run after her. To crush her into my arms and tell her that... I don't know what I will tell her. I don't know her. But my heart felt like it's been stabbed. Like it's breaking as much as hers. I've never felt like this before. And it is confusing the shit out of me. I have always been in control of my life, but Astrid... she's throwing me off-guard, off-balance.

I turned back to Alizia who was looking at the door where Astrid went through.

"Biatch. I never did like her! I don't know what you ever saw in her!" she murmured. "She's poor. She's so ordinary. So cheap!"

Hearing Alizia bitch about Astrid like that made me want to strangle her. I had to take a deep breath and remind myself, *Strict no hitting girls policy!*

"Shut up!" I told her gravely. She immediately stopped talking and stared at me. I stared at her for a long while and I saw fear in her eyes, knowing that she's angered me. I realized that Alizia may be rich and beautiful, but she's nothing but a spoiled brat who doesn't care about the feelings of people around her.

Now I remember. *That's* why we never made it past a date. I was never interested in her no matter how safe she was. She was not as beautiful inside as she is outside.

How dare she talk about Astrid like that? She doesn't even know her!

Well, I guess that proves what an ass I am, too. I also don't know Astrid, and yet I kept on hurting her over and over. Even though, every time I hurt her, something inside me is also killing me. But until I get my memories back, I would never understand why.

I took my wallet and placed some bills on the table. Suddenly, this catch up date with Alizia was not a good idea anymore.

"Seeing as I didn't drive here, I'll get you a cab," I told her and waited for her outside the diner.

"Wow! You're such a bore!" she muttered under her breath when she stepped out beside me.

I didn't have the energy to think of a smart remark to that. My mind was busy deciphering my feelings. Something inside me wanted to make me punch myself. There was a hole in my chest that I could not explain.

When Alizia's cab sped off, I decided to walk home.

I feel like a truck had hit me. And all because I saw Astrid cry rivers of tears because of me. The feel of her skin against mine is all too familiar.

I still don't know what she did to make me fall for her. It seems like a lot of my previous decisions revolved around her. I even agreed to make Paris the CEO of my bars so it could give me more time away from the business. I wouldn't normally do that. I would usually want to be hands-on. But I gave Paris full control of my own business except for Malibu, which I wanted to handle myself.

And I guess I know why. Astrid is in Malibu. Of course! It gives me a reason to be where she is. So I didn't give up my bars in the city. I even used this as an excuse to see her. *Stupid!* When did I become stupid for a woman?

Thinking about Astrid's beautiful face and curves that seem to be at the right places, I thought maybe... it's time for me to visit Malibu.

28.

GUARDIANSHIP:

Legal term which is used to describe the legal and practical relationship of a parent and a child, which includes the right of the parent to make decisions for his or her child as well as his or her responsibilities to take care of his or her child.

Astrid.

"*D*amn it!" I shrieked when I opened my office and found a tall figure standing by my window.

Then my heart hammered in my chest when I realized who it was.

I got that familiar urge to run after him and throw myself in his arms, thinking that he would catch me, like he always did in the past. But I knew I would hit the wall this time.

Then I got that usual flicker of hope that he remembered even a fraction of his time with me. Or he somehow felt our connection. Or he was even willing to work on it until he finally heals. I knew I whacked him on the face the last time I saw him in Manhattan. Did he come here because somehow, he regained some memories back?

"Ryder," I breathed.

He turned around and looked at me. "So this is what you did with my money?" he asked quietly.

Anger flared inside me again. *This Ryder is such an asshole!* He doesn't miss a chance to insult me. If I met him like this, I would not have fallen in love with him. But then, before *my Ryder* went away, he sort of warned me about this. I remembered what he said to me before he got into that stupid accident.

"Always remember that I love you, okay? I'll always be that guy who would do anything to protect you, make you happy. I want you to know that even before I met you, you were the woman I needed, the woman I have been looking for."

Maybe this was what he meant. The old Ryder Van Woodsen didn't have much faith in people, especially women. And maybe I did change him. Maybe I had a positive effect on his life, too.

I didn't want to give up on him. When he never gave up on me, on us. He patiently waited for me to come around, to realize that he was the one for me all along. And I must have broken his heart over and over too. But he never showed me signs of giving up. He stood strong. My rock. My knight.

I should do the same. I would wait until he finally found his way back to me. No matter how much he hurt me or shut me down, I knew this wasn't him. I knew this Ryder was just guarding his emotions from something he didn't understand, something he didn't know. But once he regained his memories of me, he would come back.

"I don't see why I would be interested in these," he said. "I don't believe in marriage. My father went through a lot that didn't work."

I took a deep breath. "You believed in me," I told him.

He looked at me for a moment. I held my head high and looked back at him. I didn't back down. Then finally, as if he couldn't take it anymore, he looked away.

"I'm sorry, Miss Jacobson, this is… not… working out for me," he said in an almost broken voice, as if he too, was not sure of what he's doing.

"Wh-what?"

He turned his back on me. "Call your lawyer," he said. "Let's try to do this as easy as possible. I'm pulling out my investment here."

"But Ryder…" I trailed off. What is he saying? Moreover, what am I going to do about it?

I couldn't believe this was happening! I cannot believe he could be this harsh. I will be jobless when he shuts my business down.

Just as if on cue, Adam appeared in the room, his eyes looking at me and then at Ryder.

"Van Woodsen," he greeted Ryder, his voice cold. "I guess you also don't remember me. I'm Adam Ackers."

"Attorney Ackers?" Ryder asked. Adam nodded. "You were the one who executed the deed for this company. Good thing you are here. I have no idea what went through my mind when I decided to invest in this. But now, I'd like to undo what I did."

"Great! If only you can *un-do* my cousin, too," Adam muttered under his breath. Ryder raised a brow at him. "Never mind," Adam said. "Just so you know, Mr. Van Woodsen, you're going to have to compensate Astrid a lot for this. Her contract states that you are to pay two year's worth of her salary should you decide to pull the plug on her."

"Two years?" Ryder echoed.

"Adam! That's not true! Why would you do that?"

"Because when Van Woodsen decided to put up this business, I knew he was doing it to impress you. And back then I didn't know what his intentions with you really were. So I decided to put a clause to make sure that you will be able to survive for at least two years after he's done playing with you."

"And I agreed?" Ryder asked, a little shocked.

"I'll send you a copy of the contract. You'll see that you signed for it, happily too. You told me you genuinely cared for her. And you know what, silly me, I believed you."

Ryder looked at me for a second. "I don't know her well enough to care this much," he said quietly.

"I know," Adam said coldly. "And I was afraid for her, so I made sure she would be taken care of."

274

"Adam, you don't have to do this," I begged.

Adam stared at me for a while, completely apologetic, but I could also see that he was not taking any more bullshit from Ryder Van Woodsen. He'd seen me cry more than enough.

Adam reached out and touched my cheek. He looked at me reassuringly. He gave me a warm smile that made me want to cry even more. I thought Adam was the most unemotional person I knew, but I could see now he really cared for me.

"You said you two are cousins?" Ryder asked, watching us. Right! He forgot everything, never met me, nor Adam.

"Yes and no," Adam replied. "We're not related by blood," Adam said still not taking his eyes away from me, as if assuring me to trust him and he will make it right.

"Oh really? So would you please get your hands off her?!" Ryder scowled.

Both of us stared at him. I didn't expect it, but he looked so angry with Adam... for touching me? The same brotherly way that he always does.

"Excuse me, Mr. Van Woodsen?" Adam asked, dropping his hands and raising his brow at Ryder.

As if he realized what he just did, Ryder turned away from us and looked outside the window.

"Draw up the papers. Minimize my losses. Pay her whatever severance pay you see fit. I want out," he said curtly and then he walked away without looking at me again.

Adam turned to me. "Are you okay?"

I nodded at first, and then I shook my head. And tears rolled down my cheeks again. Adam reached out and hugged me.

"Damn it, Astrid! How many more of these are we going to face? When are you going to give up on that guy? You deserve better than this."

"I can't give up, Adam. I love him," I said.

"I know. But he doesn't even remember you."

"He... he made me promise to always remember that he loves me. I will not break that promise. I will not give up. I will wait for him."

Adam sighed and then he pulled away from me. "What do we do now that he wants to pull the plug on you?"

"How much does he want? How much did he invest here?"

Adam and I looked at all the reports that we have. Apparently, about fifty percent of Ryder's investment had already come back. It's cash available in the banks.

"What if I just buy him out?" I asked Adam, a far out idea coming to my head. Can I really do this alone?

The business was doing very well. I had four weddings lined up just this month alone and I didn't want to disappoint my clients. I cannot shut down. Just because my 'ever after' is in jeopardy didn't mean I would let down the clients who put their faith in me.

Adam gave me the figure needed to buy out Ryder's investment. My heart sank. The money that I currently had was just not enough to make the fifty percent, even if I put all my savings into it.

Adam reached out for my hand. "I know you really want this, Astrid. I will lend you the money."

"Adam, it will take more than a year for me to return it to you."

"Then it takes a year or more," he said. "Or if your stupid boyfriend wakes up earlier than that, I'm sure he'll be begging to put back his investment here."

I bit my lip. Four months I had been waiting for Ryder to wake up. Nothing was happening. I was getting weaker and weaker every day. It didn't help that he was not even trying to remember me and what I was to him before his memories of me were taken away.

"Are you really going to do it for me?"

Adam nodded. "We may not be related by blood, Ash, but I've always loved you as my cousin."

"I've always hated you," I told him, laughing bitterly.

"I know," he laughed.

I reached out to hug Adam. I will always be thankful for him. He had always been there; during the times I needed someone the most. And now, it seemed that he was all I had for the second time in my life.

***

Ryder.

"You did what?" Janis almost shouted on the other end of the line when I told her that I was pulling out my investment from Astrid's business. "Why do you have to be an ass, Ryder? Astrid will be jobless when you do that. And that was exactly the reason why you invested in her in the first place! You didn't want her to be jobless. You wanted to help her, but she wanted no help from you! So you devised a way to trick her into accepting your offer..." She trailed off, realizing that she said too much.

"Thanks!" I muttered sarcastically. I specifically told her not to tell me anything about my past with Astrid until I am ready to hear it.

"Undo this right now!" Janis demanded.

"Jan, why do you guys like her so much?"

Janis sighed. "Because she is a good person. She's beautiful inside and out. And because she is a hundred times good for you. And..."

"Stop." I told her. "I don't want to hear about her again, okay?"

"Ryder, please! That business is everything to Astrid. She worked so hard to put it up. It's doing well. You didn't need the money! What were you thinking?"

"I just… I don't know." I sighed. In truth, I really don't know why I wanted to pull out my money. I just didn't want anything to do with her. I wanted no connection with her.

When I went to her office, I saw her portfolio and how good she is. The phone was ringing non-stop with inquiries. It's a good, lucrative venture. And she is probably the best in town.

But I thought maybe she used me to get to her dreams. She must have cajoled me to invest in her to make her dreams come true.

But now, when Janis was saying to me that I *tricked* her into accepting my investment, I was not sure about what I did anymore. And I'm scared that when I wake up from all this, I will regret my decision.

"Undo it! I cannot believe you would hurt her like this!" Janis said angrily.

I sighed. "It's too late. Her lawyer called." Speaking of the good-looking lawyer, my blood boiled when I remembered how tenderly he touched Astrid, as if she was a crystal ball.

But she's my crystal ball! At least that's what everybody said to me. And even if I didn't remember this, somehow I didn't like the way he touched Astrid. They may be cousins, but they are still not related by blood. I don't understand, but an ugly, unfamiliar feeling swept through me, I couldn't resist telling the guy not to touch her.

"Adam?"

"I guess that's his name," I replied. "He said Astrid is buying me out. She will continue to run the business and will return my investment to me."

"Wow!" Janis breathed, and I can hear the admiration in her voice. "She's really good if she's saved enough to buy you out."

"I think she is. I saw her portfolio," I said. "But it's too complicated for me, Janis. I want to remember Astrid… in my own time. I cannot go by what you guys tell me about her. I will not put my guard down for nothing."

"Put your guard down?" Janis echoed angrily. "Sometimes, I want to take that guard from you and hit you so hard in the head with it so you will wake up from all this."

I laughed humorlessly. "If that was guaranteed to work, I would do it myself, you know." I sighed. "Speak to you later." And I hung up.

I decided to go look around my house. I only have a faint memory of it; it was new since I just bought it.

I opened my fridge; it was fully stocked. Funny. I haven't been here for four months. But the house looked very well taken care of.

Of course.

She was here, just like she was in my apartment in Manhattan when I was in the hospital. Had I asked her to be here too?

I went to my room. I found that my clothes were all in order. The hamper was empty. One shelf of my cabinet has some pieces of clothing

277

that were not mine. I took out a pair of lavender pajamas. Definitely not mine!

The bathroom also has some tampons, a pink razor, and some other feminine stuff.

Dear God! I've been living with a woman! Somehow, it terrified me. I never thought I would be capable of doing this. And it made me even more curious. How did Astrid Jacobson make me do all these?

I never dated a woman long enough. I have had some flings. After we go to bed together, I call a cab for them. They barely even stay the night.

What has this woman done to me?

I went downstairs and took a box. I shoved all of her stuff into it. I don't know if I asked her to live with me, but all that has changed now. I am not going to let her invade my personal space anymore.

Then I fished my phone from my pocket and scrolled to find her name.

Astrid Love

I blinked at the name on my phone. What the hell? How did she make me do this? Maybe she was lying. Maybe she really was a witch and she put me under a love spell.

"Ryder." Her voice was soft like velvet. The sound is as familiar to me as it is strange. *This is so confusing.*

I took a deep breath, gathering the courage I needed. Gathering the courage to hurt her again… one last time.

"Can you come to my house? You left… a couple of your things here," I said, as gently as I could.

There was silence. Then she said, "Okay. I will also return your key. What time are you going to be home?"

"I'll be here all evening," I replied.

"I'll finish my meeting and then I will go there." And she hung up.

I looked at the clock. It was eight o'clock. Astrid is coming to the house. Somehow, an unfamiliar feeling crept through me. My heart pounded in my chest and my pulse was hammering like crazy.

What the hell is wrong with me? Am I… *excited?*

29.
KISS:
The groom kisses the bride at the end of the wedding ceremony to seal their union.

Astrid.

"I want you to stay here while I'm gone." His words echoed in my head over and over. Tears were rolling down my cheeks.

Okay, Astrid. Better cry now than later. Better here than in front of him.

I couldn't show him how affected I was. No matter how much I beg, it's not helping him. I didn't give up on him yet. But I knew that putting pressure on him would only make him run away more.

He did tell me that he was always cautious about girls. Now, he doesn't know me. So I fall into the general category of women who just might like Ryder Van Woodsen for money and not for who he is inside.

Quite ironic, actually. He accuses me of the very things that kept me from taking a chance on him. He worked so hard to turn me around. I broke my own rules, and here I am now. Accused of being a gold-digging slut by the man I trusted not to hurt me.

I guess not giving up sometimes means you only need to wait. I decided not to pressure Ryder anymore. I couldn't break my heart over and over again because I knew it wasn't going to work. He could wake up or change his opinion of me. And right now, he was not even close to doing either.

I planned to prove to him that I was not the woman he thought I was. As a start, I would have his check on hand. Adam wired the money I needed to my account. It would be a tough following months. But at least now I could say that I fully own 'Ever After', my baby, my company.

I told Adam that I would not invoke the severance clause in my contract with Ryder. I would not take a dime from Ryder Van Woodsen. That is exactly what he expected of me, and I was going to prove him wrong.

But the changes meant I would have to transfer to a smaller place to save on rent. It also meant I would have to work double time, lose a couple hours of sleep and multi-task, as I couldn't afford to hire extra hands just yet.

I can do this. I'm a rock.

It took me a while to notice that the cab had stopped in front of Ryder's house already. I paid the driver and then stepped out.

I took a couple of short breaths and then I rang the bell.

He opened the door. The familiarity of the house and the person in front of me made me want to break down and cry. It reminded me of the things that I used to have and the dreams that came shattering to the ground. Never mind the house. But the man in front of me… he was the one thing I wasn't ready to let go of.

He looked the same. God, he even smelled the same! But he was not the same man who rescued me months ago. He was not my knight in shining armor.

Before he left he told me that he wanted me to stay in his apartment. He asked me to take his car. It was his way of protecting me even though he wasn't physically with me.

I slept in his house for months. Every day hoping, always praying that one day, he would walk into that door and pull me into his arms, and tell me that everything was back to the way it was. That he remembers me. And that he loves me the same way.

But now, he was back in Malibu. The first thing he did was pull the plug on the business. And now, he was kicking me out of his apartment. Well, I didn't officially live here. But the man I loved told me I should stay until he comes back for me.

But I guess… he's never coming back.

"Come in," Ryder said politely.

I just nodded and stepped inside the house.

"Can I offer you something to drink?" he asked me.

I looked into his eyes, trying to assess whether he meant it. He was usually rude and brutal towards me. I didn't understand why he was making an effort to be nice to me now. Unless the drink he was offering me was poisoned. But even if it was, what had I got to lose, right?

"Okay," I replied curtly.

He opened his fridge. He stared at it for a while, obviously still lost and my heart just broke for him. If only, he would allow me to help him find his way back…

"Second shelf. Watermelon Vodka," I said quietly. I still stocked his fridge up until last week. He told me once that it was one of the sweetest things anyone has done for him.

He took the vodka out of the fridge and rummaged through his drawer to look for a bottle opener.

"First drawer, left side," I murmured.

He smiled when he found it. "You seem to know your way around the house," he said.

I stared at him, trying to decipher if that comment was a trap that would be followed by another insult if I fell for it.

But I was surprised to see that he had a twinkle in his eye. For the first time in months, I saw an improvement in him. Before, he looked like a walking time bomb ready to explode anytime, bottling up his anger and his confusion. His pride prevented him from admitting that he felt lost, confused, and not in control.

"Well, I lived here for a while," I murmured.

He stepped closer to me. My heart pounded in my chest. He stood so close we were almost touching. He looked down at me, searching my face. I looked away, blushing, then I stepped back, putting some distance between us.

When I looked at him again, he was biting his lip, doubtless he was trying his best not to laugh or even smile.

He handed me my bottle. "Would you like to join me on the deck?"

"Seriously?" I asked him. "Whatever happened to *'never gonna be ready to see me?'*"

He shrugged. "Maybe, I'm just bored."

I shook my head. "No, Ryder. You're never just bored." *Everything you do has a purpose.* But I didn't say that aloud. I sighed. "Are you going to turn off the asshole mode?"

"Asshole mode?" he echoed, blinking back at me. Then he laughed. I knew that laugh was real. He stared at me and saw that I wasn't laughing at all. "Seriously?" he asked.

I nodded.

"Alright," he said, raising his right hand, swearing like a boy scout. "Asshole mode—off."

He led me to his deck. For a while, we sat in silence, just listening to the sound of the waves, staring at the tower lights in the distance.

Then he asked, "How long ago did we meet?"

I sighed. This was difficult. These beautiful memories killed me as I recalled them. But if this was a way for Ryder to remember me in his life, then I could endure the pain.

"About eleven months before... before your accident," I replied.

"And we only got together *officially* a couple of days before I got hit?"

I nodded.

"What were we in between?"

I smiled bitterly. "We were... friends, Ryder," I said. "And you were one of the best." I couldn't disguise the tears in my voice.

He fell quiet after that.

Then he asked, "Why did it take so long for us to be... together?"

"Me," I replied. "I wasn't ready. I was broken. You fixed me. And then... I found out who you were."

"What do you mean?"

I sighed. "When I met you, you pretended to be a bartender. We hit it off immediately. You agreed to help pose as my boyfriend at my ex-fiancé's wedding. You covered up all the broken holes in me. You saved my face and my pride in front of my family.

"I made you a promise that I would be better, that I would believe in fairy tale romances again. I would fix myself. And I would find you when I was ready. I was excited to look for you again, actually. But I found out that you were not just a mere bartender. You lied to me. I found out who you really were. And I didn't want you anymore."

"Why?"

I sighed. "Because... I've never been interested in rich jocks in my life. Even when I was younger, I wasn't looking for some dreamboat who was out of my league. I wanted someone who I could be secure with... somebody who wouldn't look down at me, somebody who would believe in me." I stared at him and added, "I didn't want anybody to accuse me that I was in it for the money. You... did all you could to change my mind."

He stared back at me. I saw an emotion crossing his face. Guilt? Shame? I didn't know. He took a gulp of his beer and turned away from me. He fell silent for a while. I didn't know if he remembered a thing and if I was making sense to him.

I took out the check from my wallet and handed it to him. He stared at the figure in his hand.

"I am not going to ask you to pay me two years of my salary. I will always owe you for helping me get up on my feet and start this dream." I reached out for his hand and squeezed it.

He closed his eyes for a moment. Then he stared at me. His eyes were wildly confused. His face was filled with a dark emotion I could not decipher. Immediately, I took my hand away, afraid that I would trigger something in him that would further ruin the stained image of me in his head.

"Astrid... I'm..." he started then he trailed off. He took a deep breath. "What happens to you now? What will happen to the company?"

I looked at the watchtower from the distance. "I will still run it. I have to make a few adjustments. But I know I can do it. This is what I do best," I replied. "I cannot shut down. I've gotten this far. There are couples out there depending on me to make their 'ever afters' come true. I won't let them down."

There was silence again. I missed Ryder and me. We were two people who wouldn't run out of things to talk about. But I guess, it wasn't time yet. I had to tread carefully. *Walking time bomb*, remember?

I finally looked at my watch. "I better go," I said. "It's getting late."

In truth, I just want to get away from Ryder now. It was so difficult for me to be in the same room and not touch him. It was difficult for me to see him look at me and not remember me at all.

I took my bottle inside to throw it in the bin, leaving Ryder on the deck. I paused for a moment and composed myself. I let some of the tears fall. It was difficult to hold it in. It was difficult to reminisce my wonderful memories of Ryder, knowing that he didn't remember any of it at all.

When I faced him again, I would have to say goodbye. And who knows how long this goodbye would last? I may never set foot in this house again. This house that held too many memories between Ryder and me.

I told myself that I would not give up on him. But it didn't mean that I would go around town chasing him. It would only push him away. He didn't need that now. He needed time to heal from this.

I leaned on the counter and took short breaths, trying my damn best not to break down. But it was just too hard. So I let the tears fall, silently. I didn't whimper. I don't want to make a sound and let Ryder hear it.

Then I wiped my tears with a tissue. Trying so hard to compose myself before I bid my goodbye to him.

When I turned around, I found myself face to face with Ryder. He had been just behind me all the time, standing a few feet away. He'd been watching me cry.

He looked down at me, his eyes searching mine. I am sure he saw the tears I was trying so hard to conceal. His expression softened. And then I saw a flicker of another emotion on his face. An expression dark and yet familiar...

"Damn it!" I heard him curse and without warning, he wrapped his arms around my waist, pulling me to his chest and then he leaned down, crushing his lips to mine.

30.

TULLE:

A kind of textile that is lightweight and has very fine netting, usually used for veils.

Ryder.

I was dreaming for sure because I haven't felt like this before. It was like I was in a trance, and I don't ever want to wake up. I felt the surge of emotions sweep through me in tides that I could not control. I gave up fighting. I gave in.

I crushed her into my arms and kissed her the way I have wanted to kiss her since the first time I laid eyes on her at the hospital. The way I always wanted to kiss her whenever I looked at her.

I know I shouldn't let my guard down. But there is something about this woman that draws me in, and drowns me.

The minute she walked into the house, her scent captured my senses. If I close my eyes, I could swear that I know that scent well. But when I look at her, I can't place her.

I listened to her sweet voice and I could almost say it was familiar. But I don't remember a thing. I still do not remember her.

Astrid confuses me in many ways. Maybe that is why I was not ready for her yet. Everything was in place. I am okay. I am stable even with this stupid cloud in my brain. But when she's around, she throws me out of balance.

Like… my mind tells me one thing, but something else inside me is fighting for her.

When she touched me a while ago, I felt my nerves jump. I felt her skin against mine and it was comfortably familiar. But I don't know her. And I don't trust what I do not know.

She melted in my kisses. I tasted salt on her lips and I knew she couldn't stop crying anymore. And for the life of me, I wanted to make her tears stop! Something about her makes me want to protect her… always.

I carried her to my bed. I told myself to be careful, but I just didn't care anymore. I gave in to my desires. God, I wanted her with every fiber of my soul. I have never felt like this before. Usually, I'm attracted to a woman physically. No emotions involved. And it had never been this strong; it made me abandon sense and reason.

We had sex. No, this was not sex. This was not just lust. This was something else. Something I could not place.

I couldn't get enough of her. It was like I have been so thirsty for a long time and now I find myself drinking in her, getting intoxicated by her.

She was like a drug I didn't know I craved. Something I needed, and wanted without me knowing it.

When I made love to her, it was like... feeling lost for a very long time, and then finally finding my way back home. It was comforting, satisfying, exciting, confusing, and scary all at once. And I don't want it to ever end.

She screamed my name when she reached her peak, and it was the loveliest sound I have ever heard in my life. Familiar, and yet strange at the same time.

It was like a sweet episode of *déjà vu* that I did not understand. It felt like the first time for me, and yet I also felt like I have done this a dozen times before.

And when we were done, I gathered her in my arms and held her tightly, breathing in the scent of her, understanding for the first time in months, what my sister, my mother, and my friends have been telling me since I woke up at the hospital.

I was head over heels in love with this woman.

I heard her quiet breathing in the darkness and I smiled to myself. I kissed her bare shoulder and held her against me tightly.

My consciousness does not remember her. I don't recall what I see. But her scent was all too familiar, the feel of her in my arms felt like something I would die to go home to everyday.

I don't remember her, yet. But I know I am going to. And even if I don't, how can I forget this night? The feel of her in my arms, the magic of this lovemaking will haunt my dreams, even my waking hours.

Maybe she really is a witch. And she's got me under her spell—again! And unlike the time I found out about her when I woke up in the hospital, I was not mad at all.

Tomorrow...

Tomorrow, things would be different for her. Tomorrow, she will not hurt because of me anymore. And for the first time in months, I felt the lightness in my chest.

I hugged her to me tightly. I fell asleep with her skin keeping me warm, and her scent intoxicating me.

When I woke up, my arms immediately reached out for her, to gather her against my chest and hug her, as if it was second nature for me to do that. But all I felt was the cold sheet and the empty space she left.

I opened my eyes and found her gone. I felt a deep sense of loss. Far worse than when the doctor told me I lost a year of my memories.

***

I don't know how long I lied down on the bed, just staring at the ceiling, trying to get the image of Astrid, as well as her scent and the feel of her skin, out of my head.

What's worse, I was trying my damn best not to feel this… black hole inside my chest. This is new to me. I don't know why I feel like this, but damn! I hate it.

I wondered if Astrid felt like this now. Maybe even worse. And I wonder how she hasn't brought herself to hate me yet. I would hate me if I made me feel like this!

I stood up from the bed and put on a pair of pajama pants. I stared at the bed we laid in last night. Images of the passion we shared flashed through my mind. I remembered her scent again, her warmth, the way she screamed my name…

When I came down, I found that she had taken her box with everything of hers that was ever in this house. Then her check was on top of the table, along with my house keys and car keys.

I felt a stab of pain in my heart again. Something I cannot name makes me want to cry. *Shit! I'm becoming a girl!*

She returned my money in full. The whole nine yards. And that made me feel sad again, as if I just severed another connection with her. Now more than ever, I felt that pulling the plug on her was a bad idea. It was the wrong decision. Janis was right. I would regret what I did.

She didn't even take the severance pay that was stated in my contract with her. It was not a small amount. Most women would be happy to jump at that opportunity. But Astrid… didn't invoke it even though she will win in every court she brings that paper to.

Instead, I remembered how she squeezed my hand last night, and told me that she already owes me for helping her get back up on her feet, and that was enough for her.

I made myself a cup of coffee and sat on my deck. I remembered how she looked last night—sitting beside me, her hair being blown by the soft breeze, her scent filling my senses.

I just couldn't get her out of my mind!

I was not usually like this. Even after I have slept with a woman, I do not remember every single detail that happened the previous night. And her scent does not remain in my memory in the morning. Moreover, when I find her gone from my bed, I would be more than happy. I never feel like this. Lost… yearning… confused.

Just when I promised myself that I would treat Astrid differently starting this morning, she was gone.

I promised I would forever turn off the 'asshole mode' as she would like to put it. Thinking about that word brought a smile to my face again. She has a sense of humor in spite of what I put her through.

I stared at the beach in front of me. I thought about everything that happened the previous night again. Every single detail is vivid in my memory. The woman... her scent... the touch of her skin... the sound of her scream... *Damn! I need a cold shower again!*

After showering and changing into a pair of linen pants and a white button shirt, I opened the vault that I kept in the house, just curious what I will find inside. After all, I lost one year's worth of my memories. I don't remember the password. Luckily, I had fingerprint identification as a backup. The vault opened for me.

I found some papers for Oil Rig and Rig Style. Contracts and investment data. I found about four different expensive watches. A couple of diamond ear studs.

I found the copy of the contract I signed with Adam Ackers for Astrid's company. He was right, I signed it, flawlessly. The strokes of the signature didn't show signs that I had a gun to my head or I was high on something.

Then I found a small black box that said 'Harry Winston'.

My heart hammered in my chest as I opened it. *Why do I have a Harry Winston ring?*

It was a beautiful diamond ring, at least two carats, surrounded by smaller diamond pieces, set on a platinum band.

I brought my fingers to it. A flash came through my head.

I walked inside the jewelry shop and something bumped into me. Before I can even look down, I felt arms wrap around my waist and I found a sobbing woman in my arms. She hugged me. As if I was the only thing she needed to ease her pain. And she doesn't even know me, didn't even see what I looked like.

Warmth filled through me. She smelled of strawberries. She felt like fine velvet in my arms.

Then she looked up at me and I found the face of an angel. She was so beautiful, my breath caught in my throat. It took me a moment to compose myself and ask her if she was fine. She apologized and then walked away.

Even when she was gone, her memory lingered. It was the first time in my life somebody needed me... without even knowing who I was.

I took a deep breath. It's not my imagination. That was my first memory of Astrid coming back to me, bringing with it unfamiliar emotions I could not understand.

I stared at the ring again. Somehow, I remembered the girl who hired me to pose as her fake boyfriend and rent a diamond ring to give to her by the end of the night. She wanted to get back at her ex-fiancé for giving her a fake diamond ring. She wasn't just in it to get even. She was going for the kill.

I can't believe her ex proposed with a fake ring. What a loser! And my heart went out to Astrid. She was so trusting; she didn't realize that the ring that was given to her didn't hold any value. She didn't care. She was getting married to the guy and she was happy. She didn't look much on the ring to notice it wasn't really a diamond. Some women would have their rings appraised immediately after it was put on their finger. But Astrid was different. She didn't care. And she happily planned her wedding.

So I thought I would give her a real ring. I saw that ring in the shop and I immediately thought that it belonged to her, that she deserved it.

But she returned it to me. A thirty thousand ring and she wanted nothing to do with it.

"You're not going to trick me into wearing this ring," she said. "You know I will be returning the ring before I go."

"I'll find a reason soon enough. And after that, who knows? You won't be taking that ring off your finger ever," I said.

I squeezed the skin between my eyes, trying not to get overwhelmed by the memories that were slowly flooding through me.

I guess I was really wrong about her. Like what my mother, my sister, and my friends were saying to me. I was very wrong about Astrid. I immediately assumed she was like my father's wives: gold-diggers.

Damn! I called her a mercenary! She must have wanted to whack me in the head when I said that. Well, I wanted to whack myself in the head now that these pieces of my memories of her are slowly coming back to me.

I tried to think harder, trying to see if some more memories have been unlocked. When there was nothing, I checked the vault again. Searching for more clues that will help me get closer to waking up from this nightmare.

I found some pictures in the vault too. I am guessing these came from Janis. Once in a while, she would send us snapshots of our moments together.

One picture was of me with Astrid, Jake, and Janis. I was holding Astrid in my arms and we were both laughing. I looked at myself in the picture. I looked… really happy.

I flipped the picture over and there was a caption at the back. *Keep dreaming!* I looked at it closely. It was *my* handwriting. *Why would I write something like that?*

I found the manual of my house alarm. I have scribbled the password at the back page. 278743. That didn't ring a bell at all and I wondered where I got the number.

Then my eyes drifted to the touchtone phone. I looked at the buttons. 2-7-8-7-4-3. A-S-T-R-I-D.

Even my password is her name? I must have been really in love with this woman.

I took a deep breath. Maybe she's not the one who needed something from me, like what I accused her of. I was the one who wanted her in my life. Like what my best friends were saying to me. She didn't want anything. She only wanted me.

Shit! What have I done?

And even though I only have fragments of my memories back, I cannot help feeling remorse for what I did to Astrid. I treated her like shit. I insulted her more than once. I wanted her to give up on me.

Even now, when my mind is telling me to stay away, my heart feels like it's breaking into a million pieces. There was something missing in my life, and I feel like dying. I didn't know that I needed her… until last night.

I dialed Jake's number.

"Ryder."

"You've been holding off information about Astrid… because you know I didn't want to hear it," I told him. "I'm listening now."

"Why do you care?" Jake asked.

I heaved a frustrated sigh.

"I don't know, man. I never felt like this before."

Jake let out a humorless laugh. "Funny, that was the same thing you said to me when Astrid found out you were the investor in her business. You told me how you cheated Janis and me on our bet. The whole charade you put up with her and how that was the only way you thought you would be able to get her to fall in love with you, because she doesn't want anything to do with Ryder Van Woodsen.

"Had you been Ryder Woodson, the bartender, you two would have been moving in together by then. But since she found out who you were, she didn't want you as more than a friend. She said you were too complicated for her.

"Man, you were in trouble. You were so crazy about her. And you hated the fact that she didn't like you because you were rich. You got your wish. A woman who would love you for you, not because you were Ryder Van Woodsen. You can't change who you are. But you still wanted her. So much so you would have renounced all your wealth that was given to you as an option.

"She wanted to be equals. She didn't want to be called a gold-digger. She was afraid that she would be judged. She didn't want that. But you wanted her to take that chance. Because you would never let anyone hurt her. You would protect her."

I sighed in remorse. "And the person I didn't protect her from… was myself. You guys were crazy about her. You accepted her. Defended her. I was the only one who judged her, scrutinized her, and doubted her. I deliberately insulted her." I was silent for a long while. Then I said, mostly to myself. "I don't know her that well. I can't be in love with her…"

"Ryder…"

"But damn, why do I feel so… *heartbroken* right now?"

"Because it's your brain that got messed up, man," Jake said. "Not your heart. And your heart… knows her."

I closed my eyes, taking deep breaths one at a time. It was all I could do to keep myself from screaming, or throwing the phone across the room. "How bad was I?"

"Before the accident? Very bad!" Jake replied. "Man, you wanted to renounce your claims to your family's wealth. You hated being you, being *the* Ryder Van Woodsen. All because she didn't want anything to do with you. The only thing that prevented her from accepting you is the fact that you were too rich for her."

"And when she thought she could trust me, the first thing I said to her in the hospital was… I thought she was a gold-digger." I said sadly.

"Yep. You've screwed up, man," Jake said apologetically.

"I have to fix this," I said. And I knew I meant that.

"Why? Do you have your memories back?" he asked.

"No. At least not all of them," I replied. "But I know someday I will. And I don't want to wake up that day thinking I made the biggest mistake of my life. If you say that I would have risked my whole fortune just to be with her… and I feel like shit now even without completely remembering her… I must have really loved her. And I want her to be there when I finally wake up from this nightmare."

"Good luck, man," Jake said. "You're going to do need it. Astrid is a hell of a girl."

"She must be… for me to go nuts about her," I said. "She must have been really worth it."

I hung up. I went to my room to change my clothes and then I quickly gathered my car keys.

It's going to be difficult, but I knew what I needed to do. I would run after Astrid, no matter what it takes. I would make up for every single thing I said and did to her since I woke up in the hospital.

And for the first time in months, I prayed that she had not yet given up on me.

31.
SOMETHING NEW:
Brides are supposed to wear something—anything—new during the wedding ceremony. It can be as small as a trinket, jewelry, an undergarment, or the gown itself.

Astrid.

I met up with my friends at Starbucks.

"So, because Ryder forgot about you, we all have to be sober now?" Dannie asked. I knew what he meant. Since Ryder forgot about me, I had been steering clear of Oil Rig and Rig Style. It was too painful for me to go there. The sweetest guy I'd known didn't want anything to do with me and looked down at me as if I was the biggest gold-digging slut on the face of the Earth.

"No, Dannie. No one is preventing you from getting drunk out of your wits. As long as you don't do it with me and in any of Ryder's bars," I said.

"But those are my favorites!" he complained.

"Oh I feel *so* sorry for you!" I said, a little irritated. "My problems are nothing compared to yours!"

That shut him up. He smiled at me apologetically. "You're right," he said. "I'm sorry."

"So, still no development?" Nicole asked.

I shrugged.

How do I tell them that, *No, Ryder still has not remembered even an inch of me, and he still has not changed his opinion about me being after his money. But hey, he made it clear though, that he wanted me and couldn't get his hands off me in bed!*

That was a slip. I thought about last night and felt confused more than ever. I was happy that at least he was still attracted to me. But I knew there was no love in that department. He touched me last night because he wanted me. He wanted my body. I was a woman he wanted to warm his bed. He didn't touch me because I was his Astrid and that he loved me with all his being.

Last night, I didn't make love to Ryder Van Woodsen, the guy who would go to hell and back for me. I had sex with a guy who looked a lot like the man I love... the man who went to a place where I couldn't reach him.

Right from when his arms snaked around my waist and he crushed his lips into mine, I knew it was a mistake. I didn't know this man. He didn't know me. He wanted my body. I wanted a piece of the man I had been aching for for too many nights.

I told myself I would not give up on him. But I was only human. It was painful to be near him and yet I knew it wasn't really him. He looks at me with wanton lust and all I wanted was the man who looked at me with so much love and tenderness. They look the same, but I knew they weren't.

"I... returned Ryder's investment," I said.

"Oh my, you're shutting down?" Dannie asked.

I shook my head.

"Wow!" John breathed. "At least now, you won't owe him anything. He won't think that you're just using him for his money."

I didn't have the heart to tell them that Ryder was the one who pulled out his investment. That my choices were to either shut down or pay up.

I kept telling myself that Ryder was not fully aware of his actions and everything that came out of his mouth was based on the fact that he didn't know me at all. He was disturbed and confused with my existence in his life.

But I knew not everybody could be forgiving. And if Ryder came back to me again, I didn't want my friends or my family to hate him.

Speaking of my family, I hadn't even had the courage to tell them that Ryder had forgotten about me. Whenever they called and asked about him, I told them that he was out of the country, somewhere in Europe.

My phone rang. It was Rose, my assistant.

"Astrid, Mr... Mr. Van Woodsen is here," she said in a whisper. "He's looking for you."

My breath caught in my throat. *What does he want now?*

Did he think that just because I slept with him last night, it was going to be a regular occurrence between us now?

Oh no! He's dead wrong!

Okay, I slipped. I was weak for a night. But that didn't mean I would be willing to accept the way he saw me, the way he thought of me.

I want my Ryder. Not this asshole that thinks all women are trying to get into his pants to get into his pockets.

In a way, I felt like I was cheating. I should not have gone to bed with him. I had only been with one man in my entire life. And he loved me. Even that first night he touched me, I meant more to him than just a woman he wanted to warm his bed.

The last time I was in Manhattan, Ryder was having a date with Alizia. Of course, he didn't remember me. But he'd known Alizia for more than a year. It was no surprise. And if he was with her, *God! What have I done?* I should not have slept with him! If he's seeing Alizia, then he's cheated on her with me. Well, if he is with Alizia, technically he's cheated on me with her!

God, it's so unfair! I couldn't even blame him if he tried to sleep with Alizia. How can you accuse a man of cheating if he doesn't even know you were his girlfriend in the first place?

"I would never touch Alizia," he said, *"* he said. *"Because I would never cheat on you."* My heart breaks at the memory. But the man who promised me that was gone now. In his place was a man who looked exactly like him, but does not feel an inch of affection for me. The man who would go to hell and back for me… was gone. I didn't know when he might come back. And all the waiting is killing me.

"Tell him you don't know where I am," I said.

"Huh?" my assistant asked, obviously confused. Usually, I would jump at the chance to see Ryder. Now, I was running away from him.

I still had not given up on him, but that didn't mean I was ready to face him already after sharing a night of insane passion with him.

What happened between us was a game changer. We were already complicated in the first place. Why did we have to give in to our dark desires and think we could get out of it unscathed?

Because I showed him how I could go wild and mindless in his arms, I'm sure the term *'mercenary slut'* now applied! And I was not ready to hear that from him just yet. I didn't know if I could stop myself from killing him if he said that to my face.

I was confused. And more than that, I was scared. So I guess, it didn't hurt to lay low for a while, and just… take a deep breath.

"You heard me," I said. "I'm not around. You don't know where I am."

"Okay." And she hung up.

My friends raised brows at me.

"What's that about?" Dannie asked.

I shrugged. "Ryder is at the office looking for me."

"Now *he's* looking for you and *you're* the one running away from him?" Nicole asked. "You guys are so confusing!"

"Why is he looking for you? Did he have his memories back?"

"Doubt it," I said. "Only yesterday I wrote him a check for his investment. He doesn't even remember why he invested in my talents. Unless he hit his head this morning, I doubt that he's looking for me because he remembers me."

Nicole and Dannie seem to agree. But John was looking at me suspiciously and I didn't know why. When I raised a brow at him, he just shrugged and looked away.

"So why did you tell your assistant that you aren't around?" Dannie asked.

I sighed. "Because I'm only human, guys! My heart can only take a couple of heartbreaks at a time. I need a break too."

"Are you giving up?" Nicole asked.

I shook my head. "No. But that doesn't mean I cannot take a breather from all this... pain once in a while."

"Sure, sweetheart." Nicole said, reaching out for my hand. "And I hope you use that breather to think that you deserve to be loved, Astrid. You deserve a man who knows what a good thing he has when he has you."

I laughed humorlessly. "You sound like the old Ryder. Thanks for the reminder."

"She's right, sweetheart," Dannie said. "For how long are you going to keep on doing this? How long are you going to hang around and get your heart broken over and over?"

"I'm a rock!" I recited, more to myself.

John shook his head. "No." He looked at me, and I can see that his heart goes out to me, like he's so sad that I have to go through all this pain. "You're a precious stone, Ash. And you need somebody who could appreciate you and not look down at you."

That was a lot coming from John, who only seemed to see women as bedroom playmates. And it warmed me to think that, in spite of what I have been going through with Ryder, I have friends who really love and care for me.

"I had that somebody." I said to him, tears brimming my eyes again. "He looked a lot like Ryder Van Woodsen. But he's a different man now. And I don't know how to get him back."

Nicole put her arms around my shoulder and let me cry. I needed this. I needed to let it out because it gets too heavy sometimes. It felt like this time, I was the walking time bomb and I didn't know just when I would lose it and explode.

Dannie finally had the sense to change the subject. He told us about his boyfriend and how serious they were getting. Actually, I knew the guy. He's the one who broke the news to me that the engagement ring Bryan gave me was a fake and that the supposedly fake ring that Ryder gave me was the real thing.

John told us about his new apartment. He's doing pretty well in his father's company. Now, he can afford a two-bed apartment with a garage in a prime area in the city.

All day Ryder kept calling me. I just chose to ignore his calls. I wanted him to know I wasn't a booty call, if that was his intention. *Give yourself some dignity, woman!*

He needs to decide what to do with me. I'm either with him or without him. Nothing in between. We've been down the "friends with benefits" road before, and I'm not going back there again.

More than that, I need to breathe, too. Even for just a couple of days. A couple of days without hearing Ryder insult me, accuse me of things that I am not. A few days of not seeing him look at me and not place me in his past.

Last night, after we made love, he actually held me in his arms until we both fell asleep. For a while, he felt like the old Ryder… my Ryder who was content and happy to have me locked in his embrace. And I wanted that to be my last memory of him… at least for now.

***

I stayed with Nicole for the next couple of days. I could not be alone, even for just a few moments. Ryder's been showing up at my office every day.

I decided to conduct all my business outside. I can easily meet my clients at their place or at any restaurant in the city. Plus, I was office and apartment hunting. I had all the excuses in the world to not be in the office.

However, after three days of crashing at Nicole's I had to move out. "I'm sorry, sweetie, but my mother is coming to the city and well… she's gonna be staying with me," Nicole said. "You can stay with us if you want, but I honestly don't recommend it. My mother is unrelenting, you know that."

I knew. Her mother wanted to know everything about the person she speaks to and I know she'll pry on my love life. And the reason why I'm staying away from my house in the first place is because I'm avoiding the love of my life.

"Oh, that's fine," I said. I looked at Dannie. "Can I crash?"

Dannie smiled at me apologetically. "Sorry sweetie. You know I haven't been single since last month." Yes, right. And I don't want to get in the way of Dannie and *his* love life.

Rats! I didn't want to go to my place yet. I just… want to surround myself with my friends right now. Otherwise, the first ring from Ryder, I know I will pick up. And if he asks me to come to his house for some fun, I just might blindly accept it… I think. That's how vulnerable I am to him. And damn, he knows it! And even if he didn't, then I have just proven it to him a couple of nights ago.

I'm a rock. I'm standing my ground. Maybe if I give Ryder a little bit of distance, he'll have time to think about why I returned his investment… why I didn't take the severance pay that Adam is so willing to fight for. I'm not the mercenary slut he thought I was.

Adam! I remembered him. He's got a nice place and he will take me in in a heartbeat. But Adam would smell that something was up. The guy has a talent for pulling information out of me. He will know that I slept with Ryder again and he will not like that. He'll give me a good beating for being stupid. Plus, Ryder knows he's my cousin, so if he is looking for me, he might look Adam up. And Adam is already losing his patience with him. I don't want it to turn into a fistfight, particularly since Adam seems to be a fan of martial arts lately. He doesn't talk about it, but the mild bruises on his face, and the wounds on his knuckles tell the whole story.

"I just moved into a two-bed apartment," John reminded me. Right. I forgot. John owns a place big enough to crash in now.

"And the point is?" I asked, smiling. I already know what he will offer. John may be quiet most of the time, but he's such a sweet guy. But somehow, only Dannie, Nicole, and I knew that. He's a playboy. But as long as he doesn't plan on bringing home a girl while I am there, I am all for it.

"Well, I need somebody to clean up the house once in a while for the price of free night's stay in the guest bedroom," he joked. "You might sleep in the middle of a mountain of boxes though."

"Very funny," I said. "I'll take it! It's only a couple of nights anyway. Then I should be able to find a new place to move in to."

I sincerely hope I find a new office soon, and a new apartment. It's actually tough since I just paid Ryder out and I owed Adam some money. But I know that I can still do it. I still have some money left to support my relocation.

I gathered my stuff from Nicole's place. I decided to go home quickly and get some new clothes before I went to John's. John agreed to pick me up after his meeting.

As soon as I was heading out with my bag, I froze on my feet when I found Ryder standing in the driveway.

He was watching me, a hard expression on his face.

Stick to the program. Stick to the program. I recited in my head.

He approached me. *Damn! Why does he have to be smoking hot!?* My heart kept pounding inside my chest. I have to consciously remind myself that my brain needs oxygen, ergo, *I have to breathe!*

He raised a brow at me. "You can't avoid me forever, sweetheart," he said, giving me a crooked smile, which did not touch his eyes.

"Funny *you* seem to have succeeded a lot in doing that to *me*," I said sarcastically.

"I know," he said and I thought I heard a trace of guilt in his voice. "But I guess we started out on the wrong foot."

"No. *You* started out on the wrong foot. I was exactly where I was the last time you said you loved me," I said, pain evident in my voice.

He didn't say anything. He just stared at me.

Then I realized that it was not entirely his fault. I'm sure he didn't want to forget a year of his life. Nobody would want that.

But I wish he could have been a little bit nicer and little less judgmental towards me. I wish he just gave us a chance. I wish he didn't try his best to drive me away… cut me off from his life.

"I'm sorry. I know it's not your fault." I started saying to him. "I…"

I was not able to finish that sentence. I blinked and the next thing I knew Ryder's soft lips were ravishing mine. His arms were around me, holding me tightly against his chest.

I savored that kiss for a while. I knew I craved it. It made me weak and shut down all my senses.

But I also wanted to know... *why?* First, he didn't want anything to do with me, asked me to stay away from him and his family... then one day he woke up and realized he likes kissing me and taking me to bed?

If I kept on giving in to this... I know I will end up being hurt by him over and over. I cannot accept these kisses. He's not the same man he used to be. He isn't kissing me because he loved me. He's doing this because he wants me... *in spite of the ugly thoughts he has about me.*

And whatever Ryder Van Woodsen wants, Ryder Van Woodsen gets.

So I gathered all the courage that I had and pushed him... hard.

That startled him. Maybe he really did think that after that night, I would be a very easy prey; that he could play with me however he wanted.

Tears brimmed my eyes. He had no right to play with my feelings. He knew I was so in love with him and I wanted nothing more in the world than for him to snap out of his brain injury. But he didn't feel the same. He was taking advantage of my weakness... which he knew perfectly well was... *him.*

"Stay away from me, Ryder." I breathed.

He took a step forward. "Astrid, *love*..." he started.

"Don't call me that!" I snapped at him. Tears are rolling down my cheeks now. "Only... only my boyfriend calls me that. And he's not here anymore." I took a deep breath. "So please, Ryder. Don't play with my feelings again. You have already judged me. The first thing you did when you woke up was crush me. I'm sorry I slept with you. I shouldn't have because I know you're not the same man. I guess I just... missed you so much, I gave in. But I can't do that again, knowing that you think so low of me."

"Astrid..." he started saying, but nothing followed. He just stood there, dumbfounded. It genuinely looked like he didn't know what to say. His face was full of guilt and anguish. And I know that for the first time, I was getting through to him. He was listening to me and seeing how badly I was hurting... how badly he was hurting me.

"I am not giving up hope that someday, you will wake up from all this," I said. "Because if you don't... *then I will.* I will wake up and stop dreaming that you will come home to me."

I saw John get out of his car. It was my cue to go. I walked past Ryder, but he grabbed my hand.

"Astrid..." I stopped walking, but didn't turn to him. "I'm sorry." His voice was broken.

I pulled my hand away. "I know. I'm sorry too." And I ran towards John. He took my bag from me and I hopped into his passenger seat.

It seems that Ryder was about to follow me, but John stopped him.

"Leave her alone, man. The girl could only take so much shit from you."

"Who the fuck are you?" Ryder asked John angrily.

"I'm someone who will beat the shit out of you if you don't keep your distance from her!"

"Oh, I'd like to see you try!" Ryder snarled at him.

"If that would wake you up, I would have done that a long time ago. But seeing as you're stubborn, I don't think one good beating is enough to bring you back. So stay away, man! Let Astrid heal. She needs that." And John went inside the car and drove away.

Once Ryder was no longer in view, I let all the tears pour. John didn't say anything. He let me cry. I was thankful for that. I needed to feel free to cry my heart out and yet assured that I wasn't alone.

The next thing I knew, John was parking his car in his garage. He turned to me and smiled. "You're going to be okay, Ash."

I smiled at him and wiped my tears away. I took a deep breath and said to him, "Come on! Show me your crib, Daddy's boy!"

John laughed. Then he rounded the car and opened the door for me.

"Didn't figure you much to be a gentleman," I joked.

He grinned. "My deepest, darkest secret. This playboy thing... is only my disguise."

I laughed. It felt better, even just a little bit. In my current state, I needed all the laughs I could get.

I went out and looked around. Suddenly, I felt that something was wrong. The place seemed oddly familiar.

He led me inside his house. It's was big as Adam's house, also with a deck and a view of the beach.

I could not shake off the feeling that something was wrong with his place. Like I have been in this neighborhood before. John hasn't fully settled in. After all, he only moved in a couple of days ago.

"So when you said you needed somebody to clean up your house in exchange for rent, you weren't kidding," I joked.

John smiled mischievously. "I was dead serious."

"Come on, John. You're rich now! Can't you afford a maid?"

"Ah, but I needed somebody creative to decorate this place. And I am hiring the best," he said.

"I decorate wedding venues, John, not bachelor pads."

"But that's the best part," he said. "Since you're so attuned to what brides want, you can turn this place into a chick magnet."

I groaned. "I knew there was a catch to all this!"

I followed him upstairs where he showed me the guest bedroom.

"Are you going to be bringing women home in the next couple of days?" I asked him.

"You kidding me? I might bring one home *tonight*!"

"John!" I groaned. "I knew this was a bad idea! I don't want to be talking to your women about you. If I open my mouth, they wouldn't want to see you anymore!"

"Ha! I knew you were the right person to ask to be my roommate!" He said triumphantly and I hit him playfully on the shoulder.

Then I heard a sound of an engine roaring outside, followed by the sound of crashing metal, like somebody just hit a gate or something.

I looked out the window and saw a familiar car parked across the street. Its owner gave his metal gate one hard punch before going inside his house. It was the biggest house on the block. And it was all too familiar to me.

My jaw dropped. I turned to John, a shocked expression plastered on my face.

"Shit!" I cursed. I knew the neighborhood looked so familiar. I wasn't looking while John drove to his house. I was busy crying. "Did you know who lived across the street?"

John shrugged. "Well, even if I didn't have any idea before, the sight of you scrambling out of that house at four in the morning was a dead giveaway."

I was open-mouthed and I knew I was blushing from the roots of my hair. Nobody knew what happened between Ryder and me. I was careful not to tell them. But John knew right from the start.

"Wh-why were you awake at four in the morning?" I asked weakly.

He shrugged. "I just moved in. I was unpacking. I looked out the window. I saw you walking out in a rush, hailing a cab. I put two and two together."

I sighed. Again tears began to stream down my cheeks.

John took a deep breath and put an arm around me. "It's alright, Ash. I know how much you love him. So I understand why you would do it. But he doesn't remember you. I hate to think that he would take advantage of you that way. Now I understand why you were running away from him."

"And you invited me to crash in your house, when he was your neighbor?"

"Well, I didn't know the real reason why you were staying away from him. I thought you'd love the idea of stalking him. I thought I was actually doing you a favor," he said apologetically.

"Stalking?" I echoed. John just grinned, making me smile in return. That was really sweet of him. "Anyway, thanks. I know you meant well. But chances are I'm better off living at my house than here."

"Come on. You're already here." John said. "And he still doesn't know where you are. So you're still safe. My haven, your haven. Let me be your shield for a while." He grinned. "And besides, haven't you heard the saying, *'Keep your friends close, and your enemies closer?'"*

I think I got what he meant. I can avoid Ryder better if I know where he is. Or at least where his car is, since he never goes around the city without it.

That buys me a couple of days at least… some days of break. And then I will have to face my problem with Ryder Van Woodsen all over again.

32.
SOMETHING OLD:

A bride must also complete her ensemble on the wedding day with something old. It could be an heirloom piece, old jewelry, or anything that the bride owned in the past.

Astrid.

The following days, I barely left John's house. Rose was taking care of all the queries for the company. I spoke to my suppliers over the phone. I searched through the net to find a new place with a lower rent.

I was getting frustrated because the places with lower rents are really smaller. So it means that I have to rent a separate apartment for myself.

"Why don't you just rent a room instead of a place of your own?" John asked. We were eating pizza in his house.

"I suppose you're right. I mean, I can afford a new apartment, but I don't want to spend too much on that. I still have a long way to go with my company. And I still have to return Adam's money."

"Well, you know I have a spare room," John offered.

"You don't need the money." I told him.

"But you need a room," he said.

I sighed. "I'll think about it."

"Cool." He stood up from his seat and grabbed his jacket.

"Hot date?"

He grinned. "Don't wait up."

I rolled my eyes. "Player." I muttered under my breath.

Ryder's car has not moved in two days, so I assumed he's back in New York and I am safe from running into him for the time being.

I closed the deal on my lease. It's in the center of the city. It's a lot smaller than my current office, but it will do for now. Besides, it's all about the interior design. I just have to make it cute and cozy.

I had to move out, too. I took most of my personal stuff to John's place. I considered his offer, but only temporarily. He's a nice guy and all, but it's weird having breakfast with a different girl almost every morning.

I still think about Ryder every hour. I wonder how he is. I still remember our many nights of passion. It still brings tears to my eyes. And I am still praying that one day, he'll come back and tell me he remembers me and he still wants me.

One late afternoon, I was taking out my boxes from the office, when suddenly a voice startled me from behind.

"Going somewhere?"

My heart stopped beating. I took short breaths and turned around to face him.

303

He was wearing jeans and a white Armani T-shirt. He looked simple. He didn't look like a tycoon at all. His hair was disheveled and he had dark circles around his eyes, like he hasn't been sleeping at all. But God, he still looks beautiful.

"I… I'm moving," I replied.

"Why?"

I shrugged. "This place is too big for me. I am trying to cut costs so I can make more profit."

He nodded. I saw guilt cross his face, but I turned away. I don't need that. I don't need his pity. And besides, there is nothing wrong with cutting costs and laying low. In fact, I should have done this when I started the company in the first place.

I turned back to my boxes. I lifted one, and it was really heavy. Ryder stood beside me and took the box from my hand, lifting it as if it weighed nothing.

"Where are you going?" he asked.

"I've closed the lease on the new place. I have to get my stuff out of here this week."

"Did you not consider movers?" he asked.

"I don't have a lot of stuff. A couple of trips will save me the money I would spend on the movers. It's unnecessary."

He looked like he wanted to say something, but then he decided not to. Instead, he took another box out to the front. Then he went back to take some more.

What is he doing now?

"Ryder… really. I can do this," I said to him.

He grinned at me. "I know. But if I help, you will finish faster."

Is he trying to be cute? But God knows 'cute' is a huge understatement to describe Ryder Van Woodsen!

"Why do you care?" I retorted.

He shrugged. "Maybe because I would like to ask you out to dinner after you're done here. So the sooner we finish the better."

I sighed. *What now?*

"Why do you want to have dinner with me? Ryder, I can't…" To my surprise, he reached out to take my hand. His touch was gentle. Sincere. I wasn't able to finish my sentence.

"Please, Astrid?" he pleaded.

I looked into his eyes. And somehow, I saw the shadow of the man that I loved in there. The man that loved me back. Hope flickered inside me.

Hope. Is there still hope for Ryder and me?

I nodded. He smiled at me. "Thank you."

Ryder was making some calls while helping me bring out my boxes. And when I went inside my office to continue packing some more of my office stuff with Rose and Leilani, he went with me and silently helped.

Then I heard some noise out in the front. I went out and found a huge truck pulling up my driveway. The logo on the truck said *General Movers.*

I stared at Ryder in disbelief. He grinned at me.

"I told you, I don't want this. This is an unnecessary cost for me."

He gave me a crooked smile. "But it's not on you. It's on me."

"Ryder, I don't want to owe you anything!" I said in a frustrated tone.

He grinned at me again. He reached out to push a lock of hair away from my face. "I know. And you don't," he said. "Consider this a treat."

"A treat?" I echoed.

He shrugged. "A treat from your *boyfriend.*"

That irritated me. I pushed him, but he was too quick for me, as if he knew I was going to do that. He trapped both my hands against his chest and pulled me closer to him. His expression was mischievous and boyish.

"Astrid…" He said gently. "Did you break up with me before my accident?"

I took a deep breath. I shook my head.

"Did I break up with you?" he asked again.

I shook my head.

He gave me a crooked smile. And then he pulled me closer towards him, snaking one arm around my waist. Then he leaned forward, I can feel his breath on my neck, which caused all the hairs in my body to rise.

"So if we didn't break up, it means we're still a couple. I'm still your boyfriend, Astrid," he said. "Don't forget that, sweetheart." And he planted a soft kiss on my neck, before releasing me.

I felt weak when he pulled away from me. I had to hold on to one of the boxes beside me to support my weight.

Damn it! How can he have such an effect on me? And what game is he playing? He's asking me not to forget that he's still my boyfriend, when he was the one who literally forgot that I was his girlfriend!

Ryder turned and gave instructions to the movers.

"Where will they take these boxes?" he asked me. I gave him the exact address.

"So, now, you're free," he said.

"But these guys are not yet done."

"Your assistant can watch them. These guys will pack and transport everything to your new place. And then they will unpack everything there. Basically, you don't have to worry about a thing. You're free to go out with me now."

I rolled my eyes. He didn't give me a choice. I don't know what game he is playing, but to be honest, I was curious. After all, what else can Ryder Van Woodsen do to me that will hurt me even further? I'm practically maxed out!

"Okay, since I've packed away most of my clothes already, I'm going like this!" I said motioning to the jeans, sleeveless turtleneck top and thong sandals that I was wearing. I will make no effort to look glamorous to impress Ryder. The Ryder I know likes me the best when I'm wearing one of his oversized shirts.

He grinned at me. "Do you always look gorgeous in anything you wear?"

I raised a brow at him. Is he... flirting with me?

"You're kidding, right?" I asked.

He smiled and stepped closer to me. "I wish I was," he said. He looked down at me, pushing a lock of hair away from my face again. He looked into my eyes. "Your eyes are beautiful."

"Of course. I'm a witch remember?" I retorted and stepped away from him.

I can't be too close to Ryder. I have to put some distance between us before I literally jump on him and beg him to kiss me like there's no tomorrow.

He stared at me for a moment, watching my face turn the deepest shade of red. Then he grinned. "Your blush is beautiful too, you know. And I like it that I can make you blush."

I groaned. "Ryder, what's going on?" I finally asked. "The last time we saw each other, you were not nearly this nice to me!"

He raised a brow. "I don't think that's true. The last time I saw you I couldn't get my eyes or my hands off you."

I breathed heavily. "Where's the rude guy who thought I was after his money?"

He raised his hand like a boy scout. "Hey, 'asshole mode' still off." He grinned.

Somehow, this Ryder is confusing me. He's every bit as cute and as playful as the first time I went out with him in Miami... the first time I actually changed my mind about Ryder Van Woodsen being a snob and obnoxious.

He seems like the old him, but I know he's different. The arrogant guy who woke up at the hospital was so much easier to resist. This Ryder, on the other hand... I live for this man! *God, help me!*

"Are you going to turn it back on anytime soon? Because I have to be ready, you know! I have to make sure I have enough fire power to snap back at you and enough cab money to get back home when I walk out on you."

Ryder stared at me for a while, and then he laughed, a real heartwarming laugh. "You're amazing Astrid Jacobson! I guess now I understand how you got through my shield the first time around."

I raised a brow at him. Still waiting for his answer.

306

He took a deep breath and reached out to touch my cheek. "No. I promise. 'Asshole mode'... *forever off*," he said and my heart nearly melted right then and there. He looked so sincere and there was tenderness in the way he stared at me now. The cold, relentless man I met at the hospital was almost gone. "Now, can we go?"

I sighed and then I nodded.

He took me to a restaurant and chose a spot where we had a lovely view of the beach. Tears threatened to brim my eyes. This place was the same restaurant we went to when I first found out who he was. But of course he doesn't remember that.

When I looked at him, he was staring at me, watching my expression. He didn't say anything. But I know he could see that I was on the verge of crying.

"We came here before, didn't we?" he asked quietly.

I bit my lip. "Yes. First time after I found out who you really were. When I found out that you lied to me about being a bartender."

The waiter came and interrupted us. Ryder asked me to order first. I ordered pasta and Ryder ordered salmon.

"Why did you have to move?" he finally asked me.

"The place was too big for me and too expensive. I would rather divert those funds into more important things," I replied.

"You still have my investment," he said gently.

I stared at him and raised a brow. "No. I gave you the check."

He reached for my hand across the table. "I didn't cash it," he said. "And I'm not going to. I was out of line when I pulled it out."

I bit my lip for a moment and then I gently pulled my hand away from his. "Doesn't matter, Ryder. I don't want your investment anymore. I can do this. It will be difficult, I know. But I guess when you pulled the plug on me, I realized that it's time for me to grow a pair and be strong and brave enough to face the challenges in my life alone.

"Every time somebody in my life leaves me... I crumble and fall and I don't know how to get up. When Bryan and Geena cheated on me, my world just fell apart. When you... forgot about me, I felt like a part of me died and I didn't know how to recover from it." I tried my best not to cry. "I don't want to do that anymore. I have to be strong for myself."

He stared at me for a moment. I could see pain on his face. But he was lost for words again. He didn't know what to say. Of course, he can't imagine how much pain he can cause another human being he doesn't even know.

Hearing myself say those words, I know that it was the right thing to do. Ryder cannot do something out of whim and then change his mind about it and think it's just like clicking the 'undo' button on a computer program.

And besides, I cannot make my life always be a result of the consequences of the actions of the people around me.

Bryan proposed to me, and I set out to become Mrs. Bryan Bryans. *What a ridiculous name that is!* Then he cheated on me, I became homeless and jobless. Ryder came and invested in me, and I became an entrepreneur. Then he forgets about me and I *almost* became jobless again.

This cycle has to stop. I have to write my own future. I have to be who I am, regardless of who comes in and walks out of my life.

I looked at Ryder again. He was staring at me. Somehow, I see some admiration in his eyes. He reached out for my hand and squeezed it.

"I know you will not change your mind about my investment," he said. "But neither will I."

I pulled my hand away. "Why? You don't even know why you did it in the first place."

"If I didn't get into that stupid accident, I know we wouldn't even be discussing this. I'm trying to leave everything the way it would have been."

"Impossible." I murmured. "You already changed a lot of things, it's… impossible to bring them back."

Ryder took a deep breath. I know he was getting frustrated. But so am I. I've been through hell these past few months. I didn't want to give up on him. But he's got to let me know what he really wants from me, now that he doesn't even remember me.

"How are your mother and Paris?" I asked, just to change the subject.

"They're good. They miss you," he replied. "I'm going back to New York tomorrow, do you want to come with me?"

Seriously?

"Ryder… I don't think that's a good idea," I said.

"Why not? You are my girlfriend, after all. And my sister and mother both miss you."

I took a deep breath. "Because we're done putting on a show for everyone to see, Ryder." I told him. "You didn't want that. You wanted the real thing. We can't go and show your sister and mother that we're getting along well, when in truth, we could hardly make it out alive when we're with each other. I know you're only enduring me because you have to."

He stared at me for a long while. His eyes were hard and cold. I saw a hint of anger there, but he was trying to control it. "You don't know anything about how I feel right now, Astrid, so don't judge me."

"You're one to talk." I muttered under my breath.

He closed his eyes for a minute and then he continued eating his food without saying another word to me.

I didn't finish half of my food. I was so angry. How could Ryder tell me about judging people? He was the one who was quick to judge me the very first minute he laid eyes on me after his accident.

He paid for the food and then we went to his car. He opened the door for me and I went inside quietly.

"Where do you live now?" he asked, looking straight into the road.

"Across the street from you." I murmured.

He glanced at me briefly. But he didn't ask any more twenty-twenty questions. And I don't want to elaborate about my living arrangements with John either. I just want to get home. This emotional rollercoaster I have with Ryder is wearing me out.

Ryder drove home quietly. I prefer it that way. If I open my mouth again, I will either cry or curse at him. Either way, it's not going to be good.

He parked in front of John's house, got out of the car and opened the passenger door for me.

"Whose house is this?" he asked.

"John's," I replied.

He raised a brow. "You're living with... *another man?*"

"Yeah. He's one of my best friends," I replied. "And it's a two-bedroom apartment."

"He's still a guy, Astrid!" Ryder argued.

"So what?"

"And he's not even bad looking!"

"Again, so what?"

What's the matter with him? Is he jealous?

"Don't I have a say in this?!" He asked, trying to calm down.

"Of course! Feel free to say what you want! I don't guarantee that it will matter though."

"Astrid... I'm your boyfriend! And I am not comfortable with you living with another man!"

"Could you stop using the boyfriend trump card?" I asked angrily. "Only a few months ago, you were willing to pay me to stay out of your life!"

He didn't have a response to that. The look he gave me was as guilty as it was broken.

I sighed. "It's only for a few days. Because I have nowhere else to go!"

"My house is across the street!" He replied. "Why not stay there?"

I shook my head. "I used to stay in your house, Ryder. But you kicked me out, remember? Oh! That reminds me! When you kick your girlfriend out of your house, doesn't that mean you broke up with her already?"

He stared at me in disbelief. "Astrid... that is so unfair!" He said. "I returned your stuff before we spent the night together. I had no more intention of letting you go in the morning! But you... you ran away from me."

Tears streamed down my cheeks. I raised my chin to him. "I have no intention of being your toy, Ryder. *That's* why I ran away from you."

He looked at me through narrowed eyes. "My toy? Is that what you think you are to me?"

I took a deep breath. "Since you woke up in the hospital, you haven't showed me anything that will make me think otherwise. *Mercenary slut*, remember?"

Ryder took a step away from me. He stared at me in amazement. Maybe he realized that what I said is true. Since he woke up he's been nothing but rude to me and showed me that he will do anything to get rid of me. Then we slept together, and suddenly he's running around town looking for me, he's treating me to dinner and attempting to be nice to me.

Thanks, but no thanks!

If he told me that he's remembered even just a bit of me, I will not think that he's doing all these to get me to bed again. But right now, it's the only logical explanation I can come up with.

Ryder looked down and then he took a deep breath. "You're right," he said. "I don't deserve your better judgment or treatment. And I can't make you believe anything that I say either. I wanted you to give up on me. Now... I want nothing more than to undo everything I did to you in the last four months. But I guess... it's too late for that now."

He headed for his car. My heart was breaking into a million pieces with every step he took.

That's it? He's accepting it without a fight? The Ryder that I know will not give up on me too easily. He will put up a fight, even if he tricks me into accepting things, until I admit to myself that I want what he wants too.

"I'm sorry for hurting you, Astrid," he said. "I wish... I could do something to take the pain away. If I am the cause of your pains, then I'll stay away if that would make it hurt less. I only wish you happiness." His voice was broken and sad. At that moment, I believed him. I believed he was really giving up this time.

This is it. We're breaking up.

"I wish you happiness too, Ryder." I said, trying my best not to cry. "I wish... I wish fate didn't play with us."

He nodded. "I wish fate made me forget everything else... but you." He whispered. Then he went inside his car and drove off. He lives across the street, but he didn't go home. He sped past his house and onto the highway.

I stood in John's driveway for the longest minutes of my life, hoping that Ryder would drive back to me and tell me that everything is going to be okay. I didn't want to give up on him. But right now, I don't know how I could hold on to him.

I know he wanted me; he wanted to possess my body. But I cannot allow him to do that unless he gives me a space in his heart. I go packaged deal with love. He can't have fun with me unless he loves me.

Is this it? Are we really over? Did we really break up without him remembering who I was in his life?

I turned towards John's house and opened the front door. I was about to close it behind me when suddenly a force from the other side pushed the door open.

I almost lost my balance. I had to step back to keep the door from hitting my face. I stared up the intruder, ready to shout and curse. But what I saw made my blood drain from my face. He has a smirk on his face; his eyes were reddish and have dark circles around them.

"What's the problem, doll? Trouble in paradise? Does this mean you can finally come out and play with me?" Bryan asked me, an evil smile plastered on his face, and he definitely looked like he was high on something.

I have seen Bryan drunk, but I've never seen him like this. This looks like the demon version of him. The one that cuts throats and beats up girls. And when I looked into his eyes, I can only see one thing… the darkest, most evil form of *lust*.

Instantly, my blood froze and every nerve in my body was screaming the same thing… *Run!!!*

33.
SOMETHING BLUE:

The Bride must always wear something… anything… blue. It can be a trinket or undergarment. Some choose to put a blue lining on the wedding garter that they wear under their wedding gown.

Ryder.

*T*hat did not go as planned.

Astrid is a little firecracker. You don't handle her properly, she will explode. *And damn!* I did *not* handle that well.

I wanted to woo her, show her my charming side, the one that is not uptight and suspicious of all women. The real me without masks and with all my guards down.

I thought I was doing a great job earlier in the afternoon. I thought she'd appreciate the movers, but I don't think Astrid likes owing people anything, especially favors with a financial value attached to it. A very admirable trait.

Wow! I have chosen well.

The problem is how do I delete the asshole image of me in her head? How can I make her forget that even once, I called her a gold-digger! Or the fact that I accused her of only being after my money!

I wanted her to give up on me. I wanted nothing to do with her. Now, I wanted nothing more than to remove this stupid cloud in my brain so she could be with me again.

Jake was right. When I wake up from all of this, I would want to kill myself for what I did to Astrid. Damn! I wanted to kill myself now, even though I haven't fully recovered from my amnesia.

I wish I gave her a chance, right from the moment I opened my eyes. I wish I did not push her away, and made it clear that I did not want anything to do with her. I wish I'd gotten to know her first before I decided on the fate of our relationship.

If I gave Astrid a chance four months ago… I think I still would fall in love with her… even without my previous memories of her.

She is beautiful. Her eyes just enchant me. Her scent fills my senses and intoxicates me.

She is talented in many aspects. I cannot believe, in less than a year, she was able to make her company break even. I saw her portfolio. She has good taste and so much passion for what she does. She knows what she's doing, and she puts her heart into it.

She has a sense of humor. Not every girl can make me laugh. Hmmm… the 'asshole mode' still cracks me up. Do I really have that mode?

She has been badly hurt by the people close to her and yet she chose to get back up on her feet and love again. She fell in love again… because of me. She chose to take a risk in me in spite of the pains that she has been through.

Lucky bastard! I thought to myself.

Paris and my mother are not the easiest people to please. But Astrid passed their tests with flying colors. I know my mother's heart breaks along with Astrid's.

And Paris… well, she has not been speaking to me much. The last time she spoke to me was when Janis told her that I pulled the plug on Astrid's company. I could still remember how that conversation turned out.

I always remember my conversations with Paris lately. She surprises me and shocks me at the same time. I lost one year of my memories. I don't remember how much she has changed in twelve months. She was bolder, tougher. She has so much angst and she's not afraid to say what's on her mind. In a way, I admire her more. But a part of me felt sad because I realize I don't really know her as much as I thought I did.

"You couldn't choose a better knife to kill yourself with." Paris said to me over the phone. "Actually, that's not a knife. It's an F-in samurai!"

"Since when do you swear that much?" I asked her.

"F-in is not a swear word." She argued. "I should remember not to code my language, since I was gonna get scolded the same way by my big brother."

"Paris Van Woodsen! You were sent to the best schools in the country! Not just to learn business, but to learn etiquette and what differentiates a man from a… lady!"

"Funny you should say that, big bro," she said in a sarcastic tone, "because I've seen how you treated Astrid in the past few months. You were sent to the best schools in at least three continents. I thought you learned what differentiates a man from a moron."

I didn't have anything to say to that. One, because it was true; two, because I didn't know Paris would defend Astrid with such vigor; and three, because I didn't know Paris would be bold enough to talk to me like this.

"Did I… do something to you, Paris?" I asked.

She sighed. "No." There was silence on the other end of the line. Then she said, "I talk to you like this, Ryder. At least for the past year, you've made me feel like I didn't have to conform to the rules of our society. You've always allowed me to be who I really am. Not the dumb little heiress that everybody expects me to be."

I took a minute to process what she said. Then I said, "You're not a dumb little heiress. Don't even allow anybody to make you feel like you are. Even me."

"Good." I can hear the smile in her voice. "That's why I'm telling you now that what you did with Astrid's company… your funeral."

I sighed. Why does everybody keep telling me this? "Why?"

"You lost one year of your memories, Ryder. We've been telling you who Astrid was in your life and how much you loved her. I get that you don't know her now and you don't trust her. But even then... you should have trusted us."

They were right. They were all right! Even Jake warned me I was going to regret this.

I underestimated the degree of my feelings for Astrid. Darn! I didn't even know I was capable of falling in love.

I always thought I was not going to marry for love. I thought I would find a woman that was... *suitable*. And then I would marry her, have kids with her and be a happy father. I would be a good husband. It's a give and take relationship. If she's faithful to me, there is no reason for me to play around. Plus, I know how kids feel when their parents go their separate ways. I've been there. I wouldn't want my kids to go through that.

I wasn't expecting Astrid to happen; that I would find someone that I can drown myself in. I didn't know I would feel so strongly for a woman, that the sight or even the thought of another man touching her would boil my blood and make me abandon reason.

I never knew I could go to bed with a woman and would want to hold her until morning. That I could forever drown in the scent of her. That only one night of sleeping with her in my arms would make the other nights without her unbearable.

Whatever pieces of Astrid that I recalled from the past year is just enough for me to know that she's the woman I've been looking for. My match, the woman that I needed.

Damn! I hurt her!

For the past few days, Astrid has been in my thoughts every waking hour. When I go to bed at night, her memory lies down beside me. I wanted to see her smile and hear her laugh again. I wanted to hear her scream my name in bed again.

I wanted her to keep stocking up my fridge and tell me where things were in my house. I wanted to open the front door of my house and she's the first thing that I would see.

But I threw all that away. I drove her away.

I hit the brakes of my car. I had been driving more than a hundred miles an hour, not caring if I will hit something. Maybe I was tempting fate again. Maybe I wanted to get into another accident and hopefully hit my head so hard, the cloud that veils my memories of Astrid would be gone.

I don't know where I was or where I was going. I was driving without a destination or a purpose. In truth, I wanted to get away. If I went home, I knew I will be restless knowing that she's just across the street from me. Ten bucks say I will not be able to resist for ten minutes. I will cross that street, break her friend's door down, and carry her to my house and no one will be able to stop me.

But she needs some space right now. And I need to think. I need to... I don't know... strategize!

I stopped the car on the side of the road and took deep breaths.

I realized that I don't need to regain my memories to know that I am in love with Astrid. Because even now, with all these holes and missing puzzle pieces in my head, I still want to be with her. And I want her to love me back. I want her to forget what an ogre I have been to her the past few months.

I didn't tell her that I remembered a little bit of her. I should have. But I didn't. I wanted her to know that with or without my stupid amnesia, we could still work. We could still be together and I could still make her happy.

Well, congratulations for a job well done, Ryder! I thought angrily. I messed up my chances yet again.

I don't know when I will gain my memories back. There is a chance that I don't recover them at all. That's why I don't want her to keep loving the man I used to be... the man in my past. I want her to fall in love with this man in front of her now, and later realize that I'm still the same person. That nothing changed. And nothing will change between us.

This afternoon, when I reminded her that I'm still her boyfriend, a sense of joy and pride swept through me. I felt like I'm the luckiest guy in the world because she is mine.

I realized I didn't want to change that. And no amount of amnesia could take Astrid away from me, or me from her.

I will make amends for everything that I did to her in the past. But for now, she has to forgive me.

God, I was so stupid! Astrid has a good heart. All I needed to prove to her was how sorry I am about the way I acted and ask... *or beg...* for her to give me one more chance.

Because I love her.

There! I admit what my pride and my logical brain prevented me from admitting before. I don't know how, but even without gaining back all my memories of her, I fell for her anyway.

And even if she doesn't accept that, I realized that she has to know at least. I cannot have her thinking that I only wanted her for a playmate. I may have forgotten her, but I'm still the man she fell in love with. And I will never use her or take advantage of her.

But how will I do this? She must freaking hate me right now!

I am not going to wait. I will tell her now. No guards. No masks. No prides.

Right now, she could be in her room, crying her heart out because of me again. No, I promised myself I wouldn't hurt her anymore. She can do whatever she wants with what I am going to tell her. But I will say it to her anyway... I love her.

And if she choses to start over... even without our memories together... I would make that chance count. Instead of waiting for me to regain my memories of her, we would just make new ones... happier ones.

I took a deep breath and I prayed for a little bit of luck. Looks like I was gonna need it. And then I shifted the gear to reverse and turned the car back around.

34.
SOMETHING BORROWED:
A bride must complete her outfit by wearing something that is not hers.
Suggestions would be a tiara, hair clips, gloves, jewelry, and the list goes on and on.

Astrid.

*M*y heart pounded in my chest. But I knew that I shouldn't panic. This was Bryan! He was one of my best friends before we decided to become more than friends. I knew him. Once in his life, I loved him. And he loved me. He will never hurt me physically… or *will he?*

"Bryan…" I breathed. "Are you okay? You look… drunk."

He laughed. "Oh, I am more than that! And I like it!" His eyes gleamed with mischief and I got even more scared.

"Wha-what do you want?" I asked him, taking a step backward.

"Ha!" He sighed angrily. "You still don't know what I fucking want?" He took a step forward. "What's the matter, Astrid? Is your Prince Charming breaking your heart?"

"No…" I started.

"Liar!" He shouted. "I know everything, sweetheart!" He looked at me angrily. "Why do you put up with him? Why do you allow yourself to hurt over and over? You're erased from his memories. Accept that! Move on!"

I was shocked. My family didn't even know about Ryder's accident. How could Bryan know?

"How… how do you know that?" I breathed. Half of me wanted to know the answer, and the other half is thinking of a way out.

"Oh, little Astrid. I know! I know everything about you! I care for you! Ryder… just wants you for a playmate and has conveniently forgotten about you." He laughed. "You were heartbroken for months. You didn't even tell your family about his tragedy… well, now, it's more *your* tragedy! Because the only person being hurt by all this is you." And he laughed, an evil laugh that made me want to smack his face, but I didn't want to provoke him.

"I don't… understand how you… know all this." I whispered, taking a step back, and fidgeting at the table beside me, trying to get hold of something that I can use as a weapon against him, in case he decides to go *psycho.*

"Your young employee… Rose… she's a talker… especially after sex!" Then he laughed loudly.

And whatever control I have in my body, that was gone in an instant. I got so mad at him I couldn't help it. *He's Geena's husband!*

"You son of a bitch!" I said to him angrily. "How could you cheat on Geena?"

He laughed. "You expect me to be faithful to her? I don't even love her. There was only one woman I could have been faithful to." He looked at me sadly.

"You weren't faithful to me!" I hit back.

"I would have been! If you threw me a bone! I have needs, Astrid! I'm a man. How could you have forgotten that? If... if you didn't... then we would have been married by now. I would have been happy! I would have made you happy! And you won't be here, eating your heart out because of him!"

I shook my head. "Don't pin this on me, Bryan. If you really loved me, you would have waited. Ryder would have waited. He was willing to. Because I was more important than anything else."

I saw wrath in his eyes. "Ryder, Ryder, Ryder! You worship him like a god and he doesn't even remember you! He even pulled out his investment on your business! He doesn't care! Now, here you are! Homeless! Where is he, Astrid? He walked out on you! I would have fought for you! I would not have given up so easily!"

Tears stung my eyes. I wanted to shout at him and deny everything he just said, but I know he was right. Ryder didn't remember me, and he didn't even care that I would be homeless after he pulled out his investment in my business.

My defenses crumbled for a minute. And Bryan saw that window. I hate it that somehow, he still knows me. He still knows when I am being weak or defensive, or when I was lying.

In two long strides, he was able to close the gap between us. He grabbed my waist and pulled me to him.

"Forget Van Woodsen, Astrid! I'm here now! And I will never let you go again!" he said. His breath smelled of alcohol, smoke, and something else I could not place. Up close I could see just how red his eyes were and how his cheekbones were protruding, like he lost a lot of weight since the last time I saw him.

I watched in horror as his face descended towards mine. I took a deep breath, pulled back and used all my efforts to push him away. When his grip was still too tight, I started hitting frantically, scratching and screaming. For the first time, I realized that my pretty long nails have another useful purpose.

I got him on the cheek, he staggered back from the pain and that gave me a little room to get away. I ran behind the counter, putting some distance between us.

Bryan touched his cheek. It was bleeding a little bit from the scratches I gave him. But instead of getting mad, he only gave me an evil grin. The kind that says I actually turned him on rather than discouraged his advances.

"That's the Astrid I like! Feisty!" he said, starting for me again.

"Don't come any closer!" I shouted at him.

"That's impossible, sweetheart. I'm attached to you. You pull me like a moth to a flame!" He took another step forward.

There were some figurines or plates on the counter, I didn't check to see exactly what. But I just kept throwing things at him, sending each piece shattering to the ground.

I hit him hard on the shoulder. He stared back at me, his eyes narrowing from the pain. "That's it! You'll regret that!" And he lunged forward.

I ran, but he was too fast.

He grabbed me by my waist and lifted me as if I weighed nothing. He dropped me hard on the counter. I whimpered from the pain as I felt my back hit the hard countertop. He held me there, pinning both my shoulders down.

"You thought you can fool me for a second? Really, Astrid? Van Woodsen was never your type! I know that! You never go for rich jocks! Even when you were in high school, you steered clear of popular kids! You always wanted out of the limelight. They all fell to your feet, but you never entertained any of them! You didn't want guys with big egos and deep pockets! You have this stupid thing of wanting to be the center of a man's world. You wanted a man who thinks he has enough, as long as he has you!"

I struggled to get away from him. But he leaned forward and pressed his body against mine to prevent me from escaping.

"I was that man, Astrid! Van Woodsen is the epitome of the guys you were avoiding ever since you were a teenager! You expect me to believe you are happy with him?"

I took a deep breath. "Ryder didn't have to be rich! I would love him even if he were poor because he is a hundred times the man you are, Bryan!"

"You whore! You made me wait years for nothing! And what? Van Woodsen had to wait one night to pop your cherry? You sold yourself to the highest bidder! How much?"

"You bastard!" I screamed and then I gathered all my remaining strength to kick my knee up to his crotch. He let go of me, backing away, feeling the pain.

I pulled myself up and ran to get some distance between us, but he was fast to recover. He pulled my hair and I screamed from the pain.

"You slut! You will pay for that!" He screamed. "I'm not waiting anymore! I will take what is rightfully mine! You don't know how sorry you will be after I'm through with you!" Without releasing my hair he pushed my head down with intense force.

I had no way of escaping that blow. I felt my head hit the counter top with a big thump. I wasn't even able to scream.

I fell to the floor, barely conscious. I wanted to get up and fight. I was afraid of what Bryan would do to me and I wasn't even awake to defend myself. I felt a warm gush of hot liquid on my forehead. There was a sharp pain on my wrist as I realized I landed on broken shards of glass.

I tried to push up, hoping that Bryan will not come for me yet. I needed a little more time to get back on my feet and fight him off, or at least try. I waited for him to haul me up, but somehow, he didn't come for me again. I heard his voice... shouting and cursing in the background. But my vision was blurring. The noises around me were slowly fading. And then I felt darkness taking over, and I realized in horror, that this could very well be the end.

***

Ryder.

In less than ten minutes, I reached our neighborhood. I was tempted to go home instead, but I looked across the street and realized that I cannot chicken out now. Every second I spend away from Astrid, just might be widening the gap between us.

There was a car parked in front of John's house. A Boxster. I guess Astrid's roommate is home.

Great!

I didn't make a good impression on this guy a couple of days back. I doubt he would let me through the door now. He seemed so protective of Astrid. And I don't know whether to feel good or bad about it.

Good, because somebody is protecting her, while I was being an ass. Bad, because... *damn*! I'm jealous! The reason why I didn't like the idea of her living with her good-looking friend is because I was so insecure and jealous. I wanted to be the one protecting her. But I don't know how to get her back, after all the hurtful things I said and did to her these past couple of months.

I took a deep breath and stared at the skies.

Help me, God!

I was about to ring the buzzer when I heard voices from inside the house.

"*Van Woodsen is the epitome of the guys you were avoiding ever since you were a teenager! You expect me to believe you are happy with him?*"

"*Ryder didn't have to be rich! I would love him even if he were poor! Because he is a hundred times the man you are, Bryan!*" I heard her shout angrily. My heart swelled at hearing this.

But who was she fighting with?

"*You whore! You made me wait years for nothing! And what? Van Woodsen had to wait one night to pop your cherry? You sold yourself to the highest bidder? How much?*"

322

His words boiled my blood. I don't care who he is. No one can talk to Astrid like that and get away with it. I reached for the door and turned the knob, but it was locked.

"You bastard!" I heard Astrid scream and I felt cold. I knew I had to do something before she got hurt.

With all my strength, I kicked the door. The lock gave. I immediately ran inside.

The house was a mess, like somebody played tag inside it. There were shattered pieces of broken glass all over the floor. The furniture was in disarray.

An unfamiliar man registered in my brain. He had his back to me, and he was holding Astrid in front of him.

"I'm not waiting anymore! I will take what is rightfully mine! You don't know how sorry you will be after I'm through with you!"

I went for him, but I was too late, he banged Astrid's head on the counter top. She fell to the floor unconscious.

My heart pounded inside my chest and I felt a sense of terror that I have never felt before. The sight of Astrid, limp and barely breathing blocked me out. No one can hurt her! Whoever does will pay! And I saw nothing else but red after that.

I went for her assailant. I pulled him away so he could not come for her again. My leg hit a piece of furniture behind me and I slightly lost my balance. The guy launched a punch at me. He got me straight on the side of my head. I fell back. And suddenly, I felt dizzy. Like everything was blurry.

But I knew I had to get up. I had to protect Astrid. She has no one else but me. And I will die first before I let anything happen to her. I stood up and went for the guy blindly.

I didn't stop to check who he was and I didn't care. I punched him and he fell over. I mounted him, not giving him a chance to get back up, and I just kept punching.

He already had scratches on his face and his arms. It looks like Astrid put up a good fight after all, but he was just too strong for her.

My blood froze at the thought of what he would have done to Astrid had I not decided to come back for her, and if Astrid was not able to put up a little fight, buying me time so I could save her.

Wrath enveloped me at the thought that he might have killed her had I been too late. I kept punching, not caring about what part of his face would break.

Then suddenly somebody pulled me from behind, preventing me from throwing in more punches. I struggled to get away. I struggled so I could come back and beat the life out of the asshole that had hurt Astrid.

Then I heard a familiar voice call out to me. "Ryder!" He was holding me on my shoulders tightly, preventing me from moving towards the guy again. "He's out, man! He's out! You could kill him!"

I looked up, and found that it was John who was holding me back. I pushed him away from me.

Then I remembered Astrid. I pushed John out of the way and practically crawled to where she was. She was still unconscious.

I felt her pulse.

She's alive.

Relief swept through me. I gathered her in my arms and held her against my chest.

I stared at her beautiful face. Her blush was gone; her skin was almost white, except for the blood that is staining her forehead and cheeks.

She was so brave! She gave Bryan a good fight! And I was so happy because if she didn't, I would not have made it in time to save her.

I leaned down and kissed her bloodstained forehead. I held her to me. I closed my eyes and remembered the first time I woke up in the hospital and laid eyes on her. There was an unfamiliar knot in my stomach and my blood heated up just at the mere sight of the woman I didn't recognize from my past. I have wanted her, but I didn't understand those emotions yet. So instead of exploring what I felt for her, I shut her out. And I hurt her in the process.

Months before I returned to Malibu, she had been living in my house because I asked her to. My house has a central alarm system and panic buttons that would immediately alert the authorities. She would have been safe there.

But no! I pulled out my investment in her business, causing her to move out of her own place and finding friends who will be kind enough to take her in. And that asshole ex of hers followed her here.

When we were fighting, she was telling me that she doesn't want to be my toy. And stupid me! I could have kissed her senseless and told her that she was never a toy to me. I could have told her that I remember even a little bit of her. I should have told her that I loved her and I wasn't letting her go this time, no matter how many times she shut me out or turn me down. I should have told her what I really feel... I should have done everything else... except for walk away!

I looked at her almost pale face, her bloody clothes, her limp body, and I knew I shouldn't put any blame on anybody. No! Her ex-fiancé didn't do this to her. I did! I can come up with a thousand excuses, but deep in my heart, I knew... I did this to her!

From the moment I opened my eyes at the hospital, all my actions were leading her to this fate, this day. I know I cannot blame anybody else. It was all me. I did this to Astrid... the woman I swore to protect, the woman I would go to hell and back for.

And for the first time in many months, I really cried. Tears poured from my eyes as I held her to me and inhaled her sweet scent mixed with the rusty smell of her blood. Her scent reminded me how much I loved her. And the smell of blood reminded me of all the ugly things I did to her.

I was only a couple of minutes away from losing her. And I haven't even told her that I love her. I didn't even apologize for everything that I did. She didn't even know that I have changed... that I was no longer the man who woke up in the hospital not knowing who she was.

The ambulance finally came. John tapped me on the shoulder. When I looked up at him, he was beckoning me to let Astrid go and let the paramedics attend to her.

I reluctantly let her go. John pulled me up and pushed me to go outside the house. I caught a glimpse of Bryan who was also unconscious on the floor, paramedics already putting him on a stretcher.

"You okay?" John asked.

I raised a brow. "Are you trying to be funny?" I snapped at him.

"I guess you're not," he whispered.

He took out his phone and called some people, telling them what happened to Astrid.

They carried Bryan out on a stretcher. If he weren't unconscious, I would have hit him in the head once again. I can still taste bile in my mouth just by looking at him.

I tried to calm my nerves. I clenched my fists and I found that my knuckles were also bleeding slightly.

"You should let them attend to that." John said to me.

I took a deep breath. "I will live. Not the first time I got into a fist fight."

Finally, they brought out Astrid on a stretcher. She had an oxygen mask on her face.

"Who's a relative?" One of the paramedics asked.

"I'm her boyfriend," I replied, even before John could open his mouth.

"We're bringing her to the hospital now." The guy said.

"I'll come with you."

They let me ride with her in the ambulance. I was still high on adrenaline. I couldn't calm down until I knew for sure that Astrid was going to be fine.

I looked at her limp body. I took her hand and kissed it. I couldn't help the tears that were pouring from my eyes again.

God, I love her! I love her!

I always have. She was my life. She *is* my life. And now, I cannot believe that I came so close to losing her. And it's all my fault.

Bryan would not have the guts to even come near her if he knew I was still protecting her. He must have known that we were having

325

problems. He must have waited for me to drive away and then he saw an opportunity to attack Astrid.

When we reached the hospital, she was taken to the emergency room and I was asked to wait outside. I didn't want to. But some nurses pushed me towards the waiting area.

"We will take good care of her, don't worry," somebody said to me. It was a nurse, I think.

I was pacing back and forth, praying to God that she would be okay, that her fall didn't cause any concussion or severe injury.

I shouldn't have walked out on Astrid.

She was saying goodbye to me. She was wishing me happiness. I walked away thinking I only needed to give her space for a while. And give myself some time to breathe… compose myself… before I said any more that will further decrease my chances of being with her.

No! I wasn't saying goodbye to her at all. *Never!*

And I pray to God that I still have one chance to make it all right. To undo everything I did in the past few months. I didn't want to lose my memories of her. And it wasn't her fault that I did. But damn, she suffered the most! I made her suffer because I was afraid to face what I feel for her.

Adam arrived at the hospital, followed by John.

"Where is she?" Adam asked me.

"Inside," I replied.

"Bryan did this?" Adam asked John. I don't know why he didn't ask me, I was the first one on the scene. John came a bit later.

Has Bryan not done enough to Astrid? He knocked up her cousin, her best friend. They stole Astrid's dream wedding. They robbed Astrid of her faith in 'ever afters'. They crushed her dignity and self-esteem.

I remembered their conversation before I came in. Bryan was so mad at Astrid because he waited too long for her. Yes. Bryan wanted Astrid so much, but she wanted to wait until marriage. And that night I went to the wedding with Astrid… she shared herself with me. I was her first. And it was the most amazing thing that ever happened to me. I was Astrid's first… I was the only man in her life.

Dannie and Nicole came to the waiting area, a look of panic evident on their faces. Of course! They love Astrid to the core. Even John and Adam. They all cared for Astrid.

Dannie and Nicole were looking at me angrily and I know why. For the past months, I have been hurting their friend and they haven't forgiven me yet. The last time I saw them, they were all for Astrid and me. Now, if looks could kill, they would be responsible for my murder.

Just then, my head snapped up as a realization hit me. I stared at them closely.

"Dannie." I said looking at Astrid's semi-feminine friend.

"Nicole." I said looking at Astrid's girl best friend.

They stared back at me, equally dumbfounded. I'm sure I haven't seen them since my accident, so there was no way in hell I should know who they were.

And how would I know that I was Astrid's first... that I was the only man she's ever been with?

Unless...

Now, maybe the adrenaline rush died down. I finally felt what my body has been telling me. My knuckles were painful, and I felt dizzy, like everything was spinning.

I sat down on the chair, holding my temples, trying my best not to scream from the pain. Everything was getting blurry.

"Nurse!" I heard somebody shout. I think it was Adam who first realized that something was happening to me.

And after that, there was only darkness.

35.
WEDDING ALBUM:
A collection of the snapshots and pictures captured during the wedding day. The Wedding Album holds all the memories of the most wonderful day between a husband and a wife.

Ryder.

I have to meet her. The girl I spent half a day looking for around the city! I thought I would never see her again.

"I'll cover the bar, guys!" I told my bartenders. I took my jacket off and grabbed the baseball cap from one of my staff and wore it on my head. "Borrow for a while, okay?"

He looked at me like he thought I was high or something and then he nodded.

I watched her. She was alone. Now, I wish I knew some pick-up lines. Or if I did, I knew how to use them effectively! But so far the only things that I could remember hearing around were:

'Did it hurt when you fell from heaven?'

or

'I lost my phone number, so can I have yours?'

and

'If I say you have a wonderful body, will you hold it against me?'

They are so lame and corny! Who invents these things? And I doubt any of them are going to work on her. Damn! I am not good at this!

She ordered a margarita. I guess here's my cue.

"The best margarita in town for the beautiful lady," I said. Even I thought that sounds creepy! "Can you sign, Ma'am?"

She didn't answer. She just stared at me. Her expression looked... I don't know, star-struck or something. Hmmm... I guess she likes what she sees. That gave me the confidence I needed.

"Can you sign, Ma'am?" I repeated.

"Oh." She said and she signed the tab. I couldn't help but notice that her fingers were slightly shaking.

"Thank you," she said.

"You're welcome Madam," I said. "Enjoy your drink. Just call me if you need anything else." I said, grinning at her, flashing her my perfect set of teeth and the dimples on my cheeks. Flirting. Yes, I am definitely flirting with her, and she looked dumbfounded.

"And what name would I ask for?" She asked.

There! We're getting somewhere.

"Ryder," I replied.

"Alright. Thanks, Ryder," she said.

I stood there for a while, waiting for her to tell me her name. But she only smiled at me and I realized that was the only reply I was going to get. She's teasing me. Alright! Two can play this game.

"Alright. Perhaps when I bring you your next drink." I said, and I winked at her.

I felt like a high school boy reeling with excitement. What is it about this woman that unnerves me? She got under my skin the minute I laid eyes on her. And I can't forget the feel of her in my arms. Although I doubt that she recognizes me from the jewelry shop.

She was talking on the phone with her friends.

"Find me a straight guy!" She said loudly over the receiver.

I smirked. I couldn't help smiling. What would she need a straight guy for? She can have her pick here at the bar. Doesn't she know how beautiful she is?

"You shouldn't eavesdrop on other people's conversations." She said, not looking at me, but I knew she's talking to me.

I approached her. "I wouldn't have, if your voice wasn't that loud."

"Oh sorry," she said. "People talk loud in bars, you know. Well, you should know."

"Yes, I know." I grinned at her again. "So, what's the quest for the straight guy for?"

"Not just a straight guy. But a straight guy who's willing to do anything for a couple of grand."

"You're not doing porn, are you?" I asked, and God, I hope she says no.

"Oh my God! No!"

I sighed in relief.

"Now, I'm intrigued. What could a girl like you possibly need a straight guy for?"

And so, she told me the story of her life, with tears in her eyes.

For the life of me, I could not believe everything she told me. How can someone bear to hurt her? She looked so fragile, so vulnerable. She looked like she has so much light and fire inside her. How could somebody afford to put it out?

She wanted her pride back. She wanted to save her face. And I couldn't believe what I was doing. I was agreeing to her plan, letting her think I was a bartender in need of extra cash. If I was not so touched by her breakup story, I would have laughed.

She wanted to bring a guy to the wedding that could pretend that he was smart and rich, wore an Armani suit, and drove a very expensive car. Harvard Degree, investments here and there. She's inventing the man who will annihilate her ex-fiancé's pride. She wants to redeem her dignity by showing up at the wedding with a man that is like a slap in the face to her ex, even if she was just pretending.

Well, that would be very easy for me. Because basically, she wants me to pretend to be... well... '*me*'.

***

The feel of her lips on mine was... magic. It was like there were fireworks everywhere. All night, I felt myself drowning into our charade. I could not get my hands off her. I held her and kissed her, praying that the day would never end.

Her eyes sparkled when she looked at me. She erupted like a firecracker in my arms when I kissed her. She genuinely laughed at my jokes. She was not afraid to show me that she felt hurt and she needed me to hold her. She needed me to save her.

And she didn't even know who I was. She was parading me around to her family, saying that I am the rich hotshot guy who owns a chain of restaurants in New York. She thought that was part of the act. I wonder how she'll react if she finds out... that's who I really am.

Here she was, kissing me, hugging me. Ryder, the bartender. And she didn't care. It's me she wants, regardless of what I am.

She was drowning and drunk on both the liquor and her grief. But I admire her. No one could go through all that pain and live to tell about it.

Then she started crying. She hugged me. And the next thing I knew, she was kissing me.

I didn't want to take advantage of her. She was sad and drunk. But she was a cannonball in my arms. I could feel her heat radiating against my skin. Her kisses were sending me over the edge. I tried to hold on to my last string of control, but when she pushed me on the bed and mounted me, I lost it! I was only human, and my body craves this woman like a drug.

I kissed her. She melted in my arms. She was whispering my name over and over and it was the sweetest sound I have ever heard in my life.

We lost our clothes. I was lost in ecstasy. And when I went inside her, she squirmed in pain. I felt a tearing sensation. *Damn!* No wonder she was too tight. I leaned down and kissed her. She was crying.

"I'm sorry, love." I said to her. But I knew I wasn't! This is probably the most amazing thing that has ever happened to me. She was a virgin. She was mine first. I was the only one. And I knew from that moment on, I intend to keep it that way.

***

I had just got back to Malibu and my manager told me that a woman was looking for me. I was not really interested. There was only one woman I was interested in and I was getting impatient. I wanted her to

331

get over her past, her grief. I wanted her to fulfill her promises so I could finally work my way into her life. I wanted her to start fresh, fix herself, and then open herself up to trusting another man again. And I wanted to be that man. I wanted her to know the real me.

She wanted me. I know she did. Her eyes had a certain gleam when she stared up at me. She blushed at the simplest touch of my skin against hers and she went mindless with me that night. And she thought I was a bartender, desperate enough for money that I took the job of pretending to be her boyfriend for a night. But still she wanted me.

This was the woman I was looking for my entire life! A woman who would want me for me... not for my money. It's a good bonus that she's sweet, beautiful, and her touch makes me explode.

I cannot wait to pay Astrid Jacobson a visit.

"Ryder..." My bar manager said. "This woman was asking for you a couple of days ago. She left a message."

I didn't even look up from the papers I was signing. I let Donald continue.

"She told me to tell you that... Astrid Jacobson was looking for you."

Now, he got my undivided attention. I stared at him for a while.

"Astrid Jacobson?" I echoed. He nodded. "You're sure? Strawberry blond chick, enchanting violet eyes?"

Donald grinned. "Yes. Quite a breathtaking lady."

So she found me. Now, she knows who I am.

"What else did she say?"

Donald smiled at the memory of Astrid, and I wanted to punch him in the face. I controlled myself and raised a brow at him. He cleared his throat and said, "Well, she asked me to tell you that when she does find you, she cannot wait to... kick your ass."

Oh! That's why Donald was smiling. Feisty Astrid! God, as if I needed another reminder why I wanted her in the first place.

I called up Adam Ackers to ask... no... force him to tell me where Astrid was at that moment. After five minutes, he texted me her exact location and I wasted no time going to where she was.

I found her, talking to a man... a familiar man. Her ex-fiancé. Jealousy reeled through me when I saw them talking. Is she still not over him?

But as I moved closer to them I realized they were fighting. She slapped him and turned on her heel. Luckily, I was already only a foot away from her. She collided into me and I caught her in my arms immediately. Her blush told me how angry she was. I wrapped my arms around her and stared angrily at her ex.

"I see you haven't lost your touch, Bryans." I said to him. "It seems you still want the things you do not have."

"Are you really sure you have her? You don't know her as much as I do."

I raised my chin to him, feeling proud and honored, "I think I know her now more than any man does." The translation of that in my head was, *"She wanted me enough to offer me what she didn't offer you!"*

"I doubt she loves you that much!" he said. Translation: *"I'm the biggest fool for losing her! Now I want her back and I want you to give her up!"*

"It doesn't matter. I love her more than enough for the both of us," I said. The real translation of that, if he's smart enough to decipher it is, *"I am never giving her up so fuck off!"*

She was still crying when I took her away, but I let her. Then I tilted her chin up so she could look at me. I realized I missed her so much! It's so not like me because I barely really know her.

"I was told you were looking for me… and I was told that you couldn't wait to kick my ass," I said. Her temper amused me.

I didn't see what was coming next. Her palm connected to my cheek in a force that sent my head flying sideways. That should have made me angry, but it only made me want her even more. She was not thrilled with me now that she found out I lied about who I was.

"Ouch!" I took a deep breath. "I can't say I don't deserve that. Anything else?"

"Damn it! Who are you?"

I was actually excited to introduce myself to her, as Ryder Van Woodsen, hoping she would be thrilled that the date she brought to that wedding was real. That I wasn't pretending about who I was.

But damn! I should have kept my mouth shut!

When I told her who I was, she actually 'hated' me. And at the end of that night, she returned my ring. She loved it when she thought it was a cheap replica. But when she found out that it was real, she didn't want it anymore. And she wanted me less.

And worse… because of all that… I only ended up wanting her even more!

***

I knew I was crying even before I opened my eyes. I couldn't help all the tears even if I tried.

Light flooded into the room, but it has already flooded into my brain even before I woke up. It felt like I had been sleeping in the dark. I was trapped there and I was struggling to find my way out before I messed up my life entirely… before I regretted every single thing that I did.

Astrid. My love. My life.

I remember her now. Every single bit of her.

I remember that I was on my way to the airport that day. I just finished meeting my real estate agent in Manhattan. I was not supposed to come back to Malibu yet. But God, I couldn't get enough of her. I wanted to sleep with her in my arms that night! And me showing up in our house that evening would be a pleasant surprise for her. I knew she wouldn't be happy that I was stretching my limits and spending too much on flights, but I also knew she would be happy to see me.

Astrid was driving my car. Living in my house. *Our house.* I warmed up to the thought.

I wanted nothing else but to have her move in with me to Manhattan. But until she was ready, I would patiently wait. Because I meant what I said, I would never hurt her. She had to trust me and love me completely. And I would make her 'ever after' come true.

And then I felt the impact of the crash. Everything turned dark. And when I opened my eyes again, it was like I was thrown back to the past. And I have no recollection of the beautiful woman who my friends and my family referred to as the love of my life.

I remembered my conversation with Jake.

"I can't love somebody I do not know, genius! That's just the way I am. I will not fall for a woman that easily. She must have... I don't know... given me a love potion or something. I am telling you. That woman is no different from the rest. She's with me because she wants the life that I can give her. She's already manipulated me... and you!"

"Ryder, when that cloud in your brain goes away, I want you to repeat this conversation over and over in your head and you will realize just how much I wanted to punch you right now! In fact, I believe when you do get better, the first thing you would want to do is to kill yourself!" And Jake walked out on me.

And God, was he right! I wanted to hit myself with anything... just so I would feel the pain. Because I deserved it! I deserved a good whack in the head for everything I said about her... everything I said and did to her.

I promised her I would never hurt her! But right now, I couldn't help but hate myself for the painful words I ever said to her.

"I don't trust you. How the hell you made me fall in love with you, I do not know. How you made me put my money on your business, I am also not sure. You must be really good in bed. I am usually not the type of man who would fall under a woman's spell. And I stay away from girls like you."

"I don't know you well enough to judge you. But the last thing I want is to end up with a mercenary slut who is only using me to gain access to my bank accounts!"

God! She must have really wanted to kill me. I wanted to kill myself!
Mercenary slut?

That was the most ridiculous and most inappropriate description for Astrid.

First off, she's not a gold-digger. The only thing that stood between us was my money. If I were Ryder, the bartender, we would have been together a long time ago. But I was Ryder Van Woodsen. And she had this stupid idea in her head that people would judge her and look down at her if she's with me.

Boy was she right! She was judged, alright. She was looked down on. *By me!* I was the first one to judge her because she confused me. Because I was trying my best to fight my unexplainable need and attraction for her.

Slut?

It's so funny, she must have been laughing her heart out if she was not busy getting insulted by the word.

Astrid was a virgin when I took her. And she had not been with any man… except for me. I was her only one. I should have realized how lucky that made me. If it weren't for me, she would have been pure… innocent. And I had the guts to imply that she slept around to get to men's pockets!

I devised a way to help her back on her feet. I really did believe in her; I believed in what she could do. The idea of investing on her company was all me. I approached her cousin to help me out.

Her company was one of the things that made her happy and I took that away too, knowing that pulling my investment would cripple her. But I didn't care!

Just as I helped her get up, I crushed her. I took away her spirit, after I took away her happiness, which I know now, is… me.

God, she loved me. And I hurt her in more ways than I could imagine. She didn't want to trust me. But I made her. I made her fall in love with me. And in less than a week after she took a chance with me, she lost me.

It would have been better if I died in that accident. At least, she would live knowing that I loved her. She would always remember how much I cared for her, how much of myself I was willing to give to protect her. She would have gone on with her life knowing that she owned my heart, and that if love was enough for the two of us, I would always be beside her, making love to her, protecting her, making her laugh, and promising to make her 'ever after' come true.

But what happened to us was worse than death. It tore us apart, when death would have been unable to do that.

I broke her heart. I insulted her. I looked down at her. I called her names she didn't deserve. I did all that after promising her that I would never hurt her. After asking her to trust me.

She must have been worried sick when she heard about the accident. She must have feared losing me. I can imagine the tears she cried while I was at the operating room. And when she would have been relieved that I was out of danger, I opened my mouth and flung insult after insult at her.

God, I hate myself! Jake was right. Hand me a gun, I want to kill myself!

I couldn't stop the tears from pouring. I stared up the ceiling, as if looking at the heavens. In my mind, I was shouting, *"Why? Why did you do this to us?!"*

And if I realized a second too late, that I was in love with her again, I could have been too late to save her from Bryan.

I saw a different Bryan that day. Before, he only looked like a man who lost the woman he loves to a better man. He felt small, jealous, and remorseful. The Bryan that attacked Astrid was a maniac who was determined to take what he thought was his no matter what it takes. He was determined to destroy the one thing he wanted, but could not have.

And I swear to God, I want to kill him for almost succeeding.

The door opened and Jake stepped inside the room. I wiped the tears on my eyes, trying my best not to let him see what I was doing. But it's pointless. Jake is a shrink. And moreover, he's my best friend.

"You okay?" he asked.

I shook my head. "No."

He smiled apologetically. "I thought so."

"How long have I been out?" I asked.

"Doctors kept you out for three days. That would give you better chances of healing," he replied. "And I guess I don't have to tell you the results of your test. You already know that."

I took a deep breath and I nodded slowly.

"Where is she?" I asked. "How is she doing?" I was almost afraid of his answer.

"They sent her home yesterday," he said. "She got away with a few stitches on her forehead, and on her wrist and a couple of bruises. But she'll be okay."

I was relieved that she got away from Bryan without serious damage. But I know that the damage I caused her was far more difficult to remedy… and will take more time to heal.

"She was here. The moment she was well enough to stand up and walk, she's been here beside you." Jake said. "She was told that you came in just in time to save her."

"Does she know… about the results?"

Jake shook his head. "No. We never told anybody anything. I figured that's your job. And her friends weren't sure whether you really got your memories back. They didn't want to tell her anything… give her false hope that you finally remembered her."

I sighed. "Okay. Get me out of here as soon as you can. I have a hell of a mess to fix."

Jake smiled at me. "I know how you feel right now. I know you want to kill yourself now that you remember everything, and realize what we have been telling you for months."

I laughed humorlessly. "It's a good thing you didn't leave me with a gun."

Jake reached out and squeezed my right shoulder. "It will be alright, mate. If anybody can fix this, it's you."

I hope that Jake was right. I hope that I can still fix this. I silently prayed… so hard… that it's not yet too late.

36.

PRESENT:

A moment or period in time perceptible as intermediate between past and future;
The period between Yesterday and Tomorrow… Today.

It is also referred to as something special given to another person… a Gift.

Remember this quote? "Yesterday is history, Tomorrow is a mystery, and Today
is a GIFT, that is why it's called the Present."

Astrid.

It's been almost a week since I got out of the hospital. I got away just
fine with some stitches on my forehead, just above my left brow. My
wrist was also stitched up as apparently, I landed on broken pieces of
glass when Bryan banged my head on the kitchen counter.

Ryder was still at the hospital. Apparently, he took a couple of
blows for me when he came to my rescue. And I know his condition
could get worse because of that. I was getting worried sick. The last time
they kept him out to let his brain recuperate, he woke up not even
remembering who I was.

I couldn't believe the nightmare I went through. This had been a
hell of a year for me. It started when Bryan and Geena stole my
wedding… then I got up and rose above the shit hole they put me
through… I built my own company… I met the most wonderful man…
I fell in love the way I could not even imagine before… then I lost that
man… I broke my heart again a hundred times worse than the last
time… and then I almost got raped and murdered by my ex-fiancé.

When I woke up in the hospital, I was hysterical. I knew Bryan
wanted something from me, something he didn't get. I tried to put up a
fight. But sadly, I was not strong enough. Plus, the fact that he no longer
has a moral bone in his body made it even more difficult for me to fight
him.

I got knocked out and darkness took over me. I was so scared that
Bryan had succeeded in his evil plans. If he did, I don't know how I
would live afterwards. Perhaps I would wish that he should have just
killed me. I would have welcomed that. Anyway, what have I got to
lose? I already lost the person I live for… the person I love the most.

But my friends calmed me down and told me that Bryan did not
succeed at all. As soon as he knocked me out, Ryder broke the door
down and saved me. And then he beat Bryan to a pulp.

Ryder saved me again. Even if he was not the same Ryder who loved
me a couple of months back, he still hasn't lost his touch. He is still my
rescuer, my knight in shining armor.

I tried to visit him in the hospital after I got out, but Jake told me that he is keeping Ryder's visitors out. They didn't want to tell me what's wrong with him. He just said that they're running tests and it's better if he didn't have visitors for the time being.

I hope he doesn't end up worse than he was before. Yes, we did sort of break up. But he was still the man I loved. And even if he didn't want me in his future anymore, I would still want him to live... and I wanted him to live a happy life... the way he would have been happy with me if he didn't forget our life together.

I love Ryder. I guess I always will. And my heart will forever break when I remember that I got erased from his memories. I will forever question fate for being so unfair.

Everything that he said and did to me... he would not have done that if he knew who I was... if he had the background of our history together. No, Ryder, would never hurt me.

However, he's not the same man anymore. He doesn't know me. And it wasn't his fault that I got lost somewhere in his past and he couldn't see the real me. I know that if he didn't lose his memories of me, he would still be beside me... loving me... making my 'ever after' a reality.

I know I will forever have this yearning for the man who left for Manhattan that day, telling me over and over how much he loved me, and asking me to wait for him because he'll be back for me sooner than I thought.

That was the last...

The last time he would ever tell me that he loved me. The last time I would ever feel that love really existed in my life... that 'ever after' didn't seem so far away.

I left John's house. I didn't want to remember what Bryan did to me there. And John is getting it fixed anyway. That nightmare with Bryan left him with damaged furniture and broken plates and vases.

I wanted to pay him for all the damages, but he refused saying, "I'm just glad you are okay, Ash. I'm glad Van Woodsen came back for you. I would have been too late."

Bryan was also taken to the hospital. He suffered from broken bones, and his face was in bad shape. He didn't look good. But perhaps that would make him stop cheating on Geena for a while.

He will be taken to jail as soon as he is released from the hospital. Adam was more than furious with him. He filed several cases of physical injury on my behalf. He also applied for restraining order against Bryan. He is no longer allowed to come within a hundred foot radius of me.

Adam told me that he already warned Bryan that should he file a case against Ryder for beating him up, he would lose that case. Ryder is my boyfriend, and it's only natural that he defends me against him. I don't think Bryan will have the guts to go for it though. He would be nuts to go against Ryder Van Woodsen, especially if I will be there to testify against him.

Adam actually fired my telemarketer, Rose. He did give her a good severance pay, but he wanted nothing to do with her. I told Adam that wasn't necessary. Rose didn't know who Bryan was, and what he did to me. Bryan used her. But for Adam, Rose shouldn't be babbling about her boss's life to strangers at all. And he didn't want somebody like that in my company. Although I own the company now, I have to admit that Adam has special rights there. He helped me build it and he loaned me almost half of the money I used to buy Ryder out.

Even if I didn't want to tell my family what really happened, it could not be hidden from them. Geena must have been devastated to find out about it. First off, her husband was cheating on her. And then for him to even think and plan the things he did meant he was not yet over me... in spite of him being married to her... and having a family with her. Then lastly... she was married to a monster. And she deserved more than that.

And even though I hated Geena for what she did to me, I cannot help but feel sorry for her. She was trying to make it work... make the most out of the hand she's been dealt with. But maybe she just wasn't lucky enough. It only got from bad to worse. And I also could not imagine how Uncle Jack feels. Geena was his little girl.

When I got out of the hospital, I stayed with my parents for a couple of days. But I needed to get back to work. There were happily engaged couples who still needed my services and whose marriages will not be cancelled regardless of what happened to me.

When Adam found out that I was headed back, he insisted I stay with him again. I haven't fully recovered yet and he wanted to keep an eye on me. He's really sweet. And I will always be thankful that I have him. We may not be related by blood, but now, he's more a cousin to me than Geena is.

I was walking on the beach in front of Adam's house again. This has been my hobby for the last few days. Walking by the beach, listening to the sound of the waves, silently praying for the ocean to take away my misery.

Ryder and I were breaking up that day. No matter what I did, he couldn't remember me. I wanted him to come back as soon as he drove away. Even though he came back a few minutes too late, I will still forever be glad that he did.

I looked over the horizons in the beach. Back there, the clouds looked so tranquil... with no trace of grief or turmoil.

Sometimes, I'd like to imagine that somewhere within those horizons, in a different dimension, lies Ryder and me. Making love. He never forgot about me. He couldn't tell me enough how much he loves me, and how he wants to build a future with me.

"Every queen needs a prince or princess in her ever after too, doesn't she?" I remember him saying. And I giggled and cried at the same time. Those memories were bittersweet.

Tears rolled down my cheeks. It seems like ages ago, and yet it was only a couple of months back.

I would like to think that my Ryder was just there... hidden beneath the clouds, waiting for me to come to him...

Somewhere out there, my Ryder still remembers me... still knows me... still loves me... the way I will always love him.

"I love you Ryder Van Woodsen!" I shouted into the wind, hoping that somewhere in our parallel universe, my Ryder would hear it. The Ryder that vowed to protect me. The Ryder that did not forget about me. The Ryder that would go to hell and back for me...

Words are not enough to describe just how I miss him... just how much I want to be with him again.

"Do you really mean that?" A voice suddenly asked behind me.

I jumped up in surprise, completely unaware that I was no longer alone. I turned around and found Ryder standing behind me. He was wearing a pair of cream linen pants and white button down shirt.

He walked towards me, watching me wistfully. He was wearing a sad expression on his face. His eyes had dark circles on them, as if he hadn't been sleeping lately.

"You're... you're okay." I whispered, relieved to see him released from the hospital.

He nodded. He was standing so close to me, our bodies were almost touching. He pushed back a lock of hair away from my face as he looked deep into my eyes. The last time we saw each other, we were wishing each other happiness... without each other. Our happiness no longer existed as one. It was like fighting so hard, and then giving up in the end. But as I looked into his eyes, I could not remember why. I didn't plan to give up on him. I just needed a break. I did not know how to hold on to him anymore. I needed to compose myself again, to be strong for the both of us.

And then... he came back. I don't know why. But I was thankful. Because Bryan would have succeeded in tearing me apart if Ryder didn't come back for me.

I couldn't help the tears from rolling down my cheeks. I love Ryder so much! If only things had been different between us.

He wiped my tears away and he closed his eyes for a moment. He heaved a frustrated sigh. Then suddenly, he dropped to his knees in front of me, snaked his arm around my waist and pulled me to him, resting his cheek on my belly.

"I'm sorry, *love*," he said. "I'm so... sorry." His voice was weak, but it carried an intense emotion I could not place. He was crying. "I'm sorry, love." He kept saying over and over.

Emotions overwhelmed me. He called me 'love' again. And I recognized that tone… and the emotions that went with it. I don't know how long I've waited to hear him say that again… the same way he always does.

Hope flickered in my heart. The hope that seemed to have died a long time ago. The hope I didn't know still existed within me. But I guess it will never go away. I guess I will always keep on waiting for Ryder to come back to me.

I gently pulled away from him and knelt down in front of him so I could look into his eyes. He looked torn. I have never seen him so broken before.

"What… what are you saying sorry for?" I asked him quietly.

He took a deep breath. He cupped my face between his hands and looked at me deeply. Then in a broken voice, he replied, "For not coming home to you that day… for making you wait this long… and for hurting you in between."

My heart literally stopped, as well as my breathing.

Tears were rolling down Ryder's face. And when he said those words, I knew… that I know this man. The man that I lost… the man that I prayed would come back to me.

I reached out and touched his cheek with my palm. He turned sideways and kissed it.

"I'm sorry," he said. "If you will never forgive me, I would understand. Damn! I find it so hard to forgive myself." He took a deep breath. "I'm sorry… for all the hurtful things I ever said to you… the things I accused you of… that were not true. The pain I deliberately caused you… for justifying all the reasons why you didn't want to be with me in the first place.

"I'm sorry, Astrid. You know I would never… *never*… for the life of me, hurt you, after all that you've been through. It's just…" He trailed off. He looked up and as if he was praying to somebody. "I don't know why fate played with us like this!" He stared at me again.

He reached up and held my neck. Then he pulled me to him, resting his forehead against mine. "I meant to come home to you that day. I wanted to surprise you. I couldn't last another night without you in my arms. I was so excited to go home, knowing that it would be the first time that I would open the front door, and you would be there… for real… because you were mine… and because you lived in that house as much as I did."

He paused for a while, tears rolling down his cheeks. I couldn't help my tears, too. My heart broke as he told me the story that I was meant to hear months ago… had he not gotten into an accident.

He took a deep breath and continued, "I'm sorry I didn't make it. And I'm so sorry I came back as someone else! I'm sorry for all the hurtful words that I said… for all the things that I did. That I forced you out of your office, out of your apartment... that I made things difficult for you.

"God I'm even sorry I went out with Alizia, even if I sort of walked out on her in the middle... I shouldn't have been there in the first place! I'm sorry I didn't give you a chance to get to know you... to remind me of who you were in my life. That I realized too late that amnesia or no amnesia... you *are* my life!" He pulled away from me and looked into my eyes. "I love you so much, Astrid. You were the last person on earth I would ever want to forget! And the last person I would even think of hurting."

I couldn't say anything. Tears were streaming down my cheeks; I couldn't stop crying.

I felt happy and broken at the same time. I have waited for this. For months, I waited for Ryder to come back to me, for him to remember me again. And at the same time, I felt heartbroken for him... to see him torn, broken, and desperate.

In truth, none of these were our fault. Ryder didn't choose to forget me. And if he had a choice he would have gone home to me the day he got into an accident. We would have been making love these past few months instead of tearing each other apart.

He cupped my face between his palms again. "If... if you would choose to leave me, I would understand. I will not hold it against you. I know I had hurt you beyond belief when I promised you that I would always protect you. So, if you choose to leave me, I will set you free, Astrid."

He leaned his forehead against mine again, struggling to find the right words to say. He took a deep breath.

"But if you would still accept me, I would make it up to you for the rest of our lives. I would try my best to make you forget what a monster I have been the past few months. I would make you remember who I really am... the man who is so in love with you and... the man who would go to hell and back for you."

I broke down after hearing him say those words again, like he used to in the past.

I am Ryder Van Woodsen, the man who will go to hell and back for you.

And I knew that I really have my Ryder back.

He pulled away from me and looked into my eyes. They were welling up with tears. He looks remorseful... broken... and scared out of his wits. He looks like a man who is afraid that he is about to lose *everything.*

"The decision is yours to make, love," he said. "Although I am praying... So. Hard.... That you choose the last option."

In spite of my tears, I giggled. Tears kept streaming down my cheeks and I couldn't find my voice.

I stared back at him. I know what my answer is going to be. There was never another option for me. Ryder with amnesia may deserve a slap or two... but that's not who he is anymore. This Ryder now... is the man I desperately hoped would come back to me.

"I love you, Ryder." I whispered. "I will not go through life asking myself what could have been if I chose to stay with you. And I know... if fate had been fair to us... you would never hurt me."

He smiled. Relief washed over him. Tears were still streaming down his face. "Oh, love!" And he crushed me into his arms, holding me as if he will never let me go again. His lips came down to mine and he gave me one passionate kiss that felt like he was kissing me for the first time. That kiss said everything I wanted to know. It enveloped a million emotions that cannot be put into words. And I know he meant what he said... that he would spend the rest of our days making it up to me... making me forget the things he never meant to do.

Then he pulled away from me gently, and stood up on his feet, pulling me with him.

"I love you so much, Ash," he said. "Even when my mind had forgotten about you, my heart never stopped beating for you. The minute I laid eyes on you at the hospital, I felt something for you... but I didn't know what it was. So I resorted to being defensive... pushing you away instead of knowing who you really were in my life, and discovering the many reasons why I was so in love with you."

I giggled. "And now, do you remember all those reasons?"

He smiled ruefully. "I realized it even before I got my memory back," he said. "I came back to John's house to tell you that... I love you... that I am in love with you... with or without my memories of you. I was going to convince you that we didn't need those memories to be happy... because we can always create new and happier ones together. I came back to convince you that I'm still the man you fell in love with. That fact has not changed."

"And thank God you came back! At that exact moment." I said in between tears. "Otherwise, Bryan would have succeeded in what he came there to do."

He leaned his forehead against mine and took a deep breath. "And I would have killed him."

I leaned forward and kissed his lips. "Thank you, Ryder!" I whispered. "You never fail. Even when you have forgotten me, you were still there to protect me and save me."

He raised his fingers to the bandage at the top of my brow. "I wasn't fast enough."

"But I made it out in one piece," I said. "And that's all that matters."

He stared at me for a moment, then pushed a lock of stray hair away from my face.

"Ash?"

"Hmm?"

"If ever I forget you again, please hit me in the head… no matter how many times it takes… until I regain my memories of you, okay?"

I giggled at that. "Keep in mind that if it were up to me… I would never, ever want to lose you… not even in my memories. I would always want to remember you."

That made me cry even more. I giggled in spite of my tears and then I nodded.

He pulled me to him again into a tight hug. "Astrid…" He whispered, breathing in the scent of me. "I love you so much."

I took a deep breath, resting my head on his shoulders. I realized just how much I missed doing this, holding him in my arms like this, feeling the warmth and comfort that he brings.

"I love you too, Ryder."

He pulled away from me and looked at me deeply. Then he leaned forward and kissed my lips gently. It was one kiss, but it lasted longer than it should, both of us savoring the love wrapped around it.

Then he inhaled the scent of me and whispered against my lips, "Let's go home, love."

I almost burst from happiness. I know… it may be a few months too late… but I was very happy to hear him say those words again.

Ryder put his arm around my shoulders and led me back to Adam's house.

Adam was on his couch. He stared up and looked at my swollen eyes, and then at Ryder's.

"I'll go get some stuff." I said to Ryder, pulling away from him.

Adam's brow shot up. He stood up from the couch.

"Where do you think you're going?" he asked me. His tone and expression is every bit protective and big brotherly. And I had to smile at the thought, because after all these years of hating Adam, I never thought we would love each other this much now. And in a way, it's one other good thing that came out of what Bryan and Geena did to me.

"Adam… I'm going to stay with Ryder for a while." I said, smiling at him reassuringly.

"Actually she's going to stay with me for good." Ryder corrected me.

Adam shot Ryder a warning look and Ryder gave him a slight nod.

Men! How can they understand each other without even talking?

"I have the papers ready for you to sign." Adam said to him.

"What papers?" Ryder asked.

"The papers that officially say you pulled out of Astrid's company and that she bought you out." Adam replied.

Ryder's face stiffened. He took a deep breath. "Oh. That!" Then he shook his head. "I'm not going to sign that," he said.

346

I stared at him. "But Ryder... I told you that I'm not going to change my mind about giving you the check."

He looked at me. Even though it seems we are about to argue again, I can see the difference now. This Ryder still looks at me with tenderness and love, even though we don't always agree with each other. And silently, I thank the heavens again for helping him find his way back to me.

"And I told you that I'm not going to change my mind about not accepting it," Ryder said. He turned to Adam. "I'm not going to pull out my money. I want you to draw up some papers stating that Astrid has majority ownership. Give me ten percent share, I don't really care. That company is hers, but I will not pull out my investment there," he said firmly.

"We'll have a surplus of cash. We don't need that." I told him. Even after I return Adam's money, there will still be a lot of cash that we don't seem to need, especially now that we have transferred into a smaller office and operational costs are going to be lower.

Ryder stared at me with a solemn expression on his face. He took a deep breath. "Maybe it's time you seriously think about branching out in Manhattan, love. We were having this discussion a couple of months back. Maybe it's time we revisit that conversation."

In his eyes, I can see that he really wanted me to do it. And after all that we have been through... after losing him for a few months, and finding him again... he can ask me to branch out in Timbuktu and I still would say yes!

"Guess you're really back, Van Woodsen." Adam said to him. "Don't hurt Astrid again or I swear, you won't get away with it next time."

Ryder reached out and extended his hand to Adam. "If I do, you're welcome to kick my ass."

Adam nodded, shook Ryder's hand and then he looked at me. "When you two finally decide on this, give me a call and I'll get the papers done."

After about an hour of packing my stuff, we finally got to Ryder's house. He stepped inside and pulled me with him. He looked into my eyes and said, "Welcome home, love."

Tears welled up in my eyes. This house held too many memories for Ryder and me... memories that Ryder lost for a while. Memories that I thought he will never recover.

I stared up at him and then I lunged forward and kissed him. He wrapped his arms around my waist and kissed me back. Then he bent down and swooped me off my feet and carried me to the bedroom.

We didn't speak, but we showed each other how much we missed each other... how happy we are that we're back to where we were five months ago.

The last time we were together, it was different. It was like raging emotions, dark, sad, and daring. That lovemaking was like finally giving in after fighting for so long, and then savoring the stolen moments of heaven regardless of the consequences that we would face in the morning.

This lovemaking... felt just as passionate, but without confusion and sadness... and without any trace of doubt. This felt right... like every step we took in our entire lives has led us to this... has lead us back to each other.

I screamed his name when I reached my peak and at the same time I felt his body rock within me. My eyes were wet with tears, as the emotions threaten to overwhelm me. When I looked at Ryder, I saw that his eyes were teary, too. He leaned forward and kissed me.

"I love you, Astrid," he said solemnly. "And I never want to forget *that* again."

"Thank you, Ryder." I said in between our kisses. "Thank you for finding your way back to me."

We lay in bed for a while, locked in each other's embrace, feeling each other's warmth, savoring the feeling of being together again. Both of us were afraid to let go, to break the magic... to wake up from this surreal dream.

Finally, I propped up on my elbow and asked, "Are you hungry?"

"Yes," he replied. I can hear laughter in his voice.

I sat up and started gathering my clothes. "I'll cook," I said.

Ryder was quick to pull me back to bed. "You can't," he said," he said.

"Why?"

"Because the fridge is practically empty." I raised my brow at him. He chuckled. "You left a few weeks ago. It's your duty to restock our fridge, love."

Our fridge?

"Your fridge, Ryder." I corrected him.

He shook his head. "Didn't you hear me say to Adam that you're staying here for good?"

My eyes widened. "I was only half-listening then. I was more afraid of the warning looks you two were exchanging."

"*He* was giving me the warning looks. I was just merely accepting them."

"So you told Adam I'm staying here for good, but we haven't discussed this yet."

He pulled me by my neck and kissed my lips gently. "Okay, so let's discuss this now. We're only picking up where we left off five months ago," he replied. "This was my plan then, Ash. To ask you to move in with me here. No wonder I was so pissed when I found out you were staying with John." He cringed at the memory. "I'm sorry I got delayed a couple of months, but Astrid… it would really make me happy if you agree to live here with me."

I couldn't believe what I was hearing. He was actually asking me to move in with him… to start making a life together.

"I want to call my landline, and know that you will be picking up the call. I want to come home here, knowing that it's you greeting me at the door. I want to open my fridge and know that you've done our groceries… that you're taking care of me, as much as I'm taking care of you."

My heart swelled at his words. When I woke up this morning, I never thought this day was going to end like this. That Ryder would come home to me and would try to make everything right. That he would try to undo what he did when he has no memories of me.

He reached up and wiped my tears with his thumb. "Is that a yes?" he asked.

I giggled and I leaned forward and kissed his lips. I sighed contentedly. "Yes."

"Thank you!" He said in happy voice. Then he gently pushed me towards the bed and in a minute, he was on top of me again, pinning me between the mattress and his body. With a mischievous look on his face he said, "Now… Manhattan."

"Ryder!" I laughed. But my laughter died when his lips descended towards mine.

37.
RING:

A ring is round because it represents eternity… like a love that will last forever. It is a symbol of never-ending commitment. It is usually worn on the left hand, on the fourth finger, as "myth" states that this finger contains the "vena amoris" or the "vein of love", which is connected to the heart.

We were sitting on the deck; Ryder was strumming his guitar, serenading me with his smooth, soulful voice.

I couldn't help but be drawn to him and the world he was bringing me to when he sings. If I wasn't in love with him already, hearing him sing to me would probably do the job.

"How come you sing so well?" I asked him.

"Genes, I guess." He smiled.

"Did you always know how to play the guitar?"

He nodded. "Ever since I was a kid. I play the piano, too."

"So why didn't you make a career as a musician?" I teased.

"Well, it's not too late, right? If the band in one of my bars walked out, I could always fill in." He grinned.

I laughed. "You're right. But I don't think I would like that," I said.

"Why not?"

"Girls always fall for the front man, especially if he's hot!" I leaned forward and planted a soft kiss against his lips. "I'm very jealous and possessive." I kissed him again.

I can feel Ryder's smile against my lips. "Hmmm… if you're possessive, then does that mean you want to be with your man all the time?"

I felt him shift and put his guitar aside. Then he pulled me to him and deepened the kiss.

"Yes," I replied. "I want to be with you all the time." I moaned when he nuzzled my neck.

"Hmmm… then you should really consider branching out in Manhattan." He whispered against my skin.

I giggled.

"You're not going to stop, are you?" I asked.

"Nope," he replied. "I'll get you to say yes… eventually."

"You realize that might take a long time, right?" I pulled away from him so I could look into his eyes.

He smiled at me wistfully. "I guess. But I won't give up," he said. "Astrid, I live in Malibu, too. But I live in Manhattan more. And when I take over my parents' company, I will be there eighty percent of the time. And… by then, I hope you have decided to make the move." His voice was sober. There was a hint of frustration and sadness there.

It's been three days since he found his way back to me. During those days, we mostly stayed in the house. Ryder was making plenty of calls to New York to give instructions and conduct conference calls. But he never booked a flight back.

"Ryder... how long have you been in Malibu?" I asked him.

He shrugged. "Probably the longest time I have been here."

"When are you going back to New York?"

"I don't know." He leaned forward and kissed me again.

"Ryder... why aren't you going back to New York yet? Are you not needed there?"

He sighed. "I'm always needed there."

"Then why are you still here?"

He kissed me again and leaned his forehead against mine. Then he looked back at me. "Because... I keep remembering the last time... the last time I left you. We were making love. Then I went back to New York... and then it took me five months to come home to you." The look on his face was gloomy. "I don't want to be away from you for that long again, Ash. I get scared that the minute I board that plane, I may not keep my promises to you again."

"Ryder..." I whispered. God! I was so insensitive. He was right. He boarded the plane to Manhattan the last time we were this happy. Then he came back as a different person. And he did a lot of things he wouldn't have done if he were himself.

He shifted on the chair and pulled me so I was sitting on his lap. "I meant what I said, Ash. I will make up for *everything* that I did to you these past few months. And I would have a better chance of doing that if you were with me all the time."

"Geography will always be our problem." I whispered.

"You know my solution to that," he said, planting a kiss on my neck. "And nothing will make me happier."

I sighed. "Can I... think about it?" I asked.

He took a deep breath. "Sure, love. Take all the time you need."

We sat there for a long time, lost in our own thoughts, enclosed in each other's embrace, enveloped in each other's warmth.

I was scared of Ryder going away, too. We've been through a lot in the past few months. I don't want to go through another nightmare again.

Please God! I've had enough! I silently prayed. *Please let me keep him!*

I planned to return Adam's money. With Ryder's money still in my company, I have more than enough to start something in Manhattan. I could start small. Get a small office; renovate it to make it cute and cozy. Hire a fresh graduate to do my telemarketing for me.

I think I can let go of my monthly salary and give it to Nicole. She will do a great job managing the Malibu office. I will just oversee it from Manhattan. I can even come with Ryder once a week for a visit.

I can let go of the little luxuries in life, until the branch in New York takes off. I have some money saved up. Enough for me to fend for myself for the next three to six months, I guess.

Three to six months?

Can I really make it in such a short span of time? Plus, it's New York. Competition will be much stiffer there. Truth be told, I'm dead scared. Ever After Malibu is doing well, but it's not yet big enough to save another branch that is losing out. I've been so proud of myself that I almost raised Ryder's investment in such a short span of time. I wish I could do that again, in Manhattan.

Moreover, I cannot bear losing Ryder again. When he forgot about me, I desperately wanted him to remember me again. I wanted to spend every minute of every day with him… but I can't because he didn't even know he was in love with me.

Now… we're past all that. I was thankful I was given a second chance with him. And I want to make it count. I don't want to live in fear that every goodbye kiss we share would be the last kiss we will ever share. We've come too close to that. I have too close to losing him forever.

I felt Ryder's lips on my neck, his warm breath sending shivers down my spine. I giggled and turned to face him. He kissed my lips gently.

"Ryder…" I have to make a decision now. There's no point denying him this. Both of us have suffered too much already.

"Yes, love?"

I took a deep breath. "Okay."

He pulled away from me and looked into my eyes.

"What are you saying?"

I smiled. "If… if you won't pull out your investment from Ever After Malibu… I think I will use the money to… venture in Manhattan."

He stared back at me, his eyes glittering. "Really?" His smile was boyish, but genuinely happy.

I nodded.

He leaned forward and gave me a deep kiss on the lips. Then he said to me, "You know when I said move to New York, I didn't just mean move to the city, right?"

I raised a brow. I know what he meant, but still, it would feel nice to hear him say it out loud. "Just exactly what do you mean?" I asked.

"I meant… move in with me to New York, love," he replied. "As in the whole package. I don't just want you in my city. I want you in my apartment, too. And besides, what's the point in living separately there, when we live together here?"

I smiled at him. I felt warm and giddy. A year ago, I was bent on waiting for marriage before I share myself with a man. And I was so much against men with power, fame, and money. Now, I've broken all the rules and put all my bets on a man who is… the epitome of what I didn't believe in.

But I believe in him the way that he believes in me. I believe in our love. After all, it has gone through a lot… but still… it stands strong and it burns bright.

"You really want this, don't you?"

He nodded. "I promised you I would make up for the past months that I behaved like an asshole. And it will be easier to do that if you live with me. So I can show you every day, every night, just how sorry I really am and how desperately I want you to forget how much I've hurt you."

His words touched me in ways I couldn't explain. I felt his sincerity, like he truly wanted to erase everything that happened to us when he lost his memories of me.

And I won't make it harder on him. New York is a huge and scary city, but I know I'm making the right decision. "I'm scared, Ryder. Manhattan is huge! What if I fail?"

Ryder chuckled. "For a woman who doesn't have to work a day in her life anymore, you worry too much."

I raised a brow at him. "I'm not rich like you, Ryder. I need to stretch my legs if I want to eat."

He pulled me towards him and kissed my forehead. "Ahh! Are you forgetting who's taking care of you now, love?"

I laughed. "Ryder… I don't want to have this argument anymore."

"Luckily, neither do I," he said," he said. I pulled away from him so I could stare into his eyes. "I love you, Ash. And I will take care of you. Let me. You can work on your company as a hobby if you want. But everything that you will ever need… I will take care of it. You don't have to worry. All I ask in return is for you to stay with me."

Tears welled up in my eyes, as I hear him pledge those words to me. I may have a lot of stubborn beliefs in the past, but now, I know that none of them matters anymore. I will do everything to make Ryder happy, too. And he was right. We have to find a balance in our relationship. So I nodded. "Okay."

He smiled at me. "I love you, Astrid. And I mean it. Your ever after has just begun."

The next afternoon, I met with my friends at Oil Rig. I haven't seen them since Ryder came back. They were actually worried when I moved out of Adam's house.

"Are you sure you are okay?" Nicole asked.

"I'm perfect!" I said, smiling. "He's back you know."

They sighed in relief.

"We actually kind of know. We just weren't sure and we didn't want to give you false hope… just in case it was… a false alarm." John said.

I smiled at them. "Thank you, guys! Thanks for sticking with me all throughout these years. I must have been a lot to handle."

Dannie laughed. "Yeah, you are! But it would have been very boring without you! You give our lives a whole different level!"

I laughed, too. Then tears welled up in my eyes as I remembered that I would leave them soon. I surely will miss them.

I looked at Nicole. "Are you still interested to work for me?"

"Is the sky blue?" She asked. "Of course! I can start like yesterday! Fiona is about to fire my ass because I'm best friends with you!"

"Good! Cuz, I need you to start this week." I said to her.

Her eyes widened. "You're kidding, right?"

I shook my head. "I want you to manage this branch, Nic."

She was excited at first, but then her smile faded. "Wh... what are you going to do?"

I smiled at them. "I'm moving to Manhattan, guys." I croaked. It makes me sad that I will be away from them, but I know I cannot live without Ryder, too.

"Are you breaking up with us?" asked Dannie crossly.

I laughed. "Of course not! But... it's gonna be a long-distance relationship for us." I sighed. "Ryder asked me to live with him. And... he insisted on not pulling out his investment in my company, so I decided to use that to branch out in Manhattan."

"Wow! A year ago, you refused to even sleep with Bryan until you were married. And now... you're going to live with a man!" Dannie teased.

I laughed. "I know. I found it ironic, too. But somehow, I realized that this is not a question of values or beliefs. Love does get in the way of our principles. I guess what I had with Bryan wasn't strong enough to break through my pedantic beliefs. But with Ryder... I gave in the first night we were together. We have this passion that is stronger than both of us. He tried to stop it too because he didn't want to take advantage of my weakness then. But somehow, we both just gave in, stopped fighting what was happening to us. But you know, Ryder and I have more than passion, too. We believe in each other. We also have faith, trust, and friendship."

Nicole was already crying and Dannie's eyes were brimming with tears, too.

"Sweetheart... we will miss you. But I know... after all you and Ryder have been through... you deserve this." Dannie said.

"I will take care of your company here, Ash." Nicole said. "You'll be so proud of me!" She giggled in spite of her tears.

John ruffled my hair. "How often are you going to visit?"

I laughed. "Once a week or at least once every two weeks. Ryder owns two bars here, remember?"

We were all sad, but I know my friends weren't holding me back. After all that's happened to me since I dumped Bryan, I deserve this. I deserve to go after my happily ever after.

After meeting with my friends, I asked Dannie to drop me off at Adam's house. I called up Ryder and told him where I would be. He promised to pick me up after he was done with what he needed to do at Oil Rig.

Adam was startled when I appeared on his deck again.

"Jesus Christ, Astrid!" He breathed.

I laughed and then I reached up and kissed his cheek. Then I wrapped my arms around his waist and rested my head against his chest. I couldn't help crying. I will sure miss Adam a lot, including his snide remarks and sarcastic comments.

"Are you happy, Ash?" he asked, wrapping an arm around my shoulders.

I nodded. "Very."

"You will shine in Manhattan, too, Ash. You can do this," he said.

I looked up at him. "How did you know I was moving to Manhattan?"

He raised a brow. "I'm Van Woodsen's lawyer in Malibu, remember?" He replied. "I'm required to know everything that goes on in his life here." He smiled. "Plus, he called and told me already. He promised me that you will be taken care of, and I need not worry. And I was assured you will come to Malibu once a week anyway, so this is not really goodbye."

I smiled at him. "Thank you, Adam." I told him. "In a way, you've been the bridge between Ryder and me. You were the one who helped me find the love of my life. If you didn't offer to pay my date for Geena's wedding, I would not have met Ryder." I pulled away from him. "You're a great guy, if only you chose to show it. You have a good heart."

He frowned. "Yeah, but don't go telling people about it, okay?"

I laughed and hugged him again. "I love you, Adam. We may not be related by blood, but you're the best cousin a girl can ever ask for."

It took him a moment to hug me back. And then he said, "Thanks, Ash. You're not too bad yourself. And I love you too. Be happy, okay?"

I smiled. And I know, with Ryder, Adam can be assured of that. "You know I will be."

***

One month later...

Although my parents and my relatives know that Ryder and I are living together, they still didn't know that during Geena's wedding, Ryder and I were only pretending. And until now, they still believe we are engaged. I once told Ryder that maybe it was better if I told my parents that the engagement was a sham so our relatives would not feel sorry for me. Then Ryder and I fell in love afterwards and are together now. But Ryder thought it was a bad idea.

"Being engaged to me was probably one of the things that drove Bryan mad, and for you to tell them that it was a lie would break your parents' hearts, as well as your Uncle Jack's. Leave it be, Ash. We're living together anyway. We pulled it off before when we weren't officially dating. I think we'd do better now."

So we left it at that. I wondered what we were going to do if my parents came for a visit and find that I'm not wearing my ring anymore. I guess, we'll just make something up when we get there.

Ryder's apartment was lush and luxurious, but somehow, I couldn't help feeling that it was more a bachelor's pad. He did have it when he was a bachelor, but he's not exactly single now. I prefer the house in Malibu with separate rooms, a living room, and a deck.

I guess even though his apartment was huge, a part of me prefers a smaller, cozier apartment that feels more like two people are making a home out of it. But I'm not really complaining. It's such a small price to pay for being with Ryder.

Nicole had taken over my responsibilities in Malibu and I kept myself busy with setting up the branch in Manhattan. Ryder and I visit Malibu once a week together, where he conducts his business at his bars and I check up with Nicole in the office.

Today is exactly a month after Ryder and I got back together... a month after he found his way back to me.

We planned to travel back to Malibu together. I planned to surprise him with dinner. We could drink on his deck and he could play his guitar if he wanted. Then we'd make love all night.

An hour before we were due to go to the airport, Ryder gave me a call and told me that he couldn't make it.

"But Ryder, we agreed to go last week." I said, a little disappointed, especially since his tone said that he forgot what day it was today.

"Sweetheart, I'm in the middle of a meeting," he said to me, he sounded like he was in a hurry. "I'll see you tonight. Call me when you've landed back in Manhattan."

"What?" I was looking forward to staying in Malibu this weekend. "I'm going to take the last flight out?"

"The five p.m. flight out, love. Promise me you'll be back?" he asked.

I was not happy about that. But I didn't want to fight with him. With a disappointed sigh, I replied, "Okay."

"Look, I have to go. I'll see you tonight."

Has it started already? Has he started being too busy to remember anniversaries or special occasions?

I would only have a couple of hours in Malibu and so I had to make the most of my stay. I was not in a great mood when I met Dannie, Nicole and John and I only had a couple of minutes to ring Adam.

Ryder didn't give me a call all day, nor send me a text message. He usually sends me messages every two hours, telling me he loves me and that he misses me. Today is the first day he didn't. And it's only been a month since we survived his tragic memory loss.

I flew back to New York in the evening and, although I was tired and a little unhappy, I had no plans of spoiling this day. I decided to cook a nice dinner for the two of us anyway. We're going to celebrate today, no matter what.

When I got inside the apartment, a red envelope on the table caught my attention. It was sitting beside one of Ryder's car keys. I usually don't pry in his stuff, but this envelope just seems to call out to me. It looked elegant, and it smelled of floral perfume.

It was not sealed so I pulled out the note inside it.

"I was hoping you could come to see me…" printed in a neat script font.

There was a location map attached to it, as well as what seems to be an access card.

"Ryder!" I called, my heart slowly started pounding inside my chest.

No answer.

Now, I was getting nervous. I've only lived with Ryder for about a month. Maybe one of his old flames didn't know he was already living with someone and attempted to have a little tryst with him.

Ryder would never do this to me! I believe in him, I believe in us.

Besides, if he's up to no good, he wouldn't carelessly leave this note for me to find, right?

But whatever was going on, I intended to find out. I took my phone and dialed his number. His phone was off. I tried about three more times just in case he just lost signal. But still it was off.

I took short breaths to calm myself down before calling his office. Derek, his assistant, answered.

"It's seven in the evening." I told him. "You should be home."

He laughed. "But I'm fresh out of college and already a workaholic. What can I do for you, lovely Ash?"

"Where's Ryder?"

"Ah..." He took a moment to answer. "He... went off more than an hour ago. Said he has some personal things to attend to down at Sixth. I thought... he was with you."

"Thanks Derek." I said and then I hung up.

My hands were turning numb fast. I looked at the location map and found that the "X" on it is on Sixth Avenue. The address says penthouse.

Ryder would never cheat on me!

"He wouldn't." I whispered to myself. "He, of all people, knows what I have been through."

But I needed to find out. Damn, if curiosity really did kill the cat! I dashed to the elevator and raced to the location stated on the map.

I felt like a woman in pursuit. My heart was pounding loudly, my hands were cold and I'm pretty sure my face was crimson red.

I found that the address points to one of the luxurious apartment buildings on Sixth. I looked at the map once again to make sure that I was at the right place.

The man standing by the doors greeted me cheerfully. He was wearing a black suit with a nametag so I assumed he is an employee of the building. I showed him the map.

"Yes, Ma'am. This is the place. Go straight, turn right to the elevators." He gave me instructions and gave me a very bright smile. I had to smile back. He seemed very happy with his job.

The lobby of the building was posh and absolutely impressive, from the marble floors down to the furniture. If I didn't have a bomb hanging over my head, I would probably stop and admire the interior design of the building.

The person that Ryder visited is probably just as rich as he is.

"But it's you he loves." I said to myself.

When the elevator opened, I pressed P and swiped the card. I closed my eyes and willed myself to keep calm. I know Ryder. He wouldn't do this to me. There is a good explanation for all these. And in a few seconds, I'm about to find out.

I promised myself that whatever I uncover, unless what I see leaves little to the imagination, I would listen to what Ryder has to say.

Breathe in. Breathe out.

Damn! Why is it taking so long to reach the penthouse?

Finally, the elevator opened to a luxurious apartment. I gasped. Unlike our apartment, this one has a huge living room adorned with gold-accented furniture that looks very, very expensive. There is a glass staircase that seems to lead to the bedrooms on the mezzanine floor. There is an elegant chandelier in the center and everything in the house was a combination of white, cream and gold trims.

"Hello?" I called out. There was no reply.

I sincerely hope I don't get arrested for trespassing!

Just then, I noticed that the wall in front of me had a paper stuck on it. I looked closer and saw that an arrow was printed on the same paper type that I was holding in my hand.

I followed the direction of the arrow until I reached the next one, and then the last one. I was led to a huge balcony that was probably half the size of the whole house. I stepped out, expecting to see Ryder and whoever it was who left him the message.

But what I saw blew me away. There were roses and lighted candles all over the place. The balcony has the perfect view of the city. There was a table in the middle, set for two.

Then, I saw Ryder standing in one corner looking out at the view.

"Ryder…" I whispered weakly.

He slowly turned to face me. A brilliant smile was pasted on his face.

"I… don't understand," I said.

He walked towards me, his eyes twinkling.

"Who's here with you?" I asked in a small voice.

He shook his head. He pushed a lock of stray hair away from my face.

"No one, love," he said. "It's just the two of us."

I looked around. The place was romantically set up.

Just the two of us?

"But… I found a note for you…"

He chuckled. "That was for you, love."

"For me? You had me thinking…"

"What were you thinking?" he asked, raising a brow. I had a feeling that he knows exactly what I was thinking and immediately, I felt embarrassed. I sighed in relief and gave him a hug. I felt really silly.

"Nothing," I said. "I missed you."

"You don't know how painful this day was for me." He whispered.

"Painful?" I asked, pulling away from him.

He nodded. "Asking you to travel alone to Malibu. Not calling you, texting you… it bothered me all day!"

I narrowed my eyes. "You did that on purpose?"

He laughed. "I wanted this to be a surprise… and a little bit more dramatic."

I looked at the dinner table, then at the roses and the candles. "What is this all about anyway?"

"You didn't think I would forget what today is, did you?"

My heart instantly melted. "You remembered!" I said hugging him again.

"Of course I did," he said. He stared back at me and said. "A month ago, you gave me another chance to make your 'ever after' come true. So it's sort of like another date we need to celebrate every month and every year."

He leaned forward and gave me a thorough kiss on the lips. I couldn't help it, but I was crying again. I was only planning a simple dinner. Ryder prepared something even more romantic... something surreal.

After the kiss, I pulled away from him and approached the dinner table. I looked at the elegant china and crystal wine glasses on it.

"Candlelight dinner, under the Manhattan moon, with the perfect New York city view, surrounded by red roses?" I stared back at him. "You couldn't be more romantic, could you?"

He didn't answer.

I turned to look at the setup again. It was absolutely enchanting... like something you tear out of a romance novel. And this was not even a hotel.

"Perfect location too," I said. "Whose place is this anyway?"

"Ours." He whispered behind me.

My heart pounded in my chest. I turned around to face him again. The expression on his face was serious... and wistful.

"You told me once that the other apartment is an ultimate bachelor's pad. I guess it's time to give it up now that I'm not one anymore," he said. He turned towards the house. "This one has four bedrooms, a huge living room, a huge kitchen, a library, a game room, and a nursery. I think you would find this more suitable for us."

"Ryder... I'm not asking for this much. I can live anywhere with you."

"But I want us to live in a house we can build our future in... where you can comfortably spend your 'ever after' in."

My heart warmed. Tears welled up in my eyes. Every time I hear Ryder say the words 'ever after', I believe in it more and more.

"When did you buy this?"

He took a deep breath and said, "You know... that day I got into an accident, I met up with my real estate agent. I was looking for a house for us." He took a step closer and looked at me deeply. "I'm sorry, this got delayed, love. I would have brought you here sooner."

Tears rolled down my cheeks. I shook my head. "There's nothing to say sorry for, Ryder. You're here now and that's all that matters." I lunged forward and gave him a tight hug. I cannot believe this is happening to me. Somehow, I still can't believe that Ryder Van Woodsen is happening to me now, when before, I was even scared to dream about a guy like him.

When I stared up at Ryder, I saw that his eyes were teary, too. He gave me a kiss on the forehead. "Do you think you can live here with me?" he asked, smiling.

I laughed. "I will live anywhere with you, Mr. Van Woodsen."

He brushed his lips to mine again. Then he looked deeply into my eyes, a sober expression was on his face now, that it actually made me quite nervous. "One more thing, Ash." He whispered. "You told me once that I should find a reason that is good enough, and you would finally accept your ring."

I nodded, because now, I have completely lost my voice.

"I think I found one." He whispered. And then slowly, he pulled away from me and came down on one knee. He held a box in front of me and opened it. My Harry Winston ring sparkled before my eyes.

"Astrid Jacobson, I will forever thank God that I walked into that jewelry shop that day... that your friends stood you up that night we met at the bar. Little did I know that those days would change my life. That I was about to be rescued by you. I didn't believe that a woman could want me and love me if I wasn't who I am. But you wanted me, needed me, and loved me for everything I was inside. Even when I hurt you over and over... you still kept your faith in me.

"And I want to spend the rest of our lives proving to you that I am worthy of that faith. I will spend the rest of my days making you happy. I love you very, very much, Ash, and if you will allow me... I will make the rest of your 'ever after' come true... but not as Astrid Jacobson. But as Astrid Van Woodsen." He paused, looking at me wistfully. His eyes were welling up with tears. Then he asked, "Would you please be my wife?"

I bit my lip. Rivers of tears were streaming down my cheeks now. "Ryder..." I started. "I don't know what to say."

Ryder smiled nervously. "I would like you to say 'yes' actually."

I giggled, in spite of my tears. "I... love you." I said in between sobs. "If... you are the prize at the end of the road, I would... go through a hundred more breakups and a hundred more pains. Before I met you, I was asking the heavens why I had to experience that much betrayal and pain... but now, I know. Everything... had fallen into place. You are my knight in shining armor, my rock, my guardian angel. You are my real 'ever after'." I giggled in spite of my tears. "Yes, Ryder. It will be an honor for me to be your wife. I will marry you."

He smiled. He took my hand and placed my ring on my finger. Then he brought it to his lips and kissed it. He stood up on his feet. I smiled and threw myself in his arms. He caught me and spun me around. When he settled me on my feet, he took my hand so he could look at the ring on my finger.

"I told you... if I found a reason that was good enough, you wouldn't have to take this off your finger ever." He smiled.

I laughed. "I never thought I would be wearing this ring for real." I looked at the ring again and noticed something was different about it. The center diamond looks a lot bigger, like about twice bigger, but everything else looks the same. "Ryder... did you change this?"

He laughed. "It's the same ring. But I thought the future Mrs. Ryder Van Woodsen deserved a bigger rock at the center. That was the only thing I changed, I promise."

"You didn't have to, you know." I said, looking up at him.

He leaned forward and kissed me. "I know. But I wanted to, okay?"

I hugged him. "I love you, Ryder,"

He kissed me on the forehead. "I love you more," he said. Then he leaned forward to kiss me on the lips again. "See? I told you, you didn't have to tell your family that our engagement was just a sham. Because it was going to be real soon enough."

"Except your family knows and our stories do not match now."

"It's only Paris, my parents, Janis and Jake," he said. "They can easily go along with the old story in front of your family. They find our love story quite amusing."

"I find it amazing," I said. "After all that we've been through... I couldn't believe we survived all that... and we're here, happier than ever."

Ryder stared at me. "It's surreal."

I stared back at him. "Surreal? Even for you?"

He smiled and said, "Especially for me!" Then he bent down to give me a thorough kiss on the lips. When he pulled back, he stared at me for a while, tears almost brimming his eyes. "Thank you for saying yes."

I smiled back. "Thank you for asking."

"So, now it's time to celebrate... our real engagement."

We ate the food that Ryder prepared. Then we toured the house. It was screaming luxury and good taste. The floors were made of marble. The furniture was made of the highest quality materials. Everything was a perfect combination of beauty and class.

I was very happy. I loved the house. And I loved the fact that Ryder thought about buying this as soon as we officially got together a couple of months ago.

We stood on the balcony, staring at the view of Manhattan. I leaned my head on Ryder's shoulder. I felt him wrap an arm around my waist to pull me closer to him.

"How did you know I was going to pick up your note?" I asked him.

He chuckled. "I know you more than you give me credit for, love," he said. "And I know you would rush here if you couldn't contact me."

"What would you have done if I didn't come?" I asked.

"Then I would come and get you." He laughed. "Honestly, did you really think I was gonna have a rendezvous with another woman?"

I felt ashamed of this. I really did. I know I should trust Ryder more. He wasn't Bryan. Just like Ryder, Bryan is one of a kind, too.

I sighed and tiptoed so I could give him a kiss on the lips. "I'm sorry," I said. "But I did promise myself to listen to you first before… I made any judgment, you know."

He gathered me to him again and gave me a hug. "I'm done breaking your heart, Ash." He whispered. "I've done that plenty of times when I forgot about you. I promised I wouldn't do that again."

I rested my head on his chest and breathed in the sweet masculine scent of him. "Can you stay like this forever?" I asked him.

He hugged me tighter. "You once told me that I have everything I want. I told you then that… I don't have everything yet. But now, I do. Because I have you. You were the only thing missing. And I promise, love, I will do my best to stay like this forever. As long as you promise that you will always trust me, have faith in me."

I nodded. "Always."

Ryder smiled and then he leaned forward and gave me a kiss on the lips before bending to pick me up on my feet, carrying me towards the glass doors that led back to the apartment.

"Now, how soon do you think you can plan that dream wedding of yours?"

I laughed. "So soon, Van Woodsen?"

"Yes. Your father is under the impression he'll be walking you down the aisle this year," he replied.

"What was that all about anyway? What did you talk to my father about?" I asked, remembering the day we went to my parents' party and Ryder seemed to have had a man-to-man conversation with my father behind my back.

He smiled mischievously, "He made me promise not to make you cry. And if possible, marry you this year. Well… my amnesia got in the way, but hey! I still have a couple of months to work on it, right?"

My eyes widened. "How could you promise my father that? We were not even together for real during that time."

"I know," he said. "But he didn't know that. And I wanted it to happen so badly, I couldn't say no. I was sort of wishing out loud when he spoke to me. I know that I would do everything in my power to make it happen. The rest would be up to you… up to fate."

"And you want me to plan our wedding now?"

"Yes. I'm your first customer in New York. I want the best wedding for my bride. And I want it done as soon as possible. The sooner you become Astrid Van Woodsen, the better."

I bit my lip to keep myself from screaming. I felt so blessed and so lucky. I've read plenty of fairy tale romances when I was a kid. But I never knew they would happen to me for real. That someday, my knight in shining armor would come and rescue me from the pains of my broken heart, change my stubborn beliefs about love, regain my faith in myself, and make me trust in love again.

And even though he came in a shiny package, it didn't really matter. Because he made me believe that I... was absolutely worth it!

38.

THE VENUE:

The place where the whole wedding will take place. Considerations in choosing a venue could be because the place holds special memories for the couple or it could be sentimental to one of the couple's parents or grandparents. But more than anything, the venue chosen must accommodate the theme of the wedding.

*I*t was the most hectic following months of my life. I was setting up Ever After Manhattan, meeting up with potential suppliers, and hiring and training people. On top of all that, I was planning my own wedding. I had to actually get Nicole to stay in New York once in a while to help me. Leilani, my assistant in Malibu, was left in charge of the branch and Nicole and I would just fly in if there were important matters that needed our attention.

The first major problem that I had was the location of my wedding. I could easily have that in a hotel, but it wasn't good enough for Ryder. He wanted my best idea, my top dream wedding on the table. He wasn't settling for anything less.

"Really? Apart from the wedding you planned for Bryan, there could have been something else that you wanted... something you only thought was possible in dreams," Ryder said to me one night when I was showing him my notes.

I sighed. There was one dream when I was younger. The first wedding idea that sparked my passion for wedding planning.

"Tell me," Ryder said.

I shook my head. It was such a long time ago. I was barely a teenager then. I was just a kid who hasn't even graduated from reading fairy tales.

Ryder pushed me back to bed and started tickling me. I laughed.

"Ryder, stop!"

"Come on! I can do this all night!" He laughed and then he relentlessly tickled me in spots he knew I was most sensitive.

I wriggled away from him but he refused to let me go.

"Okay! Okay!"

He stopped and collapsed on the bed beside me. He gathered me in his arms and let me rest my head on his chest.

I took a deep breath and then I closed my eyes, picturing what I thought was *the* dream of dreams weddings.

"When I was younger, I used to picture a wedding in a huge estate... with a huge garden. Flowers in bloom everywhere. The ceremony would be in the middle of an orchard, surrounded by trees. It would be like a fairyland. When the bride walks down the aisle, there would be a rain of flower petals. Then at night, all the trees would be illuminated by lights like they've been infested by fireflies, and then there would be a fireworks display."

"Fairyland wedding," he said. "Suitable to seal the deal on your 'ever after'."

I giggled. "Yes."

He tilted my chin up so I could look at him.

"Now, I like *that* idea!"

My eyes widened. "But Ryder... that will be very expensive!"

He raised a brow. "So? I intend to marry only once, love. Why not go all the way? If you had to plan the wedding of your wildest dreams, with unlimited budget, what would you do?"

"But Ryder... we don't even have a location for that. Where could we find a large estate that has a forest or a garden that's huge enough to pass up as a fairyland?"

He smiled and pulled me to him. "I think I know exactly the place, love."

The next day, Ryder took me for a ride.

"Where are we going?"

"My grandmother's house," he replied.

"Your grandmother's? You... you never mentioned her before."

"Well, she's in heaven now," he said. "But she left my mother her estate. Just check it out."

It was a little more than an hour drive. Then he stopped in front of a steel-gated estate. He blew the horn and waved at the CCTV camera. Immediately, the gate opened. We were entering a huge property. My jaw dropped. It was not just a mansion. It was almost like... a freaking castle!

"Your mother owns this?"

Ryder nodded. "Soon we will own it too, along with Paris."

I stared at him, unable to believe what he's saying. "Who lives here?"

"Butlers... maids," he replied. "We come here for short breaks at least twice a year."

He parked in front of the mansion... castle... estate... whatever you call it. A man dressed in a suit greeted us.

"Mr. Ryder, good day." He greeted. Then he looked at me and smiled. "Madam Astrid. It is nice to finally meet you."

"Good day Ben." Ryder greeted him. "Sweetheart, this is Ben. He takes care of the whole estate."

I smiled at Ben and extended my hand to him. He shook it. I was actually surprised that he knew who I was.

"To what do we owe the pleasure of this visit?"

"Astrid wants to see the whole place. If she likes it, we're going to hold our wedding here in a couple of months."

Ben smiled. "Then I shall take you on a tour. A wedding has not been held here since Mr. Ryder's grandparents got married. It would be our utmost pleasure to host yours."

The whole estate was massive and completely impressive. The front of the house has a vast garden filled with flowers of different kinds and colors. There are two lavish fountains standing side-by-side each other and sculptures of angels and cupids adorn every corner.

There are two other gardens at the back of the house. One is a labyrinth. I couldn't resist going inside it. There are benches inside the pathways, as well as lamps and posts to make it suitable for walking at night. The whole structure was only about two feet taller than Ryder.

The center of the labyrinth was an even more picturesque garden with beautifully landscaped plants, cut knee high, and form patterns of circles and hearts.

I couldn't believe what I was seeing. I can barely believe I was still in New York. God, I cannot even believe I was still in the human world!

Ryder and Ben led me out of the labyrinth and we proceeded further into the estate. They led me to a line of oak trees. Some branches were intertwined together to form an arc over the pathway. The end of the arc lead to what looks like an orchard, surrounded by very tall trees that shade the whole area, allowing only a little of the rays of the sunlight, even at noontime.

We walked further, until we reached the lake at the end of the entire estate.

"We can get swans to swim here on the day of the wedding." Ryder whispered.

I stared at Ryder. Tears were brimming in my eyes. "Seriously?" I asked him.

He nodded. "It gets better," he said.

"There's more?"

Ryder smiled. "Guess what comes out here at night?"

I smiled, looking at the beautiful line of flowers and shrubs that border the entire estate, separating it from the lake.

"I don't know what else could top these. Unless you have fireflies here at night too."

Ryder didn't answer. Ben smiled. I stared at both of them.

"Oh my God!" I breathed. "Seriously? Fireflies?"

Ryder's eyes twinkled. "So, has the future Mrs. Ryder Van Woodsen found her fairyland yet?"

I nodded. I lunged forward and hugged him. "It's perfect," I said. "Just like you… it's absolutely perfect."

***

The following months zoomed by so fast. Maybe that was because I was too busy. I kept Nicole on her toes as well. Janis and Paris would come to help once in a while.

Ryder made Nicole in-charge of the wedding budget. I strongly argued, but I didn't win, two against one.

"If you handled the budget, it would alter your creativity." Nicole said to me. "You stop your wonderful ideas once you tally the bottom figure."

Ryder agreed with her. "I already told you. Wedding of your wildest dreams, love. Nothing less." He looked at Nicole. "Don't even give her the subtotals. Send all the bills to me."

Nicole smiled radiantly and gave me a triumphant look. She had a couple of out-of-this-world ideas that she wanted to try, and she was using my wedding as a guinea pig.

A month and a half before the date, a very elegant, Swarovski-adorned, white and gold scrolls encased in crystal glass tubes went out to the guests, inviting them to our big day.

A few days before the wedding, the girls planned for my bachelorette's party, which was held in Ryder's grandmother's vast estate.

On the same day, Ryder was going to have his bachelor's party. At first, I was nervous about what they were going to do. I knew Bryan was planning to do his at a strip bar. I knew it was tradition to go to those places for bachelors' parties, but I somehow couldn't help being worried about the fact that Ryder might be with another woman. And I hated that thought... tradition or no tradition.

But in the morning, I saw Ryder in his hiking boots, preparing some camping stuff.

"Where are you going?"

"Bachelor's thing," he replied.

"In hiking boots?"

He laughed. "What did you think, love? Strippers and one night stands?" I glared at him. He laughed again. "I promise. No monkey business," he said. "Jake, Adam, Derek, John, and I are going camping in the woods close to my grandmother's estate. We'll trek, we'll fish, we'll enjoy the fireflies and we'll get drunk. Then we'll head back in the morning."

"Why would you do that?"

"Because that's what I wanted to do before I got married," he said. "Something that I only used to do when I was a boy with no responsibility in life."

I smiled at him and gave him a hug, quite relieved that I didn't have to worry about him being with somebody else.

370

But it seems that my girls have planned the complete opposite for me. They wanted me to have the whole bachelorette experience. From liquor, to kinky-looking cakes to blindfolds, and really slinky, revealing lingerie presents.

After they revealed their presents that seem to lack in material and leave almost nothing to imagination, they blindfolded me and told me to sit in the chair and just enjoy the ride.

"Strippers!" They screamed and the music blasted from the stereos.

"Guys! Please! Ryder's grandmother might still be here watching us!" I pleaded.

I don't like this at all. I have never been with anyone but Ryder, so I won't really be missing out on anything when we get married.

There were cheering all around. The girls were going wild. Suddenly, I felt hot breath on my neck. I almost screamed. Masculine hands touched my nape and I felt a soft kiss on my right shoulder.

Now, I really screamed.

"Stop! Please stop!" I pleaded to the guy. I will not allow this! I raised my knees up my chair and wrapped my arms around my legs. I was almost in the brink of crying.

"Come on, sweetheart!" Janis said. "This guy is expensive! Make it worth our money!"

"I'll pay you back!" I shouted. "Just please make him leave!"

They laughed again. They kept encouraging the guy to touch me. "Come on! Her fiancé won't find out! Touch her!"

I felt hands on my waist, then on my thighs, forcing me to sit properly. I felt cold hands on mine and they were pulled behind me.

"Sorry, sweetheart." Dannie said. "We can't have you resisting the ride of your life!"

"Ryder!" I whispered. "Where are you when I need you the most?"

"Come on, Ash! One man all your life?" Somebody asked. And I recognized that as Paris.

"That one man is your brother!" I cried desperately.

She laughed. "I won't tell."

"Guys, stop this!" I pleaded to them. "I don't want this."

"You don't know that." Nicole said. "You just might enjoy it!"

Just then, I felt strong arms wrap around my waist and I was lifted from the chair.

I started kicking and trying to get away. But damn he's strong! I was being lifted again and tossed over a muscular shoulder like a piece of sack. The man walked and I knew I was being carried away from the room. I could tell that the guy was shirtless. I kept kicking and struggling but he held my thighs securely over his shoulder.

"Make her scream, okay?" One of my traitor friends said.

"Make every penny count!" Another one added.

And suddenly, I could only hear my friends' faint voices. I landed on soft mattresses and I knew that I was placed down on a bed, in a separate bedroom. I got even more scared because I suspect that we were alone.

"Damn you! Stay away from me! My fiancé will kick your ass!" I screamed.

I was pushed on the bed by a force that is a lot stronger than me. I struggled, but he held me perfectly in place, pinning me between the mattress and his body. It didn't help that my hands were tightly cuffed behind me. The combination of Dannie and handcuffs proved to be dangerous.

Why are my friends allowing this?

"I will scream rape!" I said, almost shouting.

Somehow, I know that the guy was laughing at me, but he didn't even make a sound. He reached for my hands behind me and suddenly the cuffs went off.

I prepared to punch, scratch and inflict pain, but he was ready for me, too. He captured both my hands and held it securely above my head.

"I will pay you! Ten times what they paid you." I pleaded when I knew I wouldn't be able to escape.

It didn't seem like he was listening to me at all. I was pinned securely on the mattress, his thighs covering mine. One of his hands was securely fastened on my hip to prevent me from escaping, the other was holding both my hands above me. I felt his hot breath on my neck again. I squirmed.

"Ryder!" I prayed silently. "Please... please come save me." Tears were streaming down my cheeks, a whimper escaped me.

But I knew Ryder was getting drunk somewhere in the woods, while a complete stranger was raping me here. I have to fight and defend myself.

He tightened his grip on me and nuzzled my neck. He was close enough and immediately I leaned forward and buried my teeth on his bare flesh. I think it was his shoulder that I bit. Then I struggled to be free of him while he was writhing in pain.

"Jesus Christ, Astrid!" He cursed.

Then suddenly, I realized that I know that voice. And instantly, relief washed over me.

He recovered from the pain and in two seconds, I was secured under him again. "God! You make me want you more and more." He whispered against my ear. And if before I was appalled by the thought of being in bed with him, hearing his voice now made my blood stir, arousing familiar emotions within me.

Then gently, he removed my blindfold. I stared into his familiar green eyes. There was a combination of love, lust, and amusement on his face.

I was relieved and angry at the same time. "Damn you!" I started hitting him and he laughed, trapping my hands in his and securing them over my head again.

Ryder smiled at me and leaned forward to give me a thorough kiss on the lips. I kissed him back. Then he released my hands and cupped my face between his palms.

"You don't know how proud I am right now," he said. "Hearing you pray for me to come and rescue you, when a potentially sexy stripper is about to pleasure you... is just too heartwarming for me."

"What are you doing here?" I asked him. "It's your stag party, right?"

He smiled. "Well... the bachelor usually gets laid on his stag party. But I'm not really interested in bedding another woman. And I will kill any other man who lays a finger on you. So... why don't we just sleep with each other and both our problems are solved?"

I giggled. "Sounds good to me." Then I pushed him on his back, so that he was sitting on the bed and then I mounted him. "You're entitled to a lap dance. How about I make it worth your while?" I smiled at him mischievously.

He grinned at me. He raised his arms and intertwined his fingers behind his head. "Now, my love, I guess it's your turn to make me scream."

I was a bit drunk and feeling a little bit wild. I dared to do things I haven't done before and was afraid of trying. But the alcohol and all the euphoria caused by this bachelorette thing brought out a side of me I didn't even know existed. Ryder had a big smile on his face when we woke up in the morning.

My cheeks turned red as the memories of the previous night flooded back to me. I saw that Ryder has a bruise on his shoulder where I bit him when I thought he was a strange male stripper.

"I'm sorry." I whispered to him.

"I'm not complaining." He grinned. "You, my love, are a perfect ending to the best bachelor's party a man could ever have."

My blush turned more violet. I buried my face against his neck, inhaling the scent of him. I guess last night my senses were dimmed by the alcohol and my fear of male strippers that I didn't recognize Ryder. His scent... the feel of his skin... all of these are familiar to me. I didn't need to see him, because my senses know him. How could I have doubted that he was someone else?

We went out of the room at around ten. Some of our friends were already in the gazebo having breakfast.

Ryder came with all the boys last night and everybody spent the night in the mansion.

As we got out of our room, I heard a harsh banging of the door on our right and saw John walking out of one of the rooms. He was fully dressed and looked completely pissed off, he didn't even see us when he hurried down the stairs.

Then the door opened again and Nicole came rushing out of the room. She was still dressed in the clothes she was wearing last night.

"John! What the hell is your problem?" She chased after John.

What is going on?

I knew John and Nicole had feelings for each other, although both of them were just too chicken to admit it. John was too much of a rake, and Nicole was just too scared to trust a guy like him.

Did John finally admit it's time for him to go after Nicole? Did he plan to start last night? Or this morning? And then... Oh my God! Did he come to Nicole's room and find her with somebody else? Who?

The door of the room where Nicole and John came from opened again and I almost fainted when I saw who stepped out of it.

Ryder gave my shoulder a gentle squeeze.

"What the hell is going on, Adam Ackers?" I demanded, looking at my cousin sternly.

He shrugged. "Apparently, the first girl I slept with after a long time is in love with somebody else," he said sarcastically. But he always was so good at hiding his emotions.

"Don't be smart with me, Adam! What happened?"

Adam proceeded to go down the stairs. I grabbed Ryder's hand and pulled him with me. We followed my cousin.

"Nothing happened, Ash." Adam said. "Leave it."

I touched his shoulder and forced him to stop walking and face me. I raised a brow.

He sighed. "Your friend John was being charming to everybody, except for the girl whose heart is breaking because of him. She was drunk out of her wits, okay? I... gave her assistance. I couldn't leave her alone in the room. I fell asleep beside her. And he found us in bed together." Adam said. He took a deep breath. "Good for him. Maybe now, he'll wake up and see that she's... actually not bad at all." His voice was even, but I thought I heard a trace of... yearning there. Then he turned on his heel went down the stairs towards the gazebo, whistling as if nothing happened at all.

I stared up at Ryder who has an amused expression plastered on his face. I glared at him. He pulled me to him and gave me a tight hug.

"You're getting married in three days, love. John, Nicole, and Adam are no longer kids. I'm sure they will sort this out. Our wedding preparations require your undivided attention."

I sighed and hugged him back. He's right. They're a bunch of smart adults. They can sort this out on their own and I have better things to think about, bigger plans to worry about.

I smiled up at Ryder and tiptoed to give him a kiss on the lips.

"I love you." I told him.

"I love you more," he said. "I can't wait to make you mine forever."

"Even after last night?" I asked remembering how I let myself a little bit loose in bed with Ryder. It was like I didn't know I had the guts to do half the things I did.

Ryder's eyes twinkled. "*Especially* after last night!" I gave him a pout and pinched him on the arm. He laughed and pulled me towards him in another heart-stopping kiss.

Epilogue

THE WEDDING

The ceremony that officially takes a couple to the beginning of their happily ever after... a gathering that involves a lifetime of promises.

Breathe in. Breathe out.

I looked at myself in the mirror. I could barely recognize myself. The girl staring back at me was wearing a very elegant white princess gown made from the finest duchesse satin and silk. The bodice that has a sweetheart neckline was encrusted with genuine crystals. The romantic full skirt with elaborate ruffles and folds was adorned with crystals and intricate embroidery, as well as the cathedral length veil that I wore. The famous designer who made my gown made sure that the dress was fit for fairy tale and princess romances, too.

My hair was curled and clipped in a half pony and fastened with two diamond hair combs that belonged to Ryder's mother. My hair cascaded around my face and there were very small white flowers clipped all over it. The combs were my something borrowed and something old. I wore a very elegant and expensive diamond necklace that Ryder gave me as an early wedding gift, which was my something new. Under the dress, on my right thigh, I was wearing a lace garter adorned with sapphires, which was my something blue.

I smiled at myself. I looked like a princess, indeed. And today, I will officially begin my happily ever after.

My father entered the room and smiled at me. "Sweetheart, it's time." He stared at me for a while. "You look so beautiful. I'm so proud of you, sweetheart," he said. "I am so glad you found a better man and you're going to have a better life than what you originally planned with Bryan. I am so happy because Ryder is an honorable man and he genuinely loves you."

"I love you, Dad." I said to him. "Thank you for everything."

He kissed my forehead. Then he held out his arm to me and led me out of the mansion.

A coach was waiting for me outside. Nicole and Ryder had this custom-made as a surprise for me. It was round-shaped, with gold steel carvings. The big rear wheels and smaller front wheels were made of rubber tires and white metal rims. The carriage itself looked like it was made of glass and white flowers accented the entire thing.

My breath was taken away. I'm a wedding planner, so nothing about the entire wedding was supposed to surprise me. But this... I would forever love Nicole and Ryder for this.

My father and I climbed up into the coach and sat on the white leather seats. A white horse drew it, and a coachman dressed in a white suit drove us towards the entrance of the garden where the ceremony was going to be held.

Nicole met me by the oak tree arch.

The arch was now adorned with white roses at the front. White flowers hung over the interior of the entire arch and over the head of anybody who walked inside. White rose petals covered the entire floor.

I stepped into the orchard and my breath was taken away completely. I know I planned how this place would be decorated, but seeing the final result was beyond what I imagined it would be.

The entire orchard had flowers in full bloom in different rich colors. It was right to choose white and cream for our motif, as it would be a perfect contrast to the colorful orchard and garden.

White chairs now filled half of the orchard, where our relatives and friends were all seated. Lines of white roses decorated the aisle. White flower vines hung from the makeshift ceiling we created all over the portion of the orchard where the ceremony would be held.

A choir of cellos, violins, and a piano was playing a classical music. Then the music stopped, and Pachelbel's Canon played, signifying my arrival. Everybody stood up and looked at the entrance.

My father squeezed my hand and smiled at me.

I smiled up at him and allowed him to walk me down the aisle. The minute I arrived rose petals slowly dropped from the ceiling like gentle snow. Then the machines we had installed in every corner filled the entire place with bubbles. I walked on ivory carpet that had the emblem "R&A" printed all over it in gold ink.

It was breathtaking and it was everything I imagined it would be... probably even better.

Our relatives and friends were watching me; many of them were in tears. Tears were also rolling down my cheeks even though I was trying my best not to cry.

I stared ahead and saw Ryder standing there, splendid and breathtaking in a white Armani suit. Jake was standing behind him.

His eyes never left mine as I walked towards him. And it felt like walking towards my eternity... towards the only world I would ever want to belong to.

As I took each step towards him, I saw my life flashing before me.

I remembered running away from the jewelry shop and bumping towards a warm body that enveloped me in comfort... I remembered sitting in the bar that night, desperately asking that man to help me... I remembered showing up in Geena's wedding feeling hopeful after many months of pain and heartache. I remembered being broken... and then being rescued and fixed. I remembered the joy of finally giving in to my love and passion for this man... my savior, my best friend, my ally, my knight in shining armor.

Then I remembered a little of the pain I felt when I thought I lost him in the accident… the heartbreak that came afterwards when he couldn't remember me… and the joy we shared when he made love to me even though he couldn't place me in his past.

And finally, I remembered that day at the beach where he finally found his way back to me. It felt like being lost for a long time and then finally coming back home.

Ryder was looking at me intensely… lovingly. He was crying, too. And then he gave me a gentle smile.

"I love you, beautiful." He whispered.

I smiled back at him. "I love you, too."

My father took my hand and placed it in his. Then they shook hands and then Ryder guided me towards the altar.

Ryder and I intertwined our hands all throughout the ceremony. Even until now, I couldn't believe that I'm standing here beside him. For years, I never knew happiness and love like this would exist in my life. I was content with what I had with Bryan and when my heart was shattered to pieces, I didn't know that I could be fixed again… that I could be as good and as strong as I am now… that I could be with a man like Ryder, who I thought existed only in dreams and fairy tale novels.

"Ryder… a little over a year ago, I was heartbroken and I thought I was unfixable beyond belief. I was in the dark and I didn't know how to find my way out. At the lowest point of my life, when I thought I had nothing left to lose, nothing left to hope for, I ran into you, and you offered me kindness… enveloped me in warmth… hugged me in comfort and gave me hope the very first second that I met you. I didn't even know your name… didn't even see your face and yet you already saved me in many ways. That very second was the start of my real 'ever after'.

Now, I understand why I had to go through everything that I went through… and I wouldn't change a thing. Because without all those… I wouldn't be standing here… happier than I could ever imagine… and about to spend the rest of my 'ever after' in love and bliss with you. I will forever thank you, for loving me, for fixing me and for patiently waiting for me to love you back. You are my rock, my best friend, my savior, my knight in shining armor. I love you so much, Ryder Van Woodsen… and I promise to love you forever… more than anything in this world… more than myself and more than life itself."

Tears were glistening in my eyes, as I said the words that are in my heart and the promise that I intend to keep until the rest of my days.

Tears brimmed Ryder's eyes too as he squeezed my hand in his.

"Astrid… the day you walked into my life, you changed it instantly. I knew I was in a dream… a dream that I didn't want to wake up from. You made me feel needed. You have given me a whole new purpose and my life a whole new meaning. You are everything I didn't know I needed. Our love was everything I was afraid to hope for because I thought it existed only in dreams and fairy tales. But when I realized that it was happening to me for real… I knew I would never let you go.

You taught me how to believe in forever... you saved me from my old self... you led me out of the dark and drew me into your world and I never ever want to come out of it.

You showed me that love can withstand a million storms... and that happiness can be limitless. You are my princess, my best friend, my perfect match. You needed me, and loved me for who I really am inside. Because of your faith in me... I am no longer afraid to be weak... and because of that I am stronger than I have ever been. I love you very, very much, Astrid Van Woodsen. I promise to always be the man you fell in love with... I promise to make all your dreams a reality... I promise to take care of you... and to never stop making your 'ever after' come true... now... forever and beyond."

Ryder's vow went out to my heart and engraved itself there, where it would remain for eternity. I know that he meant every word, and I felt the intensity of his love for me in every promise he made.

Finally, we put our platinum bands on each other's fingers. We opted for a simple band, no stones, no corners... only a circle that symbolizes our love... smooth sailing, strong, valuable, and never-ending. Inside the rings, my name was engraved on Ryder's, and his name was engraved on mine, along with the words *'Ever After'*.

"I pronounce you husband and wife... you may now kiss the bride."

Ryder lifted my veil. His eyes were brimming with tears and there was so much love and tenderness on his face. I couldn't stop crying too, but I know that from now on, with Ryder... I will only be crying happy tears.

He leaned forward and then he gave me a gentle kiss on the lips. One kiss... but it lasted for a long time. Because that single perfect kiss contains so much love, so much passion... so many promises that we couldn't even put into words... vows that only our hearts could understand. We were breathing together, and our hearts were beating as one.

When the kiss ended, Ryder leaned his forehead against mine breathing in the scent of me. Then he pulled away gently and said, "Astrid Van Woodsen... my love... my life... my wife."

I smiled at him and then he leaned forward again and this time, he gave me a more passionate kiss.

It seemed like we were in our own world. During those moments, there was only Ryder and me... in each other's arms, lost in the passion of our kisses.

Then we heard everybody clapping and cheering around us. We reluctantly pulled away from each other. Ryder smiled at me and kissed me on the forehead before pulling me to him into a tight hug.

We were joined by our friends and relatives who congratulated us and gave us their best wishes.

My new father and mother in-law hugged me.

"Welcome to our family, sweetheart." Mr. Van Woodsen said.

Ryder's mom hugged me. Tears were streaming down her cheeks too. "I'm so happy, Astrid. Thank you for your love and patience for my son."

"Thank you… for bringing a wonderful man into this world." I said to her.

After taking pictures with everyone, we headed out towards the arch of oak trees again and into where the coach was waiting for us. Our bridesmaids and groomsmen were already there, along with most of our guests. They were all holding white balloons.

Just as we are about to go into the coach, confetti popped and flew all over us. Our guests clapped their hands and they released hundreds of white balloons into the sky.

Inside the coach, Ryder looked down at me and smiled. "I love you… wife."

I laughed. "I love you too… husband." And then we lost ourselves again in another world-spinning kiss.

First, we went for a photo shoot along with our bridesmaids and groomsmen. Some shots we took by the lake, some we took inside the labyrinth, and others inside the mansion.

We transformed almost the whole estate into a fairyland. We decided to hold the reception in one of the huge gardens beside the labyrinth. It started in the evening and the guests were just amazed about how we created an enchanting world for them.

The sun finally set, the evening fell and the whole place lit up. The entire reception area was covered in a high-ceiling transparent dome. Again, one of Ryder's many brilliant suggestions. The purpose of that was because the ceiling was filled with tiny LED lights that lit up in the evening, making it look like a million bright stars across the sky.

To build the dome took time and, doubtless, a lot of money. So I told Nicole that I'd rather have my stars and constellations instead of the fireworks. I've always dreamed of having fireworks in my wedding. But I had to compromise. I don't want to spend more than I should, particularly since Ryder insisted on paying for *everything*. Even my father could not convince him to share some of the expenses.

Tables and chairs were covered in white linen and decorated with elaborate white rose centerpieces, tall white candles and white torches. Gems and crystal pieces were also scattered around the tables to add to the sparkle when hit by light and camera flashes.

A huge lighted dance floor was built in the center, and it too was covered in white rose petals. Again bubble machines were installed in every corner.

The trees all around were also covered in flowers and mini LED lights were installed in almost every branch to make the trees light up as if fireflies infested them. Swans swam on the lake and at night real fireflies really did fly around the bushes, which made the whole place look even more enchanting.

We served a buffet with more than a dozen main courses, a huge selection of desserts, and free-flowing drinks from juices to liquor. The catering gave me the least worries, since it's practically what Ryder's family does. Ryder's mother made most of the arrangements for the food and beverages.

The guests were given a Swarovski crystal coach figurine, which were custom-made and engraved with our names. The coach opens up on top to reveal the finest Godiva truffles inside them.

The finest wine was served during the ceremonial toast. We had an eight-tier wedding cake that had cream-colored flowers and roses cascading on it from the topper down to the base. A miniature version of "Princess Astrid and Prince Ryder" adorned the very top of our tall cake.

I tossed my beautiful rose bouquet and I was so happy it landed in Nicole's arms. She didn't even try to catch it. She was the farthest at the back, but I gave a little bit more force when I threw it, and her reflexes made her catch it.

When I sat down in the chair for Ryder to get the garter on my thigh, he couldn't resist going under my heavy skirt using his teeth. I giggled lovingly at him, reminiscing the memory from Geena's wedding when he first did that.

John was among the bachelors lined up, eager to catch the garter and possibly get a chance to dance and kiss Nicole... without having to ask her himself.

Ryder looked at the hopeful bachelors and then he turned around. He tossed it high and with force. The guys jumped and trampled on each other when they landed on the ground.

I watched, eager to see who finally caught my garter. But the guys stood up, laughing and fixing their suits. No one seemed to have caught it. My heart sank when John emerged empty-handed. The guys looked at each other blankly.

Finally a figure stood up. He was sitting behind the pool of guys. He didn't seem interested to join them, but somehow, the garter landed perfectly in front of him.

I bit my lip as Adam approached me. I saw John shake his head and retreat to his seat. Adam turned to give Ryder a secret scowl before he turned to Nicole, a crooked smile now planted on his face.

Nicole raised a brow at him. Then she gave Ryder and me a look that seemed to say *You-two-are-so-dead!* Ryder just smiled innocently at the three of us.

"What? Maybe it's fate." Ryder whispered to me.

"Or... maybe it's your perfect aim." I whispered to my husband.

I giggled to put on a show in front of all the guests while Adam knelt down to put the garter on Nicole's leg.

"Higher! Higher!"

The crowd cheered, and I swear I could hear Dannie and Garrie's voices on top of everybody else's.

Adam pushed the garter higher up Nicole's thigh, while she blushed all shades of red. John was sitting at the bar now, ordering drinks, not even slightly interested with what's going on in the dance floor.

When he had pushed the garter far enough, Adam stood up and took Nicole's hand in his in a very gentlemanly way.

"Kiss!" We heard everybody cheer.

Ryder took me in his arms, his eyes glittering. "Come on, love. Let's show them how it's done." He teased. My laughter died on my lips when he covered them with his and gave me a passionate kiss.

When we pulled away, Adam and Nicole were watching us with disbelief on their faces. Adam took Nicole in his arms. Everybody clapped their arms and cheered, including us.

I was nervous. What was Adam going to do?

He leaned his face forward, and for a while, I thought he was really going to kiss Nicole. But his lips landed an inch from her lips. And then he pulled her closer to him, bent towards her neck and planted a soft kiss on her shoulder.

When he pulled away, he looked down at her and laughed. Nicole pinched his arm as she giggled in relief.

The music played and Adam pulled Nicole into his arms again and danced with her. Ryder took me into his arms, too. He had a wide grin on his face.

I cannot describe how I felt for Adam and Nicole. I was nervous at first, but after that, my heart sort of melted. I haven't seen Adam so affectionate for a woman. Usually he was cold and heartless. But he seemed comfortable and warm with Nicole... like they've been friends for a very long time.

"You did that on purpose." I whispered to Ryder.

"No." He denied. "I threw with a purpose. The rest was up to fate," he said, placing a kiss on my neck. "Just like us, love. Fate brought us here. I didn't like that it played with us first, but then I'm happy it brought us back together again. Well, I got Bryan to thank for punching the life out of me, causing my memories to go back. But just the same... fate got us back together... so we could be here today. Happy."

Tears welled up in my eyes. I leaned forward and gave Ryder a kiss on the lips. "Yes. I am happy, Ryder. Are you?"

He smiled at me gently. Then he said, "Bliss, love. This is bliss."

When a new song played, I danced with my friends, and Ryder's male relatives, although there weren't many of them. Ryder danced with my mother and my aunts and some of my young nieces and cousins.

I danced with John, who was completely ignoring both Nicole and Adam and I was scared to ask him about it. Maybe I'll save all my questions for after my honeymoon.

I danced with Adam, who seemed nonchalant about the whole thing. And I know that if I do ask him about Nicole, I will not get a proper answer anyway, so what was the point?

I also danced with Dannie, who couldn't help asking me if I knew what was going on with the three. I told him I knew nothing and he must not press any of them. I made him promise not to meddle.

I even danced with Garrie, who admitted to me that his heart broke when he told me the first time he met me that my engagement ring was a fake. He told me that he was so glad to be part of my wedding... to see that it all turned out perfectly well for me in the end.

I was emotional when I danced with my father, and he cried a lot too. He kept telling me how proud he was of me and how happy he was that I am very happy with Ryder.

I also danced with Uncle Jack. He was very happy because he knew he didn't have to worry about me. That I've gotten over what Geena and Bryan did to me, and it all worked out for the better.

Then finally, I was back in Ryder's arms. He leaned forward and kissed my lips gently. "This is probably the best wedding arrangement I have seen," Ryder said to me.

"It was probably the most expensive too." I complained. I actually didn't know how much the whole wedding cost. Nicole knew because she spoke to all the suppliers. And of course Ryder knew because he wrote the checks.

He laughed. "It's nothing, love," he said. "The twinkle, the pride and the happiness that I see in your eyes are all worth it."

I leaned my head on his chest and sighed contentedly. Who would have thought that about a year ago, I was devastated because my dream wedding was stolen from me. And now... I got married, and I had the wedding of my wildest imagination, and my real prince made it all happen for me.

When I opened my eyes, a familiar, beautiful blonde caught my attention. She was sitting in the corner, holding a toddler in her arms.

I looked at her. She still looks pretty, but her eyes looked old, like they were hiding layers of sadness in them. I remembered sending her an invitation, but I was not really sure that she would come.

Bryan was in prison for months, and now he's being placed on rehab. Geena filed a divorce on the grounds of infidelity, physical assault and psychological incapacity. I felt sorry for her, but I know that she was also better off. No matter what she did to me, she still deserved a better man.

Geena's eyes met mine, and she smiled at me shyly. I realized that I could not hold her a prisoner of her guilt anymore because I am truly happier now. And if it weren't for her, maybe I would not have been here with Ryder, making my dreams come true. Her fate could have been mine.

Slowly, I smiled at her. Then I took a deep breath and mouthed, *"I forgive you."*

Somehow, she understood my message, like she always did when we were growing up. She always gets my sentences even before I finish speaking. Tears brimmed her eyes and she nodded at me. Then she smiled. I felt the warmth and sincerity in that smile.

"Thank you." She mouthed back.

Tears welled up in my eyes, too. And I felt like a hundred tons was lifted from my chest. I didn't know that I was still holding this anger inside me until I finally decided to let it go. And I felt better. Because no matter what Geena did to me, we were still cousins... and we were like sisters, and I knew I would always love her.

I looked back at Ryder. He reached up and wiped a tear from my cheek. He'd been watching Geena and me the whole time and he witnessed what happened between us.

"You're truly an amazing woman, love," he said. "You have a good heart and a pure soul. More than your beauty and charm, I am in love with how good you are inside. I'm so glad you're my wife. And I hope our kids will be as kind-hearted as you are."

I glanced back at him in surprise. "Kids?" The thought warmed my heart.

He nodded. "Please pass on your violet eyes to at least one of them."

I laughed. "How many kids do you plan to have, Mr. Van Woodsen?"

"Minimum three," he replied. "Two boys, one girl. Or two boys, two girls... or three boys and two girls... or..."

"Ryder, stop!" I laughed. I knew where he was going with that. It made me feel warm that he wanted many kids... because I do. I was an only child and I only had Geena when I was growing up. It would be nice to have siblings who are also your best friends. "We'll have as many kids as we will be blessed with."

He leaned his forehead towards mine. "And I will take care of all of you. You will have a lot of little princes and princesses in your 'ever after', love. I promise you that."

Just then, Nicole, Paris, and Jake interrupted us.

"It's almost time." Paris said.

I was confused. I didn't know what was going on. Ryder nodded and then Paris grabbed my hand, pulling me with her. Nicole grabbed my train and we hurried into the house.

"What is going on?" I demanded.

They smiled. "You can't go to your honeymoon in your wedding gown."

"I don't even know where we are going," I said.

"Just trust my brother." Paris said. "He's been planning this for months."

Ryder took care of the honeymoon and he refused to tell me where we were going. I don't even have a clue.

Before I knew it, Paris and Nicole were undressing me, taking out the flowers in my hair and I was being dressed in an elegant halter-top purple dress that went all the way to my knees. Nicole insisted I wear a pair of shorts under my dress. Then she handed me a pair of violet beaded thong sandals. Paris managed to fix my hair into a half-pony. My hair still looked wonderful, but much simpler than it was during the wedding.

Then they led me out to the front of the mansion. Ryder met me by the stairs. He too had a change of outfit. The suit was gone and he was now wearing a pair of pants and loose long-sleeved shirt.

He took my hand and kissed it. Then he leaned forward and kissed me thoroughly on the lips. Our guests were around us, clapping their hands, cheering for us.

"I love you, Mrs. Van Woodsen," Ryder said. Then he motioned for me to look at the skies above me.

Suddenly a streak of light sparked in the sky. Followed by a loud sound. And then the whole sky burst into a million different colors. It was beautiful and breathtaking... just like the man beside me.

Tears brimmed my eyes. I stared up at him. I completely crossed out fireworks on the list and exchanged it for the starlit dome in the garden. Ryder didn't tell me that I was going to have fireworks after all. I forgot that this man *really* listens to me. When I dream out loud, when I talk about the things that I wanted... things that would make me happy... this man was listening and he remembers every single thing.

"Thank you for the fireworks." I said to him.

"Thank you for marrying me." He whispered and then he kissed me again.

Immediately, after the fireworks display, we heard a loud sound from the sky. I looked up again and found a helicopter descending in front of the huge garden.

"Our ride is here," Ryder said.

"Seriously?" I asked. "Where are we going?"

"To the airport. We can't miss our flight," he replied. Jake handed him our bags and then he pulled me away with one hand.

Again, everybody congratulated us and sent us their love and well wishes.

"Astrid, my only wish is that when you come back, you already have something baking in the oven." Ryder's mother whispered to me.

I laughed nervously and looked at Ryder. He smiled at his mother. "I will try my best, Mother."

Then Ryder took my arm and led me towards the helicopter. Now I realized why Nicole insisted that I wear shorts underneath my dress. Ryder guided me up and then he climbed in himself. Our guests and relatives waved us off. As the helicopter ascend to the sky, tears were rolling down my cheeks. I waved back at them and threw them flying kisses.

Everything was just surreal... perfect. Even if I planned the wedding well, Ryder managed to make it even more perfect for me. He still managed to throw in a couple of surprises. I leaned my head on his shoulder. I felt a kiss on my forehead and I closed my eyes to savor the warmth, comfort, and security that I felt in his arms... where I know I will forever belong in for as long as I live.

When we arrived at the airport, Ryder told me that he was taking me to Maui.

"We'll stay five days there, then we'll go to Tahiti. Then to the Caribbean, then we'll head off to Asia. On the way back we'll pass by France and Italy."

My eyes widened. "Seriously, Ryder?"

He grinned. "Seriously." Then he leaned forward and kissed me thoroughly. "Why did you think my mother was so hopeful that she'll have a grandchild when we get back?"

I laughed. "How long are we going to be gone?"

"A month..."

My eyes widened. "A month!"

"And two." He added.

"What?" I couldn't believe what I was hearing. "Three months? Who goes on a honeymoon for three months?" I asked him.

He laughed. "Us, love. Us."

"What about Oil Rig?" I asked.

"Paris will take care of that. And I've asked Adam to look at the reports twice a month."

"And Ever After Malibu and Manhattan?"

"Relax. Nicole is taking care of that. And... Dannie and Garrie are helping as well. Plus Janis is practically not working. So on her spare time, I think she'll also give a hand."

"Wow! They really love us, don't they?"

"Yes. Plus, they're being well-compensated for it, don't worry." He chuckled.

Then his face descended towards mine and he kissed me thoroughly again. He only needed to do that and I would do anything and go anywhere with him.

I took a deep breath. "I'm glad I ran into you at the jewelry shop that day, Ryder. And I'm glad you served me margaritas at Oil Rig that night. You... are everything I dreamed my Prince would be... maybe even more. You are... wonderfully surreal."

He chuckled. "I'm glad that you still believe in fairy tale romances."

I stared up at him and smiled contentedly. "Of course I do," I said. "I am in one."

And with one happy smile, Ryder said, "I love you very, very much, my sweet Princess. Thank you for choosing me to make your 'ever after' come true... I promise to make you happy... now and for the rest of our lives." Then he leaned forward gave me a thorough kiss on the lips.

I closed my eyes and kissed him back. I thought that if this were what was in store for me from the very beginning, I would gladly go through all those heartbreaks again. Because I know I would never trade my life with Ryder for anything else. What I had with Bryan was a good thing for a while, but what I have with Ryder now... is a blessing, a reward, a present... a miracle that I would treasure forever.

Had I known this at the time I found out Bryan was cheating on me or when Ryder lost his memories of me... I would not have cried rivers of tears... I would not have lost hope. I would have had the courage because this man in my arms now... my Prince, my Knight in Shining Armor... is absolutely worth everything I have been through.

And I will thank God every day that this time... there will be no more heartaches, no more pains. This time, I get to spend the rest of my life with Ryder Van Woodsen. This time I truly get to keep him in my 'ever after'.

ABOUT THE AUTHOR

Jerilee Kaye was born under the sign of Leo in the year 1979. She graduated with a Bachelor's Degree in Legal Management and with post-graduate qualifications in the fields of Product Management, Project Management, and Procurement.

She is currently managing a global vendor portfolio for a multinational company based in Dubai.

She is married to her first love, Sam, who has been her boyfriend since the age of 16. They are blessed with a beautiful four-year-old daughter, MarQuise.

When she's not buried under stacks of paper at work, or engrossed with her writing, Jerilee Kaye spends some down time playing golf, kicking her husband's butt on a judo match, and learning to play the piano.

Visit her Facebook Page:
www.facebook.com/jerileekaye

If you have purchased this book, she would appreciate it if you could drop her a line at jerilee.kaye@yahoo.com and she would be happy to hear your feedback, and keep you posted on future stories and publications.

Other Books by this Author:

Intertwined

Coming Soon:

All the Wrong Reasons

Wingless and Beautiful

Taming a Princess
(A Knight in Shining Suit spin-off)

A preview of
Taming a Princess

Adam Ackers sat on Mr. Van Woodsen's office. He looked at his clock. The man was thirty minutes late. He would be late for his date! But he needed this deal. Not for himself. But for his father, who is currently fighting for his life in the hospital.

He took his phone and started typing a message:

Might be a bit late. You can start appetizer without me. I'm sorry. Would be there as soon as I can.

Then he scrolled through his phone book until he found Nicole's number.

A minute later, she replied:

Don't worry. I'm running late too. Just got off a meeting with a witch bride from hell.

Adam smiled. He liked his friendship with Nicole. She was sensible. She has a serene personality. And she was in love with her best friend. So Adam knows she will not try to flirt with him or go to bed with him. She's safe. If only John knew how lucky he was. Nicole would make a good wife someday. At least that's what Adam thought.

Finally, the door opened, and Mr. Van Woodsen entered the room. Although he is now somehow related to the Van Woodsens, Adam refused to use Astrid as his trump card. He would prove to his father that on his own, he could win back this account.

Adam didn't even call Ryder about the expiring contracts his father's company has with the Van Woodsens Group. Ryder's father is still the President. The old man would be the one to sign with them. He wanted to do this as professionally as possible.

"Mr. Ackers." Mr. Van Woodsen addressed him.

Adam stood up from his seat. "Mr. Van Woodsen." He extended his hand, and the older man shook it. Then he motioned for him to take a seat again.

Mr. Van Woodsen stared at him for a while and then he said, "I know why you're here. My contracts would be expiring soon. It's worth a couple of millions." He looked at him as if he was sizing him up. "I trust your father, but why should I trust you?"

"Because the fruit doesn't fall far from the tree. And I'm younger, smarter and armed with new tricks." Adam replied confidently.

"You're a lawyer, Adam."

"Which means I know how to prove a point and make people believe in it. Isn't that what you hire a marketing company for?"

The older Van Woodsen smiled. Then he stood up. "I'm still waiting for you to mention my beautiful daughter-in-law's name."

Adam smiled. "Don't hold your breath for that. She has nothing to do with this."

"You're right. But if you are as charming as she is, then maybe I will put you up on a challenge. And then you can earn my trust."

Adam raised a brow. "What challenge is that?"

Mr. Van Woodsen smiled. "You have to accept it first. And once you do, you cannot back out. And I trust you know how to keep your mouth shut."

Adam was not only desperate to keep this account for his father without Ryder's help, he was now intrigued with the game Ryder's father is playing at. And he loves a good challenge.

"Okay. But if I pass your test, you will give my father's company a decade of business... that comes with a binding contract."

Mr. Van Woodsen smiled. "If you pass, there wouldn't even be a need for a binding contract. We will do business with you for as long as this company stands."

Adam stared at him for a while and then he extended his hand to him. The older Van Woodsen shook it.

"So what is the challenge?" Adam finally asked.

The older Van Woodsen smiled slowly. Then he said, "This is a personal challenge, Mr. Ackers. I know you're smart. In fact, very smart according to your credentials. But I'm afraid that won't help you in this challenge. If it will, maybe only just a little bit."

Adam raised a brow. He doesn't know what Mr. Van Woodsen was aiming at, and he was now more intrigued than ever.

Mr. Van Woodsen sighed. "There is a girl who is... my treasure... my princess. I want to see her married to a man who has something to say for himself. Smart. Honorable. Loyal. Isn't a womanizer. With a good family background... a family fortune and a fortune of his own."

"Someone like your son." Adam suggested.

Mr. Van Woodsen stared at Adam for a while. Then he said, "Yes. But, unfortunately, a breed like Ryder nowadays is... scarce."

"But not extinct."

Mr. Van Woodsen nodded. "I have arranged many eligible bachelors to marry this girl. But she hated each and every one of them. Not only did she refuse this arranged marriages, but she also tried her damn best to make the guys surrender. I arranged for her twice, and both men came back saying they wouldn't even come within a kilometer away from her. I'm trying for number three."

Adam raised a brow. "What does this have to do with me?"

Mr. Van Woodsen stared at him for a while. "I want you to convince her to marry this guy I arranged for her. And I want you to make her do it willingly. She can't know that this guy is her arranged betrothed. The minute she does, she will employ all means to make him... cry. I want you to strategize how she'll end up in the altar, this time next year... with the man, I chose for her."

392

Adam looked at Mr. Van Woodsen as if he was out of his mind. "Do you really think I can pull this off? I don't even believe in marriage, myself!"

"Oh? Is that why you are helping your cousin and your girlfriend manage their booming wedding events company?" Mr. Van Woodsen asked sarcastically.

"That's a different matter. I'm doing it because they're very good in it. And you've been misinformed. I don't have a girlfriend."

"Then even better. No one else needs to know about our little arrangement."

Adam was in the brink of frustration, but he tried to control his emotions. This is a business meeting! Why is Mr. Van Woodsen mixing business with his daughter's personal life?

Adam gave the man a hard look. "I'm assuming you're talking about Paris, your daughter. Why... why do you need to arrange a marriage for her? I mean, are you blind? Have you seen how beautiful she is?"

Thinking about Paris Van Woodsen's long legs, creamy skin, and riveting green eyes, the word attractive doesn't even give justice to her. But Adam doesn't like spoiled, rich brats like her. When he first met her, he thought she was exactly like his sister. Rich. Pretty. But not so bright and quite shallow. Maybe all she does is shop around and spend Daddy's money. All she needed to do is to stay pretty and wait for a rich guy to marry her.

The old man sighed. "I love my daughter very much. And I have a lot to make up for. She didn't grow up with me. But I provided for her. I gave her all her whims. But she's been trying to get my attention ever since she was little. I wasn't there for her. Now, I want to make sure she ends up with a good man. One who has money himself, so I am sure he isn't trying to get into her pants, to dig into the family's fortune. An intelligent man with principles in life." Mr. Van Woodsen looked at Adam. "But I needed someone close to her age to convince her that this is the best thing for her. That she can't marry the guys she normally dates. They're all... hopeless imbeciles. I know she's only doing that to rebel against me. I know you're smart enough to strategize this. And I was hoping you would be as charming as Astrid to convince my overly rebellious daughter to accept her position in this family."

Adam laughed humorlessly. "I think you got yourself the wrong deal, Sir. I am not related by blood to Astrid at all."

The man smiled. "But blood is not the only thing that makes two people related, Mr. Ackers. I know more about you than you think. You moved out of your father's house at the age of 18. Graduated law school a year ahead of time. Became a partner in your firm after only two years. Never lost a case in your career. On your free time, you practice kickboxing and other forms of street martial arts, but you didn't want anybody to in your family to know that.

"We both know you will soon put up your own law firm because that's your dream. You are trying to win my account, not for your own gain. But for your father's company, which you have no intention of taking over. You know this firm will go to your sister someday. And you're trying to secure her future. Not yours."

Adam was shocked with what he heard from Mr. Van Woodsen. He felt like he just went to his shrink, though he doesn't have one, and read all his file.

"I love my daughter. I am trying to secure her future too." He said. "I want to make sure she doesn't end up marrying one of the bastards she's been dating for years. They are all spineless, gold-diggers."

Adam couldn't believe what he just heard. "You want me to play cupid for your daughter and this man you want her to marry?"

Mr. Van Woodsen nodded. "I'm old. I don't know what you kids 'dig' these days. I need help pulling this off, because my previous two attempts failed miserably. My daughter is tougher than I gave her credit for, and believe me, I gave her a lot!" He paused, lost in his thoughts for a while. Then he said, "I need help, Mr. Ackers. And obviously, I can't ask anybody in my family because they would never agree to this plan. Ryder would kill me if he finds out. He loves his sister very much and would want her to choose her own future. Astrid is very loyal to my son; I don't think she would be able to lie to him about this. My ex-wife... well, I don't even want to go there! Through the years, she's the woman I trust and distrust the most. You need something from me... and I am desperate to settle my daughter's future."

"If you're damn desperate why don't you just feign terminal sickness and make this your last wish?" Adam said sarcastically.

Mr. Van Woodsen was taken aback by what he said. And then he laughed. "I can't say that didn't cross my mind. But my daughter is smarter than that. Obviously, smarter than you give her credit for. Paris is a... gem."

Adam snorted. "Yeah. Real princess." He said with a hint of sarcasm in his voice.

Mr. Van Woodsen laughed hard, and Adam raised a brow. He expected him to get mad at his remark, but to find that amusing is not something he expected.

"Adam, son... I suggest you take this challenge." He said. "You just might be in for the surprise of your life."

Adam seriously doubts that. Paris doesn't rank high in his list of rare and precious gems... right where Nicole and Astrid are at the top of it. He shook his head. "I don't think I can do this."

Mr. Van Woodsen raised a brow at him in a challenge. "We already shook on it."

"That is not binding and legal." Adam pointed out.

Mr. Van Woodsen shrugged. "Yes. But after a couple of weeks, so are my company's contracts with your father."

Adam knows he's failed his father plenty of times in the past. And now that he's fighting for his life, he doesn't want to do it again. It will make his condition worse if he loses this account.

"What exactly do you need me to do?"

Mr. Van Woodsen stood up to pour himself a glass of whiskey. "Do you want some?" He asked Adam.

Adam shook his head. "Thank you."

"I want you to get close to my daughter. Close enough to earn her trust. And then do what you do best... convince her that she's better off marrying this man I chose for her." Mr. Van Woodsen said. "Good if she accepts it because her brain is telling her she should. But better if she does it because her heart tells her it's what she wanted."

"And who is this guy you arranged for?" He asked. "Does he know what the deal is?"

Mr. Van Woodsen nodded. "He's a son of one of my business partners. Wealthy and about to inherit his family's fortune. Yes, he wanted to marry Paris from the moment he laid eyes on her. He knows that it's going to be difficult, knowing about the first two guys. He's willing to cooperate, for as long as he succeeds."

"If I refuse to do this, what would you do?" Adam asked the man challengingly.

Mr. Van Woodsen stared at him thoughtfully, and then he said, "I would shop around for other companies. If your father, my old friend, Jack gets better enough to handle his company again, I would sign with him. He won't lose my account. But we both know that's not your point in coming here today, Mr. Ackers. Am I right?"

Damn! Adam knows the man is right. He wanted to get this account himself. Without his father's help or Ryder's or Astrid's. And if his father doesn't get better, he wanted to secure his sister's future.

"Fine." He said in defeat. After all, how difficult could it be? She's just a spoiled, little rich girl who probably spends all her time in the saloon or the mall. How impossible could she be?

Adam stood up from his seat. "If I break your daughter and make you win, you would sign a legally binding contract with my father's company... which I would be drafting under my terms. And since you've background checked me, you know how good I am with corporate contracts."

"I heard you were better than good. You're probably the best in your game." Mr. Van Woodsen agreed.

Adam sighed and extended his hand to the older man. Mr. Van Woodsen shook it.

Adam wanted to do this and get it over with. He wanted nothing to do with Paris Van Woodsen. He doesn't want to stay long in her world of glamor, fashion and shallowness. He's sure she's somewhere in a saloon by now, getting her nails done, preparing to go out with her equally spoiled rich friends tonight.

"When shall we start?" He asked.

"Now." Mr. Van Woodsen replied. "You can start by bailing her out of jail."

Adam stopped moving or breathing altogether. He couldn't believe what he just heard.

Jail? What the fuck?!

Lightning Source UK Ltd.
Milton Keynes UK
UKHW03f1821170418
321224UK00001B/96/P

9 781494 894351